Young Will

The Confessions of William Shakespeare

A Novel by

Bruce Cook

T·T

TRUMAN TALLEY BOOKS
ST. MARTIN'S GRIFFIN
NEW YORK

www.stmartins.com

Library of Congress Cataloging-in-Publication Data

Cook, Bruce, 1932–2003
Young Will : the confessions of William Shakespeare / Bruce Cook.
p. cm.
ISBN 0-312-33573-3 (hc)
ISBN 0-312-33574-1 (pbk)
EAN 978-0-312-33574-8
1. Shakespeare, William, 1564–1616—Fiction. 2. Marlowe, Christopher, 1564–1593—Fiction. 3. Stratford-upon-Avon (England)—Fiction. 4. London (England)—Fiction. 5. Dramatists—Fiction. 6. Theater—Fiction. 7. Actors—Fiction. I. Title.

PS3553.O55314Y68 2004
813'.54—dc22 2004046755

First St. Martin's Griffin Edition: January 2006

10 9 8 7 6 5 4 3 2 1

DEDICATION BY JUDITH ALLER

My beloved husband, Bruce Cook, died on November 9, 2003, before this book was set in type. The book grew out of a conversation we had on a trip to Dover, England, in 1999. So I would like to dedicate it to the happy memory of that trip and of our life together. I also wish to thank Dick Adler for his help.

Young Will

PROLOGUE

This morning, it being the Sabbath, I did attend services at Holy Trinity in town. These days I go oft to church, sometimes alone, and other times with wife Anne. It is a habit of age, or so I am told. In truth, I should be hard prest to give an occasion, save for weddings and funerals, during all those years in London, when I ventured inside any of the many churches that were so near at hand. There was reason for this, and I shall reveal it anon, but for the moment let me return to the event which took place early this day.

There is a woman lives outside of town, Goody Bromley by name, who appears to be quite elderly, though she is not so old as she looks. Her house, little more than a hovel, lies at a remove from Stratford on the high road to Warwick. Thus located, the place has many who pass it of a day, yet whether they go by foot, by horse, coach, or cart, those passers-by do quicken their pace. The reason, whether it be credited or no, is that she who lives within is said to be a witch. Though I have written such into plays during years past, I have not much faith that women of their sort have commerce with the Devil, or that they have special powers given by him. I might indeed say that I have no faith whatever, except that among those hereabout Goodwife Bromley is known as an "ill-look woman." She possesses, so they say, what Italians of my ken describe as malocchio, *the evil eye. These same Italians sought to convince me that the faculty to curse with a look is both perceptible and powerful.*

And so it was that while I was hardly prepared when we encountered the woman, I had at least been forewarned of her and told of her rumored powers. She had been pointed out to me, and I had often seen her about the town. As a titheholder, I was given a warm goodbye after the service by the vicar. We made our way through the church door and into the light (Holy Trinity was ever the darkest of churches). Then did we repair toward New Place, Anne and I, and our path took us through the churchyard wherein our forebears had been laid to rest. There we did pause and give unto the occasion the long faces and dreary piety that it deserved. Yet as I stood there in the churchyard, looking left and right and leaning upon my stick, I became aware that there was another, a woman, regarding us as we regarded the tombstones. Because I have with age become a bit shortsighted, I did not immediately discern the personage of her who did study us so close. That it was indeed a woman I had seen truly as she rose from behind one of the largest stones, shook out her skirts, and moved forward a few steps that she might herself see me better. Or perhaps contrariwise, she wished me to see her better—for that indeed was the effect that she achieved.

It was just then that I did spy that she was Goody Bromley, and no mistake of it. Her hair, which did cover her face, hung lank and gray down to a dress all besmirched and muddy from the winter rains. She seemed a pitiful, demented creature, more beast than human. Indeed she did so seem until she parted her hair and showed her face. In most wise it matched the untidy rest of her: snot dripped from her nose; her teeth, revealed in an ugly smile, were carious, yellow, and pitted. Only her eyes did save her from an appearance of purest idiocy.

They were most remarkable. Of a blue so blue they seemed near colorless, these orbs would have set children to terrified flight with their ghostly appearance. Yet to me they exhibited a most peculiar sort of intelligence—not wisdom but sly cunning.

Then, as she stared at me (and I at her), I was of a sudden taken by the notion that this wreck of a woman could penetrate the recesses of my soul, that without a word from me she was privy to all I would keep hid from the world.

As this feeling did overwhelm me, the grin faded from her face, and with the forefinger of her right hand she pointed downward. Then did I see what it was she pointed at: it was not a thing, as such, but a place. I had not previously taken proper note of it, but Goody Bromley had taken her stand in the middle of the Shakespeare plot. Behind her was the grave and gravestone of John Shakespeare, my father, and beside it that of my mother, Mary Arden Shakespeare. To her left was the space that Anne's earthly remains would occupy some time in the future. But direct beneath her, precisely where she brought my attention, was the place I had chosen for my own burial.

How could she know? I had talked of it with none but Anne, though perhaps I had mentioned it to the vicar, as well. But no matter—neither would have occasion to discuss it with that pitiful scarecrow of a woman. And so I could but wonder, how could she know?

And what could she mean by it? She stands upon my gravesite and points down at my grave-to-be; that sure must be an offensive act. Yet there was naught in her expression to suggest she meant it so. The smile, or grin I called it, had vanished from her face, and she did now appear as solemn as I looking upon her, though perhaps a bit more challenging. The most benevolent reading I might give such an act was that she intended it as a memento mori. "Thou owest God a death," says she to me by means of that dirty finger pointed down. Yet, knowing her reputation as a witch, and having sensed that she could read my darkest secrets—I thought that most unlikely.

A great and sudden desire came to fly cross the thirty feet or more that separated us that I might grab her and shake her and demand that she tell what she meant. And truly I believe I might have done so had not I felt Anne's restraining hand upon my arm.

Indeed it was more than restraint that she offered: her hand clamped round my elbow, and I felt a mighty tug upon my arm, one so powerful that I near lost my balance.

"Come along, Will," said Anne to me.

Having little choice in the matter, I came. And I could not but notice that the curious, wordless exchange between me and Goody Bromley had attracted the attention of those who had left the church after us or had dawdled about the entrance gossiping. A group of them, no more than a dozen, had come forward to gawk and comment amongst themselves. That, knowing my Anne, was what had impelled her to drag me off. Still, I thought it unseemly that she should do so, and I told her as much. Right masterful was I, yet I fear that I failed to frighten her.

"You were making a spectacle," said she.

"Not so," said I. "That creature from Bedlam made the spectacle. I did merely try to interpret it."

Anne waved her hand grandly, rejecting my comment. "It was as a scene in a play," said she. "One of yours."

At that I coughed out a single "Ha!" Then did I add, "How would you know?" Truly, I believe she'd seen none of them. Why should she? And she is, needless to say, illiterate.

"Oh, I hear things. There was one with three witches, wasn't there?"

"Hmmm. Yes, there was." I glanced at her. She showed me naught but gazed direct before her. I wondered she did not step into a pile of dung, or a mud puddle at least. "Do you believe her to be a witch?"

"That one? In the churchyard?" Anne laughed a proper laugh. I'd amused her. "You called her a creature from Bedlam," she said. "I think that near to the mark."

"Yes, well, of course. They do nevertheless call her an 'ill-look woman,' do they not?"

"Agh!" She let forth a guttural gurgle. "People here will believe anything. You said so yourself many a time."

"So I did," said I, "so I did." Thus I ended the matter with wife Anne, though I vowed to give the matter further consideration.

And consider it I did. Tom and Judith came to Sabbath dinner, which was prepared by Anne and cook. This is one of the customs that survives from the long periods of my absence from Stratford when Anne lived much of the time alone in this house, except for cook and Samuel, cook's husband. I find these occasions tedious. Thomas Quincy was ever dull, in particular at table. As for his wife, Judith, my daughter, though she is ever so much brighter than Tom, she is serious to a fault. They profess to hold me in awe, which I find annoying. I like better crossing swords in verbal play with daughter Susanna, though Anne does disapprove, and says that Susanna lacks respect.

Ah, if Hamnet had only lived! What a fine fellow he would have been. Or so I have said—often to myself and less often to Anne. But in truth there is no telling: children grow to be what they will in their maturity.

Tom and Judith left us shortly after dark had fallen, which was for them quite an early departure. Perhaps they'd grown as tired of me as I have of them. In any case, soon as they left, Anne declared that she was altogether spent by the effort of preparing dinner, though I suspicioned that cook had done most, as indeed she should. I bade Anne a good night and sent her off to bed. Thus was I granted the rest of the evening to give to the questions that had come to me in regard to that event in the churchyard.

Anne had said nothing of it at dinner, and for that I was

grateful. Yet to me it was clear that it had not been out of any special consideration on her part, but due rather to the awkwardness she felt that her husband had given those rude bumpkins outside church reason to gawk and wonder. She would play the grand lady before them. Yet how was she to do that if the great man who is her husband stands staring as if bewitched at the most loathly and fearful creature in the shire. How indeed? Perhaps Anne said nothing at dinner because it was understood between them that daughter and son-in-law knew all that had happened: news travels with the speed of a shooting star here in Stratford, and gossip even faster. Or perhaps Anne had seen the two among the crowd of lookers-on, simply gawking with the rest. The longer I thought of it, the more likely it seemed.

I walked about the house, searching for my pipe and tobacco and found them in the kitchen where Anne had hidden them. It is, as so many others, a habit that I acquired in London. Like all women, she despises smoking tobacco and declares it foul-smelling and harmful to my health. And so she hides them from me, though she lacks the courage to dispose of them altogether. Thus we go through life, she and I.

I took pipe and tobacco to the room at the front of the house where I kept my tinderbox and do most of my smoking. It is of modest size and contains no more than a table and two chairs in the way of furniture. One of the chairs is soft to my backside and has arms upon it to support my elbows and is quite the best in New Place for sitting during long periods of time, which is to say, it is the best place in the house to smoke a pipe and ponder matters. If I take up the pen in earnest again—though I do indeed doubt that I ever shall—it would be then in this selfsame room. I seated myself and proceeded with the pleasant ritual of filling and lighting the pipe. I have become so well-practiced at it that it took little more than a minute or two. In three, I was puffing away happily, befouling the air and ruining my health. I gave the matter of Goody Bromley a good deal of thought.

There was naught to know of her more than I already did—except, that is, how she came to know precisely where I had planned to locate my final resting place—and I managed to account for that quite reasonably. I was now quite certain that I had discussed the matter with the vicar. She, who seemed to have the freedom of the church and churchyard, could easily have overheard the conversation wherever it took place, unseen by us and unbeknownst to him and me. And for that matter, I must have talked with Anne of the matter there in the churchyard. Goody Bromley could have been hidden behind a tree or one of the larger tombstones as I pointed out Anne's place and my own. So there it was. There could be no other sensible way to it, could there?

Could she then be a witch? That pitiful thing? She could as easily be a hobgoblin or a fairy. Those witches of my own invention in the Scottish play were far more real, were they not? And in regard to her "ill-look," the malocchio, *the evil eye (call it as you wish), there seemed little likelihood she had power of that or any sort. If she could curse with a look, why had she not used it to her advantage? She could threaten to maim or strike dead. There was no end to the mischief one could make. And one thing my time in London taught me was this: If one has the power to make mischief, then one can always profit by it. That I learned early from the great Kit Marlowe himself. And as for the arguments set forth by the Italians, one argument alone can destroy all theirs: If Italians put great faith in the* malocchio, *then that is reason enough to disbelieve in it. Have I not always said that they were the most easily gulled of all peoples?*

Pleased with myself, I leaned back in the chair and took in a proper puff of smoke—more, perhaps, than was good for me, for it found its way down my throat to my voice box, and I fell into a fit of coughing. It did not last long, nor was it so deep that I did more than bring up a bit of phlegm, yet it somehow had the effect of putting me and my thoughts in disarray. Of a sudden I began to doubt all my conclusions. All were intended for one purpose alone, and that was to offer me comfort. Why, even at the gravesite I was willing to interpret her memento mori as a benevolent, even a pious gesture. Nothing of the kind! A memento mori it may have been, but she meant it ill. Of that I was most certain, for I had an instant and unwelcome repetition of that awful moment in which I sensed that she knew me, knew all that could be known about me, and in the most detail of all, she knew all my sins. She knew them. She knew their number, and she knew their extreme gravity. And that, perhaps more than likely, was the meaning of that gesture. Memento mori? Of course, though something more than that. For with her forefinger she pointed downward to remind me that I would die and my earthly remains would rest in that very spot. Yet perhaps she was also saying that my soul would also go down—down, down, down, to the very depths of hell where I should suffer for my sins during an eternity. Was she certain? Did she know? Perhaps she was a witch, after all, and if a witch she may indeed have the power to curse with a look.

I seem to have proceeded in a complete circle, do I not? My efforts to explain and account for my response to that event in the churchyard have now gone topsy-turvy. The cause of this—the reason for it all—is that I have lately had qualms of conscience. I am troubled, and do freely admit it. Is this another sign of advancing age? I hope not.

I was born, as were so many of us country men of that time, into the Roman faith, and to a certain age I was brought up Popish, as well. Except for one episode in Lancashire when I was but a young man, it was all managed most informal. The parish priests were quite out of touch with their bishops and went about things just about as they always had. Nominally, we were all of the Church of England, but in practice we were still Roman Catholics. Thus was I better acquainted than most with the sacrament of confession. As a boy, and even more as a young man, I went often into the confessional. It was not that I was scrupulous, nor even that my sins were more numerous than my fellows (though they may have been), but the very idea of confession appealed deeply to my nature. That the slate could be wiped clean again and again, that I was, so to speak, arrayed in a spotless white garment after each ego te absolvo *was pronounced over me—all this led me to presume upon the mercy of God and the generosity of the parish priest. I went often to confession, and I enjoyed every visit. When I came to London I saw no point in venturing into the churches there where the new orthodoxy was practiced. I had soon afterward put the practice of religion behind me, for the most part. There seemed little point to it.*

So now I have come back to my native Stratford to live out my days. I see no reason to return to London. This is, after all, how I planned my life, is it not? My dream of returning home wealthy, a man of property and substance, had been fulfilled ten times over. Those who expected, even hoped, that I would come as the prodigal, all rags and tatters, have swallowed their disappointment and now smile at me with the rest. Let them, say I, for I am not so easily deceived. I knew who they are, and what they thought of me thirty years ago.

Though I am often restless here and lack patience with my neighbors and even with my family, I would say that in general I am happy, but perhaps not quite so happy as I expected to be. What prevents me, I should say, is the great weight of sins brought in my baggage from London. Is sin too great a word? Perhaps. It is, in any case, one with which I am not very comfortable. Yet if I should say "misdeeds," that would seem too weak a word and not at all suitable. And so sins they shall be, and their recitation shall be my confession.

When I am done, and you have heard all, you may judge their gravity. Perhaps indeed you will be moved to separate them neatly into two separate columns, headed obviously, "venal" and "mortal." We may, however, disagree upon the matter of which should be considered which. The Church and I do often disagree on such matters, and you will find me on such questions quite argumentative and as given to controversy as any Oxford debater.

And so you are warned. Though what follows should be of interest—as, of course, the sins of others are always of interest—it may, however, disappoint some. Verse is expected of me, whether sonnets, narratives or great long tragedies—and it is prose that I offer here, and only that. To the extent that I am able, I shall eschew the pleasures of rhyme, metaphor, and simile. I am tempted to declare that you will not find them here, yet I cannot be certain of that, for so long have I been a prisoner of poesy that I can scarce manage to write in prose. Nevertheless, I shall try.

There remains but one matter to take up before beginning, and it is this: Who are you? We have not met, we two. I do not know you. How these papers in which I have begun to write came into your hands, I know not, neither do I care, for almost certainly I shall be dead by the time this is seen by anyone. And if I am dead and have embarked upon my journey through eternity, then I almost certainly have other matters with which to concern myself.

My intention is to put this in the hands of my lawyer, Francis Collins of Warwick, when I have completed it. Let it be sealed and held with Will's will. Beyond that I have not planned, nor can I till it be complete.

Whoever you be, whatever your right to read this, it should be understood between us that this is my confession, and that all of it be true.

(Signed) William Shakespeare
(on this date) January 5, 1616

I

The sins of my childhood seem unworthy of mention. What do children know of sins and sinning? What did I? Not enough, certainly, to require me to spend much time upon them here. There be certain wits in London and at the universities who will argue that all that can be known of a man is shown, or at least foreshadowed, in his first decade of life. That does to me seem the purest sort of foolishness. Taking me as an example—for what better could I find?—I had so many contrary impulses that I could scarce calculate them. I can make mention of but a few.

I was, as an instance, a tolerably good scholar and an execrably bad one. Though never so capable in Latin as my schoolmasters would have liked, I learned a good deal from the study of it. Ovid, in particular, took my fancy, and I made practical use of all he had to teach me in later days. Yet it should surprise none that I distinguished myself most in the study of Rhetoric. A succession of masters, and able men they were, taught from examples in both prose and verse. *Euphues* was introduced to me early, and though we did not get on well, it provided an occasion for a long prose satire upon the work, which I did write purely to amuse my fellows. Thus did I become an author first at the age of fourteen. Reading Chaucer persuaded me to try my hand at verse, yet what I wrote in his manner was not meant as satire, but rather was written in respectful imitation. I showed none but the young rhetoric master, Mr. Cotton, who had inspired me to try my hand at writing of that sort; he was much pleased by what I had done and, praising me, did encourage me to continue writing. When his brother was arrested for a popish priest, hostility to Catholics amongst Stratford's burgesses led to Mr. Cotton's discharge. He returned to his family home in Lancashire where later, as shall be told, he offered me sanctuary.

All of that above may be entered upon the profit side of the ledger. Indeed it was true, I was an able scholar—but only insofar as I applied myself to Rhetoric. I did passably well in Latin—but in all the rest—that is, with regard to numbers of any sort—I was a perfect dunce. My mind simply could not grasp arithmetic beyond simple addition and subtraction. I had difficulty with sums from the time I left for London till the time that I returned for good and for always.

As a son, as well, I was plagued by the same sort of warring tendencies. To all appearance, I was the very picture of propriety within the family. I was a willing apprentice to my father in the glove trade, a dutiful son to him and to my mother, and a good brother to my three who were younger and to my sister, too. I believe it might be said that it was with this role, my first, that my career as an actor began, which is to say, this was but one role of the many that I would later play. I was quite unlike the one they knew, and I am certain of that, for I am today still that secret fellow that I was then. It was in my interest, as I well knew, to satisfy my family's expectations of me. Was I then so calculating? Perhaps, for my mother was an Arden, and the Ardens were among Warwickshire's grand families. She made it clear that more was expected of me because of that, and did so convince me that I began early on to play the model son. I found that the part did suit me so well that I was loath to leave it, except away from home. Some say that a role that is so frequently played is eventually adopted, but it was not so with me. I was always outside the role, aware that no matter how cleverly I may have deceived others, I was not myself deceived. I was not the lad they thought me to be.

And what was I in truth? Oh, I was many things. To choose one of the more important: I was a poet. I continued to write verse of all kinds, yet after Mr. Cotton's departure I showed it to no one, save for the odd comic rhyme I might compose for the entertainment of my chum, Ned Wilson—but never for my family. Why it suited me so I cannot say. Nevertheless there was little I could hold back from Ned, for he played a part in my secret life: we two lads were thieves together.

Dear Ned could make claim to no trace of wit; still, he could make me laugh as no other could, for the fellow was a born clown. Every clownish role ever I wrote—the gravediggers, the gatekeeper, Bottom and his troupe of rude mechanicals—had something of Ned in them. In London it was thought quite a marvel that I might write both tragedy and comedy, and sometimes both within the selfsame piece, yet what they knew not was that I had ever my old friend in mind, and he showed me the way and the how of it.

We were classmates, and it was our custom to walk cross town together from Stratford free school; for our homes were situated quite near, one to the other. The journey took little more than the quarter part of an hour, but in that short space of time he would provide an account of the day's happenings replete with mimicry, silly faces, hoots, howls, and a phantom cast of characters on which to draw when reality failed to inspire him. To be entertained thus was the apex of my day. Many a time I would leave Ned and enter my father's workshop all jollied and chuckling.

"What tickles you, boy?" my father would ask in his customed gruff way.

" 'Twas Ned," I would answer. "He gave me a story set me laughing all the way from the miller's. Would you like me to tell it you?"

"Nay," he would say, "I've no time for Ned's foolishness—nor have you. There's three pair of calfskin in there needs sewing. So you'd best get-to, or you shall have to work tonight by candlelight."

No, he had no wish to hear one of Ned's madcap tales. Truth to tell, I believe he looked upon him as a bad example to me, a tempter to silly behavior; whereas I was quite sure 'twas I tempted Ned by my response to him: he was ever encouraged by my laughter to play the zany. 'Twas I, in fact, who tempted him in matters more serious.

I remember the occasion well enough. There were we, about at the halfway point in our journey from school to home, when Ned left off his flight of fancy wherein he was deciding what he might say in defiance to Bretchgirdle, who was then the vicar, next time he was called before the class in religious instruction. He would be daring, sacrilegious, profane. We would say—And there he stopped.

"What *would* you say, Ned?" I asked.

"Marry, Will. I know not what I would say, for of a sudden I am struck by such a horrible hunger that I have naught but a blank within me brain."

"What then, had you no breakfast?"

"Alas, no," said he, "or not enough. I b'lieve I sprouted six inches in the last month." This was a gross exaggeration, yet he had grown perceptibly in a short time. "I must eat more to put meat on me bones—or so says my mother."

"You are lucky, Ned, for look you now to your right, and you will find a satisfying remedy for your hunger."

"What have you for me?" said he as he turned to look.

That which met his eyes was a fine apple orchard which we two passed each day. I knew it to be the property of a family named Clawson. The fruit of the trees was ripe and ready to be plucked, and none of the multitudinous Clawson clan was about.

All this I called to his attention, and then I added, "What say you, Ned? Have you the courage?"

It was known that to rob that particular orchard did indeed take some courage. One of Ned's older brothers had the year before been caught relieving the trees of a bit of their burden and been punished with a birch rod by the farmer at the very spot he was apprehended.

Ned replied not a word in response to my dare. He stood but a moment considering it. Then did he turn and take a run at the low, rail fence, and in a single jump did he vault it.

"Well done," said I, applauding him. "Pick one for me, too!"

And that he did. Once committed, he wasted little time. Grasping a limb of the nearest tree, he shook it soundly. A bountiful harvest dropped down to the ground; he scrambled about, scooping up the ripest and the best. He returned to the fence at a run, dropping apples as he came. Unable now to jump over the fence with his arms so overloaded, he filled my hat with them, and then his own. Then did he make his way most careful back over the fence.

Ned's family, which was far poorer than my own, did dine upon apples—and not much else—that evening. His mother made a stew of them, which Ned claimed not be matched, not even in the kitchen of Sir Thomas Lucy. I ate but the one I had requested from him, for I well knew that if I were to return with a hatful of apples, I should be suspect most immediate. My father did indeed seem to look for opportunities to blame me for misdeeds of every sort—yet to no avail, for as my mother oft reminded him, there was not a better-behaved lad in all of Stratford.

I include this episode not merely to entertain but to make a point. Some distinction between sin and crime must be understood. What may be a sin, such as taking the Lord's name in vain (I who have God-damned and God's blooded my way through life), but is not a crime. And thus also what may be a crime, such as the act of theft I have just described, may not be a sin. Indeed, I would argue that it was not. It could be argued, too, that I had no part in it, since I did not so much as enter the orchard, yet that, I think, would be specious, for me it was who put temptation before Ned. Knowingly, I initiated the theft. I was the tempter, and therefore more to blame than Ned. And thus it became repeated in later life. I was upon occasion the tempter, the prime mover. By whatever device or manipulation, I managed to persuade others to do my will. Only once did I . . . But let that pass; there will be time enough later to touch upon that.

Our next steps down the road to crime were taken a year later. I was then sixteen years of age, as was Ned. And it all began innocently enough, for in the beginning there was naught of theft involved in it. Ned's brother, Stephen (the same who had been given a birching by old Clawson) had graduated to poaching. Ned was much interested and wished to learn a few tricks of the poaching trade, and so he did accompany him on his expeditions and was taught how he might make a snare, when to set it, and when to tend it. His brother Stephen also began instruction in the handling of bows and the shooting of arrows. So eager was Ned to demonstrate his new skills that he invited me to come along with him of a Sunday even that I might learn in turn how it was done.

We went at dusk to Stratford common. At that time of day, and perhaps especially at that time of year (the first week in November, and blustery and blowy it was) there seemed to be nobody about. Ned led me across the open field whereon the children played in the day and brought us to a thicket of birch and pine at the far side of the common. There in the fading light and the deep shadows of the close-crowded trees, I watched Ned lay his trap, bending low a pine branch that he might attach the thin rope of the snare. At last he sat back on his haunches and inspected his work.

"Have you then finished?" I asked, impatient to leave.

"All but the bait," said he.

"What is used in such a trap?"

"Depends," said Ned. "Depends upon what you expect to snare."

"And what would that be? A deer? a bear?"

"Ah, you joke, Will. A bear, or even a deer, would gnaw right through this thin stuff. A bear indeed! There ain't no bears round here. 'Cept those that come with the traveling shows."

"What then?"

"Oh, a rabbit, or a squirrel p'rhaps. I'm hopin' for a rabbit. Make a good dinner for tomorrow night." He tossed a few bits of an apple from Clawson's orchard into the center of the snare. "That should do right well," said he.

"What do we now?"

"Why, to home, heigh-ho, and to our beds, for we must rise early to see what we have caught."

And so it was. Ned came knocking upon my window next morning. I was ready for him, hopped out of bed without waking my brother Gilbert, and dressed swift as ever one could. In a trice I was through the door and at Ned's side. Together we set off for the common, saying little, for the chill in the air robbed us of our inclination to discuss, joke or jape in our usual manner. We hiked across the field, and I noticed a light frost upon the stubble of brown whereon we trod. As we drew nearer the thicket, our pace increased; I, no less than Ned, was eager to see what had been caught. We were fair running along by the time we reached the thicket.

"Hi, Will, look you!" shouted Ned. "We got us a rabbit!"

It was indeed true. A hapless brown thing hung topsy-turvy by a rear leg, suspended from the pine branch on a length of thin rope. The animal seemed dead, or near death, for it simply swung as the wind would have it, to and fro.

"Well done, Ned," said I in congratulation. "You've proven yourself."

"But alas," said he, "I must now dash out the poor creature's brains, and I do dislike it so."

"Are you sure you must? He seems quite dead to me."

"Ah, but he will come back to life soon as ever you touch him. Try it, and you'll see." He gestured toward the animal in invitation.

I accepted. Taking a careful step forward, I reached out and put a hand to him. What I had intended was the lightest of touches. Perhaps I hoped not to frighten the poor brutish thing, or perhaps again I simply wished to prove Ned wrong. Whatever be so, I did touch him so easy and light that I might well have been thought to deliver a loving caress.

The rabbit, however, did not think it so. A sudden spasm passed through it, one of such violence that he might have shaken himself free of the pine branch had the rope that bound him to it been made of weaker stuff. My hand jerked back and away swiftly, and without in any manner seeking my permission. Nevertheless, it was not an unpleasant experience. I felt a sort of tremor, a shiver of pleasure that ran through me as might a thrill come from the nether parts of the body.

Before I had even considered what I might mean by it, I blurted out to Ned, "Let me do it."

He looked at me oddly. "Do what, Will?"

"Let me kill it. Let me dash its brains out."

"You *wish* to do that?"

Ned gave that some consideration, while all the while he studied my face and its expression as if to read in them the reason for my request.

"Well . . . all right. Grasp it by the rear legs. Hold them tight as can be, for if you lose your grip on him, us Wilsons will lose our dinner. You'll hold them tight?"

"Yes, oh yes, I shall."

"Then go to that birch tree across the path—the trunk should be thick enough—and do it there."

"All right."

Again I approached the hanging form of the rabbit. It swung more vigorously, moved not by the wind but by its own power. Tiny squeals could be heard, yet only barely. I was even more careful in my movements than before, and thus was I better prepared. It was not difficult to grasp the leg by which he hung, but the other proved difficult, for he pawed the air with it unceasingly. At last, after three attempts—thanking the Almighty that I had gloves to protect my hands—I got a good, firm grip and nodded to Ned, who already had his knife poised. He cut the rope which secured the rabbit to the tree, then he nodded in return and pointed to the birch tree he had selected. Holding tight to those rear legs, I moved across to the designated birch tree. As I went, I noted that the rabbit had soiled the fur at that point where the two legs conjoined—no doubt from fear. Well, indeed the rabbit had much to fear; he did indeed fear what we all fear, not so much death as the end of life.

I swung the animal right to left and felt his head hit hard against the tree. The life seemed to go out of him then—or perhaps more likely, he was simply stunned. Thinking that to be the truth of it, I swung him again by those two rear feet, this time left to right. I heard the impact of the cranium upon the wood, and felt it, too. Yet unsatisfied, I swung him once more right to left, and then again left to right.

I felt a weight upon my shoulder. It was the hand of Ned; it was as if he sought to steady me.

I looked up at him. "What then?" said I.

"You may as well stop," said he, "whilst there is still something of him left to eat."

Hearing that, I did indeed take time to examine the damage I had done. The thing was certainly dead, head bloodied and missing an ear. He hardly had the appearance of a rabbit at all; rather did he look as some wild beast from Africa, lately the victim of a fight to the death.

"You've bloodied yourself, Will," said Ned as he took the animal from me. "You'll have some excuses to make."

And indeed he was right. Yet I had a day to prepare an explanation. Both father and mother believed, as I told them, that I had got a nosebleed, for I had suffered them before. Only Gilbert, my brother and bedmate and two years my junior, seemed to doubt me.

So long as there were rabbits to catch there on Stratford common, Ned and I continued our trapping there, laying snares once or twice a week. Yet as often as not, squirrels rather than rabbits were caught; these Ned let go, declaring there was not meat enough on them this time of year to justify bringing them home. But as time passed and winter came on, the rabbits became scarce—and finally did give out completely. Ned was most distressed.

"D'you think, Will, they've put the word out on us? D'you suppose the king of the rabbits did call an assemblage of his loyal subjects and warn them against us?"

"Perhaps they posted sentinels against us to warn their fellows."

"Ah, now that could be." He considered but a moment and added, "Or they may all have gone someplace else, one far from us. Ah, nicky-nacky, I know not."

Then did I remember just where it was on Saturday last I had seen rabbits frolicking in the snow. "I believe *I* know where they have gone," said I in my most important manner.

"Oh, where, Will, where? Tell me, and I'll seek them out, I shall. We'll be eating rabbit stew once more."

I made to give the matter some consideration, then said almost reluctantly, "There is danger involved."

"Danger? What sort?"

"Of the legal sort."

"Well, I take apples in season from Clawson's orchard, and I've no fear of punishment."

"So say you, but old Clawson is but a small farmer. Sir Thomas Lucy is a very large one."

"Ah, Sir Thomas, is it? He is most powerful."

"Indeed he is, but let me tell you what I saw."

That I proceeded to do, in a manner as briefly as possible: I was sent Saturday last to deliver gloves to Sir Thomas. My father had worked on them for well over a week—or over a month if the time spent in the preparation of the leather might be included. Leave it that he had worked long and hard upon them and wished to make a good impression on this local landowner when they were done. Therefore he sent me to deliver them. (My father, poor soul, was ever shy in the impression he made upon such people and perhaps even a little ashamed that he was a mere craftsman and not a landowner.) Because of my wit and quick tongue, he thought me best able to deal with those he considered his betters. And so I was sent, gloves in hand, well-wrapped against the snow, should a sudden squall blow up or—God forbid!—they be dropped by me in a snowbank. But I carried them careful and dropped them not, and I arrived at the Lucy manor in good time to catch the master in. Some retainer or other answered the door and asked my business. When he did hear that I had in hand a pair of gloves made specially for Sir Thomas Lucy by the master-glovemaker, John Shakespeare, he nodded impatiently and put out his hand.

"Give them here," said he. "I'll see that he gets them."

"Ah, that I might," said I with a smile meant to win him over. "But you see, gloves must fit most perfect, and I have orders to make certain these I have here fit him just so. In short, good sir, I wish him to try them on."

"Oh, *you* wish it so?" said he with a most dramatic sneer. "And who might you be, you young dollop of midden?"

I continued to smile most sweetly. "Why, sir, I am John Shakespeare's son, William. And I regret my phrasing of my last statement. I meant to say that Sir Thomas would wish to try them on."

"You think that, do you?"

He showed no signs of surrender. I was about to give in and

hand over the gloves to this boorish lackey when a door opened down the long hall, and a man I recognized as Sir Thomas Lucy emerged and came shouting towards us.

"What is all this raucous blattering about?" he demanded. A tall man, and near as wide as he was tall, he walked with a rolling gait with which he meant to disguise a limp on his left side. "I am trying to compose a letter, Arthur, a *very important* letter. And whenever I seek to gather my thoughts, your ugly voice does make it impossible. Now what is the cause of all this?"

"He is, Sir Thomas," said the fellow, pointing to me.

"And *who is he?*"

I bowed. "William Shakespeare, sir, son of John Shakespeare, who has made for you the most beautiful pair of gloves in the shire. They want only to be tried on and approved by you."

"Ah yes," he grunted, "the glover. Give them here."

I attempted to make a formal presentation, bowing once again and unwrapping the flannel in which I had carried them so carefully hither. He grabbed up the gloves most rudely and began to pull one onto his right hand. Sir Thomas was indifferent to all this. He thrust his hand in so roughly that I feared for a moment that he would punch his fingers through—but no, the gloves were too well sewn for that. Once on his hand, he held the glove out before him and looked upon it with disdain.

"It's too tight," said he. "There's no room in it for shrinking."

"Ah, but Sir Thomas," said I, "it will not shrink. My father has treated it in such a way with water that it has already shrunk to its limit. Why not try on the other?"

He did nothing of the kind but rather looked at me coldly, saying nothing for an awkward moment. At last, as he pulled off the glove, he spoke. "You dare gainsay me? You suppose yourself to know more of choosing gloves than I? Bring these to your father and tell him there is no room in them for shrinking."

Then did he wad up the gloves, right and left together, and throw them in my face. I caught one of them as it fell and scrambled on the floor for the other.

"Arthur, throw him out."

Just as I recovered the fugitive glove, Arthur delivered a kick to my backside. He inflicted no damage; except to my dignity, which by then was hurt beyond helping. By the time I had managed to regain my feet, Arthur had the door wide open. He grabbed me by the scruff of the neck and the small of my back and propelled me through the opening and down three steps to the gate. Though I had managed to save the gloves, I fear the flannel in which I carried them was altogether lost. There was no going back for it; that much was plain. Rather, I did smooth out those handsome doeskin gloves, fold them but once, and set off down the road for town.

God's blood! I did hate, loathe, and despise those two men!

I was not yet to the stone that marked the end of Sir Thomas Lucy's considerable holdings, yet long out of sight of the manor house, when I noted movement through the trees that ran along the road and served as windbreaks. Curious, I climbed the fence, squirmed in amongst the trees, and peered out at the snowy field beyond. What awaited my gaze was a most strange sight. There a considerable number of rabbits played—more than twenty, though less than forty. It was, in truth, difficult to fix even their near number for it was impossible to count them as they dashed about so madly, chasing and being chased, leaping one over the other, burrowing into the snow and popping up again. What games were these? What did such wild carryings-on betoken? Whereas my mood till that moment had been a dark one—I was full of bile and bad feeling—it was raised and lightened by the sight before me. More, so envious was I of their evident happy spirits that I found myself wishing that I might, if only for a little while, assume the shape of a rabbit and join them in their wild careering.

Nevertheless, it grew late, and though I much dreaded my return home, where I should have to tell my father of Sir Thomas's boorish rejection of his fine work, I knew I would have to leave this field of play and hurry home ere it grew dark. Though I wished to stay longer, I could not. Turning to withdraw from the trees which had given me cover, I pushed hard against a low-lying branch—indeed, a bit too hard, for it broke with a loud snap that seemed to ring through the cold air like the roar of a fowling piece. With that, all activity in the field did cease. I looked back and saw the rabbits sitting up in a state of keen attention, their ears raised and their forelegs aquiver. Yet I saw them thus only an instant, for at the end of that brief space of time, all dropped down and scurried off together for the nearby wood, which was but a rod or so distant. And in less time than it takes to tell, they had all vanished. I made note of the location of that wood, counted off the paces to the stone marker, which were many, and vowed that I should return.

What more to tell? When I arrived home, I told my father what had happened, and what had been said. I half-expected to have my ears boxed by him to relieve his frustration and anger—though as I saw it I was in no manner at fault in this. Perhaps he saw it as I did, or perhaps he felt frustrated beyond any such misguided action, but to tell it in truth, he said nothing—or next to it. After listening closely to my tale, he kept silent for a time; then he did heave a sigh and say, "Ah, well, he probably would not have paid for them, anyway. *He* may break the law, but when a poor man seeks to better himself . . ."

I had naught to reply to that.

———

None of what I told my father did I tell to Ned Wilson; nor, for that matter, did I tell my father what I had told Ned. All that my friend heard was contained in these few sentences: "I delivered a pair of gloves to Sir Thomas Lucy for my father. And whilst returning, I happened to see a great congregation of rabbits at play in one of his fields. When they saw me they all took flight and ran to a nearby wood."

"Could you find that place again?" asked Ned.

"You mean the field, or the wood?" I asked, all-innocent, in return.

"You find the field, and I'll find the wood," said he, "and I'll get more furry critters than you."

"And how many snares will you lay?"

"Why, nicky-nacky, Will, as many as there are rabbits to be snared. If we take some and leave the rest, those left behind would be sore disappointed."

And so it was agreed between us that we would go out as dark was falling and lay a number of traps there in those woods which were hard by the field wherein I had seen the rabbits at play. Since twine was then scarce at Ned's house, he had asked me to bring along as much as I could find at my own. I had done as best I could, but all I found at home was rope, thicker and more substantial than was needed to trap what Ned called the "little furry critters." But it would do, said he. Better to have it too strong than too weak.

On the way, tramping through the snow, we two discussed the morality of what we were about—or perhaps better put, the legality of it.

"Ned," said I to him, "you understand, do you, that to take from Sir Thomas's holdings constitutes thievery?"

"*Rabbits?* Rabbits is pests, Will. If Sir Thomas knew what we were about, he would thank us, sure."

"Well, perhaps." It occurred to me that Sir Thomas Lucy seldom offered thanks to many. "But poaching is what they call it, and poaching is a crime."

Ned had no ready reply for that. He simply trudged on in silence through the snow along the side of the road.

I considered that I had done my duty in warning Ned, but I did secretly hope that Sir Thomas Lucy would be greatly angered by our visit and would demand that the culprits be found and justice be done. Would it matter to him that they were only rabbits that had been trapped and taken? No, what would matter most to him was that they were *his* rabbits. I delighted in the certainty that Sir Thomas would be enraged by our adventure, yet at the same time I was aware that we must indeed use care that we leave no trace behind.

By the time we did reach the stone marker, darkness had fallen. The moon lit our way as I began counting paces off to the point where I had climbed the fence and made my entry into the domain of Sir Thomas. When, at 157, I stopped counting and indicated to Ned that it was here that we were to go through the trees and across the field, he said nothing, but with a gesture indicated that I was to lead the way; he then would follow.

I looked up the road and down and decided that there were none in sight who might witness our ingression. It had not earlier occurred to me to wonder why this fence was so much higher than others I had seen round Stratford. Since I could not answer the question I had put to myself, I let the matter go for the present. Yet there was no real problem posed by the fence: I went over it just as quickly as I had earlier, and Ned followed. Through the trees we went; then quickly we crossed the snow-covered field and entered the dark wood.

Quickly we separated and went about our business; Ned went off in one direction to lay his snares with the ball of twine that he carried, and I went in another with my wound length of heavier stuff. I had long before learned from Ned the manner of laying snares. He said indeed that I exceeded him in sequestering, though his were more swiftly laid. I found a trail through the wood and tied my snares along the way of it. But because he was more practiced than I, it was not long before he was beside me and announced that he was ready to leave.

"So soon?" said I. "Would you like some of this rope of mine?"

"No, let us be off. I heard an animal moving about in this wood bigger than any rabbit." He seemed disquieted in a way I had not known him before.

It was not until we were well on toward home that it came to me that if the unusually high fence served to keep some out, it might also serve to keep some in.

Next morning—or was it just past the middle of the night?—Ned came to my window and tapped lightly upon it. I must have been sleeping lightly, for I came awake most immediate. It was almost as if I had awaited his arrival at my house the moment I had left him at his. Gilbert did not so much as stir. I dressed quickly and left by the window.

The first thing I noted about him as he waited there in the dark for me was that he had with him a pole that seemed about a foot taller than he was. Without a word he led me to the road. Only then did he explain for what purpose he had brought the pole.

"It's for the furry critters, Will," he said. "We'll tie them to it by their feet and be able to carry off a great number."

"Do you truly believe we shall trap so many?"

"I hope so. So long as this snow does last I can keep them packed in it and keep them from going rotten. There's naught this time of the year in the way of greens—not that we could buy anything anyways, not with Papa taken sick. It looks like we will live on rabbit and not much more the rest of the winter."

He went silent again, as he had for much of the journey the evening before. After long, empty minutes of this, I began to wonder what he was thinking of—and so I asked him.

"I told my brother Stephen where we was last night. He said—"

"Stephen, the poacher?" I asked, interrupting.

"No more does he poach. He works instead for farmer Clawson."

"Clawson who birched him?"

"The same," said Ned. "Stephen heard the old man needed a cowherd. My brother's always been good with animals, so he screwed up his courage, put his hat in his hand, and asked for the job. Through the winter Clawson is paying him in potatoes and apples."

"So you'll not starve."

"Nor will we be made to go beggin'."

We fell silent again and tramped on thus for near half a mile more. Then did I remember that brother Stephen had made some comment upon our last night's work, and I had been too impatient to hear it. And so I then put it to Ned:

"What had your brother to say about laying snares in Lucy's estate?"

"He said we should go with caution and get out swift."

I little liked the sound of that, yet did I say naught.

"Also did he say we would be fools to return by the road," said Ned. "He drew me a map that we might travel back through neighbors' fields."

I was some little encouraged by that, though not overmuch. Yet enough was it so that by the time I had counted off the 157 strides and still had met no one along the road, I took greater heart in our enterprise. And when together we plunged into the dark wood and together went searching for the snares laid hours before, all went well enough, except the crop of rabbits was not quite so grand as Ned had hoped. There were four collected from the ten snares he had laid and two from my four.

The fifth snare yielded a great astonishment. I had tied it to a pine limb stronger and higher than need be; why I did it so I cannot say. Yet it was because I had done so that the good, strong rope of wild hemp held against the weight of a fallow deer of middling size. Upended it was, not quite dangling but in a position that made it impossible for her, a doe, to chew through the rope.

Ned was so excited by our find that he dropped his knife as he fumbled for it. It fell to the ground, but he scooped it up and did what had to be done. He fell upon the nearly prone animal and, holding her down by the antlers, he cut her throat. Had we not come upon her quietly and remained so, she might well have taken a three-legged stance and kept us at bay until dawn would have sent us scurrying for home.

We scurried in any case. Ned waited with improvident impatience until she had panted her last and given a final tremble. Only then did he tie her hooves tight to the pole.

"Come along, Will, grab the pole at t'other end. That's it, up on your shoulder. Together . . . *now!*"

Thus we carried it, he at the fore end and I at the rear. He led us along the trace and out of the wood. Ned pulled out the map given him by his brother, gave it a glance and pointed left which took us away from the road. There was then a short bit cross the corner of the field, then down a path, which led at last to a fence of the same style and height as the one that ran along the road. Somehow—I do not yet understand quite how—we managed to get the pole with its burden of dead flesh up and over the fence.

From that point onward, it was not so hard a piece as I had feared it might be. Our way took us through open country, and there were no more great barriers, natural or those made by human artifice, to overcome. Nevertheless, Ned called for a halt at several points along the way that he might consult the map. He could now read it better as the dimmest daylight did begin slowly to break in the east. Each time we stopped I was more delighted than the last, for the weight of the doe and the rabbits on the pole seemed to cut deeper and deeper into my shoulder. By the time we reached the outbuildings behind the Wilson house, my shoulder and also the arm with which I had attempted to support the pole and its weight were both altogether numb.

"Into the barn with them," called Ned in a kind of throttled cry. "I'll butcher them there."

"All I want," said I, "are the back and belly of the doeskin."

II

Later that morning, whilst I was at school, a constable and Sir Thomas Lucy's man, Arthur, appeared at the Wilson barn and detained Ned on suspicion of poaching one female fallow deer from the estate of Sir Thomas Lucy. It seemed that they had been led there direct by following a faint trail of blood which had dripped from the doe onto the snow as we struggled to bring it across the open fields.

They demanded that Ned tell them who had helped him, for they were certain that he alone could not have carried the carcass so far. Yet Ned refused, saying that he had no help. Further, they had heard from a farmer who had glimpsed us in the light of the dawn; he described us as "two lads floundering in the snow with a deer swinging from a pole they carried between them." In spite of this, Ned insisted he had been alone in the deed.

It was Gilbert brought me the news. He ran to meet me that I might be prepared when it was discussed at home. My brother, feigning sleep, had been witness to many of my early morning departures with Ned to tend the traps he had laid there and about, and he was certain that I should at least wish to know what had befallen my friend. Yet Gilbert was not prepared for my response:

"Look you, has the constable been to visit Father yet?"

"Why no," said he, "why should he? I heard of Ned's capture from his sister, who was quite beside herself with worry.

Three months in gaol and a considerable fine is the punishment, said she."

"I must away," said I.

There was little more to say. I hurried home with Gilbert at my heels, begging to know if it were true then that I had been with Ned that morning; and if so, what did I plan to do? Where did I plan to go?

All these questions but the last I answered in a letter which I left for Father in lieu of a proper leave-taking. I did more than hint that I had done it all for him, that he might have fine doeskin from which to cut gloves, which was true enough, I suppose; nevertheless, I well knew that my request to Ned for the back and belly of the deer came only as an afterthought. But in such ways—in particular, the loving and respectful tone of the letter—I hoped to keep the door open to me if and when I should return.

What was it sent me out on the high road in the wintertime? After all, if Ned had withheld my name thus long, I might expect him to keep it back through an eternity (and in fact that is just what he did). If challenged, I would have been forced to admit that, even as I set out upon my journey. And so it could be said that even then I knew that I had another reason for leaving Stratford, deeper than I could measure and so strong that it would succeed in driving me from this town of my birth again and again. The truth is, you see, that I was in a terrible state of *ennui*. Though it is a French word, it describes a state known all the world over. You've had it, haven't you?—that dull feeling of sameness, day after day—that sense that life has lost all flavor, all sense or meaning. Of course you know it or you would not have read this far in these paltry "confessions," without hoping to be recompensed with some titillation, some base thrill. Though I have lived all my life in England, this blessed plot, this prison of the soul, I know a bit of the great world and its workings—more, I vow, than any other man in this backward hamlet. In any case, what I know of them tells me that many enterprises are undertaken by the very rich and most powerful—and these would include wars, voyages of discovery, and missions of peaceful diplomacy—simply to alleve these same feelings of *ennui.* It is the one great unacknowledged force in human affairs. And it was easily strong enough to lure me—nay, drive me—from Stratford at the age of sixteen with little more than a shilling in my pocket.

Whilst this considering mood is yet upon me, let us look back over what has thus far been said in search of sin. I do contend that you will find little of it in this episode which I have related. If sin there be, then it be venal, surely, and Ned Wilson was its victim; for true enough, I did quite knowingly tempt him a time or two—that I do admit. Nevertheless, when it came to the commission of a crime, I warned him most plain. I said, "Poaching is what they call it, and poaching is a crime." He did, however, put forth an interesting argument. He defended the setting of snares, and rabbits were pests, no more nor less. And it was indeed true that the rabbits we took were not even mentioned when his arrest warrant was handed down.

Yet if rabbits be excepted as pests, why not also deer? Were they not also pests? Ask any farmer who tends land in country wild enough to have a herd of deer about. Ask if deer or rabbits are the greater threat to his crops; he will put you aright on the matter. They are capable of consuming whole fields at a time, or so I am told. If it is thus a pest in one set of circumstances, then it is a pest in any and all. In any case, we saw it as no more than meat upon the table—for purposes of argument, a very large rabbit.

As I look back at what I have just written, I do confess that I am pleased with it. My arguments are specious and sententious enough to be presented in any court of law. I heard often after my first Venetian play that I should have been a lawyer in consideration of the argument put forth against the Jew

("... if thou dost shed one drop of Christian blood ..."). Ah, indeed I was clever.

Though I did not tell my father in the letter I had left for him, I had chosen a destination when I left home, and I had chosen it well. I was off to Lancashire to visit John Cotton, my former schoolmaster. He it was who had encouraged me so generously in my efforts at versifying, and it was he who had been turned out of his teaching employ when it became known that he was a Papist and his brother a priest. We had exchanged letters: I sending him new poems of mine (my first efforts in the sonnet form among them), and he lavishing praise upon them. His was the first post that ever I received. I well remember the pride I felt in calling for it, and the postman noting with interest that it had come "all the way from Lancashire." He had given me a sharp look as he inquired, "Who do you know there?"

"A friend," said I as I grabbed the letter from his hand. A curse upon the curiosity of small town clerks!

In that letter, which I had received but three months past, Mr. Cotton had extended an open invitation to come for a visit of any length of time I might choose. "I should like nothing better than to see your face at my door, Will," he wrote. "I have room aplenty here and naught to occupy me but caring for my father who is, I fear, mortally ill." Having read that, I began saving my farthings and halfpennies toward a walking trip to Lancashire in the spring.

Well, indeed it would be spring by the calendar in a few days, but the ground and even the trees were laden still with snow. This was not the time of year to undertake such a journey, yet undertake it I must, for in truth I had nowhere else to go. I wondered, did Mr. Cotton know how greatly I depended upon him for succour and salvation? How could he? I could not write in advance to tell him of my visit, for the day before I left, I had no notion that I would be coming soon. Should I beg paper and pen someplace along the way that I might write him of my arrival? No, I could not afford to reduce my small store of coins by paying the post charge. I could do naught but make the tramp up to Lancashire and hope that I found a welcome as warm as the one I had been promised.

There is little point in dwelling upon the details of that dreadful journey. They are better left undescribed. And in addition, I have purposely forgotten most of the worst of it—simply put it out of my mind completely, as I am sometimes wont to do. The trouble was that just a bit beyond Warwick, the weather changed of a sudden, and it became quite warm for the latter part of March. The snow began immediately to melt, of course, and I thought that reason to rejoice, yet I did not reckon upon what would succeed it. The snow went in little more than a day, replaced by a gray slime of about equal parts melted snow and road dirt. Thus I tramped through Birmingham and beyond. Another day of it, and the good, soft boots made for me by my father were wet beyond drying, and my feet were cold and sore, as well. I slept in barns along the way with naught but my cloak to warm me during the night. As a result, I caught a chill in the cold night air and traveled the last two days with a mounting fever. I crossed the River Mersey on a bridge that was under half a foot of water at each end. I pressed on, light-headed and unsure upon my feet, powered with the knowledge that I was drawing nearer to my goal, the village of Atherton and the manor house of the Cotton family, Riverdale, which stood just outside it. I asked my way through chattering teeth and at last came upon an imposing building of two floors—three in its middle portion—with land aplenty surrounding it. I staggered up the path, reeling with fever, and knocked upon the door. My summons was answered by a retainer of advanced years who seemed to take pity upon me in my sickened state; he brought me to a chair and seated me upon it as he went off to fetch John Cotton whom I had asked to see.

My former teacher came forthwith, hurrying down a great staircase, then came to a halt at the bottom as I struggled to rise on unsure legs.

He stared, unable for a moment even to recognize me, so wasted was I with fever and exhaustion. But then, of a sudden, did he call out my name and come forward, a great smile upon his face. I sought to meet him, yet the effort was strangely too much for me. Perhaps my feet became entangled. I cannot say in certainty what led direct to my collapse, but just as I approached him, I fell; and falling, I swooned.

What happened to me then I know not. For days I was in delirium, passing from consciousness, then into a faint, which brought strange dreams. Faces appeared and vanished. Most often came that of Mr. Cotton; and less often that of the retainer; and a few times did a woman come to visit me wearing a look of great concern.

It was she, however, who was present when I did come to myself completely. I noted that I was in a proper bed, the first I had known since leaving my home. I sought to raise myself for a better look at my surroundings. Only then did I glimpse the woman as she came closer. Her face brightened as she saw that I was much improved. Then did she open her mouth and speak; what came out sounded a bit like English, yet only a bit; indeed it was quite the strangest tongue I had ever heard spoke.

Though I could not understand her, she seemed to understand me when I asked for water. She turned away from the bed for what seemed but a moment and returned with a cloth she had wetted. She put it to my lips, and then gave my face a wipe. She turned away again and brought me a cup of water. Again I propped myself upon my elbows and drank greedily from the cup—a bit too greedily, I fear, for the water proved hard to swallow, and I commenced to cough. This distressed her, and she left the room for a brief period of time and returned with Mr. Cotton.

"Ah, Will," said he, "you are with us at last, it does seem."

I nodded and attempted to smile.

"You've been a sick young fellow," he went on, "a terrible pleurisy, rattling away for days it was. But now you seem much better. Could you eat something?"

Again I nodded.

"I thought you might, and so I sent Celia to boil up some soup. We can talk later when you've gathered some strength."

Saying thus, he pulled a chair over to the bedside, sat down in it, and looked upon me with great sympathy—and something else. I knew not quite how to name it, yet it seemed to me a kind of eager rapacity, which bothered me no little. I turned slightly from him, fearing to look him full in the face. But then, in answer to an unspoken prayer, the woman named Celia—the cook, surely—came through the door and bustled to my bedside, bowl and spoon in hand. Mr. Cotton pulled back his chair and made room for her. She immediately began spooning the contents of the bowl into my mouth. I took much, perhaps most of what she offered, but at last I signaled that I had had quite enough. She looked at me in a sharp way and said something that again I could not understand. Thinking that she wished only to confirm that I had done with her potato and leek soup, I answered as if that were the question. With that, she nodded and left the room.

"So," said Mr. Cotton, "you *can* speak."

"That is what I have just discovered," I responded. "Could you tell me, sir, what language that woman speaks?"

Mr. Cotton smiled at that. "It is the dialect spoken here in Lancashire. But even if you can't understand her, she can understand you well enough. You should get on with her."

Then did he begin to tell me things—that the chamber pot was under the bed, that I might find him in the next bedroom if I felt needful of anything—of the kind that said that he was about to take his leave of me. Yet still he lingered, now standing, and smiled down upon me. He looked as if he had much more to say but could not find the words. At last he put an end to it.

"Well then, Will, it is quite late. Good night to you." And so, with a kiss upon my lips, did he leave me, taking the candle with him.

I did have occasion to use the chamber pot during the night and discovered when I did that quite all of my clothes had been taken from me. Ah well, I assured myself, they would be clean and dry when I had them back.

The next morning I was fed more soup and bread by Celia, who then returned with a bowl of warm water and a cloth. She threw the bed rug from the bed, stood me upon my feet, and gave me a good, sound washing over all my body. I tried to cover myself, but she would have none of it. She washed me and then she dried me, and then she put me back into the bed and threw the rug over me once more. I might have been less embarrassed, might even have been pleasured a bit by all this had she been in the least comely. Yet she was thick at the waist, had lank hair, and had not many teeth left in her head.

Mr. Cotton did not come to visit me until late in the afternoon. I inquired after his father's condition, supposing he had somehow been occupied in caring for him all through the earlier part of the day.

"Oh," said he with a sad shake of his head, "he lingers on. He will get no better—only worse, I fear."

"How sad," said I, thinking that an appropriate response to such a dismal prognostick.

"I looked in on him early in the day, as I do most days, to ask his wants and needs. Sometimes he wishes only to talk. I believe him to be more deeply saddened by my brother's certain death by execution than by his own." At this point he faltered, no doubt absorbed by these mordant thoughts. But then did he press on: "Most of the day I spent planning the spring planting with the overseer of our holdings."

"Are they so vast?" I asked rather brashly.

"Tolerably vast," said he with a smile. "All this falls upon me, you see, for my father is so deep in melancholia that he is quite incapable, and I have much to learn about these matters. But I have not given myself up to them completely. If I were to do so I should lose touch with the man that I was, and I do not wish to do that."

"I should not wish you to do that, either," said I with a simper. "It was that man I walked so far to see."

"Yes, we must talk of your journey. I must hear all the details. But first, Will, I have a confession to make."

"You, sir? What sort of confession?"

"When Celia took your clothes away to wash, I asked to have the bag which you had slung upon your back that I might see what new wonders you had brought me to see."

"Wonders?"

"Poems, Will, poems," said he. Then did he declare, "Each of your verses is something of a wonder. Any true work of art is in its own way just that—a wonder. But that you write so well at so young an age, that is something more, something of a higher order. That, it does seem to me, is quite a miracle."

I knew not what to say. To hear my poems—nay, more, my gift for writing them—spoken of in such a way was more even than I had hoped for. And since I knew not what to say, I said nothing. I simply cast my eyes down most modestly and waited, hoping that he would continue.

Yet he surprised me by pulling from his doublet the very poems he had been discussing. I knew them instanter, for I had wrapped them in an odd piece of leather I had found in my father's workshop and sewn the papers whereon the poems were copied into the leather. I wanted it to have the appearance of a true book.

He went to the chair on which he had sat the night before and collapsed upon it, as he began rummaging through the sheaf of poems. "There is one here I wished to ask you about," said he. Then, discovering: "Ah, here it is. This, which begins,

'Two loves I have, of comfort and despair . . .' " He looked up expectantly, as if he had already asked the question and was awaiting the answer.

"Yes? Yes? What about it?"

"Well, I may be presuming too much, dear Will, but I do see myself as one of the two. Am I . . . presuming too much?"

"Oh, no, no, certainly not, sir. But two lines down it is put most plain," said I, and then did I recite from memory: " 'My better angel is a man right fair.' "

"Yes, I see. That is most flattering. But this next line—" He read, " 'My worser spirit a woman colour'd ill.' " He frowned. "Who is this woman?"

"Why, sir, she is no one at all. I simply thought to set the bad angel against the good, as has been done often before. Yet I would give a certain novelty to it by casting a woman in the role of the bad angel. That conceit, I think, has never been used before."

"Perhaps not," said he, "but it all seems rather confused. You seem to predict that your bad angel will fire your good angel out. Can you have meant that, Will?"

"Again, sir, that was simply to give a certain freshness to it. In such poetic struggles between the bad and the good, the good seems always to win. Well, indeed we know that to be contrary to experience. Why not let the bad for once banish the good?"

"Hmmm, well," he mused, "but I want you to know that I should never allow myself to be banished from your side. I shall be your good angel forever." That last he gave most solemnly as one might make a great promise, or a binding oath.

Again at a loss for words, I chose discretion and said nothing at all.

Yet he seemed to expect naught in the way of comment from me, for without hesitating, he went on: "That said, I do nevertheless think this the weakest of all these you have brought. It is confused. There is nothing in it to compare with that phrase in the first line in the next poem, '. . . the heavenly rhetoric of thine eye.' Now, that is true poetry, pure beauty. But here, you read it, Will. Read them all aloud and let us discuss each one."

And that was indeed what I did and what, in turn, we did. Youth, of course, wishes to hear naught of criticism; only praise will do. And if, at times, he played the critic, he was far more often so generous in his praise that I felt elevated, yea exalted, by the experience. He even lauded my reading of the poems.

"You've a good voice, Will," said he. "A strong tenor, it is. I believe it would carry well." (What he meant by "carry well," I had no notion at the time, though I would soon learn.)

As afternoon passed into early evening, the room grew dark to the sound of our discourse. But then, of a sudden, he grew acutely aware of the time, rose to his feet, and made to go. "I'll keep these a bit longer, if I may," said he, waving my sheaf of poems. "And then I'll send Celia up with supper for you, perhaps something more substantial than soup. You can handle it, can't you?"

"Oh, yes sir," said I.

He bent to kiss me and indecisively planted a buss upon a point midway between my lips and cheek. He seemed suddenly vexed and cast his eyes away from mine. "I must go," said he and hurried to the door. But there he paused, and with his back turned to me still, he did say: "You must be quite perishing with nothing to read. I'll see that you get something most immediate." And saying no more, he left.

His abrupt departure troubled me a little. I knew not quite what to suppose had caused it. I feared that perhaps I had taken too much upon myself by presenting myself at his door, all sick with fever, wet, and dirty. Perhaps I was not near so welcome as I had hoped.

Yet as if in contradiction to that, following a perfunctory tap or two, the door opened wide and the old servant entered—a man of at least fifty, an age which I then thought to be quite ancient indeed. He had in one hand a volume of modest size, and in the other, a candleholder with a new candle stuck in it. He greeted me, then set about lighting the candle with flint and steel from a tinder box which was tucked away in his jerkin. As he did this, Celia entered through the open door, supporting a tray in her ample arms. Once the candle was lit, I saw that the tray had on it a sumptuous meal—a beef chop, a good bit of pudding with dripping thereon, beer to drink, eating utensils, and even a napkin, which I thought only for use on special occasions. But this, after all, was a special occasion, was it not? A successful escape from Stratford, a recovery from illness, enthusiastic praise from one whom I admired above all others—what more did a fugitive from the law, such as myself, need for purposes of celebration?

I ate well, taking my good time, wiped my hands carefully upon the napkin and picked up the book which had been delivered to me. It was *The Shephearde's Calendar,* by Edmund Spenser. Mr. Cotton had spoken of it to me during his last weeks in Stratford, even mentioned it in one of the letters he had written. It was, he had said, a collection of twelve eclogues, a form known to me (though not well, I confess) from my studies of Latin. These, however, were not in Latin, but rather in English—and very beautiful English it was—And near as beautiful as the texts were the woodcuts that accompanied them. It was quite the most beautiful book that ever I had seen.

Just as I was about to begin a serious reading of *The Shephearde's Calendar,* Celia reappeared, bearing the clothes I had worn to this grand house. Why did they look to me so tattered and worn, so plain and fustian? Had I already taken to me the standards of dress of this manor house where even the servants seemed to dress better than I? But at least my clothes were clean. That much was evident when she laid them out upon the foot of the bed. Then did she gather up the tray, which contained a few unfinished morsels of food and the greasy plates from dinner. All the while she was in this room wherein I had made my home, she said not a word. She intimidated me somewhat, and I believe she knew that. At the very least Celia must know that I was made uncomfortable by that strange dialect which she spoke. Thus we did not speak one to the other whilst she busied herself in the way I have described. And so I was not at all prepared when, without so much as a by-your-leave, she bent over and blew the candle out. I must have let out some outcry of protest, for she sniggered at my distress and muttered something under her breath, a phrase which seemed to end in "sleep." No doubt she was telling me simply to quieten down and go to sleep. Whatever it may have been, there was neither point nor opportunity to argue the matter with her, for she turned and left by way of the door which opened into the lighted hallway. She pulled the door shut behind her, and I was left in complete darkness.

Well, perhaps not complete. There was light from a half moon, still low enough in the night sky that it could be spied through the window. It was enough for me to make out the sparse furnishings of the room—the chair wherein Mr. Cotton had sat but an hour or two before, the table whereon he had laid my sheaf of poems, a stool off in a far corner; more I could not see from where I lay. It was a rather odd and austere sort of room, just the right sort for a poet's cell. I would make it so if he let me.

I noted about that time that the room had grown cold in more than temper. A shiver passed through me. Not wishing the chill to return and provoke a fever, I bounded out of bed and pulled on the homespun shirt and woolen hose which lay across the bed; then did I burrow back into the bed and under the rug, much relieved by the added warmth of the clothes.

There were footsteps in the hall. They passed my door and continued on to the room next to mine—Mr. Cotton's it was. The door shut behind him; and then began a restless pacing within. It continued without ceasing for more minutes than

I could count. As I later thought upon it, near half an hour must have been devoted to this strange exercise. At last did it cease. He must have sought to exhaust himself with all that pacing, thought I, that he might fall soon to sleep. What could have distressed him so?

Silence then from the room next door, yet that fit of pacing had put me in a state of unrest so that I myself could no longer sleep. Then did I detect the slightest noises—a squeak, a creak, the sound of a door opening and closing, and the softest ever footsteps in the hall. I thought he might be coming to discuss with me this matter that weighted so heavy upon him. And yes, my door opened, and there he stood, dressed in a handsome robe. I raised up in bed, about to speak, yet he put his forefinger to his lips, warning me to silence. Then did he close the door behind him and proceed to my bedside.

He arranged my body in such a way so that I faced away from him. There was then a moment's delay, but next I knew he was beside me in bed, quite showering me with kisses upon my back, my neck, my cheeks and ears. Yet then, when he began tugging at my hose, I turned and pushed him away. He approached me again, more gently this time; still I pushed him away—and again—and again. Nevertheless, with each approach my will weakened, until . . .

Ah well, there is no need to continue. No doubt I have gone too far already. So if I have thus offended, forgive and do not reprehend. But my description counts for little here; my words are not the point. The question is not whether or not the description may have offended you, but whether it offended God. In other words, was it, or is it sinful? It was in some sense pleasurable.

And yet is pleasure alone sufficient justification for what is forbidden by Holy Scripture and even more roundly and specifically condemned by the Church? Ah, sin is a mystery—and not least to the sinner! I admit that in the years to come when

I repeated the act with others, there was less pleasure, yet still I felt some.

Is it not human nature to feel carnal desire? Is God not the author of human nature—and therefore also of carnal desire? And did He not provide the remedy for satisfying that desire? Indeed He did. Heterodox questions such as these do trouble me still, and thus I find it difficult to accept it that scratching this itch (if I may lean upon a metaphor) be taken as a sin like any other—as, for instance, a violation of one of the Ten Commandments would be.

And so at last the question: Did I sin with Mr. Cotton? Perhaps—but perhaps not. More likely did I sin with those others who succeeded him—but then again, perhaps not. The question to me is yet moot.

Afterward, he and I lay together, wide awake, yet saying nothing. We must have passed near an hour in this attitude, but then again signaling silence, he rose from the bed and slipped on the robe which he had tossed over the chair. He bent down then and kissed me on the lips. Raising his hand in a gesture of farewell, he departed. I found it difficult to sleep. Laying there quietly, my mind going over and over again what had happened, the experience seemed to take on a fantastical quality. At one point I found myself wondering if perhaps I had not dreamed it all. But I knew that was not so.

The next few days were passed most pleasurably. We had deep discussions of poetry during the day and practiced sodomy at night. Thus had I the benefit of both his Oxford education and his great passion. This was indeed heady stuff for a youth who was some five years from his majority and from a town of no consequence, such as Stratford. As my recuperation proceeded apace, and I grew stronger, we two began to take long walks about the estate and into the village of Atherton. Spring was upon the land. All trace of the snow had disappeared, and the trees were beginning to bud. I recall the setting well, for this proved to be one of the most important conversations of my lifetime. Yet indeed I did not discover this until somewhat later.

We were, as I remember, walking along the roadside path to the village on some errand or other. Conversation had lagged for but a moment, then did he turn to me and ask, "Why did you come here, Will?"

Though it was said gently, I felt an immediate panic. Did he wish me to leave? "Well . . . well," I flustered, "I came because you invited me—or perhaps you don't remember. It was in your last letter. You said—"

"Oh, I remember very well," said he, interrupting me. "But to come at the time of year you did! Midwinter may have been worse, though I am not at all sure of that. You know what this west-country is like when the thaw comes. From the time you came into the house I have had the feeling that you were running from something."

He stopped and peered at me; when he looked at me thus solemnly I could hold nothing from him, much less lie. And so I told him all, that which was in the letter I left my father, as well as the probable fate of Ned Wilson.

"Ah, poor Ned," said Mr. Cotton. "And all he did in truth was to try to put food upon their table."

"Yes, sir," said I, "and that is the whole of it."

We resumed our walking, and for a good long space of time he said nothing, musing upon what I had told him. But when at last he spoke, he told me something I did not know.

"Sir Thomas Lucy," said he, "led the movement to turn me out of my teaching employ there at Stratford."

"Truly?" said I. "I'd no idea of it."

"Oh yes. There are enough recusant Catholics in the town that I would have been safe had it not been for Sir Thomas threatening them with disclosure. 'I will have no priest's brother teaching our children,' he declared—or so he was quoted to me. His own two sons were sent to the cathedral school at Winchester. He would not think of allowing them to attend Stratford free school."

"That is most interesting," said I.

"It was all for reasons of politics, that he might gain favor at court and with it perhaps a title." He sighed and gave me a canny glance. "I don't suppose your father could afford to send you to university?"

"Oh no, sir. Though we are in better circumstances than poor Ned's family, we are by no means rich."

"Yes, well, I thought that. But it is plain you cannot return to Stratford, not for some time. We must think of something to do with you. I believe I have an idea."

I hesitated, but then did I blurt forth: "I was hoping that I might stay here with you, sir."

"I fear not, Will. It simply cannot be."

"But why, sir?" Of a sudden I found myself near tears. "I know that I could make myself useful."

"Why? Because in less than a month I'm to be married. She brings with her a fortune that we badly need if we're to save the estate from these recusant fines and taxes."

"But do you *love* her?"

"That plays no part in this. She is a decent girl—but she is no fool. If she found you installed in the house—if she but saw us together—she would know in an instant what is between us."

"Is it so plain?"

"Yes. It is written upon our faces each time we look one at the other. Yet as I said, I believe I have an idea that will see you through. In any case, we shall know of it in less than a week."

Naturally, I wished to know what that idea might be, yet I was so overwhelmed by the news he had given me that I feared to ask.

III

It was but three days later that the players came up the Prescot road, beating their drums and tootling their flutes, as they were able; and those who could not did dance along behind, twirling and skipping about in imitation of children at play. This was a part of their show—quite an important part, for it was meant to draw farm families and those of the surrounding villages to Prescot which had the only public playhouse in all of Lancashire. Inevitably, there would be a following line of louts, bumpkins, ill-mannered farm lads, and their impudent female counterparts. Last of all came the parti-colored wagons, two of them, which contained costumes, flats, and all the rest of the physical necessities for play-making.

And so was it a noisy procession, but the mood of it was jolly and it served well to excite interest among the local residents in the offerings at the Prescot playhouse. I suspected (correctly, as it turned out) that there was little to excite the populace in these parts. People kept their places here, just as they did in Stratford. They would no more have thought of changing their village than they would have done changing their station in life. To see a troupe of actors, gaily dressed and behaving oddly as they moved freely about the county, awakened awe and envy; such did seem as visitors from another world.

I was out at the gate with the first sounds of the drums and flutes. There I was joined by the doorkeeper, by Celia and her kitchen helpers, and even a few farm workers who had left off their swinking in the fields; all had come to witness the spectacle and join in the arrival celebration. They knew, as I did, that this troupe of players were coming direct to Riverdale, the Cotton family manor. While Prescot had a playhouse, it lacked quarters for the troupe; these Mr. Cotton had agreed to provide, as had been done in the past by members of the Cotton family. I spied the procession coming round a bend in the road. As the din grew louder, Mr. Cotton, which is to say John, appeared at the entrance to the manor in the company of his father, who leaned heavily upon his son's arm. Both were richly outfitted for the occasion. The elder Mr. Cotton looked specially grand, wearing a long cloak of velvet for warmth, if also perhaps to impress the assembly. He appeared quite frail. Indeed I was surprised that he could stand at all, even with his son's assistance.

Once the entire procession had passed inside the gates, the two Mr. Cottons, father and son, stepped forward; one of the players came up from the line of dancers—a tall man he was, and a most impressive figure. The elder Cotton gave a short speech of welcome; he spoke in brief phrases and a weak voice, so that all that he said had to be repeated by his strong-voiced son. Nevertheless, it served well and provided him I took to be the chief of the players with a proper occasion both to thank their host and advertise their wares—and all in the most eloquent words and handsome tones. From what was said I learned first, that the troupe was that of Mr. Alexander Houghton of Houghton Tower, Rufford. Secondly, I heard that they would be in Prescot at the playhouse but a week, during which they would offer two comedies—*Ralph Roister Doister* and *Gammer Gurton's Needle*—on alternate days. Great favorites they were, he assured one and all, and they would be well-advised to see both. With that, he bade a good day to the crowd of stragglers who had followed them through the gates. The drummers struck up a beat, the flutists found a tune, and the local residents filed back out onto the road where they dispersed in twos and threes.

Once they were gone, there was a sudden surge of activity among the players. They ran to the wagons and began unloading baggage and personal effects of all sorts—books, papers, boxes, even a parrot in a cage. I watched, fascinated, wishing I might help; yet they knew me not and might suppose I was attempting to make off with their belongings. And so, having seen Mr. Cotton and his father enter the house in the company of the man whom I rightly took to be the leader of the troop, I followed them inside, seeking them out, yet wondering at the same time if it might perhaps be too early to present myself. Yet I found no one about.

The day after Mr. Cotton had made clear to me that it would be impossible for me to remain there in the house, he revealed to me his plan for my future.

"The theater, Will," said he to me, "it offers you what you want and need most."

"And what is that, sir?" I asked him in a manner more challenging than was my usual. (I liked not the notion that others—even Mr. Cotton—would tell me what I wanted and needed; I had already heard from my father too much on that matter.)

"What you want, my dear young friend, is to write poetry. Am I correct in that?"

I made a show of giving due consideration to the question, but in the end, of course, I nodded. "Quite right, Mr. Cotton."

"And what you *need*," he continued, "is a way to earn your keep that will permit you to write—is that also not so? You cannot go back to Stratford to continue your apprenticeship in glove-making for reasons we both understand. Yet neither would you wish to do so—unless I am greatly in error."

"True," I acknowledged, without hesitation.

"Likewise, you cannot go to university for want of the cost."

"Again, true."

"Farm labor would exhaust you and drive all thought of poetry, art, and beauty from your mind."

"I fear you are correct."

"Domestic service is beneath one so gifted as you."

"I'm glad you realize that, sir."

"So," said he, "shy of inheriting a great fortune from a rich relation, or marrying a woman with a dowry even larger than the one I'm to marry—" He broke off and looked at me intently. "Any chance of either happening?"

"None at all," said I with great certainty.

"Well then, I would say that your best chance, and perhaps your only one is, as I suggested, the theater."

"I was hoping to teach school, as you did, sir."

"Well," said he, "first of all, I must say that it is not near so easy as it looks, so you would not have as much time to write as you might suppose. And there are a number of other practical difficulties that you must consider. First of all, you have not been to university, and scholars from Oxford or Cambridge usually fill any post that comes open. My recommendation would mean nothing, for I am officially in disgrace."

"Oh," said I, somewhat sadly.

"And another thing stands in the way of teaching. You would have trouble of a sort similar to what I had."

"I don't understand," said I quite honestly.

"Your family on both sides—not just the Shakespeares but the Ardens, as well—are known to be Catholics. Your father has only escaped the recusant fines because he is so respected that none would point a finger at him."

"I had not known that."

"I heard all the town's gossip whilst I lived there. Quite simply, you have the wrong relations, Will. The Ardens, it is said, talk sedition quite openly. And look ye here, lad, most of the schools where you might seek employment are church-run schools—the Church of England, as they now call it. They would have naught to do with one who had a name such as yours."

He had given me much to consider, so much in fact that

I remained silent for a good long period of time, thinking of all that he had told me.

"I am afraid," said I, "that my name would also cause trouble for me if I were a player, for is not acting the most public of professions? If word were to reach Stratford that Will Shakespeare was a player up in Lancashire, then a constable might soon be here to see if the Lancashire were the one he sought."

"Ah," said he, "certainly you would have to adopt a new name. Yet still, there is more to be said for acting because I believe I can help you into the profession—if indeed a profession it be."

Thus much of our conversation I remember well. I even remember its setting: there lazing upon the bank of the river Mersey, taking our ease beneath the budding trees, lying upon new grass.

What I do not remember is when it was that I began to think of just what name I might use *if* I were to pursue that life of the theater which Mr. Cotton had chosen for me. Did I put the matter before him then and invite him to choose a name for me, as well? I think not. I believe the choice must have been mine and mine alone. I'm sure it was, for the one I settled upon was that which my grandfather, Richard, went by earlier in the last year-hundred. "Shakeshafte" was that name. My father, who took to himself the name of Shakespeare, declared to me that his family was ever indifferent as to names, and that his own father also signed a few documents as "Shakestaff." Why then was it necessary to change his name to Shakespeare? I remember putting that question to him long ago when he revealed to me these curious facts. His answer—"It had a certain sound to it which I liked"—was said in such a way that it said he had hoped that one day a multitude of men might have it upon their lips. Why? For what purpose? Surely not to praise his skill in glove-making. He had other ambitions, loftier ones no doubt, though I know not what they were.

You may think it odd that a lad of sixteen (though soon to be seventeen) should have hesitated an instant when offered a career as a player. Did I truly hope to find greater happiness as a teacher of ignorant and unruly boys? If so, then it was I who was the more ignorant! No, I was aware of what such a life might offer—travel, applause, the chance to mix with the gentry, even perhaps the nobility. Why then did I hold back? You may not credit this, and indeed I reveal it now for the first time, but up to that time I had never seen a play. It is true—neither tragedy nor comedy.

I had read them in Latin, though there were then none to read in English. I understood the idea of a play well enough: that it was in some sense an imitation of life whereby a story was told in the speeches and comments written by an author to be spoken by the players. In fact, I had even been in a play of a sort—some tragedy of Seneca's, I believe it was, though I cannot for the life of me think which. This was a plan put forward by Mr. Cotton to make more tolerable to his class the teachings of Latin. He distributed copies of the play, cast it, and decreed that all would have to learn them by heart. I was the only one capable of performing this miracle (as Ned called it), and so in the event our single performance resulted in the most absolute chaos.

There was a band of strolling players who visited Stratford a time or two, yet on each occasion I was ill or overburdened with work. I had heard reports from my mother's family of plays attended in Warwick, where strolling companies did often visit; it all sounded quite interesting to me, yet I myself had never been in attendance. How, with all this, could I be expected to show enthusiasm for Mr. Cotton's plan? I had no idea what a life in the theater might be.

And what then did I discover at the Prescot playhouse on the day after their arrival? I learned what had been omitted by my cousin from his description of the play he had seen in Warwick;

what Mr. Cotton had neglected to mention in lectures in class; what had never been bruited about, nor even hinted at, was a fact of the utmost importance: plays were pure magic.

That was, as I considered it afterward, the only way to explain the curious effect of what I had seen upon me. Now, you may have it from me that *Ralph Roister Doister* is a silly play; indeed it is such a silly play that it is no longer even performed—except perhaps in distant, rural corners of Lancashire. Nevertheless, knowing after the first few minutes just how silly it was, I could not hold myself from laughing. I did not wish to seem callow, ingenuous, nor inexperienced, but once I had begun, I was quite lost: I giggled; I chuckled; I bellowed. In the end I seemed to be howling like some possessed canine, and all the while was I reminding myself of just how ludicrous, how silly, all this was. And yet I laughed on—not so much at the words spoken by the players, but at their red noses, at their exaggerated expressions—the leers, the eyes rolling—the excitement onstage as they ran on and off, colliding, bumping, ducking left and right. Nor was I the only one so wildly amused by all this folderoling; the entire audience was one with me in rowdy delight. Even Mr. Cotton, normally so judicious, so rational, seemed quite as carried away as I; and as he later confessed, he had seen the play many times before.

When at last it was done, I rose slowly from my chair, quite weak from the experience, coughing, sore at my sides from the strain caused by such protracted hilarity.

Mr. Cotton regarded me with amusement. "Well, you certainly seem to have enjoyed yourself!" said he in a teasing manner.

"As did you!" said I, returning the jibe.

"Have you now been swayed? In a way, I would have wished that you had seen something more serious—*Gorboduc* perhaps or *Edward I*. Houghton's Men, as they call themselves, are quite capable in tragedy, as well."

"I'm sure they are," said I. "Have I been swayed? Well . . ."

In truth, I had been so lost in my pleasure during the length of the play that I had quite forgotten the matter which I had rather rudely kept open. Was I swayed? Of course! Won over completely! Yet I was reluctant to say so. "Oh, swayed, certainly," said I with a smile. "Perhaps I might meet some of the players? I am sure that would give me a better notion."

"That was indeed my thought, as well. Come along, Will, and I shall present you to Mr. Peter Ponder who commands the troupe of players."

Mr. Cotton, who knew his way about the playhouse, led me down from our box, then forward through the tide of groundlings who were making for the exit, to a door next the stage. He opened it confidently, and I followed him into that place behind the flats and curtains, which I have ever found more exciting than any play mounted upon the boards.

Backstage is a drama in itself, more comedy than tragedy—though there be events, and I have known them, which would rend even the most hardened heart. Ah, but most of the time, following any performance, it is *Ralph Roister Doister* all over again. Which is to say, silliness, childish pranks, and horseplay abound; laughter is heard, boasting and gloating, what amounts to an expense of energy in a waste of high spirits. Though I felt quite overwhelmed by all that I saw and heard about me, I tried not to allow this to show upon my face, though it was not, I admit, at all easy to maintain an indifferent air. Into the depths of this jostling, bustling mad world we went until at last we came to another door.

There Mr. Cotton paused, and I with him. He turned to me with a smile and asked if I had ever before been backstage after a play.

I made a great show of calling upon my memory. Then said I: "Why no, forsooth, I don't believe I ever have."

"Surely you'd remember this great bedlam."

"No doubt you're right, sir."

Then, laughing, he turned back to the door and beat upon it.

A great loud and hearty "Come ahead" was heard from inside, and Mr. Cotton threw open the door. There inside, the three principal players sat, each before his own looking glass, carefully removing from his face the paint which had so amused me. One of them I recognized as the actor who had played Ralph, and him I also knew as the tall flutist who had spoken out following the welcome given by the elder Mr. Cotton through his son.

"Lads! Our host!" cried he to his two fellows. They jumped from their chairs, did a quick little dance-step that ended for each in a bow.

I chuckled in spite of myself, and Mr. Cotton threw back his head and laughed without restraint.

"Ah, Peter," said he, "thank you for your kind welcome—and you two gentlemen, as well."

"How did you like the play?" asked Peter. "But before you tell me, keep in mind our season's just begun."

"Ah, well," said Mr. Cotton, "you had only to hear the laughter of the audience and their applause to know that I felt completely in agreement. And judging by *his* response, my young friend, Will, liked it even better. Gentlemen, may I present William . . . uh . . . Shakeshafte?" Thus did I meet Peter Ponder, and also Francis Herbert, and Anthony Parker, his principals. Mr. Cotton concluded his introductions by urging all three to their chairs.

Once settled, Peter Ponder asked: "Is this the young man you told me about earlier?"

"Indeed, yes, he is."

So they had been discussing me behind my back! What had they said? I could but wonder.

"I noticed," continued Mr. Cotton, "a good bit of doubling in the cast. One lad played three roles, did he not?"

"Ah yes, that was Gyllome, a Welsh lad, though you'd not know it by his speech. But yes, it's true, we're not yet a full crew, but as I said, our season's just begun. We usually pick up a few more as we go through the summer." Then did he thrust himself somewhat in my direction. "What about it, Will? Would you like to join our troupe? We do not offer much," said he, "but travel and keep and a bit of money at season's end. How much depends upon how well we do. You'll learn theater, though. That I promise you."

I had not quite expected to be rushed into it in this manner. "Well, I know not quite what to say." That much indeed was true.

"What's your wish, boy? Do you want to act upon the stage?"

"I'm sure I should like that, sir, but my true wish is to be a poet."

"Ah, well, let me tell you something, Will Shakeshafte. We have boys, and sometimes full-grown men, come to us each month and ask to join our troupe. Some we take on, but most we don't. Some of those prove later to be actors, but most do not. Now, if you was to come to me and say, 'Oh, Mr. Ponder, the actor's life is the one for me,' then I might invite you along with us just as a favor, as you might say, to Mr. Cotton who spoke up for you, him being so good as to put us up and all."

"Ah, but Peter, there is no such debt between us," Mr. Cotton put in hastily.

But Mr. Ponder held up his hand, asking for silence. "Let me finish, John," said he, and then turning back to me: "This I might have done in a grudging sort of way, but when Mr. Cotton showed me these—" He reached into a bag upon the floor wherein his clothes were stuffed, rummaged a moment, then pulled from the bag a most familiar-looking sheaf of papers, wrapped in leather they were so that they had the appearance of a small book; indeed they were *my* small book of poems.

I was quite horrified to see them in the hands of this stranger, this player, Peter Ponder, yet I tried my best not to display my feelings. How had they come to him? Why, from Mr. Cotton, of course, as had been said. I meant those, my poems, for his eyes only; perhaps someday they would be published for the world to see—yes, I hoped they would be—but for my master (as I thought of him) to casually offer them to another without so much as asking if he might, that exceeded all limits. And so far as I was concerned, it broke all bonds between us.

"When I saw these," Ponder repeated, waving my own work under my very nose, "I said to myself, 'Peter, old fellow, this lad is a poet, or the closest to it we've ever had in our troupe.' Now you may wonder, what need is there for a poet in a company of players? Well, I'll tell you. These plays we do an't the best. *Gorboduc* is beyond our audiences, and *Edward I* is a bit too heavy for them, too. So now, what have we got? The comedies—they go over well here in Prescot which has a big house where we can sell a lot of tickets, but we play them over and over so they need new jokes, new lines to freshen them up. But as for the tragedies, they need new scenes, new characters, new lines. There's not a one of them, nor *Cambyses,* nor *The Troublesome Reign of King John,* couldn't be improved. Even a writer such as yourself could save *Edward I!*"

"And you wish me to do this for you?" I asked.

"As you're able, and as you learn a bit about the theater. The way to do that, lad, is to get up there on the stage and speak some lines yourself. There's many as looks good on paper can't be spoken aloud. I don't know why this is so, but it is. Yet when you've been up there on the boards, then you know what will work and what won't. I can make a passable actor of damn near anyone—but versifying, doing it *right*—that's a gift. I know that, 'cause I an't got it."

I could tell that he was sincere, which so far as I was concerned at that moment gave him a considerable advantage over Mr. Cotton. Peter Ponder did indeed esteem my writing, in his own, more practical way, perhaps a good deal more than did Mr. Cotton. And I believed what this rough Londoner told me: that the plays they worked with needed improvement; but that one couldn't expect to do that until one had had some experience of acting. And so I was better prepared for him when he put the question to me a second time.

"You tell me now, lad. Would you like to join our company? I offer you my hand on it."

"I would," said I and took his hand. "There is but one thing more."

"And what is that?" asked Peter Ponder.

"May I have my poems now?"

Thus began my career upon the stage. Perhaps it could have begun a bit different. What sort of beginning should I have preferred? As I consider it now, I believe I would rather have begun it in London, having just come down from Oxford or Cambridge. Yet that would have meant starting out much later than I did, and there would have been no advantage to that. No, taken all in all, I believe that I did as well as any lad of my station, born and raised in Stratford, possibly could have done. Given our cards by fate, we play them as best we can.

By intention I was rather cool toward Mr. Cotton along our route back to Riverdale. I suppose I sought thus to punish him for what I deemed his betrayal of my trust in him. Though it affected him little, he was quite aware of the reason for my sullen silence; indeed, toward the end of our short journey, he commented upon it.

"You should not concern yourself overmuch that I passed your poems on to Peter. When it comes to gaining favor from another who has it in his power to advance your cause, you are well-advised to show your greatest strength."

"Your meaning escapes me," said I, which was true enough, though I felt I had caught the drift.

"I mean," said he, "that your ability as a versifier is that which sets you apart from lads your age—from all of them, so far as I can see. You are, you know, something of a prodigy. And so it does seem to me that rather than put forward your physical attributes—which is to say, your voice, your face and body, which are all any actor has to offer—it would be far better to demonstrate to Peter what it is that you have to offer that is unique."

"Hmmm, well now, I understand certainly, but why did you not at least tell me in advance? Or ask me? Would that not have been proper?"

"Oh, a pox upon propriety! See there, Will, we are almost to the gate. What say I race you there? Stop here now, and we shall go together at the count of three. Ready?"

I succeeded in winning our footrace. Sometime later it occurred to me that this was perhaps the only occasion in which I had bested him. He was far more calculating in his intentions than ever I had supposed: in effect, he succeeded in pushing me out the back door only a little before his wife-to-be entered by the front. I was dismayed to learn that wedding preparations were under way by the time I departed with the players. Had I known better the ways of the world, that would surely not have surprised me.

Yet far more dismaying was it to learn that very evening that the arrival of Mr. Houghton's Men meant that I was expected to share my room with a lad of about my own age. I fear that when I entered and found him unpacking his play-clothes, I was somewhat less than hospitable.

"Just who are you?" I asked—nay, demanded—of the fellow whose back was then still turned to me.

He came round with a smile and made a little dance ending in a deep bow quite like the one with which Peter Ponder had introduced himself. "Ffoke Gyllome," said he, "of Houghton's Men and earlier of Swansea."

"You're Welsh," said I in a manner most accusing.

"That is my pride and my boast."

I looked at him closely. Though he was familiar, I could not for a moment place him. Then of a sudden it came to me: "You were in the play!"

"Ah, so I was," said he. "Three roles and five jests—so you might say the play is half mine."

"Hmmm." The fellow seemed too sure of himself by half. "What did you mean by 'five jests'?"

"I meant precisely that, nor more, nor less. Did Mr. Ponder not tell you that some of these old plays need new jests in them to keep the locals amused?"

"Oh. Oh yes, indeed he did."

"Well, 'tis I who supply them. I've done *Jack Straw,* as well, and am now working on *Gammer Gurton's Needle.* Mr. Ponder said you was to do what you could to save some of the tragedies, didn't he? You supply the words, and I'll show you where to fit them in."

"I doubt I shall need much help in that regard," said I.

"That's as may be," said he, "but that's why Mr. Ponder wished us to partner together, which we must do till he tells us otherwise. Since that be so, would you then be so good as to tell me *your* name? Mr. Ponder was unsure of it."

"William . . . Shakeshafte," said I, hesitating awkwardly.

"How ever did you get such a curious name? Perhaps you should change it."

I know not how I responded to that, nor if I did, for just then it did strike me that if young Mr. Gyllome were to partner with me, then there would be no more nocturnal visits by Mr. Cotton, no more bawdy play between us, no more sodomy. Alas! And I thought our embraces would continue until my departure with this company of players. I realized at last what should have been plain far earlier: that I had been—

At this point in my tale I tossed aside my pen and ran to the door that I might discover the source of a most frightful noise from without the house. Indeed it seemed more animal than human in nature, as if some huge-voiced tomcat had positioned himself nearby and were emitting screams, one after another, in vain courtship of his night's mate. Yet when I threw open the front door and peered out into the gloom, I saw that I was mistaken: that no animal, but rather a human figure, stood just beyond the gate. Not only that, but I saw, too, that it was not a male but a female who made these terrible sounds. Then did the moon emerge from behind the large cloud which had hidden it, and I saw that the woman at the gate was none but Goody Bromley, who had given me such a start following Sabbath services at Holy Trinity. I could see no reason for this visit. If she believed that I would invite her into the house, then she was most dreadfully mistaken. Yet she seemed not in the least disturbed by my presence. She continued to scream, yet do so in such a way that she seemed to be jeering at me, screaming in derision.

"Silence!" *I shouted out at her. "I know who you are, and unless you cease and leave here at once, I shall give a report to the magistrate.* Now go!"

I waited and heard only silence for a good long moment. Then did she begin to laugh. Great loud peals pierced the night's quiet so that they seemed near worse than the screams.

"You poxy, sluttish old trull, get from here. I order you."

Then did she cease altogether, turn, and lumber awkwardly off down the road. I marched back into the house and shut the door loudly after me.

From up above at the top of the stairs, I heard Anne's voice calling down to me, "Will," said she, "who was that? What was that?"

"Naught but a visit from Goody Bromley," I replied.

"Oh, dear God, will there be more of them?"

"No, I believe I gave her a proper fright."

"Come to bed, Will."

IV

Where was I? Ah yes, looking back, I see that I had been recounting some conversation with that Welsh lad which took place all those years ago. But all that matters little now. Leave it that we got on well, though there were awkward moments at the start. With him, I learned a good deal of theater. Together we were scholars of the stage, apprentices in that antic art. Peter Ponder was our principal instructor, though Mr. Parker and Mr. Herbert also taught us much. All the company, in fact, contributed to our learning. Just to be upon the stage, speaking lines, giving unto those of the audience the laughter, the bit of emotion they all seem to need—all this gave much to our education, perhaps most of all.

And so yes, as you may gather from that, they wasted no time putting me up before the crowd. By the time we left Prescot, I had developed my falsetto to the point that I might relieve Gyllome of one of his three roles. It was, of course, a female part, as most of those we played were. Lads as lithe and slender as we were ever cast as women. As I found out, however, a few of the company continued to confuse our sex long after the curtains had closed. Gyllome, who had been the previous year with Mr. Houghton's Men, advised against such activity with our fellows. "A few, I think, is poxy, and those that an't may be by summer's end." Instead, he suggested we enjoy each the other, which we did, trading about.

When we left Prescot, we did not simply go into the wilderness and wander. Indeed nay, a circuit of manor houses round Lancashire had been established; at each we were welcome to perform in the great hall and were well paid for it in food, lodging, and shillings. Among the gentry and the nobles, high-minded verse tragedies were much favored, but occasionally a comedy was requested, as well; *Ralph Roister Doister* and *Gammer Gurton's Needle* were the best liked of all. As summer progressed and it grew warmer, these same comedies were played on scaffolds outside the manor houses, and for a fee the townsmen in such places as Preston and Lea were allowed inside the gates that they might enjoy the same pleasures as their betters. There were, in all, nine stops to be made in order to complete the circuit. As it happened, the next stop north, Knowsley, was quite the grandest of any we would visit. And indeed it should have been, for it was there that the Stanley family made its home and Ferdinando Stanley grew to his majority and eventually became Lord Strange, the fifth Earl of Derby. He, who fancied himself a poet and was no more than a poetaster, did, upon claiming his title, form his own company of players in London, Lord Strange's Men. It would not be claiming too much to suggest that he did draw his inspiration for this from Mr. Houghton's Men, which was the first such group in Lancashire. We were not acquainted; though I liked his players well, I always thought him an execrable poet.

This was indeed a rowdy and amusing way to spend the summer of 1581, and I learned more of stagecraft and practical poesy than during any time that followed. That I learned well was attested by Peter Ponder who brought me forward to meet Mr. Alexander Houghton, who had given his name and his purse to our company. This meeting took place at the eighth stop on our circuit, Houghton Tower. Mr. Ponder introduced me by the name that he knew me.

"Good sir," said he, "I should like to present to you the newest member of your company, Mr. William Shakeshafte."

I bowed low and upon returning to my erect height, I had

my first full view of our host and benefactor. Forsooth, I was not favorably impressed: the poor man appeared near as infirm as Mr. Cotton, the elder, and he had no one to lean upon.

"Shakeshafte," said he, musing. "What a rare name. I know of none other who carries it. Are you from Lancashire, young sir?"

I assured him I was not.

"Where then?"

"Why, from Warwick, sir. I came north with the purpose of joining the company." (This was a lie, I grant, but certainly a harmless one.)

"Has its fame spread so far?"

"Rest assured, sir, that it has."

"This young man," said Peter Ponder, "had the role of the queen in this night's presentation. And not only that, sir, he also indited the version of the play which we offered."

"*Edward I?* But Mr. Ponder, I know it to be the work of George Peele. You cannot fool an old fox like me."

"We would not dare try, sir," said I most brightly, hoping to ease the doddering old fellow swiftly past Mr. Ponder's well-intended overstatement.

"Ah, indeed," said Ponder. "'Twas not our intention. I meant only that it was his *version* of the Peele play."

"He changed it, did he?" Mr. Houghton went silent, his face screwed into an awful frown of concentration. Then did he say: "I cannot recall a single word out of place, nor added."

"Nor missing? I asked young Will here to cut half of an hour from the play. The lad did it with such skill that I myself who have acted the role of Edward many a time, could not at first find the missing parts—yet they are gone, and together they total a good half of an hour."

Mr. Houghton was for a moment altogether dumbstruck. But then did he regard me with new respect. "Ah," said he, "I must confess that I did ever think the play a bit too long. That was quite bold of you, young man—and of you, Mr. Ponder for ordering it done."

Ponder ducked his head in a swift bow, acknowledging the praise.

"But tell me, Mr.—Shakeshafte, is it?"

"Yes sir."

"Tell me then, do you add as well as you subtract?"

"Sir?"

"You have proven that you can cut Mr. Peele down to size, but can you write lines yourself for the players?"

"If I may make so bold as to respond to that," Ponder put in. "The lad is a true poet, Mr. Houghton. I have read pieces of his that would do credit to any man who calls himself a poet, to one indeed twice his age. It was after I had seen these that I invited him to join the company."

"So you do write?" The old man put the question to me.

"A few things, sir—sonnets and shorter poems."

"Shorter? Shorter than what?"

"Shorter than Mr. Peele's play, which is still much too long in my view."

At that, Mr. Houghton threw back his head and laughed quite lustily. Yet perhaps he should have used a bit of restraint, for it seemed that he had no sooner begun when he fell to coughing; and once begun, he could not stop, not for an intolerably long time. Yet as he coughed we scurried about—Mr. Ponder to fetch a chair and ease him down in it, and I in search of water or some other mild liquid that he might quench his cough. Yet as I ran about looking in vain, I spied a servant across the great hall rushing to his master with a cup in his hand. By the time I returned, Mr. Houghton was breathing normally—or if not quite that, at least with fair regularity. Ponder chafed his hand, seeking to revive him completely. Why such treatment should have worked I cannot suppose, but after a minute or more of it, our host and sponsor was able to speak. He beckoned me toward him. I leaned close and listened.

"I would . . . I would . . ." Clearing his throat mightily, he began again: "Could you show me some of these verses of yours? I would so like to see them."

It was not an order, it was a request—which I believe gave me a certain choice in the matter. Therefore I hesitated, remembering my ill feeling when Mr. Cotton passed them on without my permission. There was an awkward pause as I sought an answer that would satisfy him. Mr. Ponder must have sensed this, for next I knew I had got a sharp blow in the ribs from him, which took me altogether by surprise. Thus it was made plain to me that I had but one option in the matter.

"I shall have them for you in the morning," said I to Mr. Houghton.

"That would please me greatly," said he.

Then, of a sudden, came Ffoke Gyllome approaching the chair wherein the old fellow sat, nodding his satisfaction at my tardy response. Yet he came in a manner most peculiar, tiptoeing from behind as one might across the stage, making a great show of it. I glanced at Ponder to see if he approved of such odd behavior, yet he, for his part, seemed amused by it all; I knew not what to think of either of them.

Even less did I understand when, having reached the chair, Gyllome reached over the back of it and clapped his hands over Mr. Houghton's eyes so that the poor old man could see nothing. I was shocked, dismayed, and quite puzzled.

"Who is it?" asked Mr. Houghton in a manner which said that he knew very well who it might be.

"Who do you think it is, nuncle?" said Gyllome in a false voice meant to sound ghostly or ghoulish, as one might use to frighten children.

"I believe it is my . . . *jester!*"

With that, Gyllome removed his hands and flew round the chair. Then did he pull a silly face which sent old Mr. Houghton into a fit of giggles. The Welsh lad kept dancing about in front of our host and pulling faces that he might prolong the idiotic and unseemly laughter; I feared he would. I looked to Peter Ponder to step in and put an end to this foolishness, but this look in his direction told me that he seemed near as amused by all this as Mr. Houghton.

The latter did at last leave off laughing—and did so, to my relief, without falling into another coughing spell.

"Do come and sit down beside me and entertain me," said he to Gyllome. "I would hear all your newest jests. Mr. Ponder, could you find a chair for my young friend?"

Dutifully, Ponder went off, as he had been asked, in search of a chair. I saw no need to remain. I took a step back, bowed, and said, "With your kind permission, I shall take my leave."

I waited. The two, old man and boy, had their heads together and continued to whisper one to the other, paying me little heed. Having no response, I backed away some distance from them until Mr. Ponder returned. As he set the chair down, he waved me off, and I left, all but running for the stairs.

I had a great deal of work to do on that evening. Once in the room (which again I shared with young Gyllome), I sought the sheaf of poems from my bag, and finding it, I settled at the table. It would serve me as a writing desk, for it was my intent to copy all of them. I had no notion how long it might take. Nevertheless, I was determined to present him with a fair copy, rather than give up the original. And indeed the writing did continue late into the night. I cursed Peter Ponder and Mr. Houghton for imposing this labor upon me, yet had I any foresight of what it would bring me, I would indeed have worked twice as hard twice as long.

It grew late. I began to wonder where my room partner might be. But then, not so very much later, I heard a slow step in the hall. Could it be young Gyllome? Indeed it was. The door creaked open, and there he stood, half-dressed and half-undressed, disheveled and quite exhausted.

"Where have you been?" I asked.

"Where do you suppose? Pleasuring the old man."

"Is he yet so virile?"

"No, he is not, alas. Therefore be I so late in coming to bed." With that, he shut the door behind him quite carelessly so that it slammed loud against the frame.

"How did you manage? What did you . . . ?" I could not quite finish the sentence.

"What ought I to say?" said he. "He has little juice left in him, though he has desire still. Still and all, I try, and he tries, and there is naught but good will between us."

"I find it all quite disgusting."

"Do you?" said he. "I don't. What is it that gives you disgust?"

That stopped me. "Well," said I, having thought about it a moment. "It is that old flesh of his—the thought of touching it and being touched by it."

"Is that how you feel? Truly? I don't. I think it well to give him pleasure and him so late in life. We will all someday be so. When I am, I hope only that I have one as obliging as me about."

We had no more to say on the matter. He undressed and, with a great sigh, put himself to bed. I continued my copying and stopped only when the candle guttered and went out. In the dark I readied for bed, then climbed in beside my partner. Up with the first light of the sun, I finished what little was left of my task, read the poems over, and delivered them to his place at the table.

And then I waited. I waited through the entire day for some comment upon them—or at least some thanks for presenting them so promptly—yet neither came. We were at Houghton Tower for near a week. We charmed the old fellow's cronies with *Edward I* and *The Troublesome Reign of King John* and excited the local populace to laughter with *Ralph Roister Doister* done out in the fresh and up on the scaffold. Mr. Houghton had many words of praise for Gyllome's additions to the text, though not one for those verses of mine—not during the entire six days we were there. And what did I feel? Not sadness, certainly, but anger, rather. Yet no matter how I felt, we left on the seventh day for the next trip round the circuit.

I had, by that time, performed in a number of plays, which were bad. Indeed Peter Ponder was correct in his assessment of the material which we had to work with: which is to say, it was *all* bad, differing thus not in general quality so much as the specific manner in which each was bad. Some were windy and verbose; some were crude (indeed, all the comedies were so); some of those in verse might well have been in prose, so poor was the quality of versifying; some were sententious and others were base and vulgar (Peele's *Edward I* managed somehow to be both). There did yet seem to be something to be said for *The Troublesome Reign of King John*. In the state in which we played it, it was no better than any of the rest. Nevertheless, it seemed to promise something that none of the others did. In the years ahead I rewrote that play so often that eventually my version had nothing to do with the original. Then did it become a play of my own—not one of my best, nor even one of the better. Still, I learned a great deal from my work upon it, and eventually I found a proper use for it all. It has always been my practice to waste nothing.

Another point with which I credit Mr. Ponder and his good sense; He was right in his prediction that as I gained experience on the stage, I should also gain ability in writing for the stage. The ordinary actor, who may indeed be a rather dull-witted fellow, may lack the sense of invention that a writer must have, but he will be able to tell you when a word, a speech, or a scene does not play as it should. If, however, he be an actor who can also write, he will be able to change that word to the proper one; to alter that speech so that it moves well across the tongue; or, finally, to recast that scene so that it pushes the action forward. And without such knowledge gained from experience upon the stage, the writer is likely to make all those same mistakes which the ordinary dull-witted actor will recognize in an instant. To write for the stage, even to rewrite for the stage one must first have been *on* the stage. This I do firmly believe. (It is a point which took on great importance but a few years later.)

And so I acted. I gave unto it my earnest efforts, as I have always done since, yet I cannot claim a great deal for myself in this regard. Neither in the beginning nor later on, did I take the matter as seriously as one must to be an actor of the quality of Richard Burbage or Alexander Cooke. I played always in secondary roles, attendant lords and the like, even when well-established. Had I been more ambitious as an actor, or for that matter more successful, I might not have been the poet that I am.

During that first year I played women for the most part, as Gyllome had predicted I would. The largest role I had came toward the end of the season when I played one of the *Three Ladies of London*. If only it had been a better play! I had done what I could for it, but it was at cross-purposes with itself, half-tragedy, half-comedy, one that mixed poetry with prose in a manner that only confused things. Mr. Ponder seemed to think I had done adequately with it and in it. Gyllome, bless him, thought I had done quite well.

I remember that we were on the longest leg of our circuit round Lancashire—from Bryne-Scoulis down to Preston and Riverdale, the Cotton family's manor house. In spite of myself, I was eager to see young Mr. Cotton. As Gyllome and I walked along behind the second wagon, I told something—though not all—of my relation to my former schoolmaster.

"So that's how you come to know him?" said Gyllome when I had done with my tale. "He'd been your teacher, had he?"

"And something more," said I.

"What more?"

"Well, he told me of the world beyond—of London and Oxford, and he gave me hope that I might know it for myself some day." I wasn't near so foolish as that made me sound, yet I wanted Gyllome to understand that there was something more to my friendship with Mr. Cotton than that which he had already guessed.

Yet he ridiculed the over-earnest nature of my words—all but laughed at me, he did. "And you call Lancashire the world beyond? There is naught here to entertain them, except what we ourselves provide."

"I admit it's not London."

"Have you been there?" he asked me. "I have."

"Truly? Why did you never mention it?"

"Because, forsooth, I was sore disappointed." This then is the tale he told:

In the autumn of the year before, when Mr. Houghton's Men had completed their season, Gyllome had set off with the older men in the troupe for the great city in hopes of finding employment as an actor in one of the companies there. Fed by the praise of Peter Ponder and old Mr. Houghton himself, the Welsh lad had great hopes and a pocketful of money to sustain him till those hopes were fulfilled.

At last, having tramped high roads and back roads for over a week, they came to London. Mr. Ponder and Mr. Parker knew all the inns and taverns wherein the actors congregated. They went from one to the next, listening for rumors of new companies forming, auditions, rehearsals. And yet it seemed that when news found its way to them, it was always a day too late.

"Things are tight in London," said Gyllome. "There are but three theaters there. The companies are filled up. More actors coming in from the provinces each season. Troupes form to do plays out in the fresh and in the tents. Ponder and Parker managed to get parts in one or two such."

"But you got nothing at all?"

"Nothing."

"Would they not even try you for a role?"

"Oh, I went and read for them a good many times. They laughed at me."

"Laughed at you? But why?"

"They said I sounded Welsh."

"No you don't. You sound just as I do."

"Well, one or two said I had a 'west-country accent.' "

I walked in silence for a spell, seeking to understand all this. Whatever else might be said of Gyllome, I knew him to be a good actor, particularly for one so young. I also knew his speech to be free of that drawling sing-song peculiar to the Welsh. If they thought otherwise of him, what might they think of me?

"My money from the summer had near run out," said he, continuing, "and it was getting on to December. What ended it for me was falling into the Thames. I nearly drowned. I would have, too, if a waterman had not thrown me a rope. Can't swim, you see."

"So you walked all the way home to Wales?"

"I did. There was naught else for it."

Again silence from me as I mulled over what I had just heard. At last said I: "And I, too, had been thinking of trying my fortune in London this autumn."

"My advice, though you've not asked for it, would be to think about it twice, then think further upon it."

There are but a few important incidents to add to the events of that summer, and they came toward summer's end. So I shall hurry through the events which led up to them.

First of all, as to John Cotton, when we arrived at Riverdale, I learned that he and his new bride were off upon their wedding journey. And where, I asked, had they journeyed to? To London, I was told, where all the newly-married gentry go. When at last I did see him on the final trip round the circuit, he was in the company of his young wife who was either with child or grown stout; it was, it seemed to me, a bit early for the former possibility, and so I accepted it that my handsome and slender friend, my Adonis, had taken unto him a bride fat as a Sussex sow. He did avoid me most studiously, even to the extent of turning away when we passed in the hall. Shall I give him the benefit of the doubt and allow that he may have been ashamed to look me in the face? Indeed, why not? He had, after all, behaved shamefully, had he not?

With regard to Mr. Alexander Houghton, he had misplaced the sheaf of poems that I had left at his place at the table. They had not been located till we—his company, his men, his troupe—had left Houghton Tower for Bryne-Scoulis. He read them and reread them and wished for my swift return that he might tell me what he thought of them. All this I heard from his own lips, and with those lips he planted a kiss upon my cheek. Only then did he proceed:

"Young Mr. Shakeshafte, my dear lad, I cannot tell you how proud I am to have you in this company of players which bears my name. It was precisely my hope that I might uncover such a talent as yours here in the distant provinces that led me to sponsor you and your fellows. You have justified all! Such talent! Such artistry! Such . . ."

He gushed on, informing me that if there were one thing at which he was expert, it was judging the quality of a line of verse. "In other words, young sir, I know poetry and what talent goes into writing it . . ." And so on.

The point is, I suppose, that he liked what he had read, and sought to make up for his earlier lack of response with the most excessive and outrageous praise. It pleased me, of course, specially when he cited as his favorite the sonnet which begins, "Two loves I have, of comfort and despair," the very poem which Mr. Cotton thought the poorest of them all.

My only fear was that his esteem for my verse might move him to draw me closer to him—physically. I had no wish to take Gyllome's place in his affections. Yet there was clearly no need for me to worry, for even as he praised me so abundantly I saw

Gyllome come through the doorway and move stealthily across the room toward Mr. Houghton's chair—again approaching from the rear. Once arrived, he leaned forward and clapped his hands over the old man's eyes. And as he had done before, he moaned in a ghostly voice, "Nuncle, nuncle, do you know who this is?"

"My jester! Oh, my jester!"

Then did Gyllome come round and kneel beside him, so better to accept the kiss of greeting which he was offered. I retired a step or two; and Mr. Ponder, who had listened proudly to the praise heaped upon me, went off in search of a chair.

So it went. Yet this time when my bed-partner returned to our room, I chided him not and made no mention of "old flesh." Nevertheless we talked about Mr. Houghton and did agree that ill as he had appeared the last time we had seen him, he looked far worse on this occasion. By the time the troupe left again for Bryne-Scoulis, he had taken to his sickbed.

There he remained through our next visit, attended by a doctor from Preston and family members from Lea and Rufford. It was clear that the end was near. We were brought in one at a time to bid him goodbye. Gyllome was first, and he came from the room quite blinded by tears. Mr. Ponder and Parker and Herbert were next and on and on through the entire company—I last of all, for I was the junior member. I think he was quite unconscious by the time I entered. His hands were folded upon his chest; his face, pale and bloodless, seemed set already in the death mask. All that persuaded me that there was life left in him was the sound of labored breathing which issued from his throat. I could but look at him and shake my head sorrowfully. As I turned to go, I caught sight of a figure in the corner whom I had not earlier noticed. I had seen him before about the great house and taken him for one of the servants. Yet peering at him in the darkened room I saw that he wore the vestments of a priest—unmistakably Roman. I nodded soberly in his direction and blessed myself with the sign of the Cross. Then did I leave, and as I did, it occurred to me that I might ask him to shrive me.

Alas, there was no time for it. Peter Ponder gathered us together and told us that Mr. Houghton had expressed to him his wish that we continue on our circuit round Lancashire, and that after each performance we offer amongst ourselves prayers for the repose of his soul. We left early the next morning.

Mr. Houghton must indeed have hung on to life most tenaciously, for we had gone all the way to Lathom when a horseman sent from Houghton Tower caught up with us and informed us that Mr. Houghton had passed on two days before. We packed the wagons and set off most immediate, for we knew that by custom he would be buried on the third day. By traveling late into the night, we reached our destination and even managed to get some sleep in surroundings to which we were well accustomed. The funeral, which was held in a private chapel of the house behind closed doors, took place at ten and lasted an hour. We were ready, when the doors were opened, to serve as mourners and follow the procession; Mr. Ponder and Gyllome were pressed into service as pallbearers.

The graveside ceremony, held in a small cemetery just behind the manor house, was brief and to the point. There was naught in it that could be considered peculiarly Romish. Once the coffin was lowered into the ground and the small crowd at graveside commenced to disperse, I was surprised to be summoned by one of the servants into the library where a number sat round the great table waiting rather impatiently for another ceremony to begin. Gyllome and Mr. Ponder were also there at the table, but they sat far up from me, quite close to the head of the table.

A man of serious mien, unmistakably a lawyer, strode into the room with papers in hand and took that place at the head and began reading in a voice loud enough for all to hear the last will and testament of Alexander Houghton. As he read through it, he would stop from time to time to explain the late Mr. Houghton's intent. His much-younger brother, Thomas, was the chief beneficiary of the will—"all lands and holdings," et cetera—which seemed quite proper. Those at the table, in any case, seemed to accept it as such. There followed a number of individual legacies to servants and friends, some with particular purposes and some without.

Toward the end of the reading, it was suddenly apparent why we three from the company had been invited to be present. As for Mr. Peter Ponder, his interest came in a declaration by Mr. Alexander Houghton to his brother:

"It is my will that Thomas Houghton shall have all my musical instruments and all manner of theatrical costumes if he be minded to maintain the company of players that bears my name. And if he not be so minded, then it is my will that Sir Thomas Hesketh, Knight, shall have the same instruments and costumes. And whichever of the two carries the acting company forward, I most heartily require to be friendly to Ffoke Gyllome and William Shakeshafte, now in my service in said company. Mr. Peter Ponder is to continue as head of the company."

So there it was: The late Mr. Houghton had done all that he could to assure the continued life of the troupe after his death. The rest was up to his brother or brother-in-law. Mr. Ponder caught my eye and smiled in a sort of guarded manner; Gyllome ignored us both (I never would understand the fellow). Yet there was more to be learned from the reading of the will.

In the matter of individual legacies to servants and the like, a number of beneficiaries were named—and last of all were we two, Gyllome and I. Hearing my name read out again, I sat up in surprise. What was it had been said? "Annuities of forty shillings each are to be given unto Ffoke Gyllome and William Shakeshafte."

That struck me as, well, a pretty gesture—and little more than that. Forty shillings was the smallest amount mentioned in the will, but it was, after all, to come to me each year. It might be possible to live frugally upon it for a twelve-month. Then again, thought I, it might not.

The lawyer then looked up from the paper from which he had been reading and found Gyllome and I at our separate places at the table. "You lads," said he, "may not appreciate the nature of Mr. Houghton's generosity in leaving you this annuity. According to the Act for the Punishment of Vagabonds passed by Parliament in 1572, single persons between twelve and sixty who possess less than forty shillings a year, shall be forced to work as servants. That is why you players in the acting company are officially listed as servants. But I shall give you each a document worded from this section of the will. Whether or not you continue in the acting company is your affair. You are free to do what you like, for you have your liberty. If you are challenged, all you need do is present the document which I shall prepare for you, and you may go your way. To put it to you, directly, you lads have been given a great gift by Mr. Houghton. Be grateful."

All this was intoned in a most solemn voice.

Mr. Ponder called together the company and explained all to them. Our season was done, of course, for it would not have been proper, pious, or respectful to the dead to continue our play-making during the period of mourning. Yet Mr. Ponder had already talked at length to Thomas Houghton, who had not only agreed to assume the sponsorship of the company, but also offered to pay each man fifteen shillings for the month of touring they would miss.

At that bit of news a great cheer went up from the company, which Peter Ponder quickly silenced. "Please! Please!" said he. "Show some respect. Show a long face. You're *supposed* to be in mourning."

Next day brought the final accounting and payment. Gyllome and I did also receive our document of manumission and forty shillings each. We made ready to go. He refused to be enticed into another trip to London, which I thought wise of him. And I, for my part, had decided to return to Stratford—and the devil take the consequences. By my petty standards, I was now a man of wealth; if need be, I could pay the fine for poaching the deer and still have money in my purse. Gyllome and I had thus agreed, since we were both proceeding south, to go together as far as Birmingham; there were, after all, dangers on the road if one carried money. We would protect each other and keep company together. After all, were we not, as Gyllome himself had called us, partners?

The first day of our journey went well enough. We marched the distance talking of our plans and expectations for next summer. Staying at an inn the first night, we left early the next morning—perhaps a bit too early, for we had not gone far before we had fallen to quarreling. I cannot even suppose the reason—simply that we were both, for some reason, out of sorts. Nor did it ease the ill feeling between us when I insisted upon stopping at a shop in the town of Prescot wherein clothes were sold that had previously been owned and worn by the gentry. If I were to return to Stratford as a man of substance, then I must dress the part—or so it did seem to me.

He waited impatiently as I tried and tested coats and jerkins, listening with obvious contempt to the shopkeeper's unctuous words urging the purchase of this coat or that doublet. At last I settled upon a brocaded coat and a leather doublet. I wore my new purchases out of the shop.

We went along in silence for many a mile, Gyllome and I, until ahead we spied the River Mersey at its widest. We would have to turn east and walk the riverbank until we came to the nearest bridge. It was just there and then that the quarrel that had been at a low boil from the moment we had left, suddenly bubbled over into a bitter affray.

It was growing dark, and neither of us had any wish to be caught out on the road at night. There was a light ahead. I spied it first and suggested that if it be an inn, we had best put up there for the night.

"Be it an inn or a peasant's cottage, I think we must seek shelter for the night," said Gyllome.

"I have no wish to sleep in a barn on this night. There is sure to be an inn at the bridge. Indeed, I remember such."

"Yet we have no true notion of how far from here the bridge might be," said he.

"Just a bit farther. That may well be it ahead."

"I know why you will not sleep in a barn."

"Oh?" said I. "And why is that?"

"Because you've no wish to get a spot of dung on your pretty new clothes." He paused, then spat out his choice of invective: "You . . . popinjay."

I was incensed. "Popinjay? You dare to call me a popinjay? I, who have seen you spend an hour at a time before the looking glass."

"That was when I painted for a role."

Up to that time we had kept a good steady pace along the river path, but then we slowed and stopped that we might better confront each the other as we baited with insults. I had a ready reply for him.

"No, on the occasion I've in mind you were making ready to meet your sweet master, you male varlet!"

"If you must insult me, do not hide behind words that none could understand. Say what you mean!"

"You male whore! He paid you off, didn't he?"

"You must take that back!" he shouted at me. And so saying, he gave me a shove that sent me back a step or two.

"There is naught to take back, for I have but said the truth!"

Then I, who was taller and heavier than he, gave him a push in return. If he had fallen at that spot, there would have been no cause for grief, but he stepped backward, trying to keep his balance. His hands waving in the air, he took another backward step, and then another. And then he fell over the embankment with a plaintive cry and down into the river. I had not realized that we were so close.

Going to the edge, I looked down. The Mersey did not run swift there. Why did he not swim to the bank and pull himself out by grabbing some weed or branch? But then I remembered his London story—the fall into the Thames—he could not swim. He could but splash awkwardly with his arms and call my name: "Will!"

He repeated it thrice more in rapid succession before he disappeared beneath the dark waters.

V

It was an inn whose light we had seen; and it stood, just as I remembered, hard by a bridge across the river. For a few pence I had a bed, and all to myself—yet it did me little good, for there was not much sleep for me that night, nor for many to come. All the way back to Stratford I thought of little else but the mishap I had witnessed.

Witnessed? Did I immediately cast myself in the role of a witness? Was I so reluctant to accept blame in the matter? Was I not the cause? Was Gyllome's disappearance not the result? Ah, but you see? Even at a distance of so many years I think of it as his disappearance. Is that not strange? Had I thought he grabbed some great tree branch and thus saved himself? No, forsooth, I had not supposed such an unlikely end.

I pushed, after all, and he fell into the river. Nevertheless, I had not wished it so. I had not known, or even suspected, there would be such dire consequences from my act. Neither of us, I think, had any notion that he stood so close to the embankment. It was near dark, and as lads will, we considered only what was foremost in our minds. Ah, if only what was then foremost had not been rancor and anger! To part in such a final way with one I thought to be a friend—and in such a bad spirit! That was the shame, the tragedy of it all. Even at so late a time as this, it is possible for me to feel the sadness of it all, to feel my eyes moisten as I hear my name in my mind's ear as it was repeated so desperate, so amazed.

No, indeed I was not to blame. I would have given all that

was in my purse to have him up on the bank beside me—or I do think surely I would have done. Why do I think so hard upon this matter of blame? It is plain enough, for if I am to blame in the matter, then I did commit a sin. And if this be a proper confession, then I am obliged to put it before you in just such a way. Am I without sin in this? Right reason persuades me that I am, and yet I feel a lingering sense of guilt in this which I simply cannot account for. Perhaps it has less to do with what I did than what I did not do.

I own that I might have dived in and made an attempt to save Gyllome. Yet if I have heard tell of seamen who could not swim, I have heard of swimmers who dived in to save a drowning wretch who were themselves drowned for their trouble. To have pushed him into the river may indeed have been a mishap and nothing more, yet to have made the attempt to save him would have been an heroic act; while such are laudable, they are not required of us. There is no sin in failing to perform one.

I shall not pretend that all this was thought through in the course of that long journey back to Stratford. I know only that I brooded hard upon it whilst on the road, and by the time I drew close to my destination I was in a better state, able to look ahead to my homecoming to think what I might say as to where I had been for the better part of a year. In general, I wished to know something of what had transpired in my absence. And so, having dallied the last miles that I might make a propitious arrival at my old school at about the time I might expect my brother, Gilbert, to emerge. When at last he did, he was but one of a crowd, so much like the rest that I did not at first recognize him. Forsooth, I let him walk past me, and only then did he circle back and present himself to me.

"Will? Is it you?"

I turned to the voice, which I knew well enough as Gilbert's, but the tall youth before me was as a stranger to me.

"Gilbert? You are much changed."

"And you, as well, Will."

How long had I been gone? Less than a year, only months, yet both of us had altered so that we barely knew one another. Yet once we did, we threw our arms one about the next and, laughing, did dance about like a pair of lunatics from Bedlam. A class of younger boys came running wild out the school door and stopped to stare, but we paid them no heed.

"Brother," said I, "you are near half a foot taller than when last I saw you."

"And you, Will, you've the beginnings of a beard." (True, for I had not shaved since Alexander Houghton's funeral.) "And those clothes!" he continued. "I've seen naught like that coat in these parts. Wherever did you get it?"

"You'll hear all that in good time," said I. "But here, let's walk on home together, and you must tell me all the news as we go along."

"Well and good," said he, "but only if you let me carry that big bag of yours."

"You're twice my size, so indeed, why not?"

I unslung it from my shoulder, and he took it upon his. It fit him well.

"Is it filled with gold, Will?" he asked, joking.

"Nay, brother—with dreams, rather." I'm sure he had no notion of what I meant by that, but since I was unsure myself, I made no attempt to explain; instead, I gestured to the path, and we set out together. "Tell me first," said I, "what sort of welcome—if any—am I likely to find when I show them my face?"

"About what you might yourself predict," said he. "Father will without doubt be reserved and grumble of how you left him without an apprentice—the apprentice now is me. And Mother, well, she will throw wide her arms the moment she sets eyes upon you. After all, you were always her favorite. She may even kill the fatted calf and roast it whole."

"But I refuse absolutely to play the prodigal son."

"Oh, I can see that, indeed I can. You've never been good at playing humble. But in his way, I think Father will be just as pleased to see you, Will, for he thought you did well to take that doe to punish Sir Thomas Lucy. Or I think he did."

"You *told* him then?"

"Well . . . yes. What was I else to do? How was he to be prepared with a proper tale when the constable came calling? And besides, you did not say I should not tell."

I sighed. "No, I suppose I did not. But tell me, did the constable come?"

"Oh yes—that very evening."

"And what did Father tell him?"

"That he had sent you up to Warwickshire to visit the Ardens, and that you had left the day before."

Gilbert went on to describe the scene which was played at the dinner table once the constable had gone. Mother had defended me to the entire family and specially to Father. "'Twas Will," said she, "who suffered the humiliation meant for us all. He took the gloves in the face, did he not? Is that not taken as a challenge to a duel? Imagine putting a lad in such a situation! The shame is his."

According to Gilbert, Father listened solemnly to what Mother said, nodding, though not necessarily in agreement; it was as if he were giving her his attention—and nothing more. When she at last fell silent, he asked if she were done. She said that she was, then did he make a pronouncement, and indeed his only one, on the matter. "I wish," said he, "that the lads had invited me to go along with them, for that is one poaching party I would not have missed."

Thereafter did Mary Arden Shakespeare visit Ned Wilson in the gaol every Sunday, bringing him hot food and dainties of every sort. And John Shakespeare made certain Ned's family made it through the winter, feeding them from our own larder when necessary.

"And so," said I to Gilbert, "dear Ned survived his term in jail?"

"Oh yes," said he, hesitating in an odd way, "he did survive."

"And did he never say that I was with him?"

"Never. He always said he'd been alone."

"I believe I shall visit him tonight."

Gilbert said nothing for a bit. Then, with brotherly sympathy: "You didn't know? Of course you didn't. How could you?"

"Know what? What have you to say?"

"Ned is gone, Will. He's dead."

"Dead? But how could he be?"

This is the tale that Gilbert told.

When Ned's three months in gaol were done, he had still to pay the fine which was fixed at three times the value of the animal. Who could say what the value of one fallow deer, a doe, could be? "Only I can say that," said Sir Thomas to the magistrate, "for I was the owner." And the magistrate was forced to admit that it would be difficult to attack the logic of that, but was not two pounds rather a great amount for a deer? "Nevertheless," Sir Thomas declared, "that is the value I set. The poacher may work it off at a rate of ten shillings a month, which is to say, six months' labor in compensation for the death of the doe."

And so it was set. The added six months was like the gaol term made lengthier—or worse. Nay, it was indeed worse, for in the gaol they did no bodily harm to Ned, whereas in the hands of Sir Thomas Lucy, where he was kept under lock and key, he was frequently abused by Arthur, the churl who had kicked me in the backside, and by Sir Thomas himself. It was rumored that what they most wanted from him was my name as his partner in the theft—but Ned refused, thus incurring further beatings and deprivations. All this and more came out in the course of the coroner's inquest which the Shakespeare family had insisted upon when Ned did suddenly disappear. He had died in a mishap, Sir Thomas declared, and was buried immediately. When Ned's body was exhumed, it was shown that he had died of severe injuries to the head: his skull was crushed and his face was smashed. It had all happened, said Sir Thomas, in a fall from the roof of the manor house, where Ned had been placed to make repairs. "The lad was always clumsy," said he; it was his final word on the matter. Yet others spoke at the inquest who called to question the claim of death by mishap. These were the few who had spoken to Ned during his term of "imprisonment" at Charlecote, Sir Thomas's estate—among them, Ned's brother Stephen, John Shakespeare, and the old vicar at Holy Trinity. All told the same story of beatings and general mistreatment; Ned had at least been consistent in his complaints. Yet none of this could be proven, and in the end Ned's death was ruled a mishap.

"It was not a popular verdict," said Gilbert to me. "All through the month of June little else was talked of here in Stratford. And it did Sir Thomas Lucy no good at all. Folk liked it not that his word was given greater weight than those of the town."

Once it was all out, and I had heard what had to be heard, I wished to talk of it no more. Ned could not be brought back. All that could be accomplished now was to take revenge upon Sir Thomas and his man, Arthur. How that could be done, I was not at all sure; I was certain only that it would be done.

"Will?"

"Yes, Gilbert?"

"You were so silent," said he. "I'd begun to wonder." He hesitated, then added: "I wanted only to assure you that because of all this, you have nought to fear from Sir Thomas. Father says he has no influence here now in Stratford—none at all."

"Oh . . . well . . . good," said I and once more fell silent.

My homecoming went about as Gilbert had predicted, except that Father made no complaint about losing an apprentice. Instead, he boasted what an able one he had found in Gilbert, and that had much the same effect as a parental grumble would have had, did it not? Of course it did.

Mother did indeed throw her arms wide to welcome; then did she proceed to plant kisses upon every exposed part of my body. None could have been more demonstrative than she. And she did set to work quite immediately to prepare a feast worthy of the occasion. Considering that she had no more than a loin of pork to work with, she acquitted herself quite admirably, for she supplied every sort of side dish one could suppose—from potatoes to carrots to sugar cakes and all manner of sweet delights.

'Twas when we all sat down to table that Father, a taciturn man at best, truly had his say. All were there, even including my baby brother Edmund. Father took the opportunity to joke in his heavy manner, praising the grand table Mother had set, saying that one thing only would he change.

"And what is that, husband?" she asked, quite taken in by his serious mien.

"Had we proper notice of Will's return," said he, "I would have searched three counties over to find a side of venison."

"And one thing only would *I* change," said I.

"And what is that, Will?" asked Father.

"Only that Ned Wilson might be with us on this evening."

"Aye," said he, "that is a good and proper wish. Let us pray a dinner prayer and remember him in it." Which he then did offer up, thanking God for my return and praying for the repose of Ned's soul. I remembered, as well, to add Gyllome in a silent way to the prayer.

We were never silent at table (Father put no such caution upon us), and I told all of my summer as a player in a company of players. In the telling of it, I described it in such a way that it sounded like a grand adventure. All did laugh and exclaim with pleasure as I gave unto them a dazzling picture which never did quite fit the reality I had known.

Then at last, with dinner done, Richard sent off to bed and little Edmund tucked away for the night, I sat with Father and Mother still at table whilst Joan and Gilbert attended to the washing up. Conversation dawdled until it was that Father put before me the question I had known that he would ask.

"And now," said he, "what will you do? Go to London? You're a bit young for that."

"So I am," said I. "And in other ways, too, it seems a bit early."

"You do plan to go there in the future?" put in Mother.

"When I am ready." Gyllome's unhappy experience the previous autumn had made a strong impression upon me. When I went to the great city, I planned to stay. I was in no wise ready to make such a plan.

"Well," said he, "you have not yet reached your majority, and until you do, I've an obligation to keep you. And near as you are to manhood, you've an obligation to earn your keep. The problem is this, Will: You've no interest in continuing, and besides, there is not work enough for you both, at least not for this season—though perhaps in a month or two there might be. I've no way to know that. So tell me, what have you in mind?"

"Nothing in the way that you mean," said I. "Perhaps I could have some time to think about that. I've some money with me."

"From your summer with the players, I suppose. But that can't be much. What will you do when it's gone?"

Then did I tell them of the annuity that had come to me in the last will and testament of Mr. Alexander Houghton. Both were duly impressed by the news—Mother quite obviously and Father in spite of himself.

"Every year, you say?"

I nodded, indicating that this was so.

"Well, that changes things some."

"Indeed it does," said Mother.

"All right, I'd say that earns you some time to consider matters. But if you think forty shillings will keep you till next summer, then you've little notion of just how dear things are these days."

"In the meantime," called Gilbert from the kitchen, "you can share the bed with me, just as you used to do, Will."

Mother laughed long at that. Then did she declare: "And you may consider yourself invited to dinner until your father decrees otherwise."

Though it be difficult to remember at this late date, I believe that I had some vague thought of working at home upon my version of *The Troublesome Reign of King John*. I also had an idea for a more original play, something wholly of my own invention. The idea for it came whilst I was rummaging about in Mr. Houghton's library and passed the better part of an afternoon with Holinshed's *Chronicles*; eventually, that play would be written, played, and published as *Arden of Faversham,* yet there is a tale to be told about that which I shall reveal anon. It matters little what my plans were, however, for it would be months before I had the opportunity to work in great concentration upon writing of any sort.

If it be a sin to lie with man or woman, then I confess it—but we have been through all that before. There be no need to reiterate my arguments here and now, for I mention this only to make a point. Not one of the men—or boys—with whom I did so engage, ever gave me a tittle of trouble. All the trouble that I have had in that regard has come from women or girls.

What can it be with such as they? Understand that I mean to hurl no general insult at the entire sex. I speak only from my own experience, and that, I fear, has only been of the sort that would embitter any man. Oh, certainly they spread the pox and give the itch, and if that were not enough, even worse to my mind are those who, unlike the plain-thinking whores, invest every such transaction with such a deal of passion and sentiment. They will speak always of love and never of pleasure. They can be, and usually are, the most contrary of creatures.

If I seem now to rant a bit, to lose control and sputter, it is because I now welcome upon the stage Miss Anne Hathaway—eventually to be Mrs. Anne Shakespeare. She trapped me. There is no other word for it, for she baited me with honey; I took the bait and was hoist in an instant like a poor rabbit in one of Ned's snares. Nor did she ever admit that the game that she played was in any wise unfair to me.

When I went to London, I first worked for Philip Henslowe, who hired me as an actor and writer for the Rose theater for which he had a deed. He was in great need of new plays, or so he said, and he wished me to supply them. Because of that he wanted me to work where he might keep me under close observation. He was a great whoremaster, was Philip Henslowe, and so he installed me in one of his houses of prostitution there on the south bank of the Thames. Thus did I become intimately acquainted with the ways of whores. And in her way, Anne was bawdier than any whore Henslowe ever kept. Oh, you would not think it of her today. How well she has hidden that woman she once was! But had she not—which is to say, had she not altered so completely from that seducer, that female rapist who seized upon me at first opportunity—then might I have remained longer in Stratford and put aside completely and forever the dreams I realized in London; and so perhaps it has all been for the best. My view has always been that if one thing in a life is changed, then all has been changed, so there is no point in wishing something were otherwise. (No point perhaps, yet nevertheless there are deeds I wish had not been done by me, else I would not have been moved to write this which I am writing.) Still, it is alternately amusing and annoying to see Anne strut about Stratford, playing the grand lady, the mistress of New Place, when I know that at heart she is, or once was, naught but a wanton.

But I was ever given to poetic overstatement; do I now exaggerate in prose? One has only to look upon the facts of the matter to see that I do not. Think upon it: Here was I, a lively lad of eighteen, for the most part innocent of wrongdoing of the carnal sort, and certainly of any evil intent in that way. And what was she but a woman of six-and-twenty, well-experienced in all the amorous ways and with a ravening hunger to match. No wonder she was so long unmarried: she would have frightened all the swains in Stratford away. I was but a poor Antony to her Cleopatra. So what was I to do when—Well, I shall describe the matter as it did happen, and let him who is without a stone find one and cast it.

Anne's father had died. Richard Hathaway had been a friend unto my father ever since Father had pledged surety on a debt owed by Hathaway many years before. His was a big family—seven children from two wives, and Anne was the eldest. Though I knew Mr. Hathaway by sight and had been brought up to greet him politely whenever we did meet, I knew of Anne rather than knew her, for she was not often to be seen around Stratford. There were two reasons for this. First, the Hathaway farm, which was fair-sized (being over a hundred acres), was located not in Stratford but just outside the village of Shottery. The farm is nearby but can be reached better by paths through the fields, rather than by road—which is to say, by the back way. Secondly, she, as the eldest daughter, was at twenty-six long past an age where she might expect to marry, and there was disgrace sufficient in this that she kept to the house, did a deal of the cooking and planting, and the milking of the cows. And how did she acquire her knowledge of carnal love? It did not occur to me to wonder until it was too late.

As I said, I did not know her, though I knew of her through things that were said and left unsaid by my father and mother. On the few occasions she was discussed by them, it seemed to me that it was done always in low tones, in gestures and facial expressions. Was it always so with women of a certain age who were unmarried? No, I thought not, but what would I have known? I had given no attention to matters that had to do with marriage, for all that, I felt, would be years in the future. Yet the few times I saw her about, I did indeed wonder, for she was neither ugly nor disfigured but to me then quite ordinary-looking.

Again, as I said, Richard Hathaway did die, of what I cannot say, though from that which was said of it, I supposed it would have been a common sort of heart stoppage. He was quite advanced in age, near sixty or past it, and a farmer who continued to work his land until the very end. Though Father was saddened by the death of his friend, he did not think it untimely.

Upon hearing of it, Mother set to work a-cooking and baking. She made all manner of dainties and cakes to be passed about and eaten whilst neighbors and friends attended his corpus and mouthed the usual pieties. Having made so many, she sent me ahead with a great load of them and a caution that I carry them with care. I had not taken that path through the fields for years, yet I was surprised at how quickly it all came back to me once I was on my way. Even when the path forked, I remembered that I was to take the right branch and not the left. And having taken it, was soon rewarded with a sight of the Hathaway house and barn, remembered from years before. I had walked no more than a mile and probably less.

Because both hands were burdened, it was necessary for me to put down the cakes and dainties on the doorstep so that I might knock upon the door. I knocked stoutly, stepped back and waited. The door came open slowly and there stood the mysterious spinster, Anne. It had to be she—and no other—for though I had looked at her full in the face on one occasion, and I retained no exact memory of it, the woman who looked out at me bore a mark of mystery upon her, as only Anne of the Hathaways would. Dark-haired and dark-complected, she wore a rather somber expression, which was appropriate to the occasion, yet when she looked at me the corners of her mouth took a downward turn as if she were seeking to suppress a smile.

She pointed to the plates upon the doorstep. "Were you going to leave them there and run away?" she asked.

I bent to pick them up, fumbling for words to save what seemed to me an awkward situation. "What? I . . . no, certainly not," said I. "It was just that I was unable to knock upon the door . . . and . . ."

"Had you thought to sell us those dainties?" She had not budged from her place in the doorway, so that she now seemed to be barring my way.

"By no means," said I. "My mother asked that I bring them ahead. They are for your visitors on this sad occasion."

"And who might your mother be?"

"Mary Shakespeare is her name."

"Ah, then you are the player—Will."

"Yes, I suppose I am, though I think of myself as—"

"As a poet," she put in, interrupting. "Yes, so I have heard." She seemed quite unimpressed by that. "Well, come ahead, why don't you? I'll show you the way to the kitchen."

She threw the door wide and stepped out of the way. I followed her through the house, which was a good deal bigger than most. The rooms we passed into and out of were empty, though I heard movement on the floor above.

"Mind you don't knock Father down," said she as we went by the coffin. It stood upon two trestles in the middle of the largest room. As we passed, I looked into it at Richard Hathaway. So shrunken and shriveled was he by death that I did barely recognize him (who I had often seen with Father). Her caution struck me as odd if she had meant it seriously and cruel if she had not.

And at last into the kitchen, where she indicated I was to put the plates down upon the big table there in the center. "I suppose I should go and return with the rest of my family," said I, wishing to be accommodating. "You must have things to do before your visitors arrive."

"Oh, no, stay," said she. "What must be done has been done. My mother and sisters and I have worked the day long to prepare the house for them. I was sent down to play the role of doorkeeper—and that is all *I* have to do." All this was said in a somewhat sullen manner, but she then did add in a brighter voice: "I saw you in town but a few days past."

"Are you sure it was me? I've not been here long."

"Two days ago? I remember you wore that coat and jerkin you have on now."

"Oh yes, that would have been me. I'd been sent off to buy thread for my father's workshop." I hesitated, thinking it questionable to go on as I had intended. Yet in the end, I continued: "Do you like them? They were newly bought."

"Indeed I do. You cannot get such clothes in this miserable place. Where did you get them?"

"In Prescot."

"Where is that?"

"Lancashire. Just the other side the Mersey."

"My God," said she. "How you say that! As if 'twas no farther than Warwick. You certainly know more of England than I ever will." She paused. "Or I hope that is not true. I hope someday to see it all."

"Just as I do," said I.

"Ah, you, too?" she smiled, really for the first time since she had presented herself at the door. "I wonder," said she, "would you mind if I touched the stuff of that coat? Ran my hand over that doublet?"

"Not in the least," said I, "if 'twould give you pleasure."

"Oh, it would, it would."

"Then please yourself."

She did indeed. The coat especially—oh yes, specially the

coat—seemed to interest her. She ran her hands slowly over the brocade, tracing each separate pattern with her eyes closed. It was as if in that strange manner she might see better with the tips of her fingers. Standing very close to me in that kitchen, she seemed quite transported by the experience, as I did, too. How she did touch me! Lightly but firmly, her fingers wending over the threads of the coat from the shoulders down to the hips. She ran her hands along the bottom of it where the trim formed a border that ran the diameter of the coat. Her fingers came together at the front where it did open, and there they delved inward and examined my codpiece and that which lay within it with the same slow, intent interest that she had given the coat.

Then, of a sudden, she did stop. Her eyes came open, and the smile on her face faded into an expression of concern.

"Ah," said she, "but perhaps I go too far."

"That had not occurred to me," I told her.

"Yet to be interrupted would make us both unhappy."

I intended to argue her into continuing, but just as I organized my own thoughts and opened my mouth to voice them, there came three strong knocks upon the door. Her case was thus proven.

She started to turn away, then came back to me and, looking most solemnly into my eyes, she did say: "You came on the path through the fields, did you?"

I nodded eagerly, mayhap a bit too eagerly.

"Do you remember," said she, "a copse of maple where the path divides?"

Again I nodded.

"Meet me there tonight."

"When?" said I, my throat so tight I could hardly utter that single syllable.

"Just after dark."

Once again the knock boomed thrice upon the door. She ran from the kitchen.

And so it did come about that after that evening of prayers and pieties, dainties and drink, we did return home at twilight all the Shakespeares together, down that same path through the fields. I noted the copse as we passed it and found myself peering into it as if in expectation that Anne Hathaway might already have taken her station there and be waiting for me. Quite impossible, of course, we had left her with the rest of her family and a few late-staying visitors milling about the coffin. It was her mother stood by the door and bade us goodbye.

Though I found myself staring at her from time to time, not a word was spoken between us all during that unendurably long evening. She gave me but a few fleeting smiles, yet they were enough to feed my impatience. When would it all end? Well, eventually it did, and as we tramped the last steps to home, I noted that the twilight had turned to dusk, and that it would soon be dark. The time had come to leave them. I did not even enter the house, but rather took my leave of them at our doorstep. I pled restlessness and said I had need of a walk in the pleasant night air. They accepted what I said indifferently and cautioned me not to be too late nor roam too far from home. Promising that, I left them and started off in a direction opposite the one I would eventually walk.

When, after circling round, I found my way back to the path, I considered what lay ahead. To me it seemed a turning point in my life (as indeed it was), an end to childish pursuits of the carnal sort—chasing girls, playing the dame for Mr. Cotton, all that rolling about with young Gyllome. No, with Anne Hathaway I anticipated my first experience of sexual congress with a mature woman. She had not run from me, nor would she—oh, quite the contrary! This was a different world that I was entering, was it not? It was inhabited by others such as she who would gladly give themselves to me—and I would have them all. What an exciting life this would be!

There was no trouble in finding the path, nor in keeping on

it, for a bright half-moon was above in a cloudless sky. It was a mild night, almost warm, perfect for what lay ahead. There would not be many more nights like it in September—indeed, not many more that year.

Entering the copse, I expected to find her awaiting me, for that was my phantasy. Yet it was not long until I heard her footsteps upon the path. I thought to leave the copse and meet her on the way and was about to do that when it occurred to me that it might not be she. How could I then explain my presence? And so I waited, standing still as I was able, holding my breath.

"Will? Will?" It was Anne.

"Here I am," said I, moving toward the sound of her voice.

Then did I see her clearly. She stood in the path and peered in my direction. She wore a cape and her face was hidden from the moonlight by the hood which she wore. Nodding that she had seen me, she left the path. A moment later she was by my side.

I took her to me and pressed a kiss upon her lips. As I did so, I ran my hand over her breasts, thinking to excite her. Yet it was she who excited me. Throwing off her hood with a toss of the head, and holding tight to me, she returned the kiss, thrusting her tongue between my lips. I had heard of such kisses but never once known their like. With her right hand she undid my codpiece, which even then was too small by half for its load. Freed, my man sprang out as if sent forth by some mechanical contraption. The next moment her hand surrounded it gently.

"Careful," said I. "I should be loath to deliver too early."

"Oh, aye," said she, "that would be a loss to us both—though you've no worry. The midwife says I'm barren."

VI

Our daughter, Susanna, was born the following spring, on the twenty-third of May, 1583. By that time Anne and I had been married about six months.

To write it so upon the page can give no sense nor notion of all the grief, trouble, and frustration that lay behind those words. And perhaps, though Anne did ever deny it, there was a bit of mischief involved in the matter, as well I remember all the details very clearly, as one might those surrounding any great calamity.

Anne had been acting oddly during those last days in October. We had been conducting our carnal frolics in that same grove of trees for some weeks when at last, seeking shelter from the cold, we made the Hathaway barn our place for trysting. It required stealth to enter it and quiet once inside—yet she would be there, dependably, like a faithful mare awaiting her young stallion. She used just such words to praise me, which flattered me no end. Nevertheless, she took her payment in the demands she made upon me: Duration and frequency mattered greatly to her. There were also certain special requests that she made to me which, if satisfied, would surely have been considered as sins; indeed, they seemed sinful to me. Since, for the most part, I resisted, I shall not need to embarrass myself by naming or attempting to describe them here.

On the night in question I had declined one of those strange requests, and when she fell silent following our sport, I took it as mere sulking. Yet as I soon learned, there was more to the matter than I had supposed. Much more.

"Will," said she, "we must talk of something—something important."

"What will you, woman?" I asked her. "What has talk to do with such play as ours? Consider the birds which do court and mate in the springtime. They—"

"*Please,* Will!" she said sharply. "None of your pretty poetry, not now, please. There be more to life than your fancy."

I liked the sound of this not one tittle. Yet she had got my attention. "Tell me then, Anne."

"I'm with child."

"*You're what?*" I fear I shouted it out in surprise.

"Will, please. You'll wake all in the house. I do not wish them to find us so."

"But . . . but," I did sputter. "You said that you were barren."

"I know, I know," she wailed in a whisper. "That is what the midwife told me. I am as surprised as you are."

"Well, are you sure? After all, you could be wrong, couldn't you?"

"Not likely." She sighed. "I've missed my bleeding time twice, you see. And my mother says twice makes it certain."

"Your mother? You told her? When?"

"Yes, I told her. I had to. I knew not what to do. Just this evening I sought her advice."

"And what did she say?" As if I had to ask that question.

"Why, she said that we must marry. Your mother agrees. They talked of it whilst you were in your father's workshop."

Where I had taken a corner that I might have a place to write. I felt trapped as surely as any of the rabbits snared by Ned. The noose was tightening about me. What could I do? I made one last effort—and a feeble one it was indeed.

"But," said I, "think of the difference in your age and mine. Must I remind you, Anne? I am but eighteen."

"Must I remind *you,* Will, that you did not concern yourself with that difference when we were busy making the child." She smiled sweetly at me. "Besides, eight years is not so much. By the time I am forty and you are thirty-two, we shall no longer give it a thought."

Oh, there were difficulties aplenty, yet naught, it seemed, that my parents and the widow Hathaway together could not overcome. Because I was but eighteen and the time had passed for the wedding plans to be announced before Advent, a special marriage license had to be granted and issued by the Bishop's Court. That was negotiated. And because of my age it was necessary for two Shottery farmers to stand surety that there were no impediments to the marriage. Would that there had been!

There was no escape—I could see that. Father swore that he would not allow me to betray his old friend, Richard Hathaway. My mother formed an alliance with Anne's to ensure that I would fulfil all the obligations of a public courtship. They made certain that we two would walk out together; that we would sit together in church; that we would be seen all round the town, ever smiling, always attentive, one to the other (but never to be seen thus at night). And during all these peregrinations about Stratford and Shottery the widow Hathaway trailed us at a discreet distance. My rutting days with Anne were done, at least for the foreseeable future.

One evening after a long, solitary walk, I came to our door and was about to enter when I heard voices beyond it, those of my mother and Joan Hathaway, mother of Anne. I realized that they were speaking of me, so I remained outside and listened.

"He's not a bad lad," said the latter. "I'll give him that. And if him and Anne got a little ahead of themselves, well, who's to blame? It's not all on him, I'm sure."

Ah-hah! thought I. Now had my mother the opportunity to end this farce of an engagement by declaring that it was obvious all this had been planned and executed by Anne, as I by then was certain had been done. If even Anne's mother admitted her daughter was partly to blame, then it was certain Anne deserved it all. Go on, Mother, tell the woman! Remember, as you so often reminded me, you are an Arden.

Yet she said nothing of the kind: "Indeed," said she, "Will needs marrying. It will knock out of him all those notions of London and writing verses and such. It matters little to me just how the marriage comes about."

I stood before the door, quite unable to enter. So disturbed was I by what I had heard from the lips of my own mother that I felt that I had somehow lost my sense of inner balance. I left the door, having not so much as touched the latch. Wandering about aimlessly, I felt as one who had gone ill in the head. I thought upon my situation: To run away once again was quite impossible. I had not money enough to go anywhere and besides, had nowhere to go. London was out of the question: The little money I had left would not keep me long there; more important still, I was not yet ready either as an actor or a versifier to attempt such a bold endeavor. Yet when I was ready, I would go. I would show the mother who had, I felt, betrayed me that I was not to be so easily led away from the path that I had chosen. And I would show Anne that while she might have me as a husband, as soon as I was able I would make myself a husband in absentia. She had often said to me that her dearest wish was to leave Stratford and Shottery behind and never to return. While that had endeared her to me in the beginning (for I shared the same desire), I now saw it only as a means of punishing her for putting me to all this distress. So long as I was her husband, this is where she would stay.

I returned late that night to home. Mrs. Hathaway had left long before; Mother and Father had gone off to bed; the fire in the hearth had burned to embers behind the screen. Yet having thought through the matter of my future, I felt the fire in me burning even brighter now that it had upon my return to Stratford. By God, let them do what they like! Let them plot against me—I cared not! I would best them all in the end. And have I not? Indeed I have!

Anne and I were married in a chapel in Luddington, a village even smaller than Shottery, which lay across the Avon. The curate, whose name I forget, served both villages. Had either my family or Anne's taken any pride in the union, the wedding would surely have been held at Holy Trinity in Stratford. There were few present beyond the members of the two families, and I knew none of them. As for the exact date, I cannot call that to mind, either, for it is certain that I never celebrated its anniversary. Nevertheless, it was sometime in November.

Anne brought with her into the marriage a little under seven pounds; this was according to the terms of her father's will. We were also given the use for an unlimited time of a cottage that stood on the Hathaway property. All we had to do to take possession was clean the place out. Since it had been used to store grain and hay and earlier as a chicken coop, this was not easy. Yet Anne was equal to the task. Indeed I give her credit: she made the place habitable within a week.

And while she was thus employed, I would trudge off on that well-worn path across the fields to my father's workshop. There I worked in the manner of an apprentice, though out of respect to my rank in the family as a newly married man, I was paid something. It was no more than a pittance, but it was enough to buy our food; when it was not, some was given us by the widow Hathaway.

It was a simple life we lived during those first months, huddling together before the fire for warmth during the winter. She sewed by candlelight, making clothes for the baby which would come in the spring, whilst I did read.* I could no more

---

*At that time my library consisted of but a single book, Spenser's *Shephearde's Calendar,* which I had stolen from Mr. Cotton. I acknowledge this to be a sin and hereby confess it, though for all the grief he caused me, I think it small recompense.

than that, for we had not a desk for writing in our small collection of broken-back house furniture; and further, I had not money enough to buy more paper with which I might proceed with *Arden of Faversham,* which I did think of as my first play. And so I simply put things off, dangerously comfortable in this post-nuptial period. The unvaried nature of the days and evenings did suit me well. But then, not long before the birth of Susanna came an event that would alter our situation utterly. After it, Mother would never again boast of her heritage as an Arden.

Her cousin, Margaret Arden, had married a wealthy Warwickshire squire named John Somerville, who was of rather an unstable nature. He, a recusant Catholic, maintained a Catholic priest named Hugh Hall in his manor house as his chaplain—all in secret, of course. At the priest's urging, Somerville hatched a plan to go to London with his fowling piece and shoot the Queen dead, thus restoring the One True Church to its rightful place in England. (Just how he expected to get close enough to do this, I cannot suppose.) Mr. Somerville then boasted to one and all of what he planned to do. One of those to whom he boasted was his father-in-law, Edward Arden, who no doubt thought (and may indeed have hoped) that this was just another of Somerville's hare-brained notions and that he would think better of it as soon as he was once again sober; in any case, he did nothing about it and certainly did not report his son-in-law to the authority in London. Someone did, however, and mentioned Father Hall as prime mover in the plot and Edward Arden as one who knew of it but did nothing. Then one day, surprising them all, the Queen's men appeared in their part of Warwickshire and took all three men into custody; and while they were about it, they brought along Margaret Arden Somerville, as well. All went to London, and all were imprisoned in the Tower.

Sir Francis Walsingham, ever eager to prove and root out a great conspiracy against the Queen and the Church of

England, prescribed a course of torture for all four of the prisoners that they might provide the names of all of those in the west country who had joined with them in the plot. He sent his spies out to Warwickshire to see what might be learned *in locus solus*. This much was known, and widely known, throughout the two shires, which were strongly Papist in their preference. What was suspected by one and all was that there was no conspiracy but that which Somerville and perhaps his chaplain, as well, had fashioned in their phantasmatical imaginings.

All this had I, forsooth, learned from the Hathaways, Joan, the widow, and Bartholomew, her eldest son. They sat before our fire, in hushed tones and with eyes wide, told us the story, then asked to know what my parents had told me.

"Why . . . nothing," said I. "This is the first I had heard of it."

"We thought you might've heard more from them," said Bartholomew. "Your mother being an Arden and all."

"She is an Arden, an't she?" asked the widow.

"Well, in a manner of speaking, I suppose," said I, then of a sudden feeling rather evasive about our connection to the family.

"She said she was. Many's the time she mentioned it."

I jumped to my feet and began pacing about the small room. I continued just long enough to note the fearful look in Anne's eyes as she watched me.

And so did I turn to her when I halted to declare that I must go back across the fields and discuss all this with them. I half-expected the Hathaways to rise and accompany me as far as the farmhouse. But no:

"We'll just stay and visit with Anne a little longer," said her mother.

Pushing up from her chair with no little effort, she went to the door with me, risking each step in the awkward manner of women in their ninth month with child. She took down my hat from the hook where it hung and offered it to me.

"What does all this mean?" she whispered.

"That is what I wish to discover." And with that I bade goodbye to all in the room and went out the door held open for me by Anne. Just outside I mused how odd it was that she seemed to look to me more and more as her master—this in spite of her seniority in age, her earlier bold manner. It often happened during those days that I knew not quite how to respond to her and to these changes in her.

Having just turned nineteen, I was then in my physical prime, taller and stronger than ever before, given to running distances simply as a means of expending my youthful excess of energy. And though I ran swifter than ever before to my old home in Stratford, I had better reason for doing so than mere high spirits. It was the urgency I felt to know more, to learn our situation, to find out what lay in store for us.

We Shakespeares were ourselves recusant Catholics, as were indeed the majority of those in the shire. Father, who had been an honored member of the Stratford Town Council, was forced into inactivity and finally into retirement from the Council as it became obvious that he failed to attend services at Holy Trinity—and for obvious reasons. Once the old parish priest—Father Dickerson was his name, I believe—was replaced with a bona-fide Church of England vicar, John Shakespeare let his children know by his example that there was no longer any need to attend holy services where once we had been most regular. I missed the sacrament of confession but little else. The children in the family younger than Gilbert received no religious instruction whatever; they simply did without. There were fines, but with the help of loans and gifts from neighbors, Father paid them. He was no longer an alderman, no longer a bailiff; he was no more than a tradesman in the town, and that to him was sufficient.

Predictably, I arrived out of breath, panting at the doorstep as I beat upon the door, perhaps a bit louder than needed be—yet I knew not if there were yet any about on the ground floor. Would I be heard? Would my visit be for naught?

But then, sooner than I would have expected, the door flew open, and there stood my father, his jaw set in an expression of restrained anger. Yet it took him but a moment to recognize me, and when he did his face softened and his eyes lit in a look of relief.

"Will!" said he. "What are you doing here?"

My mother appeared behind him. "What does it matter, John? Let him in."

Father stepped aside and I stepped forward. It was only when I entered that I saw that all my brothers and my sister were there at the far end of the room, runged upon the staircase. My mother turned to them and clapped her hands. "All right, children, up the stairs with you. We've had our talk now, no more tonight. Joan, take little Edmund and put him to bed." She waved them up and reluctantly they went. Gilbert and Joan bade me good-night; the younger children ignored me. Soon I was alone with Mother and Father.

"I came to hear what you know of this matter of cousin Edward and Somerville and cousin Margaret."

"What do *you* know?" asked my father.

"Only what I heard just now from the Hathaways."

"You see?" said Mother to Father. "Even they know about it."

"But how much do they know?" he demanded. "Will, sit down, please, and tell us what you got from them."

We took our places before the fire, and I quickly blurted out the entire matter as related by the widow Hathaway, with reminders and interjections from her son. I summarized, and thus it took me not near so long to tell as it had the two of them. When I had done, Mother and Father exchanged glances and an elaborate series of shrugs and muttered words. This sort of secret language was quite beyond me. When had it developed? Why?

"That is all you heard?" asked Father.

"Is that not enough? What more is there to know? *When* did you know, and *what* have you kept from me?"

Thinking back quickly, I realized that my father had been even more evasive and distant than usual during the past week, and Mother had been absent from the house without explanation for one whole day. There had been, to put it in other words, signs to be read, had I but read them.

"All right," said she, "you deserve to know, and so you shall. After all, we told a bit of it to the children this evening, but because you know more, you shall hear more."

As she explained it, the Earl of Leicester was the moving force behind it, for he and Edward Arden had long been enemies. Somerville, a loose-lipped drunkard, probably had boasted in some public place of his "plan" to murder the Queen. That gave Leicester all the opportunity that he needed to bring the matter to Walsingham.

"But how were Margaret and Edward brought into it?" I asked.

"Well, there was one small matter that dear Mrs. Hathaway had wrong. Father Hall was Edward's chaplain and not Somerville's."

"Hiding a priest?" I said. "Then, from all I have heard, I fear cousin Edward is lost."

"I know it," said she glumly. "But I shed all the tears I have to shed for him when cousin Lawrence came down from Warwick with the news."

"Was that when you first heard? When was that?"

"Oh, I don't know." She threw up a hand dismissively. "Five days ago perhaps."

"Why did you not tell me?"

"Well . . ." Again that dismissive gesture.

"You told the children tonight."

"More or less."

"Then why did you not tell me?" I demanded.

At that, Father intruded, asking with all the force of his paternal authority: "We're telling you now, are we not?"

"Well, yes, but—"

"The situation is altered," he declared. "Matters change by the day. You were told, were you not, that spies had been sent into Warwickshire?"

"Yes, go on, tell me."

"Indeed they are here. A friend—never mind who—came by early this evening, just after you'd gone home and I'd closed up the shop, and he gave me some news." At this point he lowered his voice to little more than a whisper as he leaned forward and continued: "Two of Walsingham's men were at the Swan tonight—they may still be there for all I know—and though they named themselves simply 'travelers from London,' spies was what they were."

"How can you be so sure?" My father was a cautious man, one not much given to such certain pronouncements.

"Because they asked too many questions and because of the kind of questions they asked." He paused a moment, adding to the drama. "They asked about us."

"You mean our family? The Shakespeares by name?"

"I mean your mother and me in particular, but"—he hesitated—"they had questions about you, too."

"What kind of questions?"

"Oh, they said they'd heard we had a preference for the old Faith. Would we be willing to put up a priest if one was to come through on his way someplace else? Only they asked it in such a way that you would suppose that they, too, were Roman by persuasion and were truly looking for a family who might shelter a priest passing through here in disguise."

"And what were they told?" I asked.

"That they'd have to ask us about that."

"Yes, well, that's good. But how did I come into it?"

"Well, you didn't quite—and that was strange—for they seemed to be asking questions of a different sort about you. They knew of your marriage, the wedding over in Luddington and all. What they wanted to know about was where you had been the rest of the year. They had heard that you had been a player and would know more about you so that they might see you perform. There was evidently a deal of such fanciful nonsense told."

"But why would they want to know about me?" I asked myself aloud.

"You really don't know?"

"Of course he doesn't, John," said my mother. "He has no idea of the politics of this infernal place." And then to me, "Will, I would suppose they were asking at the request of Sir Thomas Lucy."

"What has he to do with it?"

"Why, he's the Earl of Leicester's creature. He was but a middling squire until Leicester took him up, arranged his knighthood and made him his man in this part of Warwickshire. Sir Thomas wishes to know more about you—and that is a bad sign—for the more he knows the greater harm he can do you."

"All this because of that deer we took without intention."

"Such men," said she, "cannot easily bring themselves to forgive and even less to forget."

"Still," said I, "it does seem strange."

"You took it ill that we had spoken to the children before we talked to you. We simply told them all to say naught about us or about you, if asked either by a stranger or by someone known to them and to us. John and I were talking about what we might say to you when you came to the door. We'd come to no real decision, but now that you're here I have some questions to ask you."

"Ask them then, and I shall answer."

"How many, outside the family, have you told of where and how you spent the last summer?"

"I told a few *how* I spent it—in a boastful way, I fear, hoping to impress or gain favor. But I don't believe I've been truthful to anyone—outside the family—about *where* I spent it."

Thus far I had managed only to puzzle her. "What do you mean?"

"Well, I give the impression that I was in"—I hesitated—"in London."

"You lie about it?"

"No,* but I describe life there, the sights, the sounds, and if I am asked questions, I answer them as my powers of invention may dictate."

Mother and Father wore similar worried frowns as they considered this. I fear I had shocked them deeply.

"And what about Anne?" my mother persisted. "Where does she think you were all those months past?"

"In London."

"That may make it easier for me." I knew not what she meant. "Just one more question," said she. "Did you tell anyone about the name you used up in Lancashire?"

"You mean Shakeshafte?"

"Shh! Please! No need to cry it out to the four winds—but yes, that silly name."

At that Father took umbrage. "It is *not* a silly name," said he to her. "It was good enough for my own father. If I chose to vary it, then that was a matter between him and me."

"Oh, all right, it is *not* a silly name." Then to me, "Well? Did you tell anyone?"

"No."

"Excellent."

The next evening I left Stratford by stealth as soon as it was dark. I took the same route—going by way of the Warwick High Road—that I had walked the year before. It was Sir Thomas Lucy had driven me out then just as he had before. I had come to resent the man most profoundly. Yet someday, I assured myself, I should have my own back at him. And that day did indeed come.

---

*Alas, this also was a lie. If it be a sin, then I confess it, yet what more did I do than entertain with my tales of London Life.

Ah well, I was, forsooth, leaving only a week or two earlier than I had planned. I had promised Anne and her mother that I would stay on but a few days past the birth of the baby to be certain that both mother and child were not in danger, then was it my intention to journey north to Lancashire.

My mother had visited Anne and the widow Hathaway in the morning whilst I was pretending to be busy at work with Father. Yet I was much too agitated by last night's discussion to sew a good stitch during that day, so that I fear that most of what I did that day had to be redone by Gilbert or by my father.

After a long and no doubt arduous session with the Hathaway women, my mother returned when the sun was near its zenith and informed me that I was free to leave but that she thought it best that I wait until after dark to make my departure. It had been difficult for her to persuade them that it was necessary for me to leave before the baby was born without telling much (or as much as the widow wished to know) about the troubles of the Arden family or my difficulties with Sir Thomas. Having argued unsuccessfully that loyalty was owed me for the exemplary manner in which I had accepted my responsibility going into the marriage ("And why shouldn't he?" the widow demanded; "Because by law he is yet an infant," said Mother), cooperation and a promise of silence was wrung from them at last only after Mother's promise that she, too, would assist at the birth and that we would bear the expense of the midwife.

"It seems," said she to me, "that they had expected that of us, but the promise to do so was what won them over."

(I wondered, though I said naught, if this were the same midwife who had told Anne that she was barren; if she were, I hoped that she was better at delivering babies than she was at discerning female conditions.)

And so this difficulty, as with so many others in life, was overcome by an offer of money. I took a lesson from that, and when I returned to Anne in the afternoon, I told her that I had left a sum of money with my parents, and that it should be sufficient to cover expenses whilst I would be gone. That indeed seemed to satisfy her, and she offered no complaints until our parting.

"Oh, Will," said she then, "I am a bit fearful of the birth. I do so wish you would be here."

"You've no need to fear," I declared with greater confidence than I felt at that moment. "As you've told me often, you're a big, strong country girl. You can best any such threat."

She was silent for a moment, but she then gave a good, firm nod. "I suppose I can," said she.

Then did we kiss, and indeed I felt closer to her at that moment than ever I had before. I was quite amazed to find tears blurring my sight as I made for the high road to Warwick.

Ah, there is my dilemma revealed. I had either to consider myself Anne's victim—she so desperate at age twenty-six to be married that she seduced an eighteen-year-old boy, one quite innocent of women's ways; or, contrariwise, I was to think of her as *my* victim—herself an innocent victim of my lust, one who had proven herself a dozen times over in the brief period since we were married as possessed of all the wifely virtues. Still to the present I am riven between these two opposing views.

I do often rant within at Anne in the same tones and in terms similar to those I did use in the chapter previous. In a sense I have never forgiven her—and probably never shall. When I have taken it up with her, as I have often done, she has ever affirmed that she had been told by Mrs. Tillyard, the midwife, that her womb was tipped and she would always be barren. This was disappointing to her in one way, for she had always assumed she would have children, yet it removed the fear of an unwelcome pregnancy and left her free to adventure "as a man does" (she readily admitted I was not the first with whom she had sported, though she named no names). And further, as she put it to me but a week or two before we wed: "Would I likely get myself with child by you with so many women dying each day of childbed fever and Mrs. Tillyard telling me that with my particular condition I'm likely to have a difficult delivery if I ever did get pregnant?"

All this, forsooth, made great good sense, and I could not deny that she had been a good wife to me. In cooking and sewing she showed herself without equal, and up to the end of our time there she kept the little cottage a deal cleaner than her mother and sisters together did keep the grand house that faced out upon the road. Whenever we slept in the same bed, she was a good and loving wife, nor was I ever given reason to believe that she ever allowed anyone else into her bed. I never thought her unfaithful, which is more than can be said of most of the other wives I have known.

All of this together may make it plain why I wept a few tears that evening as I walked out from our cottage. I was sad beyond telling to leave her thus. Yet I accepted it that there was danger to me so that I must go, for had not my mother captained the entire maneuver and got me out of town? And was it not she who was eager to get me married that I might lose my notions of London and the theater? She knew well, surely, that the road that led to Lancashire would lead eventually to London. And indeed Anne must have known that, too.

I know not if it was sinful to leave Anne; I do know that to do so left me feeling guilty and unhappy as many of those I knew to be sins never had done. Had I deserted her upon her occasion of greatest need? I hoped not. Surely many men must leave their wives and suffer such feelings of guilt. Is that not the situation in which a soldier finds himself when he must answer the call to battle? And when the seaman attends his ship, must he not go with the tide? Soldiers and seamen also have wives they must leave—and indeed they leave them. Even merchants are often gone from their families for great periods of time, yet if they are successful in their dealings, they are applauded and respected. So was I then a kind of merchant gone off to Lancashire to learn the trade better that he might eventually go to London to sell his wares to be rewarded with riches. That was the way that I came to look upon my role. And my justification for all those departures and for the absences, which grew longer and longer, was the money that came my way. And so did I ease my guilt, if such persisted, by sending home to Anne pounds, shillings, and pence—first by way of Father and then later through Gilbert.

Nevertheless, whenever the occasion demanded, I have been able to work myself up into a fine fury at her for tricking me into marriage. Poor Will Shakespeare had been tricked into marriage, had he not? Could he even be certain that it was he who had fathered their firstborn? Might Susanna be the natural child of some nameless, faceless Stratford male? No, I think not. She is more like me in every way than she is like her mother. Still, such dark thoughts have always served me well in driving away the pangs of guilt.

VII

If I were inditing a play, instead of this—what shall I call it? confession? examination of conscience?—I should at this point cleave it in twain. All that has preceded this might then be called William I, Part One, and all that follows, William I, Part Two.

Each treats matter separate and distinct from the other. The first may be taken as a *souvenir* of my youth—if I may once again resort to the French language. The sins described therein, if sins they be, are of little moment. Nevertheless, the events of this part do bear direct upon what is later taken up in that which lies ahead.

The second part deals with a later period, which is to say, with London and my beginnings there as a poet and a writer of plays. This is, forsooth, a darker tale, and I flinch from telling it at all. Yet tell it I must if I am to realize my intention to reveal the worst. Still, though this be no history of my self, before I start I must give summary to facts and events which connect the first part with the second. Let me then begin.

Though there were many questions from all parties regarding Ffoke Gyllome, I was welcomed most heartily by all members of Mr. Houghton's Men. The company had come together at Houghton Tower and was about to embark upon the first trip round the circuit. I had foreseen the questions about Gyllome and had prepared my answers: "Not here? Nothing heard from him? Not even his family knows?" et cetera. "How terrible! I left him in Birmingham. Perhaps he lies in some shallow grave between there and Swansea." Et cetera. All that I had learned of acting the summer before aided greatly in my presentation. What I had not anticipated was that Gyllome's work of fabricating new jokes and jests for such as *Ralph Roister Doister* and *Gammer Gurton's Needle,* and the like, fell to me. I protested and declared that such was not at all in my scope; that I was a poet and not a jester. "That may be, Will," said Peter Ponder to me, "but you're all we've got. And until we find another with Gyllome's knack for jests and silliness, which may take some time indeed, you're the one who must do his work. Come now, be a good lad and do as I ask. We'll help you all we can." Which "all" was no great amount, certainly.

Our clown, Jingo Torkey, was full of suggestions—jests and bits of business which struck no one but him as funny; he thought them sure to arouse great hilarity. Yet I wished to create comedy from the differences between characters, and draw laughter out of their misunderstandings. At the start, I could not always succeed at this and would then be forced to fall back upon Jingo's paltry inventions. But by the end of summer I had managed it often enough that I had earned Mr. Ponder's respect and, reluctantly, Jingo's as well.

A few old plays had been added to the company's list—Gascoigne's *Supposes* and another by one Richard Edwards, which I had never even heard of, *Damon and Pythias*—all of this made more work for me. Yet I welcomed it, just as I did my turns on the stage, whether in female parts, or whatever.

My only disappointment that season had to do with *Arden of Faversham,* which I did finish by August and offer to Mr. Ponder. It was in his dressing room after the show at the theater in Prescot. I had, I fear, made an error in presenting it with a title page in my most ornate hand. It did say:

Arden of Faversham,
An historical drama
By
William Shakeshafte

Peter Ponder looked no further than the title before giving a disapproving shake of his head.

"This name, Arden, troubles me, Will. Has the play to do with the treasonous plot upon the Queen which was so much discussed when I left London?"

"Oh no, Mr. Ponder, by no means. This is something quite different, a play about a murder some years past in Southwark."

"Then the name could be changed for another," he suggested.

I took a moment to think about that. Much as I should have liked to accommodate him, I feared it was not possible.

"No sir, I don't think that could be done, for it is written after a true history, you see. I found the story in Holinshed's *Chronicles*."

"I see," said he with an unhappy frown and a deep sigh. "Will, I fear this just an't the time to do a play about anyone called Arden."

"Not even in Lancashire?" I asked.

"Nowheres in England," said he.

And so it was to be for years to come.

That was August. In September, however, there were no disappointments for me. First of all, I learned at our division of the season's spoils that I was to be paid a double portion. Mr. Ponder explained that I was entitled to Gyllome's share as well as my own, for I had also done his work, had I not? Well, I had to agree that this was true, and so without ever asking, which I could not have done, I did benefit from his death. That left me feeling very strange indeed.

And the next day, which was to be our last there at Houghton Tower until the following summer, I was approached by Mr. Thomas Houghton and invited into the library that we might talk about a matter which, as he said, concerned me. Not knowing what he meant by that, I confess that I felt some anxiety as I followed him into the great room which I had last visited for the reading of Alexander Houghton's will. Thomas, his much younger brother, was chief legatee and was also now the patron of the company of players that Alexander had assembled.

He took the place at the head of the large oaken table which the lawyer had occupied the year before. And, taking the place at his right hand which he had indicated, I slid into a high-backed chair which was exactly like his own. I said nothing but simply waited with mounting trepidation.

"This is, if you please, a rather delicate matter," said he to me.

All my fears seemed justified by that beginning. My eyes shifted wildly about the room. Books and more books filled the shelves which lined the walls; they seemed to be pressing in on me from every side. But then did I spy a door at the far end of the room. It would be through there that I might expect the constable to enter. Or would it be a constable? Perhaps Sir Thomas Lucy's man, Arthur, had come to convey me back to Stratford; him I feared more than the law.

"I've sought you out," said he, resuming, "on the advice of Mr. John Cotton, our neighbor in Prescot. He, I was surprised to learn, was your schoolmaster down somewhere in Warwickshire. Is that correct?"

Breathing normally once again, I answered with assurance that he was quite correct.

"Your Mr. Cotton"—was he *my* Mr. Cotton?—"told me that you were quite an exceptional student, Mr. Shakeshafte, and he felt that you would also make an exceptional teacher."

"Teacher?" I echoed.

"Well, perhaps not *teacher* quite. I suppose *tutor* would be a more accurate description of the position which I am offering."

"Offering?" Again I found myself repeating him like the hollow echo in a cave. "I'm afraid I don't quite understand, sir."

"What? No, I suppose you don't. I fear that I am not making myself very clear, am I? You see, it's my son. He is in many ways a most satisfactory lad—rides well, hunts with the best—but you see, young Jude simply cannot read—English, that is—and at the age of twelve, I'm convinced he should have some ability in that regard, don't you think? After all, he'll be a Member of Parliament when I give up the seat, and he'll be called upon to read there. More reading to be done there than ever before."

"Oh, I should think so," said I, "indeed, yes—speeches and the like and, well, legislation, that sort of thing."

I wished to be helpful. After all, it seemed he was about to offer me the job of teaching his son to read. Yet I found there was more to it than that.

"Ah, yes, that's something I wished to take up with you, too."

"Oh? How is that, sir?"

"Well, the truth is, you see, I'm not much good at letters myself. That's one reason I'd like you to teach my son to read. A good father does ever wish his son to best him, at least in some way. But I have need of you, too. I was thinking you might serve as my scribe, reading my post, answering what needs be answered for me. Not that there would be much call for you to do that sort of work. But what I'd thought, you see, was that you might teach reading to my son and, as you were needed, serve as my scribe . . . or . . . there's another word for that."

"Secretary?"

"That's it, of course. Well, what do you say?"

"I would not wish my duties to interfere with my summers with the company of players."

"Oh, that's not a problem," said he with great assurance. "There's not much happens up here in the summer. And as for teaching my son in the summertime, that would be quite impossible—a twelve-year-old boy, after all."

"And would I have the run of the library?"

"You mean this, in here? All these books? You wish to read them?" He laughed. "Do so with my blessing. They are my late brother's, of course, and so far as I can see, they are only gathering dust."

There were other details to be brought up, of course. Whether I would eat with the family or with the servants, which holidays I might have as my own, where I would sleep, and so on—but not least, what the payment would be for such year-round employment. All these were settled to my advantage with the exception, perhaps, of the matter of remuneration. I might have coaxed more from him, had I told him that I had a wife and child back in Stratford, but my over-riding intention was to keep all such personal details beyond his ken. Yet I did manage to persuade him that our arrangement should begin at the start of the next month, and that I would be given the days between to return home and describe to my family my new situation. Mr. Houghton did even offer me an amount sufficient to pay for post coach fare to Stratford and return; I took it and gladly.

My mother had kept me informed of matters in Warwickshire through her letters addressed to "William Shakeshafte, Esq." I had come to think of the name almost as my own. Almost. In the text of her letters she made no reference to my summer activities, and commented upon the political conditions there at home as if writing about the weather: "In general, things are a bit brighter here. I cannot say, however, that they have cleared up completely on your side of town. Why not come by for a quick visit? It may be possible to look in on us, see the new arrival and her friend, and then be gone before the clouds gather and the rain begins."

And that was what I had planned—an arrival after dark,

keeping indoors whilst the sun was out and about, and departing after the sun had set. An arrival by post coach would put me in the middle of town in the middle of the day. Word would no doubt be brought to Sir Thomas Lucy, and he would do whatever he would do. There was naught could be proved against me—of that I was certain. Still, I feared him, and even more did I fear his man, Arthur. Yet returning with such a report as I had to give provided me, I felt, with a certain strength. It seemed that each time that I returned home I was stronger than before. Soon I hoped to be powerful enough to do Sir Thomas and his man real harm.

And so, quite willingly, I took the post coach to Stratford-upon-Avon and happily did I descend the coach steps at the old inn, the Swan, which I knew quite well. Who but I could know just how happy I was to return! Who could say just how long I might stay!

The answer to that proved to be not long at all, as I was quite unprepared for the amount of crying and weeping of which a three-and-a-half month old baby may be capable. I was quite surprised—shocked may not be too strong a word to put to my feelings—by our daughter, Susanna. I had left a cottage so quiet that Anne and I spoke in tones hardly louder than whispers, and returned to one in which it was necessary to shout to be heard above Susanna's screams. And it was not just the volume of these cries but their unpredictable frequency which did so unnerve me. Yet there I speak somewhat carelessly for at least in one sense the baby's weeping was all-too predictable. You could be certain that in the middle of the night, well after twelve, announced by a few introductory bleats, there would come the worst fit of screaming of that twenty-four hour period. I, who am no light sleeper, would come immediately awake and remain so for the remainder of the night. Anne, on the other hand, was quite capable of taking Susanna up from the cradle, shoving a pap into her little mouth, and letting her suckle till full—all this without ever having emerged completely from a sleeping state; she amazed me thus.

Without sleep, I could not remain for long; I left, indeed, after only five days in Stratford. I had intended to stay longer, yet I could hardly ask my parents if I might have my old place back, sharing the bed with Gilbert. Who could tell what conclusions they might draw from such a request? No, I simply had to get away; and that I did, though not before I had learned more from my mother and father regarding the fate of the Ardens and their party. Of those who had been arrested, only two were left. Robert Somerville had gone quite mad in prison; because a public trial and a public execution were intended, it would not do to put a gibbering madman before all as a conspirator, and so he was quietly strangled in prison. Father Hugh Hall, the priest, enfeebled by age, could not endure the torture to which he was put and died upon the rack. And so only Mother's two cousins were left.

"How came you by all this information?" I asked her when she had done.

"We have our sources, Will, even among Walsingham's minions. They take a bribe quick as the next."

"Then surely," said I, "there is danger for one and all. I shall go deeper into hiding up north."

"Why say you so?" asked Father. He seemed truly confused by what I had declared.

"Well, because they will be put to torture as Somerville and the priest were, will they not? They cannot hold out forever. By the end, they will be giving every name they know just for a day's rest from the rack and the thumb screws."

"You think so, do you?" Mother demanded.

"Yes, I do. Forsooth, I do!"

"Well, you are wrong, Will. They will not, in any wise, compromise the innocents or give false witness."

"Why should they not?"

She looked at me rather coldly, as if I should know better than to ask such a question.

"Because," said she, "they are Ardens."

I looked at Father and found him staring at me, as if daring me to take exception to what my mother had said. Then, seconding it, he gave a firm nod—another challenge.

As it happened, that was the last time I heard her speak of what it might mean to be an Arden. And though she never again mentioned it, I believe she never let go her conviction that by an accident of birth she and all the rest who bore that name were in most ways superior to the rest of mankind.

Still, there must have been some basis for that belief, for the search for Papist conspirators did gradually die out with no further arrests made. And according to those sources within Sir Francis Walsingham's organization, Margaret Arden Somerville and Edward Arden went to their deaths without offering names of any who had joined in the conspiracy, insisting that there had been no plot against the Queen. Their deaths were predictably ignominious and horrible. She, as the wife of one who had talked openly of his intention to murder the Queen, was burned at the stake. He, as one who had hidden a priest of the Roman Church was drawn and quartered; his head was used to decorate London Bridge for some years afterward.

Since there was no need for me to return to Houghton Tower before the date I had promised, I decided that it would be as well to walk back. Thus would I keep the coach fare and also have the opportunity to open an account for myself at the Bank of Warwick (Stratford then had none). I arranged that my father might also draw upon the account should money be needed by Anne beyond what I had left with him. From that time on did I handle my affairs, first from Lancashire and later from London. When Father died, I named Gilbert as my factor.

It was a fine time of the year for such a walk. Though nights were cool, it mattered little, for I had money enough to sleep in inns along the way. To tramp along and view the red and gold of the countryside in September was so much more pleasant than bouncing about on my poor, lean arse in a coach full of foul-smelling fellow passengers. I promised myself that ever afterward I would walk, rather than ride, and by and large I have kept that promise. To this I owe the handsome figure I now still possess even into this, the sixth decade of my life.

I arrived at Houghton Tower punctual to my promise, upon the morning of the first day of October. There I found waiting for me a pile of unanswered and unopened correspondence of such a size, I feared it would take me a year to work through it. Nevertheless, working through what I was able to do by myself, and making insistent demands upon my employer's time to take care of the rest, I was able to handle the accumulation of correspondence in not much more than a month.

The boy—Jude was his name—was in the beginning quite a trial. Oh, he was a nice enough lad, good-looking in a pudgy peasant sort of way, willing to work, and no doubt he was a good rider and a promising young huntsman as his father said; yet he had no interest whatever in books of any sort. I could see that I would have to start from the very beginning, find a slate-board and chalk, and begin my tutelage with the most basic words, from which we constructed the most dull and uninteresting sort of sentences. Ah well, the poor boy let slip one day that I had had three predecessors and that all of them had tried to teach him Latin along with English; one added Greek, as well. As a result, Jude seemed unsure which words belonged to which language and which language was which. When I told him that I thought it best that he get some notion of writing and reading English before attempting to master any other, he seemed ready to lick my hand like a puppy.

The boy's mother was at fault—or so it seemed to me. She had not wished her son to attend the Preston free school, for it would have put him in a class with the sons of peasants and small farmers. On the other hand, she was too protective of him to allow him to be sent off to one of the cathedral schools far from home. She herself could neither read nor write, nor do sums, and therefore dismissed her son's deficiencies in learning as of little importance. Mrs. Houghton was pretty enough, even at the age of thirty, that she could have her way in such matters. Thomas Houghton may have given in to her on the matter of the free school and that of keeping him close to home, yet he knew the boy needed instruction—therefore the succession of tutors, of which I was the latest.

Because of his dissatisfaction with those who had preceded me, he asked that at spring's end and summer's beginning I offer some proof of his son's progress. That I did, directing Jude to write a letter of two and a half simple lines to his father in his father's presence. Not wishing to embarrass Mr. Houghton by asking him to read it, I told Jude to read it to him. The father was greatly impressed with both his son's newly discovered abilities as a scholar and mine as a teacher. Toward this result Jude and I had struggled for months. He knew a few more words than those he had set down on paper for his father—but not many more. In any case, his performance was sufficient to assure me another year of tutoring.

And then on to another summer with Mr. Houghton's company—friendships renewed, the season planned, work to be done upon this play and that. How wonderful it was once more to feel myself back in the theater! *If*, forsooth, I could so name this vagabonding about Lancashire in the company of ruffians, doing tricks onstage for bumpkins and their masters. Theater indeed! With each year that I spent with Mr. Houghton's Men—and this was my third—I was more acutely aware that the only real, the only possible theater, was in London—and certainly not in any one of the provinces. And yet I stayed on, summer after summer, even as my conviction grew that this was so. True, each year I learned more of acting and of writing plays. I advanced to the level of principal player, which permitted me to grow a beard and do female roles no more. (As Mr. Ponder had once declared, and I myself observed, there were always boys enough about to play such parts—and some of them quite comely.) In short, I grew in my knowledge of my craft far beyond the point at which I could any longer be considered as an apprentice; nay, I had at least attained the level of journeyman. Then why, after my fourth or fifth summer, did I not simply hie off to London?

The truth is, my life there at Houghton Tower did suit me. I ate well, and with the family, and was therefore considered something more than a servant. I had a room to myself with a writing table, and though the place was cold in the winter, it served me well the rest of the year. And best of all, I had access to one of the best libraries in Lancashire; I spent hours alone with Chaucer, with Spenser, and Holinshed; I pushed my Latin to the utmost and read Ovid, Plautus and Terence. I taught myself French after a fashion that I might struggle through Ronsard and Villon. That library proved to be my university, my Oxford, my all.

Nor was I naught but a bookworm. If I read, it was to feed my writing. In those years wherein I educated myself in the manner I have described, I did some of the first writing which I deemed worthy of keeping. Most of *Venus and Adonis* was writ there, and a few of the sonnets in *The Passionate Pilgrim*. Perhaps more to the point, I wrote much for the theater, tore up or burned nearly as much but eventually came away with a few that were produced (though not always in the form in which they were writ): one part of *Henry VI*, *Arden of Faversham*, the ever developing *King John*, and *The Comedy of Errors*.

The last-named was read aloud by Jude to his father upon the lad's sixteenth birthday—or a good bit of it was—much to Thomas Houghton's delight and astonishment. It was in the nature of a valedictory exercise, my farewell through Jude to all at Houghton Tower; and equally was it Jude's farewell to daily drills, rote repetitions of amusing didactic texts of my devising—and finally, to me, as well. They had wanted a boy who could read, and now they had one. Mr. Houghton understood all this, for I had put him on notice that I would be leaving. Yet he was so well impressed by his son's demonstration of his skill that he pressed upon me a parting gift of money that was nearly equal to my entire year's remuneration. I, who was quite proud of what had been accomplished, accepted the amount without protestations of unworthiness.

Thus did I take my leave. I had already made clear my intention to Peter Ponder, telling him that it was my intention to make the season just completed my last with Mr. Houghton's Men. He understood quite well and though I would be welcome back at any time, he thought I was quite ready to make my move to London. Promising to help me there in any way he could, he told me where to look for him. For my part, I thanked him for the opportunity he had given me to learn and for all that he had taught me. Our eyes glistened as we turned away, one from the other.

I took my usual route through Warwick, and continued to Stratford, and deposited money with my father, which he would "invest." In addition to Susanna, there were two-year-old twins to greet me at home. I remained a week with Anne. Then, ere winter set in and it grew too cold to make the journey by foot, I left for London.

VIII

Sometime it was during my first week in London that I left my lodging in the South Bank early one day and made my way to the Thames. I had not yet customed myself to the foul misery of my new home (though it seemed only weeks until I was completely inured to it). And so I remember well the disgust I felt as I looked close upon my surroundings. Stratford—and for that matter the parts of Lancashire I had come to know well—could not be considered clean in the fabled manner of Dutch towns and villages. What I had known was, after all, farm country; where there are farms, there are animals—cows, horses, sheep—and where there are animals, there is always dung about. In these narrow streets of Southwark, however, though they were not so far from the fields of Kent, the houses seemed to be built one atop the next in such a way as to make all but foot travel quite impossible. Even so, there was no shortage of dung about; yet all of it seemed to be human ordure which, mixed with piss and vomit, smelled so much worse than any animal smell I had ever encountered. All this came from the practice of emptying chamber pots and slop buckets out into the street. One had to be watchful not to be splashed upon.

All this required care from me in picking my way through the streets. There were spots along the way where it was necessary to hop from one dry island to the next, and a place or two where this was impossible. Though thus I made slow progress, I did at last reach the river, and the London Bridge, where I wished to cross over it. There were houses built upon the bridge, so that the alley which led across it, though no wider and no cleaner, was a bit straighter. I was able only to catch glimpses of the river between a few of the houses, yet I knew always that it was there, for it did furiously stink.

I had resolved this day to find the head of Edward Arden. As I commit this to paper, I am aware that this is the first time that I have ever revealed this. I think it odd that this is so, but still more odd that I should have set out upon this errand at all. How may I account for it? If mere curiosity, as I told myself at the time, then there was naught that was sinful about it. Nevertheless, I suspected then and more than suspect today that it went deeper than that, and if I was curious, there was a perverse element to my curiosity which certainly did make it feel wicked, yet as is so often the case, also pleasurable. If it were a sin, then I do now confess it as such.

As I had heard, my cousin's head had been stuck on a spike on the far side of London Bridge. To the bridge I did go, and from there I did first spy the hill which led up to the Tower of London, where even then a crowd was gathering, for what event I knew not at that moment. At the far end of the bridge I found, looking above me, that there were indeed many of the headsman's trophies mounted up there. I knew not which of them might once have belonged to Edward Arden. Considering the length of time it had been there, his was doubtless one of several from which the skin had been quite worn away by the rain and sun to reveal the skull beneath; one skull, I fear, looks much the same as another. Others there were with shreds of leathery skin left upon them. It could be said that two of them almost had faces. They were, as might be suspected, not at all pleasing to look upon. Neither bore the slightest resemblance to cousin Edward.

Having satisfied my base curiosity, I turned away and made for Tower Hill where the growing crowd I had noticed a few minutes before had, in that short time, grown thus much larger. As I approached, I saw that at the highest point of the hill, just outside the walls of the Tower, a scaffold had been erected. Since in appearance it was quite like the scaffolds which we of Mr. Houghton's Men did put up to do our plays upon, I wondered if there would be entertainment offered—and just when it might begin.

I put that to a rough-looking fellow who happened by just at that moment. "Entertainment, is it?" said he. "Yes, they'll be givin' entertainment of a sort here. And if this an't to your taste, then I might be able to advise to what is."

"I must say, I do not quite understand what you mean. What is it goes on here?"

The crowd streamed past us. I liked not the way the fellow looked at me, and I noted that he had taken a grasp upon my sleeve; that I liked even less. He leaned close then as if to whisper, but he raised his voice, so that some around us did stop to stare and listen.

"Well," said he, "first they strings him up, hangs him by his neck, so he's doin' a dance at the end of the rope. And just when the kicking slows up, they cut him down, so he's still alive. They take a moment to revive him, throw water in his face an a' that, 'cause they want him wide awake for what follows. First they cut off his arms, and then off comes his legs—a lot of blood spurting with each chop of the axe, so you want to be careful how close you get to the platform. Now, where was I? Ah yes, once he's down on his back, rockin' about like a turtle turned on his shell, they opens him up, and out comes his guts. By that time, though, he's most dead, so one last chop of the axe, and his head rolls—and there's another Jesuit priest for mounting up on London Bridge."

Those who had stayed to listen to the fellow seemed much amused by his recitation. There had been laughter of the giggling sort as he revealed each sordid detail. And well there might be, for this fellow who had fastened himself to me told his grisly story with such glee, dancing about and acting it out, that from such horrific matter he made a most amusing show. And by the end, he had about him an audience of about a dozen in number. About half that number applauded him when he had done, and there were calls of "Well done, Mr. Tarlton!" and "Bravo!" Then they began drifting away. Still, he stayed on.

"Now, you must remember, young man," he admonished in a tone most schoolmasterly, "that quick as I did tell this, an't the same as how long it lasts. A good executioner and his assistant can draw it out so that it's a show lasts about an hour."

"You, sir," said I to him, "are an actor, are you not?"

"Is that a guess, sir? How can you tell? Have you seen me perform?"

"Why, I saw you perform just now, did I not? The way you pulled faces and bounced about, playing to your audience—only an actor would know to do that. And when they applauded, it seemed all you could do to keep from taking a bow."

"It was," said he, laughing, "it was indeed!"

"Besides," I declared, "I heard you called Mr. Tarlton, which means to me you must be Richard Tarlton of the Queen's Men, of whom I've heard much."

"So I am and at your service, sir." With which he bowed low to me.

"And I"—returning the bow—"am Will Shakespeare, who is most pleased to make your acquaintance."

We set off together in the direction of the scaffold. In the few minutes we had spent together, the crowd seemed to have doubled. There was a hum of excitement in the air as they waited. I noted that there were women as well as men present and even a few older children about.

"Shakespeare?" said Mr. Tarlton. "That is quite like a name given me by an old friend name of Ponder. Shakeshafte, was it?"

"Peter Ponder? My friend, as well. And I am indeed that same Will Shakeshafte."

"Then you, too, are a player. Forsooth, I should have known. But tell me," said he, "how comes it that you have two names?"

That, of course, took a bit of explaining, though not so much as the complete and absolute truth would have done. Which is to say, the story which I gave to him had been edited by me in advance, for I had anticipated difficulties of this kind and put my story to fit. At any length it would have satisfied Mr. Tarlton however, for I learned through him that half the players in London performed under an alias of some sort.

"You don't suppose that Tarlton is the name that I was born with, do you?" Then he laughed a great laugh, exciting a certain hostility from those around us where we stood upon the hill. The action upon the scaffold held their complete attention, and they thought it rude of us to prattle on with such apparent indifference. Nevertheless, we continued to talk, though out of deference to the occasion we did lower our voices somewhat.

He asked quite politely after my situation, and I modestly explained that in addition to acting I did a bit of writing as well.

"Yes, so did Peter Ponder say. He declared you a prodigiously talented young man, so he did."

"Mr. Ponder did put in a word for me with Mr. Philip Henslowe, who quite generously offered to read through the plays that I had writ, and in the meantime put me up gratis in one of his lodging houses."

"Which one? Where is it?"

"In Southwark," said I, "next his theater, the Rose."

Richard Tarlton threw back his head and let loose a great howl of amusement which was utterly lost in the great roar that erupted from the crowd just then—no doubt some specific moment in the drama played out there on the scaffold; it was difficult dividing my attention so. Or impossible, really, for the next moment Tarlton had grasped my arm and was barking hoarsely with laughter. What could I have told him to set him off so? At last he recovered from his fit sufficiently to tell me.

"Why, Will, he's put you up in one of his whorehouses!" Then did he resume his cackling and giggling.

"Is that true?" said I and was answered with an affirmative nod. "Why, I had wondered why the women who lodged there were so carelessly dressed and so aggressively friendly."

"They must be so," said Tarlton, "for how else will Henslowe get back his money? You say he allows you to stay there gratis. That is all well and good, yet he expects you to sample the wares that are so temptingly offered by his whores and thus would you end up paying him through them many times the worth of the room you occupy."

"And yet if I resist their temptations?"

"Then he will put it about that you are a complete hermaphrodite, and that would do you no good."

"He cannot do that, for I have a wife and three children back in Stratford."

"And if that got out, it would do you even less good." And that he punctuated with a great growling chuckle.

Thus we talked on in a jolly manner, ignoring the annoyed glances of those about us. It had evidently been our bad fortune to situate ourselves in a nest of black-vested puritans who took events such as those that occurred upon the scaffold most seriously indeed.

At some point in the proceedings, certainly well beyond the middle, Tarlton leaned close and muttered through his beard: "What say you, Will, to a quencher of ale? I've a powerful thirst come upon me."

"Why," said I with a nod, "I was about to make the same suggestion to you."

"Let's away then."

And we managed to squirm and shove our way through the tight ranks of those wearing the dark uniform of piety. Though it was not easy, we managed to fight our way free and find a path down the hill in the direction of London Bridge. Along the way we found an ale house open where a tankard was served us each.

Tarlton laid tuppence down, which the innkeeper took and kept.

"I'll buy the next," said I.

"So far as that concerns me, it will have to wait till our next meeting," said he. "I've a curtain to make in a couple of hours, and I have no wish to report drunk and lose my place in the company."

"The Queen's Men is said to be the best in London."

"I think that be so, right enough," said he, taking a deep draught of ale. "And that's as it should be—the *Queen's* Men, after all." He took another deep gulp from the tankard.

"Ah yes, of course. I see your point."

"Absolutely. The Queen is the Queen, an't she?" He drank deep once again, finishing off the pint as quickly as I had ever seen it done. "P'rhaps I'd best be off."

I rose with him from the table to bid him goodbye and was about to do just that when he added: "Stay here as long as you like. But it won't be but a short time until the show is done up there on Tower Hill, and this place fills up to overflowin'." He paused a moment, and then brightened. "But say, Will, this play I'm in is really quite a good one. You might like to see it. I could leave your name with the ticket seller, if you like."

"Where does it play?"

"At the Curtain," said he. "The title of the piece is *The Spanish Tragedy*. It's by one Thomas Kyd. Do you know him?"

"Never heard of him," said I, perhaps a bit dismissively.

"No, nor had I, but it's good. Oh, I know we all say that to pull in a house—but this one is a little different—truly good it is."

"Well, all right, do leave my name with the ticket seller."

"Shakespeare or Shakeshafte?"

"Shakespeare."

"Consider it done. And come back to see me after the final curtain."

"I promise," said I.

"Good enough, then; Curtain at two."

We said our goodbyes, and he was off quick as any twenty-year-old.

It was, as Richard Tarlton had predicted, not long before a great multitude from Tower Hill, having adjourned till next execution day, descended upon the ale house and filled it in a minute's time. I quaffed the tankard of ale, finishing all that was left in a single great gulp. Then I squeezed through the door and out onto the street only to find myself swept up in a rushing tide of the black-suited brethren who suddenly, without warning or reason, burst into song: a hymn it was glorifying Divine Justice. (I'm sure the Jesuit priest, whatever his name, who provided the occasion for their rejoicing, would have sung a different song.) They were farm folk and villagers from Kent and Sussex, in for the morning to witness yet another instance of God's wrath directed against the Papists. They would then be returning by way of London Bridge—a good reason to go off in the other direction.

Swept along with them to the bridge, I managed at last to extricate myself. I stood off to one side and watched them, two and four abreast, pour down the passageway which spanned the Thames. As I looked, I wondered at them, asking myself where they found that sort of fervor and certainty, telling myself that I would not want such if they were offered me; qualities of that sort were not assets for any actor and were absolute liabilities for a poet.

I decided I would take a long and easy amble to Shoreditch, discovering streets and sights of London as I went. I should arrive at the Curtain theater in time aplenty for *The Spanish Tragedy* by this fellow, Kyd, whomever he may be. But as I turned away from the bridge, my eyes rested for a moment upon the gallery of heads which I had studied with such keen interest that very day. Idly I wondered how long it would take for the latest to be added to the collection and resolved to check the number tomorrow. As for the execution I had more or less witnessed, it had gone just about as Tarlton had described, yet his comic satire of the event was far more entertaining than the event itself—another instance of art exceeding life. It was yet a pity to think of poor cousin Edward subjected to such indignities—humiliating when you think of it. He would not have liked it at all.

The Spanish Tragedy was all that Richard Tarlton had claimed. Of all the plays I had seen, or acted in, or read, this one was by far the best. Dark and bloody, it was as no other tragedy that I had known, for there was naught in it to inspire behavior or caution. Its appeal was for blood and blood alone. Vengeance was the motive that drove it forward and the reason behind every action of every character. Revenge was such a force in the tragedy (if tragedy it might truly be called) that it was made one of the persons of the play, given lines with which others were tempted and demands made which urged the action forward. From the first scene, Revenge was the prime mover.

Not the leading role, please understand—but an important one, certainly, and it was played by none but Richard Tarlton, who had made a personal appeal that I come to see the play. It was evident, to me at least, why he wished to be known in this part: Mr. Tarlton had achieved some degree of fame as a clown; that, in any case, was how he was known to me, and having seen a sample of his ad lib efforts earlier that day, I would say that whatever degree of fame he had achieved was indeed well deserved. Yet there is not a clown in all of England, nor was there ever, nor will there ever be, who does not wish to be a tragedian. You may count upon it.

And how did Mr. Tarlton play his part? Adequately, no better and no worse than that. Wearing a long gray robe which looked quite like a monk's habit, he made his appearance with a ghost and presented his speech so solemnly that 'twas he who seemed to be the ghost. To him, tragedy called for such colorless monotones.

Ah, but I should be dishonest if I were to leave the notion that the audience was not moved by Tarlton's appearance and even more by the eerie voice in which he spoke his lines. Forsooth, there in the daylight on that autumn afternoon, among the groundlings, a palpable shiver passed through all, myself among them. Nor could I have helped it, nor would I have wished to. Nevertheless, in this poet's heart, I was sure that he should have played the role with more color, greater variation. Yet what do I know? The audience said otherwise; they spoke for him, the Spirit of Revenge, just as they did for the entire play. I had not, until then, been at a performance that was so well received.

Now, how was I to communicate this to Mr. Tarlton? How much need I tell him? I had promised, after all, to visit him following the performance, and I could not fail to do so. Uneasily, fearing the worst, I waited until the crowd had thinned and the way was clear, then did make my way backstage by the obvious door, asking as I went for Richard Tarlton.

I know not what I might have expected to find there at the Curtain, something perhaps a bit grander than the crude arrangements we put up with backstage at the Prescot Playhouse, yet it was no better. But why should it have been different? The theater is for the audience and not for the actors—as indeed should always be so. It was in a large dressing room that I found Mr. Tarlton, one which he shared with five of the cast. And to my happy surprise, I saw there was another present who talked earnestly with Tarlton; he was immediately known to me as my old fellow, Peter Ponder.

"Ho, Will, Dick said you might be along today. When did you arrive in London?"

"But a few days past," said I. "And everywhere I go I find you've preceded me, singing my praises to the heavens."

"I told Peter of the arrangement you've made with Henslowe," Tarlton said to me with a sly smile and a wink. Then did he return to the task of removing his makeup.

"You want to watch out for that fellow," said Ponder.

"What fellow? This fellow?" said I, pointing at Tarlton.

"No, that fellow Henslowe—a very slippery individual."

"You wonder just why such a one got involved in the theater, anyways," said Tarlton.

"Why?" said Ponder. "For one reason alone—he thought he could make a profit at it."

"I don't know why he thought so," said Tarlton. "None of us has ever managed to do that."

"None of us has ever owned a theater."

"Why, true enough! Why did I not think of that? I shall go out and buy me one tomorrow."

As was so often the case with Tarlton, it was not what was said, but *how,* which amused his audience. And we, who were his audience, were indeed much amused. The face he pulled would have fitted well a village idiot who had, for the first time in his life, got a hold upon an idea. We exchanged glances, Peter Ponder and I, and burst out laughing, drawing the attention of the other actors in the dressing room. (If I remember aright, they were Joseph Taylor, Richard Burbage, Nicholas Pringle, and Alexander Cooke, though I cannot, for the life of me, put a name to the fifth.) They looked at us with indulgence, thinking us merely two more of Tarlton's lunatic friends.

"What ho," said Tarlton to me, "what thought you of the play? I have already heard Peter's judgment upon it."

"Too bloody by half," Ponder put in.

"By no means," said I in reply. "How much blood is spilled does matter little, so long as it be spilled with good reason. And"—I added, somewhat sententiously—"there can be no better reason than revenge."

"Bravo!" I heard from a far corner. I looked. It was Burbage, son of the great actor, eventually to be an even greater actor himself. "Well said," spoke Burbage, as he came forward to where we three had taken our places. "I have argued the same myself and would again argue it with anyone." Then at last did he introduce himself as Mr. Tarlton presented me to him. We bowed politely, each to the other. Then did young Burbage surprise me by asking forthwith: "Would you like to meet the author?"

"Thomas Kyd? I should like nothing better," said I.

Then, turning to Tarlton: "Had you thought to bring him along tonight, Dick?"

"I had indeed," he replied. "I thought we might all walk over to the Duck and Drake together."

It was agreed then, though Mr. Ponder declined the chance to meet Thomas Kyd for fear he might be struck by a sudden fit of honesty and tell the poet exactly what he thought of his play. And so, telling me the location of his lodging house, and how he might best be reached, he took his leave of us. I was sad to see him go. Tarlton later whispered in my ear that poor Peter had not yet found a place, permanent or temporary, with any company. "He may well have to take work in the tent theaters again this advent season, if indeed there is any to be found."

The Duck and Drake was like most of the other taverns and ale houses which lay along Shoreditch, except perhaps a little larger. Its chief advantage over the rest, however, lay in the fact that it was almost exactly equidistant between The Curtain and that which was known simply as The Theatre. As a result of this there were a great number of theater folk about the place every evening. Since actors are known to be great drinkers, it did a great trade and stayed open late into the night. (Indeed some said that it never closed, yet since I was among the last to be turned out of the place on a number of occasions—and had the door locked after me—I know that to be false.)

A big table off to one side had been held for us. Burbage and Tarlton were treated as nobility; the innkeeper bowed and scraped before them as we—Pringle, Cooke, Taylor and a few others who had tramped over from The Curtain—followed them in and to our place. It was a noisy place, though I've been to many a country inn louder and less suitable for talk. I looked round at those at the other tables, wondering which of them might be Mr. Kyd, yet saw none who fitted the casual description I'd been given by young Burbage—"about ten years your senior, losing his hair already, with a scholarly appearance." Burbage saw me surveying the tavern and guessed that I was looking for Kyd.

"He's not here yet," said he, calling across the table to me. "He was over at my father's other theater. A friend of his has a play running there. *Tamburlaine*, it's called. It's even longer than this Spanish thing of his."

Tankards of ale arrived, slammed down upon the table by the serving girl. She collected from us, one and all, and I kept my word, paying an additional pence for Tarlton's ale.

"Ah, you remembered!" he exclaimed and raised his tankard to me.

I touched mine to his and we both drank deep. "I always do," said I, which was such an obvious lie that there could be no sin attached. Yet it was both an obvious lie and a conscious one—which is to say, indeed I knew it was a lie when I told it, for even by that time I had a deserved reputation for parsimoniousness, of which I was never ashamed. Still, wishing to make a good impression upon this man of the London theater, I claimed always to remember my obligations—some slight taint of sin there, I suppose, though perhaps I have become in this instance a bit scrupulous. If sin there was, I received my punishment most immediate.

"Tell me, Will, what did you think of my performance?"

"Ah yes," said I, playing for time and inspiration, "I'd meant to talk to you about that, but surprised by Ponder, as I was—"

"Of course, but what you do not know of me is that I commonly take those roles given a clown."

"No," I cried, "I should never have guessed. You do tragedy so well! None could fault you for want of seriousness, after all."

"Ah well, indeed it is but a small part—"

"But a very important one," I put in quickly.

"True," he allowed.

"Vital, one might say."

"One might say that. But Will, my reason in bringing up this matter of my performance is that, well, I didn't like it much myself."

"You . . . what?" I had never before known an actor who had unfavorable comments to make upon his own performance in any play. (Naturally, I would have to include myself in that.)

"No, the author of the piece and I had a disagreement about how the role should be played, and, well, I suppose he won and I lost."

He went on to explain that from the earliest rehearsals Thomas Kyd had insisted that he speak his lines in a sort of disembodied monotone. When Tarlton objected, saying that if he did them so, he would be putting an extra burden upon the audience to attend to their import. "It an't human to talk all on the same note," Tarlton had told Kyd. "The audience wants you to talk the way people talk, a little up-and-down, if you get my meaning." But he made little impression upon Kyd, who reminded him that what he played was not human, was not a person, but rather "an abstract, a mere idea." Then did he ask Tarlton in a most condescending manner if he understood what he meant by an abstract; Tarlton admitted that he did not. Kyd then said that it was not necessary to understand, and that he should simply do them as he was told. When Dick Tarlton looked to Richard Burbage for backing, he got none. Burbage simply said that Thomas Kyd was likely a "university man" and suggested that perhaps it was best to do it his way.

"Burbage is a great admirer of the play," said Tarlton to me. "And for that matter I am, too. Didn't I urge you to see it just because it was a good piece of work?"

"Oh, you did, you did."

He sighed a deep sigh. "I just think it a pity that I manage to get a decent role in a tragedy—an excellent tragedy, if you will—and I am not allowed to play it as I believe it should be played."

Dick Tarlton had stated his case well, and I was about to agree—oh, more than agree—with him when Burbage rose at his place like a soldier coming to an exaggerated stand, chest out, arms stiff at his side. He looked ready to offer a salute.

"Here he is now," said Burbage.

And I rose, as well, though I noted that Tarlton kept his seat, and turned to see a man such as Burbage had described to me approaching our table in the company of another who of a sudden interested me more.

The next few minutes passed as in a dream. I remember being presented to Kyd by young Burbage, exchanging bows, and then in turn presented by Kyd to the young man of my own age who had hung back so modestly.

I managed to stutter out some words of appreciation for *The Spanish Tragedy,* which Kyd took lightly, and was informed by him that the young man I had just met had written an even better one, which now played at The Theatre.

"Ah yes," said I, "*Tamburlaine.*"

"That is correct," said the young man, "*Tamburlaine, the Second Part.*"

Yet as I have declared—and indeed it was true—all this passed as in a dream. The intensity of the experience quite overwhelmed me, made me forget what was said, and even what was thought. It was as though there were but two people in that noisy tavern throng, he and I, William Shakespeare and Christopher Marlowe.

Does this seem most fanciful? Not to one who has experienced it, as indeed many have done. As that young man himself would later write, "Who ever loved that loved not at first sight?"

Ere I continue, I must register still another complaint against Goody Bromley. The woman is becoming quite intolerable. I cannot suppose why she should be allowed freedom of the town. Perhaps she cannot be kept out of the church and the churchyard; she is, after all, one of God's children (though I have my doubts about that at times). But now, I have noted that since the weather has gone better, she roams freely about Stratford. Why, it does seem that I must leave the house every day in the expectation of encountering her somewhere in my roundabouts.

Yet if meeting her were all, foul and ugly though she be, there would be naught to complain: I would simply tip my hat, reward her with a grin, and be on my way past her fast as ever I could make my legs go. Ah, but she will not have that. At each of our meetings she has attempted to cause an incident, to attract a crowd, to embarrass me to the extent that she, pathetic creature that she be, is capable.

Just today she was passing by as I left the apothecary shop, where I had gone to buy a balm against the old complaint. Or perhaps I should strike that, for though I saw her approach once I was out of the shop, I had—and have still—the distinct feeling that she had been waiting for me. (Yet she could not have known I was inside unless she had, by chance, seen me enter.) In any case, the moment I stepped out into the street, she was there. What was I to do? It had been my intention to turn left, but to do so would have taken me in the direction in which she was walking. It would have, forsooth, put me directly ahead of her; she would have then, I was sure, been walking beside me in a trice. Now as I saw it, only two choices were open to me: I could have retreated into the apothecary's and waited until she was well past before going on; or I could have turned right and gone well out of my way simply to avoid all but the briefest contact with Goody Bromley.

I turned right. It seemed the surest course, and would, I hope, appear the most natural to any who looked on. A little theater for them then. I was not an actor so many years for naught.

"Good day to you, Goody Bromley," said I, then added under my breath, "you benighted old trull." And I fixed my face in the pleasantest simulation of a smile that ever I produced onstage or off.

And yes, we had an audience, dame Bromley and I, and those watching seemed to take my performance as comedy. Two wives talking in the shade of a tree did turn and giggle at the honor I did give to the lowliest of Stratford's citizens. I doffed my hat to them.

But Goody Bromley did not take well to my little show. We passed close, so close indeed that I caught the set of her jaw and the glint of anger in her pale eyes. It was plain to me that I had displeased her in some particular way. And I caught something of a distinctive odor in the air—hers, certainly, though it was not what I might have expected. After all, she looked foul—a snotty nose, dirty skin rife with pustules—so I assumed that she would give off a foul smell, as well. Yet she did not. Hers was rather a mysterious odor—heavy, near to overpowering, certainly, but of a scent strange, earthy and eastern. I found that once it was inhaled, it was never forgot.

Thus was I soon aware, after I had passed her, that her scent lingered. She had not touched me (nor would I have allowed that), and she had not settled upon me any cloth, nor rubbed my clothing with any substance. Yet still I smelled her.

It took me some time to realize that she was following me at a close distance. She had clearly turned round and now pursued me from about ten yards behind—or a little less. I turned and looked over my shoulder, confirming this; the breeze I felt upon my face carried her pungent odor to me.

"Will!" she cried, "Will! Will! Will!"

Was she asking that I stop? If so, to slow down and wait for her? I scowled my answer back to her in a manner which she could not fail to understand.

"Will!" she repeated her cry, "Will! Will! Will!"

Then, of a sudden, was I struck by a memory which brought with it a chill of fear—nay, something beyond fear; call it terror. For I remembered that just so—my name, then thrice repeated—had Ffoke Gyllome called to me for his salvation just before he drowned in the River Mersey. Did she know that? How could she?

And if she did know that, then indeed she was a witch.

I resume. Yet there is more that I would tell of that first evening in the Duck and Drake.

By asking questions of Dick Tarlton, Richard Burbage and of all the other theater people with whom I crossed paths, I learned a good deal about this young man, Christopher Marlowe. One from whom I learned nothing, however, was Marlowe himself. He and Kyd had spent little time at our table—and all of it on their feet. They stayed just long enough to gather the praise that was due them and then drifted on to another table in the back corner where three of their fellows awaited them.

I was standing yet and staring after Marlowe when all others had returned to their chairs. When I realized this, I glanced in embarrassment left to right and sought the safety of my place at the table. As I did, Burbage caught my eye and smiled in a friendly manner (there was never a jot of spite or condescension in the man).

"You may wonder, Will," said he across the table to me, "just who could attract the poets away from this table. After all, our charm, our cleverness!"

"Yes," said I, "who are those three?"

"Poets, like our two fellows—each has written, or at least has tried to write a play or two. Poets, it seems, like to hold themselves apart from us mere players, crude fellows that they think us to be."

He turned and took a long look at the table in the corner which Kyd and Marlowe had joined.

"But to give names to the three, Burbage resumed, "they are Thomas Nashe, Robert Greene, and George Peele."

"George Peele?" I laughed. "Why, I've rewritten him many times."

"Then you know the limits of his talent. Only Kyd and Marlowe have anything to offer."

"Will, too, is a poet," put in Dick Tarlton. "He brought four plays of his own composing with him to London."

"Ah, but is he a *university* poet?" said the fellow beside young Burbage. (I do believe it was Alexander Cooke, my first meeting with him.)

"Beg pardon?" said I. "Well . . . no, I'm not, but—but I've put in years as a player in Lancashire, and I believe that qualifies me as . . . as . . ."

"As a poet for the theatre," said Burbage. "Bravo, Will. At least you know when a scene plays and when it does not. But indeed you must show us what you've done. Bring us your plays."

"I'll hold you to that," said I boldly.

"See that you do."

More elated by that invitation than I could then properly express, I was in such a state of pleasure that I barely heard when Dick Tarlton, beside me, took it upon himself to explain that reference to "university poets."

" 'Twas not meant at your expense," said he, "but rather at theirs." And with that, he made a vague gesture toward the group of five at the table in the corner.

"Oh? How was that?"

"Well, they and a few others—John Lyly and Thomas Lodge come to mind—are called the 'university wits.' "

"Who calls them that?" I asked in all innocence. "Whoever does is giving them credit for a great deal."

"Who calls them that?" roared Burbage (as only a Burbage could roar). "*They* call *themselves* that. They're all university men. They lean heavily on the Latin poets—Ovid, Seneca, and the like."

"And Marlowe is, as well?" I asked, all innocent. "He is one of them?"

"What have you with this fellow, Marlowe?" asked the fourth at the table (let us assume that indeed he was Alexander Cooke).

"Well," said I, having thought through my excuse in advance, "I am to see his play tomorrow, and I wished to know something of the author."

"Marlowe went to Cambridge," said Burbage, "and if you must know, Will, he's rather a slippery sort, not the kind you'd wish to get too close to."

"Oh? I don't quite understand. Slippery in the way that Henslowe is slippery?"

"Oh no," said Tarlton, "they're two different birds altogether. He's much smoother than Henslowe."

But now, it seemed, I had them talking, and once actors get on with it, there can be no holding them back. Bits and pieces came together from rumors and gossip, from what had been heard, and what was merely suspected. Yet in the end the picture of Marlowe that emerged was one of an individual of dubious character, but nevertheless one of great talent.

Christopher Marlowe, the son of a shoemaker, was born in Canterbury in 1564, which was the same year as my birth. He attended the King's School and was awarded the Archbishop's scholarship which sent him on to Cambridge. He had spent a long time there, taking leaves of absence or simply disappearing for weeks or months at a time. He was said to be a Catholic while he was there and was, anyway, often in the company of known or suspected Catholics; these were scholars who, upon finishing at Cambridge, vanished into the Continent to seminaries where they might take Holy Orders before returning to England.

I recall that when this was tossed upon the table, I quite boggled in amazement. "This is known about him? Did *he* go to France? Is he a . . ." I dared not ask the awful question.

"No," rasped Burbage in a sharp whisper. "He's not a priest, very far from it, you might say."

"Oh? Then what . . ."

"He's been a spy." This was said so soft I had to lean across the table to catch it. "One of Walsingham's own, or so it is said. He still has a way of disappearing from time to time."

I nodded my understanding; but not wishing to appear even more ignorant than I had already, I kept silent and listened.

With all that I had heard thus far, I was surprised that they held Marlowe's work in such high regard. They had naught but praise for the play at The Theatre, which was the second part of *Tamburlaine*. As for the first part, it was such a success when it was played earlier in the year at the theater that those who had seen it asked for—nay, demanded—a sequel.

"Besides," said Cooke (yes, I'm sure he was present as the fourth at the table), "the first part ended a bit sudden. You wanted to know more about this man who started out a mere shepherd and wound up ruling near a quarter of the world."

"Of course you wanted more," said Burbage. "He planned it that way, I'm sure. Wanted to be invited back for more, he did. He's nobody's fool."

"A long way from it," Dick Tarlton agreed.

In any case, I learned, last of all, that Marlowe had come down from Cambridge only this year with his degree and two plays he had writ whilst at the university. (Between trips to the Continent, perhaps?) I assumed they were the two parts of *Tamburlaine*. But no. They were the first part and another that seemed to have disappeared. None of my willing informants was able to think of the title of it, nor what it was about.

"Why don't you ask him next time he's about?" said Burbage. "He comes in here just about every evening to collect the last full measure of applause from those here. He would be loath to let any of it go unheard."

"Are you suggesting he has great self-conceit?"

"No greater than any of us—which is to say that of course he has self-conceit! Which of us does not have? Perhaps in his case self-love might be closer to the mark. But who am I to say? Has a poet not the right to puff and preen as we players do? If not, why not? Will here is both player and poet, which no doubt gives him the right to puff to twice the size of any of us. What about it, Will? Have you great self-conceit?"

I knew enough of the baiting and teasing that passes between players to know enough not to take offense at what was said, nor even take it with serious intent.

And so I mimed my response, giving unto the rest at the table the most pathetic face I could muster. Then said I in a quaking voice to match: "I? Oh no, sir, not I, for I am the most humble of God's creatures."

The response to that was general laughter all about the table—for yes, I joined in with the rest.

"A clown!" yelped Cooke. "The lad's a clown!"

Then from Burbage: "Your job an't safe no more, Dick!"

Yet just as we settled down I happened to glance over at that table in the corner whereat the five "wits" sat. I caught Marlowe looking directly at me, and he, too, was laughing. Quite beside himself, he was, enjoying my show.

I wondered then if the fellow could read lips. It would be just the sort of skill a spy might cultivate.

IX

"So you saw Kyd's play, did you? What's the name of it? Is it any good?"

Having asked the most obvious questions, Philip Henslowe leaned back, feet upon the desk, and waited for my answer.

"*The Spanish Tragedy* is the title, and yes, it is good—quite the best play I've seen."

Henslowe waited, frowning. Then at last he prompted, "The best you've seen since . . . since you came to London?"

"No, the best I've seen ever."

"Hmmm." He rubbed at his beard. "Really."

"Or ever read."

"You don't say. I must see it then."

Yet Henslowe seemed unenthusiastic. Or had he simply other matters upon his mind?

He had sent his clerk over to summon me to his bureau in The Rose theater the morning after my visit to the Duck and Drake. Though I should have appreciated prior notice, I was happy to get such prompt attention from him. He had had four of my plays for little more than two days, but, as soon became evident, he had read them all. He discussed each one at some length; then, a bit petulantly, he had asked where I had been the day before when he had first sent for me. That was when I told him I had been out to Shoreditch to see Thomas Kyd's new play, and the conversation ensued which I have just quoted. Having stated his intention to see the play, he fell silent. He seemed to be sulking. Yet then did he rouse himself.

"I should like to hold two of your plays and hold on to them for a bit," said he.

"Two?" I was quite overjoyed at the news. I hoped not to show it, however. And so I, too, resorted to the obvious: "Which two?" I asked.

"*Arden of Faversham* and this history play of yours on Henry VI. Both of them need a bit of work, though."

"Oh? Well, I should be happy to do it," said I.

"I'd rather get you started on something else."

"What sort of something else?"

"Here now, let me explain to you how I like to work. The general thing, you see, is for one such as yourself to write me out a plot—can be made up, can be out of history, can be stolen from another's work. I don't care where it comes from just so long as it interests me, and I can see it up on the stage. Then I pay you a bit for that—a third, let's say, to get you started writing. You do an act or two—enough, anyways, so I get an idea of the persons of the drama and how you're going to have them talk, and all that. Then, if I think you're on the right path, I pay you a second third, and you proceed from there to the end. If I accept the whole of what you've got—*when* I accept it—then I pay you the last third, and you've been paid in full."

He ended his explanation with his open hands raised slightly, as if to say, What could be simpler?

"I understand," said I, and I did indeed understand so far as he had taken me. Nevertheless, a question or two had occurred to me which I should like to have answered. Yet before I proposed even one of them, Henslowe had resumed.

"This is why I'm having a bit of trouble with one of these two plays of yours."

"You've quite lost me," said I. "That I *don't* understand."

"Simple enough. With *Faversham,* I like the plot quite well—murder is always good for an audience, and the characters seem to work right enough. Yet the whole of it don't quite please me, so the best I could do there would be two-thirds payment—and if you'd like you could rewrite the end and go for full pay."

"And if I didn't?"

"Then I'd probably hand it over to some other writer and let him try."

I liked not the sound of that. I would not have another poet muddying my lines or twisting my plot to fit some new notion or persona. On the other hand, the prospect of money this early in my London stay was indeed most attractive. It would silence many in Stratford (even among the Hathaways) who had sneered at my plans and prospects. I was sorely tempted.

"What about the King Henry play?" I asked, delaying my decision.

"Ah, I have no difficulty with that—no difficulty at all—*except* I do feel there's more of the story to be told."

"You mean you want the ending rewritten?"

"No, oh no, it's quite right the way it is, and I'll take it so and pay you full price—but only with the understanding that you'll write another play to follow it up as part two. Oh, you know the sort of thing I mean. That one at the Theatre now is a part-two. I haven't seen it yet, but I saw the first part of it, and the fucking thing finished up in the air—no proper end to it at all! He had to follow it up with another."

Then, perhaps a bit impulsively, I leapt at the opportunity he had offered.

"I'll do it! I certainly will," said I with greater enthusiasm than wisdom. "And I accept what you propose on *Arden of Faversham,* as well. I'll get to work rewriting it most immediate."

"No," said Henslowe firmly, "I don't want you to do that. There's something else I have for you."

"Oh yes, I'm sorry. You said so earlier, didn't you?"

"This is where my way can work in your favor," said

Henslowe. "Some time ago, your man Kyd wrote out a plot for me."

He brought his feet down from the desktop, opened a drawer, and began rummaging inside it. Grunting something to himself, he pulled out a sheaf of papers and threw it down before me.

"Here it is," said he. "*Titus Andronicus,* one of those Roman things. Kyd stole it from one of their poets, I forget which one."

"Seneca?"

"Oh, don't ask the name of me. One such is much the same as the rest, so far as I'm concerned. But it came to me that since you were so taken with this new one of his, you might be just the fellow to write this one from his plot."

"But wouldn't he want to do it himself?" It was a stupid question, and I regretted it the moment it had flown from my lips.

Henslowe shrugged grandly. "It does not matter to me what he wants, for the plot is mine. I paid him a goodly sum for it, and he did naught to bring it forward. Now is he the darling of that crowd in Shoreditch, and he will not so much as speak to me. Take this, and read it. If the matter of it does appeal to you, then I should like you to do what you can with it."

Without hesitating, I said, "I will."

"Good," said he, rising, "Now, if there be nothing more . . ."

"There was one thing."

"And what was that?"

"What do you know of this fellow, Christopher Marlowe?"

Henslowe looked at me queerly. "Is he a friend of yours?"

"No, I met him only last night. But I shall soon see his play—this second part of *Tamburlaine*—and I wished to learn what I could about him." It was strange how false that sounded in my ears. When I had said something quite like it the night before, it had the ring of truth. Why, I believed it myself. Yet now only did it seem untrue. The look upon Henslowe's face told me so. Nevertheless he responded.

"Well, if you get to know him better he may tell you things about me that an't true. He has been goin' about London telling that I cheated him, which I did not. It all got to do with this play of his, *Dido, Queen of Carthage,* which he presented to me, all complete. That's why I was reluctant to take on your two, all complete. Do I make myself clear?"

Of course he had not. Yet I wished him to continue. "In a way, I suppose."

"Let me put it so: What I shall do with your two plays is sell them to somebody else. I am, among other things, a playbroker. I an't got a company of actors to put them on, but I do have a theater, one of just three in the city—or out the city, as must be—and therefore I have money enough to buy plays, which are always in demand. I buy from the playwright at a low price and sell to the play company at a high one, as any broker would do—you'll not get rich on what you're paid by me, Will. And sometimes it behooves me to hold on to a play when I think that him who wrote it will get to be better known for other work. That's what I did with this *Dido* by your fellow, Marlowe. I paid him no better than I shall offer you tomorrow when the contract is drawn up. But now that he's a great success with his *Tamburlaine* he says I should pay him for his *Dido* what the Queen's Men paid him for the second part of *Tamburlaine,* which is the highest price anybody got so far for a play. He wants me to pay him the difference!"

"How much did he get for the second part of *Tamburlaine*?" I demanded. I was eager to know.

"I've heard different amounts from different people, so I'm not sure what the right one would be. Better you ask him if you really want to know."

"I shall, but tell me, are the two plays of mine you propose to buy of the sort whose value you believe will appreciate? Do you plan to hold on to them?"

"Well, an't you the bold one, askin' me my business matters? But all right, you asked, so I'll tell you. I like a man lets you know what's on his mind. One of yours I'll sell off just as soon as ever I can, and the other I'll hold on to."

"Which is which?"

"*Arden* I'll sell quick with a new end on it. Your *King Henry* is worth holding back—particularly when you get on to writing that next part. As for the other two you showed me—"

"Yes, what about them?"

"You should be able to sell them to one of the companies and get them produced. I hope you do, for that's what will push up the price of *King Henry,* if you get my meaning."

Indeed, I got it clearly. And so long as Philip Henslowe was inclined to plain speaking, I had more to ask of him.

"Tell me then, Mr. Henslowe, what advantage is there to one such as me to sell my plays to you? Why not wait and sell directly to the companies?"

"Good question," said he. "Thought you might ask it. A young man newly come to London like you has two advantages. First of all, I may pay low, but I pay cash—ready money which may be spent at any ale house or whorehouse in town. It all depends upon your need, so it does."

"And the second advantage?"

"Hmm, you may credit this, or you may not, but I'm respected in this theater trade—that is, my opinion is. I got a sense of what audiences like. And when word gets round that I've bought a play—or even a plot—from this fellow or that, then the people in the companies want to see what else he's written. The doors are open to him. He an't quite what you'd call established, but you'd have to say he's on his way."

"What about Marlowe?" I asked. "Would you say that he's on his way?"

"Oh no. He an't on his way, Will. With this *Tamburlaine, Second Part,* he's well established."

"Now, you may not care to answer this, I being the questioner, but since you have read Marlowe's work and my own, which of us do you hold to be the more talented?"

"Ah well, if you don't mind hearing this, I don't mind telling it. I'd have to say, Will, that *he's* the more talented—or let's say he shows more *skill* in his work. Talent an't as important as you might suppose. There's a lot of it around. It's what you do with it that matters most. You may catch him yet—and pass him by."

Though it does not today, it seemed to me then that Henslowe was merely trying to improve upon his judgment with his remarks upon talent and to make the bitter pill he had given me somewhat more palatable. Yet at this distance in time I must concede that there is much to what he said regarding these matters. Forsooth, I did catch Kit Marlowe up and pass him by in just the manner Henslowe had suggested I might. Who today remembers Marlowe? His plays are no longer performed, nor are his poems read. His name is as dead as he is.

Yet I quote Philip Henslowe here because I think it important to note that the seeds of corruption had been planted in the relation between Marlowe and me even before there was, properly speaking, any relation. This was only the first time that I heard that I was talented yet not so talented as Marlowe. In the next few years, even when he and I were closest, I would continue to hear this same judgment iterated—and hear it indeed all too often.

Yet before I leave Henslowe, I must record herein his final word on Kit, for that, too, would prove to have great, though unintended, weight. My memory tells me that Henslowe walked with me to the door of his bureau and did throw it open. He clapped a hand upon my shoulder and sent me on my way with a bit of Southwark wisdom.

"Talent or no," said he, "I do not like the fellow. And if you should come to know him better, I would advise you to watch your step. I sense about him the smell of brimstone."

And so, leaving later in the day for Shoreditch, I went forewarned. All parties seemed to agree that Christopher Marlowe was a dangerous fellow to know. Yet pulled across the river by the memory of that moment out of time when I first met Marlowe, I went obediently enough, though not unquestioningly. Indeed I had questions aplenty and had answers only to the first: *Who* was Christopher Marlowe? What I had, of course, were answers but not *the* answer. It was so great a question that details would continue to come to me and fill out the portrait of the man for as long as he lived and longer—so many, forsooth, that I wonder, did I ever know him?

The way across the bridge was as narrow and foul as ever it had been. The houses which crowded the way seemed to hang over me, darkening the path even at noon by making narrow the corridor of the sky which ran above me. Last night I had found it most threatening. As I crossed the bridge returning to my lodgings, I heard voices along the way, indifferently in conversation (or just as often whispering direct to me of illicit pleasures available just inside a door.) What was most disturbing was that none of those who spoke was visible to me. I liked it not. Time and again I started at strange voices nearby. My hand went to the dirk at my hip. I was ready to cut and run. Even better prepared for this night's crossing, I wore a hanger dangling from a chain at my belt. With a rapier in one hand and my dirk in the other I would send all but the boldest villain scurrying. Even at that young age I could seem quite a frightening fellow when I put my mind to it.

Though I came to know it well, the way through London to Shoreditch was so winding and tortuous that in the beginning I frequently lost my way. That, as I remember, is what happened to me on that day. The narrow streets, each with houses, shops, and churches so much alike, were like unto a maze to me. I wandered about in them, asking directions as I went, yet somehow I always seemed to miss that landmark I was told I couldn't miss, or would turn left at it when I should have turned right. In this way, I did manage to arrive at The Theatre only a minute or two, or possibly three before curtain time. I went straight to the gatherer, put down my thrupence and was promptly but firmly turned away.

"Sold out," said he. "No more room."

"No more standing room?" said I, all incredulous. This never happened in Lancashire, except perhaps once or twice at the beginning of a season. "Surely there's something."

"I'm giving back money to the groundlings already."

"Well, how much are seats?"

I dug deeper into my purse.

"No matter. They were all gone long ago."

Then did I feel the tap of a finger upon my shoulder. I turned and found the one I had come to see; he who had so enlivened my life with his very appearance the night before; there, forsooth, stood Christopher Marlowe.

"Are you not Will Shakespeare, whom I met the night before?"

"Yes. Yes, I am."

"Then come. Come with me. I'll find you a place."

And with that he turned and started away; I could do naught but follow. He took me up a stairway which led to the first level of seats and beyond. There in the farthest corner were two which yet stood empty. He stopped, stood, and pointed them out.

"There, you see them? Of course you do. Now, take—"

Then was he interrupted from the stage.

"The general welcome *Tamburlaine* received"—the audience hushed as an impressive-looking man (tall, well-fed) swaggered out upon the stage, blattering forth the Prologue in true stentorian style. He did continue:

"When he arrived last upon our stage
"Hath made our poet pen his second part,
"Where death cuts off the progress of his pomp
"And murd'rous Fates throw all his triumphs down.
"But what became of fair Zenocrate,
"And with how many cities' sacrifice
"He celebrated her sad funeral,
"Himself in presence shall unfold at large."

And then he, having finished, did turn and bow, then march off the stage.

Marlowe resumed: "Take the seat and keep the other free. I'll come and fetch you when the play is done, and we shall talk of it."

"I don't know how to thank you. If I—"

He silenced me with a wave of his hand. "'Tis nothing. Those two are mine to do with as I choose. But now I must go. I'm prompting Alleyn. He's still unsure in the part."

Marlowe did then turn and disappear down the stairway whence we had come. I struggled through the row of seated patrons to the prize at the end. And as I settled into the seat, a goodly number of actors entered from the wings, ushered on by the beating of drums and the blowing of trumpets. The royal procession was led by two gaudily dressed in particolored garb, all in the royal oriental style.

I found it thrilling to look upon them and to hear the grand clamor that rose from the stage. Within me, it wakened those feelings of delighted awe that I experienced when first I saw a play. But this show of pomp made it so much worthier of these exalted stirrings than those paltry stagings of Mr. Houghton's Men in that distant provincial world. This, thought I, was true theater!

If Marlowe had achieved a great success with his *Tamburlaine,* and by all reports he had, then much of the credit for this had to go to the production given it by Leicester's Men there at The Theatre. Indeed so, for there were further scenes of garish vainglory throughout the piece, as there were also moments of action and true horror. The costumes, made of good materials, were well conceived and well executed. There was little could be said in criticism of the play's presentation—perhaps nothing at all.

And this, of course, included the quality of the acting, as well. It, too, was in the old, bold manner. The "Alleyn" mentioned by Marlowe was, of course, Edward Alleyn, who was increasingly the great leading actor of their company. (James Burbage, father of Richard, seemed then to be retiring more and more into the running of the two theaters at either end of Shoreditch; he it was spoke the prologue of the play.) Alleyn, however, had become, with his ascension, an actor in the grand style. He had always had, as I understood, a good voice; it gained now in volume. Yet most pronounced was his use of his body: he would thrust and bound about the stage and prowl like a caged animal as he spoke his lines. He was a tall man and slender, and only one such could have managed all that movement with grace. If he was, as Marlowe said, "still unsure in the part," you would not have guessed it looking on from the gallery, for he filled the few awkward lapses with pacing and did it so well (with Marlowe's help) that they seemed not awkward at all. He may not have been the right actor for every role, but he made a perfect Tamburlaine.

As for the play, not having seen the first part and only having heard a little about it, I had to find my way a bit through the first act of the second part. By the second act I knew my way well enough—but should it have taken even thus long? Was it not important to keep each part as much as possible independent of the other, so that each might stand by itself as a separate play? That had been the source of Henslowe's difficulties with Part One of *Tamburlaine,* had it not?—that it had no proper ending, that it finished up in the air? Here, I told myself, was a lesson for me when I set out to revise *Henry VI* and provide another part for it.

I also learned something of Christopher Marlowe's talent as I sat a-listening to his lines, and what I learned I remembered. He was, as I suspected, a finer poet than he was a teller of tales. He was indeed a great poet. The images he painted with words were the finest I had known since Spenser; yet he had a way of piling image upon image, or perhaps taking one, perfect in its brevity, and extending it to an unnecessary length. In sum, he was verbose. He would not use one word when ten would do. And such verbosity, such riches of words, does predictably slow down the telling of the story. That I had learned in rewriting George Peele.

And so, as I put my reactions to *Tamburlaine the Great, Part Two* upon display, it may be evident that even as I sat, anticipating the promised meeting with the boyish impatience of a young suitor, I was at the same time coldly assessing Marlowe's strengths and weaknesses that I might best him. I had perhaps not quite realized how deeply I had been stung by Henslowe's assessment of our separate talents. Equalling Christopher Marlowe simply would not do: I must best his efforts in every way.

How odd to think that even then I saw myself both as his lover and his rival. Had ever a friendship begun in a manner so strange as ours?

The audience was as appreciative as ever any could be, which did surprise me, for there was little to admire and naught to like in this cruel and ruthless eastern potentate who conquered so much of Asia. Yet whatever it was had held them in thrall through the length of the play, did move them to applaud mightily at its end.

I waited, as I had been told, in my corner seat as those round me had drifted away and down the stairs. I stayed on, though I confess I did indeed grow a bit anxious, fearful that I might have been forgotten up there, away from all.

But no, when all the seats were empty, except for mine, I heard footsteps upon the stairs; then appeared that familiar face of Christopher Marlowe—then he from the waist up. He beckoned to me. I went to him.

"Come," said he, "let us be out of here."

I bounded out of my seat and was beside him on the stairs before ever I could form my response. But then: "Where would you then? To the Duck and Drake?"

"By no means," said he. "If we go there, we should, I fear, have an evening much like the last—you with your crowd and I with mine."

"Are they so set in opposition?"

"You might say so. After all, they represent rival factions."

"In a way perhaps," said I, "yet I should have thought, rather, that yours was the writers' table and mine the actors'."

"Hmmm," said he, putting hand to cheek in a gesture of consideration, "I see your point, indeed I do. You, I take it, are an actor?"

"I am, well yes, but—" Of a sudden, it occurred to me that it would be best to say naught of my poetic ambitions just then.

"But are not actors and writers always in opposition?" he put in hastily, there relieving me of the need to finish a sentence ill-begun. "Though they need not be."

"So they are! And I agree there is no necessity of it. So lead on, Mr. Marlowe. I'm for wherever you wish to take me."

We went off to a tavern close by the theater with a singularly odd name: The World's End. It was in many ways just as odd as its name. The Duck and Drake, as well as every other alehouse, inn, and tavern which I had then known, were quite loud—loud and jolly or loud and bellicose, as depended upon the temper of its customers. The World's End was, contrariwise, the quietest drinking place I had ever been to—and among the darkest, too. When my eyes became used to the gloom there, I saw, to my surprise, that the tavern was not near empty, as I had supposed, but well-filled with men at tables about who seemed all to speak in little more than whispers. Women were quite absent. There were usually a few whores hanging about such places—except those deep in the country in villages and in such towns as Stratford—but here there were none. And finally as we sat down at a table, which stood in the center of all (almost it seemed, it had been saved for us, special), I looked round me and noted the strange pictures upon the walls. If intended as adornment, they did little to inspire or entertain. They were, if I read them correctly, representations of the Last Judgment—demons torturing sinners—and some of them were to my untrained eye rather crude and low images. Perhaps oddest of all, all the sinners were daughters of Eve; indeed there was not a man among them.

A serving lad, hardly more than a boy, appeared immediately at our table, welcomed us, and asked our pleasure. I was about to call for a tankard of ale when Marlowe spoke up.

"I think a bottle of wine would be good, don't you?" said he to me. And then to the young server: "A bottle of claret and two glasses."

The lad departed swift as he had come. I glanced about me and noted that some at the tables around us seemed to be staring. I wondered at that.

"What think you of this place?" asked Marlowe.

"I've not been in one quite like it before."

"How do you mean that?"

"Oh, well, the pictures for one thing. Rather indecent, don't you think?"

"Perhaps," said he, "it all depends upon how you stand on the woman question."

"What is the question?" I asked, all innocent.

"What is the answer? Or to put it another way, I note that you wear a ring. Are you married?"

"Oh yes, with three children."

"And does your wife bring you pleasure, Will?"

"As much as to any man, I suppose."

"Which means, I suppose, at least thrice."

"No, not so many," said I, "only twice. Once was a twin birth."

At that Christopher Marlowe laughed mightily. He threw back his head and ended all in a fit of giggles. I looked round me, wondering at the reaction of our near neighbors. They looked up, yet showed no great annoyance. Then did the serving lad arrive with the bottle and glasses.

"Pour them," said Marlowe to the lad. "It matters little how it tastes, so long as it does what we wish."

He was not near so eager to drunken himself as he was to bring me to a state in which I might compliantly acquiesce to his every proposal. I knew what he was about. No doubt this was how he had seduced lads from the provinces in the past. Yet had he but known, there would have been no need for such an expenditure of wine and charm; all he needed to have done was ask, and I should have immediately obliged. Still, I was curious at what sort of direction he might take—and how he might phrase his suggestions, and so I let him continue.

To begin with, he asked a few questions about me—where I was from and what sort of experience I had as an actor, where was I now living—that sort of thing. I was flattered at his interest. Yet I soon found out how thin it went, for he abruptly switched to a topic that seemed to satisfy him far more: himself.

He told me a few things about his history, though most of them I had heard the night before from those at my table in the

Duck and Drake: that he was from Canterbury; how he had come to attend Cambridge on scholarship, what his ambitions were. (I had said naught of mine.) But not a word, of course, that he, Christopher Marlowe, was one of Walsingham's spies.

"At heart, I am a poet pure and simple," said he. "But woe unto him who tries to make a living from poetry alone. I've found, however, that it is possible to make a proper little fortune by writing plays. And so I shall let that support my poetry. Yet I do confess that I like having money. The truth of it is, Will, I wish to be rich."

I did not say so, but that was my wish, as well. Yet I was unused to hearing such desires expressed so openly. Clearly, London was not Stratford-upon-Avon.

It must be said that as we conversed in the manner I have described, he continued to fill my glass with the strong red wine as I drank from it. Because up to then I had drunk little else but ale in such situations, the wine had its affect upon me. I was beginning to feel light-headed, though not unpleasantly so. Perfectly able was I to respond to him, to take delight in his wit and beauty, and to study him. Nevertheless I was light-headed: feeling confident and clever and perhaps also a bit mischievous. I would indeed teach him that I was no bumpkin.

"I should like to discuss *Tamburlaine* with you," said I. "Seldom is it that one sees a play and has afterward such an opportunity to talk about it with its author."

"Oh, well, by all means," said he. "What of it did you wish to discuss?"

"The first part of it," said I. "That which I did not see. Had you planned the second part when you wrote the first?"

"Well . . ." He seemed to hesitate.

"Or perhaps you wrote one great long play and found a place where it might be divided in two?"

"Oh no, no, nothing like that," said he. "Forsooth, it was as

I described in the prologue. You remember? When it was spoke by James Burbage?"

"Ah, so that's who it was!"

"Yes, but you remember what was said, of course: that *Tamburlaine* received such a general welcome when part one was done earlier in the year that the poet—myself, of course—was moved to write a second part. Indeed, neither old Burbage, nor I, nor anyone else had any notion how it might play before an audience."

"But historical plays, even *bad* historical plays"—I was thinking of that anonymous *King John,* which I continued to rewrite year after year—"seem well-liked by audiences."

"True, but those are bad historical plays which treat English history, and ours is an English audience. Tamburlaine, if known to them at all, was known to be a Scythian—and certainly no Englishman. The question was, would our English audience accept him?"

"And they did."

"Oh, certainly they did. The play did so well that . . . that Burbage contracted with me to write the second part."

Then did I put to him many questions of a detailed nature, some of them of a technical sort: With what event in the conqueror's life did he end the first part of his tale? Why his marriage in particular? Why had he used a line of four stresses? Would not a longer line have served him better? Et cetera. There were so many such, and I fear I posed them so swiftly that it may have seemed to him that I was attempting thus to confuse him—yet that was only partly so. I did truly wish to know the answers to all the questions—and more. I wished to know all that he knew.

At last he held up his hand and begged for surcease. "Please, Will, I am quite reeling with all you ask. But I have an idea will answer the many more you may think of. Let me loan you a copy of part one and part two. Would that satisfy you?"

"Why, I should be honored," said I to him.

"As well you should be," he responded with a smirk.

"Nevertheless, I have one last question for you."

A deep sigh. Then: "Ask it then."

"What is it, do you suppose, which made the audience so adore that fellow, Tamburlaine? He was cruel beyond telling, ruthless, and had no conception of honor."

"All to the good," laughed Marlowe. "The audience would gladly see these qualities in him, for this is how all would like to be."

"Surely the groundlings only," said I.

"Not at all! We in England have such foul weather through nearly all the days in the year, and long nights three seasons out of four. We have time to brood upon our miseries, and chief among them for each of us is the station to which we have been assigned. We all wish to be greater than we are. We care not what rules we must break to ascend, nor whom we need hurt, so long as we ascend."

I then heard murmurs of agreement, quiet laughter, and a snigger or two. I looked round me and, to my surprise, found all the faces at the surrounding tables turned toward us. Not only were they looking, they were listening, as well.

"Tamburlaine raised himself. He had been a man of low regard, a shepherd, but by the time of his death, he ruled all the world he knew. Now, tell me that you, too, would not wish to live such a life."

"I . . . I cannot."

"There—you see? We all do so." He looked at me in a manner quite triumphant, as if we two had fought a great battle, and he had won. Allowing that leer of victory to linger, he leaned close across the table and muttered: "There is yet another reason."

Was it secret? This new attitude of his seemed altogether strange. I knew not what to expect from him. He fascinated me.

"And what is that?" I asked.

"We will soon be at war."

"With . . .?"

"Why, with Spain, of course." His surprise at my ignorance prompted an exclamation and a curse: "God's blood! Do they tell you nothing back there in Stratford?"

Chastened, embarrassed, I could say nothing. I could but gulp my wine and wait for him to continue. Eventually, he did, though not before replenishing my glass.

"Drake's raid on Cádiz this year put them off a bit, but mark you, sir, they will be here soon with a great fleet and a great army, that they might add England to their empire and make Papists of us all." He frowned at me. "By the way, you're not one of them, are you?"

"One of what?"

"You're not a Papist?"

"I? Of course not!"* Then, though I did listen carefully, I heard no cock crow.

"There are many out there in your part of the west country. Don't take it ill that I asked."

"I'll not, but you must tell how the certainty of war works in favor of your play."

"Ah yes, well, I should think that evident. It is because it is at bottom a martial play. Makes the blood run faster, it does. And there is war in the air, my lad." He did pause but a moment. "But since all this has come from what you assured me was your *last* question, I now have one or two questions for you. And you must promise to answer them honestly. Do you so promise?"

"You have my promise of a certainty."

"Well enough, then. You yourself have said little of the play you saw except to ask me about. So now, Will, you must tell me, what did you think of it?"

"I thought it quite marvelous, of course."

"Only that?"

---

*Not truly a lie, for at that time I considered myself neither Catholic nor Protestant.

"I should call it the best I have ever seen."*

"Very gratifying," said he, "but not quite what I meant. I thought perhaps you might have more detailed comments. Praise or blame—I care not, so long as they be specific."

For what it is worth, I tended at that moment to believe him. Nevertheless, I declined.

"I fear," said I to him, "that if I were to try to be specific, I would end by improvising comments. You said I might have the loan of the two parts of *Tamburlaine*. I should like to study them and have them before me ere I make to criticize."

Christopher Marlowe did then give me a long and evaluating look, as if he were, in some sense, seeing me for the first time. He ruffled the hairs in his chin beard as he studied me. A sly look—call it that—came into his eyes. I half expected him to burst into laughter, yet he did not.

"Will Shakespeare, who are you?"

"Why, I am who you see before you now."

"Well, I know who you are not. You are not an actor—that is to say, you are not merely an actor. Your refusal to offer criticism without the text at hand was what one would have expected from a scholar. And a few of the questions you asked were poet's questions. Now, tell me, who are you? What are you?"

I smiled, even managed to laugh a little. "I am certainly no scholar."

"But a poet?"

"Something of the sort. I dabble."

"Competitor or colleague?"

"Oh, I am neither," said I. "I am not near so far along as you. Perhaps some day a colleague. That is what I aspire to."

"We shall talk more of this later," said he. "I'm sure we shall." There was a brief silence, not at all awkward. "What

---

*A lie, I fear, for though I admired much of the poetry in *Tamburlaine the Great, Part Two*, I thought all in all, *The Spanish Tragedy* was the better play.

shall we do about you?" he asked. There was indeed a sly look in his eyes this time.

"What do you mean?"

"Why, it is now well after dark. There are too many places between here and Southwark where you might be attacked. Even Southwark is a good deal more dangerous than you might suppose."

"Yet I made it across London Bridge armed with no more than a poniard. Tonight I wear a sword."

"Last night you were lucky. They shall be waiting for you tonight. You had best stay here in Shoreditch."

"What am I to do?" I asked, all innocent.

"Well, you may stay with me, if you like."

"Would that not be a great deal of trouble?"

"On the contrary, it would provide me with a great deal of pleasure."

X

What distaste I feel for the young fellow I was. As I read, with sinking heart, through what I have written thus far of my first evening with Kit Marlowe, I realize that what I have written is indeed accurate—or as accurate as I could make it. And having realized that, I now must acknowledge what an absolute simper-de-cocket I was at the age of—oh, what was it?—twenty-two or twenty-three, something like that. How eager to please, and how naif!

Could I truly have wondered at what sort of place The World's End might be? It had even then the sort of ill fame that made it known well beyond London; its reputation as a house of assignation for catamites and their patrons must surely have reached Lancashire in tales of the great city told by Peter Ponder. Thus informed, could I have wondered at Kit's intentions? Could he have doubted mine?

In any case, our bargain (if never our troth) was sealed that evening in The World's End. I went with him to his room atop a building of brick in an alley off Shoreditch. Though ample enough and reasonably tidy, Kit's quarters were somewhat disappointing when one considered that they housed one who, in the words of Philip Henslowe, was "well established" in the theater. Thinly furnished with a bed, writing table, and a chair, it had but one window, and that facing north, so that it must be continually dark in the daytime. Was this the best I could hope for?

(In truth, the places I lived in whilst in London were never much better than this; still, it fell to me to support a household in Stratford all those years, as well. For his part, Kit was simply improvident with such monies as passed through his hands.)

There was but one way in which this room of his might have seemed remarkable: it was filled, as few single rooms are, with books. Until that moment I had seen a larger collection only in the library in Houghton Tower. More than impressed, I was quite overcome by the display, so much so that I was moved to exclaim the moment I set foot in the place and a candle was lit.

"God's blood, what a library you have!"

"A poet needs books," he declared in high sententious style. "They are the food on which his talent feeds."

"I would not gainsay that. But so many? Why, you must have spent every last farthing you've made in the theater on them."

"Nothing of the kind," said he with an indifferent flap of his hand. "Most of them I stole."

At that I laughed, thinking he had intended it as a great jest. Then did I perceive that no such jest was intended. He frowned at me, and the laughter died in my throat.

"Well," said I, "I *am* impressed. There must be well over a hundred here."

"Nearly two hundred."

"I've been known to lift a book now and again, but I've nothing like this to show," said I. "You must have carted away a wagon load from some old manor house."

"Nay," said he, "what you see before you here was not gleaned in a single day—or night. It is, rather, the harvest of a decade of years of dedicated thievery."

"Ten years?"

"More or less. Hear me, Will. I am naught but a poor cobbler's son from Canterbury, and all that I have, I have earned—or if not earned, then simply taken. When I began at King's School there, books began to disappear. I was warned that

I was suspected of the thefts, and though I did not stop, I was more careful. Corpus Christi, Cambridge, proved a treasure trove: I could beg, borrow, or steal whatever it pleased me to read. When on holiday and invited to the homes of my fellow scholars, I never failed to make a visit to the library to pore over those unread and dust-laden volumes, choosing one or two which I might take with me when I left.

"That was just it, you see, Will," he continued. "Those books, most of them, were dusty, with pages uncut, obviously unused. All I ever took I have read, and what I have read, I have used, sometime and in some manner. What say you to that, Will?"

"Why, I applaud it, so I do," said I, "and understand perfectly well, for I myself am a glovemaker's son. We fit well—hands and feet."

At that did Kit Marlowe throw back his head and laugh a jolly laugh. I joined in, thinking it only polite to do so. But then, as his laughter subsided, he looked upon me rather severely. I quailed before him, fearful of displeasing. I was like unto some foolish country girl who, having played at love with winks and smiles, has been backed into a corner and must now face the consequences of her play. Yet it was not the act in and of itself which did intimidate me so (I, who had known quite a few?), but rather the possibility that I might disappoint and be thought no more than a rude country boy. Was I ready? I wasn't sure. I thought it best to play for time.

"Would you mind if I took a look at your books?" I asked, all innocent. I put out my hand at random, and it fell upon *The Prince,* by Niccolo Machiavelli, a work of which I had heard much but seen rarely.

He took the book from my hand and replaced it upon the shelf.

"Later, perhaps," said he, "afterward."

"Afterward? After what?"

"After we have disported ourselves."

And so saying, he eased me back in the direction of the bed and began to undress me.

To judge from the moans of pleasure and pain (at times much the same thing) that issued from us both that evening, I did not disappoint. Yet each time we coupled in the year to come—and such occasions were abundant—I could not avoid a sense of uneasiness, a fear that I might not come up to his expectations.

Why was I so eager to please? Why should I have felt such a burden?

A good question that, one that has troubled me these many years. To this day I can see him well in my mind's eye, and forsooth I know him to be less comely than I. Slight of body and weak of countenance, Christopher Marlowe was the sort you would not notice in a crowded room. Let him stand close, however, and you would be instantly in his thrall. What was it held you? His eyes, first of all, for they were a deep, dark brown and could, it seemed, peer deep within those of another; with those eyes he could, as a matter of will, stare for minutes at a time without blinking (proof, some say, of madness). His voice, too, was like unto none other. Soft and deep was it and lulling in tone, so that when at last we had done with our sport, and he first began speaking at length, the low, humming sound of his voice near put me to sleep. It was not what he said, but rather how it was said which brought me so near. For much of *what* he said did seem to me at first as errant nonsense.

We had wrestled together for at least an hour, or so it seemed to me, when at last he heaved a great sigh and rolled off me, completly spent. He relaxed, yet I dared not: I ran to the chamber pot. As I returned, I found Kit sitting up and drinking deep from a bottle of brandy he had fetched from some dark corner of the room. Once done, he wiped his mouth with the back of his hand and passed the bottle to me.

"You're stronger than you look, Will," said he.

"Often it is so with country boys like me." I took but a single swig and handed the bottle back half full.

"You bucked so beneath me I thought I'd never get you tamed."

"What makes you think you succeeded?"

To that he did not reply but chuckled merely in a manner most pleased and gulped thrice more from the bottle—and then drank again. Then, without reason or proper occasion, his drooping eyes did suddenly go wide and a shout came from him of a sort that might be heard three houses away.

"Why, this is hell, nor am I out of it!"

I fell back from him in fear. What manner of delusion had he? What did he misperceive this simple room to be? Did he suppose me some lesser devil? Satan himself? Yet before I could find an answer to any of these questions, he shouted forth once again.

"I charge thee to return and change thy shape. Thou art too ugly to attend on me."

Too ugly was I? Indeed I liked not the sound of that. I was a pretty enough fellow for him moments before, was I not? Now he would have me return—to where or what?—and change my shape. What new style of insult had his poet's brain devised? Yet I, too, was poet enough to cut him with one of my own creation.

Nevertheless, before I could then cobble together a proper insult for this cobbler's son, his mood and temper had altered completely. He clasped me to him and kissed me passionately upon the lips. His breath smelled most foul of brandy.

"Come live with me, and be my love," said he to me, "and we will all the pleasures prove . . . that hills . . ." His eyes, which had shown bright at me but a fraction of a moment before, did suddenly droop and go dull as he struggled to continue: ". . . and valleys, dales . . ." There he stopped altogether, let out a sigh, and swooned in my arms.

No, he was not ill. As I then understood it, the dear boy had found it necessary to fortify himself with brandy in order to overcome his natural shyness. Only then, having talked a good deal of mad claptrap, could he then come forth with the invitation that had so thrilled me. I had heard him say it, had I not? "Come live with me, and be my love!" How the words did echo in my ears. Kit Marlowe would have me live with him—and I in London for only a matter of a few days! This was more than I had hoped for, more than I had even dreamed of. I wanted to plant kisses all over his body, but rather, as a good room-companion, I did something far more generous; I eased him down upon his pillow and spread over him the woolen blanket I found upon the floor where one of us had kicked it. Then, taking up the clothes I had worn, I pulled on my thigh leggings and shirt before diving under the blanket next to the naked Christopher, for of a sudden did I feel the cold. It took some time for me to fall asleep with those words there in my mind's ear. And as I woke next morning the invitation sounded there still. The light of day had barely broken over London town when I rolled out of bed and finished dressing. It would have been useless to try to coax myself back to sleep. Yet further, I had much to do that day. Yet ere I was to leave, I penned an acceptance to my bedmate's kind request.

I had noticed that he had framed his message to me in rhyme—poets do often enjoy speaking thus—and so, in like spirit, I answered him in a quatrain and left it upon his writing table:

I'll live with you and share the rent,
And together we'll be so well acquent
That the streets and alleys, and courts and lanes
Of London town will chorus an echo of our names.

A paltry thing it is, no doubt, and not well counted, but it was composed at the speed it was written down, and these four lines communicated that which I wished to say: thus they served my purpose.

I was wise to leave at first light, for even then the streets had begun to fill with those poor souls whose lot it was to earn their bread by their daily labor. How I pitied them! Yet it was not long till I found myself glad of the many round me, for it took but a few minutes' time for me to lose my way twice; I was set properly on the right path by strangers, once with a smile and once with a scowl. From that time on, I kept to the broader streets and thoroughfares and ignored the narrow, twisting lanes and alleys, no matter how attractive they might seem to me. At some point along the way I must have passed near the Smithfield Market, which I knew without ever viewing it. The smell of the offal and blood, and the lowing of the frightened cattle made it unmistakably a place of slaughter. Then to the river and on to the bridge. And by the time I joined the crowd crossing over to Southwark, I found an equal number flowing across into the city. What a monstrously large place this was! In every way it exceeded my expectations.

Once within the room in which I had slept during the last few nights, I set about making myself presentable for my meeting with Philip Henslowe. I washed as well as I was able, trimmed the beard I had so proudly begun but a few months past, and set about to change for fresh those items of clothing which smelled foul. As I set about this, I found myself reconsidering my decision, wondering if I had truly done right in accepting Kit's invitation to live with him. It was oddly offered, after all. Perhaps he had but given in to the impulse of a moment. As I often do in such circumstances, I decided to proceed with caution, for it would not do to embarrass Marlowe or myself. To begin with, I would say nothing to Henslowe about where I was moving, or with whom I should be living. Well I remembered Dick Tarlton's warning that if given the opportunity, Henslowe might put it about that I was an hermaphrodite. Marlowe, I was sure, had a reputation. I should not like to give Henslowe reason or cause to gossip.

Having completed my ablutions and given proper attention to my clothes, I examined myself in the cracked looking glass which hung inside the wardrobe. And, approving what I saw, I walked out the door, locked it, and made for the stairway to the street. There were two drabs blocking my way, the same two, indeed, who lodged in the rooms each side of my own. They stood, similarly dressed in shift and skirt, leaning over the rail to attract what attention they could from the street below. I had had words with one of them, the younger of the two; with the other I had a mere nodding acquaintance.

"Marry, sir!" said the younger (whose name, as I recall, was Margaret). "Don't you look fine! Where could you be off to?"

"Off courting," said the other. "You can be sure of it."

"Is it true, sir. Have you a darling?"

"Has he a darling? 'Deed he has. He were out the whole night long, he was and then come back sober as a vicar. Ain't that so, sir?"

I was a bit surprised at that. Was she my gaoler, one appointed to keep watch over my comings and goings? To whom did she report?

"Forsooth, I did return sober," said I. "And I was out the night long because I was advised that London Bridge was a dangerous place at night."

"Well, you got told right," said young Margaret. "Them stews on the bridge is truly dangerous. You'll catch the clap there for certain, maybe even the French pox."

"That an't what he means, Margaret."

"Oh? What *did* you mean, sir?"

"Danger of another sort," said I. "I was told I might be accosted, robbed, even murdered."

"Don't he talk pretty, Kate?" said Margaret. "Such words! Just like a real gentleman, I vow."

"Very kind of you," said I to her, "I am a poet, plain and simple. But I am a poet who has matters to attend to next door at the theater with Mr. Henslowe. And that, to answer your original question, is where I am off to."

"Oooh, Mr. Henslowe, is it?"

"God's bones, an't he a marvel!"

Thus they teased me, but I noted that the use of his name brought results most immediate. With a bit of artful shuffling they retreated and no longer blocked my way to the stairs: I was free to pass between them, which I did. As I descended, the one named Kate called after me:

"If you gets any money out of that greedy sod, it'll be a miracle. He does naught but take from us."

Had I any need for confirmation of Dick Tarlton's theory of Henslowe's way of giving with one hand and taking with the other, then had these two women provided it. Thus informed, I guided my steps to the Rose theater and up to Henslowe's office. There I found him awaiting me, and what I saw upon his desk convinced me that the miracle of which Kate spoke was indeed about to be accomplished. There were three separate sheaves of paper and upon each a pile of coins of varying denominations—shillings, pence, and crowns.

Mr. Henslowe rose when I strode into the room, yet he neither offered me a greeting, nor explained how it was he had so accurately anticipated my arrival. An inkhorn and a quill sat near to his hand. He turned it round so that it was well within my reach and gestured to the display before me.

"Here they are," said he, "contracts and payment."

"Shouldn't I read them?" I asked.

"No need," said he. "All is set forth just as I said yesterday—four pounds for all rights to *Arden of Faversham,* five pounds for all rights to *Henry VI,* with the proviso that you write a second part; and a single pound to get you started on *Titus Andronicus,* following the outline from Thomas Kyd. It's all as I said. Still, it's my guess that you would sign, no matter what terms were there on paper. Am I right?"

"I suppose so," said I, all in a mumble.

"You've no reason to feel ashamed," said he. "We must all begin somewhere, and I've given you the same terms I would to any other in your place."

Forsooth, I didn't resent it, nor did I feel ashamed. Though there was much about this man I didn't like, I was particularly pleased by his frank manner in commerce. While I did not quite trust him, I accepted him. Yet all I communicated to him of this came in a nod of my head as I stepped forward, took the quill and dipped it, and then signed each of the three contracts. Having thus committed myself, I took my reward, scooping each pile of coins into my purse.

"Aren't you going to count them?" Henslowe asked, making clear where his true interest lay.

"No need," said I in careful imitation of his voice and manner. "In for a penny, in for a pound."

"So they say. Why, young sir, you do seem confident and pleased with yourself—as well you should. After all, you've just taken into your purse what one of your elders might earn for an entire year of work. Do you feel rich?"

"Not yet, but I shall be."

"Well then, with that ten pounds you're on your way."

"Indeed," said I, "and far enough along that I can now afford to pay rent. I shall be moving from the room which you so generously supplied." Let him wonder where and with whom. He would hear soon enough.

"Soon?"

"Today."

"Ah, that is soon. Well, it seems to have served you well. I'd heard that you spent last night in other quarters. Trying out a bed, were you?"

I ignored his question, most provocative, and offered him, rather, a polite bow. He took it as his due and nodded in response.

"Good fortune to you then," said he. "And bring me *Titus Andronicus* in a month's time."

"Six weeks," said I.

"Five weeks," said he.

"Soon," said I—and flew out the room before he could whittle me further.

Returning to my room, I threw clothes and odds and ends into my travel bag and vacated the place, leaving the key in the door. The two whores had vanished, and so must take my departure without a farewell. They would understand well enough soon enough—mayhap better than their whoremaster ever would.

By this time, having made so many false turns in the past, I had the proper path well in mind—Bishopgate to Norton Folgate—as I set off upon my march. Thus did I make my return to Kit Marlowe's modest dwelling in the shortest time ever, even weighed down as I was by my traveling bag.

It was not yet noon when I stood at his door—but late enough. My fist was poised to beat upon his door when, thinking better of it, I pushed my bag off to one side and out of sight. Only then did I knock upon the stout oaken door. After waiting for a response of some sort and receiving none, I beat harder and longer upon it. Then at last I was rewarded with sounds of waking from beyond the door—coughing, hawking, groaning, then creaking from the bed and footsteps moving unsteadily across the floor. The door opened, Kit was revealed.

He looked quite ghastly. Standing naked before me, there was naught to hide. His skin, which had seemed healthy enough yesterday at the theater, was now a sickly pale with a bit of gray beneath; I had seen better color on dead men. There were bruises and scabs about his upper body—souvenirs, I supposed, from some recent brawl; these I had not noticed by last night's candlelight. He was much less impressive in this state.

"Yes?" he croaked. "What will you?"

Yet this was said with his puffy eyes tight shut. I don't believe he even saw me before him.

"Kit, 'tis I, Will Shakespeare."

"Oh?" The sound of that rang most hollow. "I seem to remember the name."

"Yestereve were we together. Do you not recall?"

He was silent for a moment. His face twisted into a grimace, as if he were thereby forcing his memory into some awful terra incognita, here be dragons, et cetera. He ventured a squint at me.

"You look familiar, but . . ." He sighed. "But I seem to have drunk a deal of wine last night."

"Oh, and brandy, as well, most of a bottle, 'twas."

"Ah well, there you have it. Brandy destroys my memory quite utterly. What was it you wanted, Mr. . . . uh . . .?"

"Shakespeare, Will Shakespeare."

"Ah yes," said he, "what was it?"

Oh, dear God, thought I, this is every bit as embarrassing as I had feared it might be. How was I to tell him that he had spoken to me of love and invited me to come live with him? Yet I decided that for want of a place to sleep that night, I had better tell some of it, if not all.

"We met night before last at the Dog and Duck, and yesterday when you spied me at The Theatre, you offered me one of your seats in the gallery, from which I viewed your puissant and mighty work, *Tamburlaine*."

"Enough of that," said he. "Get on with your story."

"Yes, certainly. Afterward, you did take me to a most bizarre sort of place, the World's End—"

"Ah, the World's End!" he exclaimed. "Then did we . . ."

"Yes, we did."

"Here?"

His eyes were fully open by then. He seemed to be studying me with increasing interest.

"And was it pleasurable?"

"You seemed to find it so."

"Ah, well then . . ."

"You did noise some to that effect."

At that he smirked as a child might when caught out at some clever bit of mischief. He waited to hear more.

"Then did you take up that bottle of brandy," I continued, "and having drunk deep from it, you began to say some remarkable things."

"Remarkable? In what way?"

"This is rather embarrassing," said I.

"You needn't be embarrassed. If I said it, then I should be man enough to hear it repeated. Don't you agree?"

"I suppose so, yes."

"And I assure you, uh, Will, I believe everything you've told me so far."

It later struck me that that was rather a strange thing for him to say—yet quite like Kit Marlowe. Why should he not believe me? What reason should I have to lie to him? Yet I mention this because it seemed to say something of the society in which he moved, one in which truth-telling was not the rule, but the exception. He had given me my first glimpse into the world of the spy—for that was what Kit was from first to last.

"Well," said I, "having got yourself properly drunk, you rather sweetly asked me to come live with you and be your love. Those were the very words that you used, I believe."

At that, Kit threw back his head and laughed in high mirthful manner. This, I thought, was most unforgivably rude of him. I believe I could have accepted almost anything from him—any lie, any excuse, no matter how far-fetched—anything, that is, but laughter of that sort. At that moment, I thought him quite the cruelest I had ever known. And while I later thought this quite a childish notion, I am not sure, as I write this now, if my first response were not, mayhap, the more accurate.

I said not a word, but with cheeks burning and eyes blurring, I grabbed up my traveling bag and ran for the stairs.

"Come back!" he shouted after me. "Do come back, *please!*"

Too late, I thought, halfway down the stairs. He'll not persuade me to return, no matter how clever his words.

But then, shouting so loud he must have been heard all the way back to Norton Folgate, he announced to one and all: "I was RECITING!" And full-throated, he cried out those words which had so inspired me the night before:

> **"Come live with me, and be my love,**
> **"And we will all the pleasures prove**
> **"That hills and valleys, dales and fields,**
> **"And all the craggy mountain yields.**

"Come back here now, and I shall say you the rest."

My steps faltered. I looked up and found him staring down at me, naked but for his two hands which he wore cupped over his male organ. I glanced down and saw the crowd of boys he had attracted, laughing, jeering, and pointing upward. Here was I then, caught between those below and him above. Seeing no other way for it, I turned round and returned.

He, already inside, beckoned me swiftly through the door and slammed it after me.

"Sit down, sit down," said he, making a swift motion toward the chair. "Give me a moment to pull on hose and breeches, and I'll explain everything."

I said nothing, neither did I sit, but simply waited till he be ready to convince me; I realized that in spite of all thoughts to the contrary, that was what I most wanted. In that silence which came between us I heard the noise of shouting from below—a yoo-hoo chorus in falsetto, calling out, "Bugger, bugger, bugger" in a kind of marching rhythm. The crowd had not, as expected, dispersed.

Kit caught my eye.

"Listen to them down there," said he. "I'd like to send them flying, and I think I know how to do it. Open the door, Will."

As I did so, puzzling at his plan, he went to the chamber pot and inspected its contents.

"Stand clear now. Ready?"

"Ready."

He went not quite at a run through the door I held open, for he was loath to spill the contents of the pot in the room, but he did move quickly, all the way to the porch. There he paused but briefly—just long enough to plant his feet and heave the excrement over the side and down upon the boys below.

"Bugger yourselves!" he cried.

And they, in their turn, shouted back all manner of abuse. I was by then beside Kit looking down to see what damage had been done—forsooth, not much. There were a few splatters about, but only one of the little urchins seemed to have taken a palpable hit; he must have been slow taking the shelter of the stairs. The rest emerged from beneath them, apparently untouched, snarling and laughing like a pack of mongrel dogs.

"That will do them, the little bastards," said Kit. "Of course I'm a bugger, as they well know, for I've buggered them all one time or more. I just don't like them spreading the word round Shoreditch."

Then did he give me the brightest of bright smiles and gesture politely toward the door.

"Let's inside, Will. You see? They're leaving. Now we may make clear between us this misunderstanding and be good friends, as we were meant to be."

Indeed he did make clear the misunderstanding, which was easily done, for he searched out a fair copy of "The Passionate Shepherd to His Love," showed it to me and let me read it through. I thought it a good piece of work, and think it so still today. (It must be, for it is of all his works, the only one remembered and read today, and was good enough to be, for a time, attributed to me.) With such evidence before me I could not deny that this was the reason for my confusion, nor could he blame me for my embarrassing mistake. I asked him the meaning of that rather frightening line that had to do with hell, something about being in hell and not out of it, and he was quick to tell me that it was one of those contained in the play at which he was now at work.

"You're writing a play about hell?" I asked, impressed and even a bit frightened.

"No, 'tis a play about a man—a great scholar—who would stay out of hell."

"And does he?"

"Alas, no. He has made a bargain with Lucifer himself, and Lucifer does drive a very hard bargain."

"So I've heard," said I lightly, "though I've no direct experience of it. I assume that other puzzling line which you shouted out was also from this new play?"

"Which one was that?"

"Which one indeed! It had to do with returning in a more satisfying shape."

"Ah, that! It is said to one of Lucifer's emissaries to earth, a lesser devil by the name of Mephistopheles."

"And does he return in a more pleasing shape?"

"Oh, no doubt, for he must do what I tell him at this point."

"You order devils about, do you?"

"As it pleases me, for in the writing of the play, I may do as I like," said he.

"I had not considered it quite so."

"And you a poet? You see, I do remember something of our talk of the evening past." He fixed me with that cold, unblinking stare as he continued: "Truly, you disappoint me, Will. Had you never thought that we rule our characters' fates as we are ruled by Divine Providence? I say that merely as an analogy, of course, for I myself have no belief in Divine Providence or any other attributes of that which we call God. Briefly put, I do not believe in God."

That gave me pause. No one had ever said such a thing in my presence before. I knew not how to respond to such an assertion. I could not have said, "Nor do I," for that would have been a lie. (Well, I've told lies before—surely we all have—yet it was the sort of lie for which I saw no profit or gain.) It may also have been a trap, for I recalled the warning from Burbage that Marlowe had been a spy and mayhap was one still; a common enough trick used by such a one is to tempt another into agreement with some provocative statement or belief and thus to catch him out. And so, not knowing what to say, I said nothing. There was silence between us for more than a moment. It became a bit awkward.

Finally, he broke the silence with a laugh and a welcome wink of his eye. I wondered, had all that before been said in jest? Or did he simply wish to lighten the heavy mood? The latter, no doubt, for what he said next had the effect of moving us into shallower waters.

"I must say, Will, this misunderstanding, which was my own drunken fault and not yours, may indeed have had an advantageous effect—for me at least."

"Oh? And how is that?" I asked.

"Why, it does so happen that from time to time I have difficulty meeting the rent on this desirable room. You, uh, do find it desirable, do you?"

I looked about me, pouched my lower lip judiciously, and gave a grudging nod.

"A bit dark," said I, "but it's really quite large."

"Too much for one man alone."

"Do you really think so?"

"I simply *mean*, Will, that *if* you were to move in with me here, we wouldn't be bumping into each other whenever we turned this way or that." He had raised his voice. Was I exasperating him?

"One might even say that it could use a bit of furniture—another chair, certainly."

"One might say that—and you positively must leave Southwark!" He hesitated then but the merest fraction of a second. "Then what say you, Will? Come live with me and share the rent?"

That sounded familiar, did it not? I gave it a moment's thought and remembered the lame-rhymed quatrain that I had lain upon his writing table. A glance in that direction told me that it was yet where I had left it, untouched and—thank God—unread.

"Will?"

"Oh . . . well . . . yes," said I. "But that depends upon the rent, doesn't it? How much is it?"

"Uh, two shillings on the month."

"Two shillings, is it?" I thought, though said not, that the landlord would be fortunate to get one shilling for such a place as this. I'd no doubt Kit was trying to cheat me. Let him. I had money enough to indulge Christopher Marlowe, if I so chose. Besides, there were also very practical reasons for me to share this space with him. And finally, though perhaps not quite as beautiful by daylight as he had been by candlelight, Kit was nevertheless quite the most attractive young man I had ever met and ever hoped to. And so I accepted his terms on the rent and dropped my traveling bag upon the floor; there were other of his terms upon which we found it far more difficult to agree, and some we never came to terms on.

He made it clear, as an instance, that though we shared the same bed, we were to lead separate lives. That meant that *he* was to lead his own, yet have me whensoever he would. Just to make sure that I understood that, he took shelter that very night with one of his "university wits" and was, no doubt, at his wit's end two or three times before the night was through.

I did manage to get to the writing table and filch from it that execrable little quatrain I had written in imitation of his own. I would not have him look upon any work of mine which I considered inferior, for if my lust for him had cooled ever so slightly, my desire to equal and eventually excel him in the crafting of plays burned in me just as hot as ever. I mentioned in this account but a moment before that there were certain "practical reasons" for my keen desire to share room and bed with Christopher Marlowe, and I now shall make it plain that in so doing, I hoped (nay, expected!) that I might learn better from him. And I must confess now that even though I have derided him and his talent thus far, I knew then in my heart that I had much knowledge to gain from him and that Philip Henslowe's assessment of our respective talents was not much in error. Mayhap it was no more than my envy of his university education that made me feel as I did. Perchance it was something stronger, for I came to feel, and feel yet today, that fate had chosen us two as actors in a play of our own, a comedy which would end in tragedy. The sense of competition that drove us on was but the theme which sustained the early acts.

I went to school to him. And most ironic was it that because my teacher was so often absent, I succeeded in learning so well from him. It was Kit's way, as I soon found out, to work as little as possible so long as money flowed in; and for a while—that is, for the length of time that *Tamburlaine the Great, Part Two* played at The Theatre (its run was twice extended)—he would have wealth aplenty. He spent it as it came to him—standing the table to drinks and dinner at the Duck and Drake, buying boys at the World's End. Ah, it was a merry time as long as the money lasted, and I must admit that more often than not he included me in these reckless pursuits of pleasure. Nevertheless, when *Tamburlaine* closed, he had so little money left that I feared that I should have to support him till he finished *Doctor Faustus,* which was the devil play from which he had quoted on our first night together. In any case, he set to work upon it with an industriousness I had not seen in him before.

Still, I had underestimated Kit's financial resources, for he had not worked long upon *Faustus*—much less than three months, as I recall—when he was called away to perform a service of some sort. I remember quite well how the summons came: 'Twas a night in midwinter, damp and dour. The room had gone cold, for the fireplace wanted fuel in the worst way; neither of us would budge, hoping the other would fetch wood up from below. Each of us sat at the writing table, I upon the chair which I had had made for me. Thus, sharing the table, we sat each across from the other; he, as it happened was nearest the door. We heard steps laboring up the steep stairs and then a knock upon the door.

"You get that, will you?" said he to me.

"Get it yourself," said I rather testily: I was tired of playing servant to this young master.

"I've but a line or two to write, and I shall be done with this scene."

I gave in. I wished to do all I could to keep him working. Jumping up from my chair without a word, I went swift to the door and threw it open.

There was Thomas Watson, a poet and an occasional visitor, a friend of Kit's and one of the "university wits." He was older than both of us by eight or ten years, bearded, grizzled, somewhat threatening in his manner. I liked him not. He frightened me a little.

His eyes barely grazed me as they moved on to Marlowe.

"Come here, Kit," said he. "I've something for you."

"What then? What have you, Tom?"

"A job to be done, and some crowns and florins to send you on your way to do it."

"I'm for that," said Kit, bolting from his chair and rushing to the door.

"Then come out here on the porch, and we'll discuss it."

He accepted the invitation and followed Watson out into the cold night, shutting the door in my face. What, I wondered, did all this mean? Danger? A threat of some sort? If 'twere me, I'd not go out alone with such a one as Watson for fear of finding a poniard stuck between my ribs. I returned to my place at the table and, finding I was unable to resume my work, simply waited for Kit to return. It was not long before he did, and in his hand he carried a small bag which, I judged, contained a quantity of coins. He rattled them at me, that I should have no doubt.

"Ah, Will," said he, "fate has come and rescued me from this drudgery. You hear that, don't you?" He jingled the coins once again. "It is the sound of freedom, of liberation; in short, dear boy, it is the sound of money."

He emptied the purse upon the table before me. I saw immediately that there were crowns and florins there, right enough—as well as angels, nobles, and a pound or two. Verily, I was impressed by that great pile of coins.

"I must away for a while," said he. "How long that while shall be, I cannot rightly say. But I'd like you to keep some of this for me for my return. So shall I not be put in straits, as I now find myself. I trust you, Will. You're better with money than I shall ever be."

Having said as much, he began counting out the coins and arranging them in piles of a single pound each. There were six such piles when he had done. Two of them he sent over to my side of the table. The remaining four he dropped back into the purse.

"Thus much shall I need for my journey," said he.

"And where will it take you?" I asked.

"That I cannot say, but I shall need a bag to carry a few things in. May I borrow yours?"

"Oh . . . well . . . yes, I suppose so."

I fetched it for him, and he began tossing inside it all spare items of clothing he had hanging on pegs about the room. It appeared that he would be gone for quite some time, judging from what he took, more than a week, certainly.

"You're leaving tonight?" I asked. Even to myself I sounded distressed, and I wondered why that should be.

"Yes, oh yes. These things come up sudden or not at all."

"I see," said I, though of course I understood little or naught, which was as he would have it.

"Tom Watson will be back soon with a mount for me." He hesitated but a moment. Then he dressed in a great rush for the cold night, strapping on his hanger and tucking away his poniard. As he did, he delivered me a set of instructions which had to do with what I was to tell visitors (generally, as little as possible) and what I might say about the time of his return ("next week, next month—whatever suits the situation best"). There was one specific message to impart, however, and that was for James Burbage, manager of the Queen's Men and owner of The Theatre and The Curtain.

"Should he come by," said Kit, "or send someone in his stead, he will no doubt want to know how I am proceeding with *Faustus*. Tell him I went back to Canterbury where I might write without interruption. If he wants to know when it will be ready, say that he'll have it the moment I return from Canterbury. Yes, you may use that for them all, if you like. Now, a book or two." He went to the bookshelves and pulled from them *The Prince* and a Latin Bible.

"An odd combination," I commented.

"Not at all," said he. "Machiavelli would have understood Christ perfectly well. But forsooth, I'm reading for my next play, the one after *Faustus*."

"Oh? Tell me about it."

"Not now, Will. When I return, perhaps. You can—"

A shrill whistle sounded from below.

"That would be Tom," said Kit. He shouldered the bag, now well-filled with odds and ends of clothing, and I managed even so to wrap my scarf about his neck. "If I'm not back in a year, you may consider the two pounds your own."

"A *year!*"

"Goodbye, Will." And so saying, he kissed me hastily upon the lips and ran out the door.

He was not gone a year, but he was away for well over a month, and it seemed like a year to me. I had grown used to him, and he to me, specially during that time when we two worked day and evening across from one another at that great writing table. I was surprised at first at the sense of privacy which I felt with his absence. This was new to me, for though I had been out and away from Stratford since I was but sixteen years of age I had not, forsooth, spent much time by myself, neither in Stratford, nor in the various parts of Lancashire wherein I had dwelt. There was always Anne and the children, Ffoke Gyllome or someone like him, or a manor house filled with servants, to divert my concentration.

And so, with much time alone, did my writing prosper. Already had I done with *Titus Andronicus* and delivered it to Henslowe. He seemed pleased by it, and showed his pleasure by paying promptly, yet I never liked the play. The reason, as may be evident, is that it was not wholly mine. I had worked from an outline prepared by Kyd for Henslowe and as I attempted to put meat upon the bones of that skeleton, the weakness of the plot became to me all-too plain. And, most paradoxical, its weakness lay chiefly in its excess (meat pies made of the flesh of sons and the like). I did all that could be done with it. None could have done more, save perhaps for Kit and Kyd himself. I'm sure, as an incidental to this, that Kyd gave up the play because, having written out the plot, he saw its weakness. Yet Henslowe liked it and wanted it written just as it was. And when I gave him what he wanted, he liked it even more. If the play did not please its audience—though truly it did—then let the blame or credit fall on Philip Henslowe.

I had written *Titus Andronicus* during those weeks when *Tamburlaine, Part Two* ran so successfully at The Theatre, those same weeks during which Christopher Marlowe sported his money away—at the playhouse each day and out drinking each night. He seemed to know that I was working on something, yet he showed no interest in what it was. Or perchance he had looked at it whilst I was off on an errand (I did the buying for us both) or was otherwise occupied, and thought it the poor stuff that it was. But willy-nilly, he never mentioned it to me.

When, however, I set to work upon *Henry VI,* 'twas but a week, or not much more, before the night of Kit's sudden leave-taking. Though I had started, I had set down not a word of the sequel, for in making my beginning, I had thought, quite reasonably, that I must carefully re-read all that I had written a year before. In doing so, I discovered two things. By reading through to the end I saw, first of all, that Henslowe was quite right: For the story to be told satisfactorily, it must reach a true resolution; as it was, it ended with a strong hint of dark things ahead and nothing more. My second discovery was far more discouraging. It was simply that all I had written thus far of *Henry VI* was bloody awful.

Had I learned so much in a year? Had my standards risen so in such a short time that what I previously thought admirable and my best work, did now seem merely trite and tired? Yes, tired: Through whole scenes the lines lumbered along so that I was made to suspect that I had simply put Holinshed and Halle into iambics. (I hadn't, though the effect was much the same.) It was clear to me that before I was to write the Second Part, I should have to rewrite the first. And so was I greatly desponded on that late evening in February when Thomas Watson called upon Kit and took him away, wondering how I might put some life into those year-old lines of mine.

Then, however, with Kit gone, I was left alone to my devices. And with my new-found privacy came the realization that I had at hand the material with which to enliven my play. Across from me, laying upon the desk at which I worked, were great piles of papers whereon were writ the complete works (to date) of Christopher Marlowe. All that I needed was there for the stealing. Yet was it theft, or mere mimicry?

I went rummaging through those paper piles on Kit's side the writing table until I found fair copies of *Tamburlaine the Great, Part One* and *Part Two*—both of them sewn together. Then, with mine upon the right and his *Tamburlaine* on the left, I started revising Henry—which is to say, lifting here and appropriating there from Kit, adapting, altering, editing, giving to my play a bit of that oriental potentate's force and sense of urgency. Marlowe loved to bombast; given room, he would have his characters striding about the world in seven-league boots. That is his style. And I daresay I caught a bit of it early on:

> **Is this the scourge of France?**
> **Is this the Talbot, so much fear'd abroad,**
> **That with his name the mothers still their babes?**
> **I see report is fabulous and false:**
> **I thought I should have seen some Hercules,**
> **A second Hector, for his grim aspect,**
> **And large proportion of his strong-knit limbs.**
> **Alas! This is a child, a silly dwarf.**

Et cetera. I am most proud of that passage, for in it I managed to imitate his manner and at the same time twit him for it. A small victory that, yet by and large, I must confess that this exercise was a rather humbling one, for going back and forth, over and over again through these two plays, instilled in me a greater respect for his poetry than I might have had previous. Poetry covered his weaknesses and faults. When the pace of a scene slowed, he would resort to poetry. When the action grew repetitive, he could divert attention with verbal fireworks. Yet while my original estimate—that he was a greater poet than he was a writer of plays—was yet true, still I had to admit, if only to myself, that he was indeed a great poet. It would not be easy to excel him. Yet I knew I must try, and I knew that ultimately I should succeed.

There were but a few visitors come to ask about Kit, not so many as he seemed to have expected. But as he had anticipated, a representative of the Queen's Men came to call—in fact, it was Richard Burbage, son of James, whom I had met that first night, backstage at the Curtain Theater. I liked the man, and he'd been most friendly to me, and so it pained me to tell him the ready lies that Marlowe had given me; yet tell them I did, and he accepted them as truth. All went well with our conversation until the end of his visit when he happened to mention upon leaving, what a shame it was about poor Dick Tarlton.

"Why?" said I, "what has become of him?"

"Had you not heard? He passed on but a week ago."

"What was the cause?"

"Ah," said Burbage. "The doctors differed, as they always do. One said 'twas apoplexy, and another that the cause was heart stoppage. In any case, it was merciful swift. He got up from the table at the Dog and Duck to go outside and have a piss. He made it near to the door and plain fell over. After he'd quivered a bit, he died."

"What a pity," said I. "I liked the man well—and there was no better clown in London."

"We all felt so." Burbage sighed—then brightened a bit of a sudden. "Listen, Will, we're in need of a clown. I remember you pulled a few good faces for us. Why not come and try out for Tarlton's place? I'd like well to see you in the company."

"Ah, well, so would I, but I lack the manner of a clown."

"Well, you know best. There can be no doubt but that it's a particular sort of talent, bein' a clown. But do come by, won't you? As soon as spring comes, we'll be starting our season—a great many plays and a great many roles to be cast outside the company. Try us, Will."

We left it at that, and he departed. Yet I promised myself I would indeed try my luck at both theaters. By the end of the next year I should tread the boards in London for the first time, though I promised myself not for the last.

Of Marlowe's close friends (or had he any, really?), only Kyd, Greene, and Thomas Watson attended our room, making inquiries. Kyd was easily handled: he accepted it that Kit had gone to Canterbury and asked no further questions of me. That pleased me well, for I doubted not that Henslowe had let it out that he now had a completed play on Kyd's outline of *Titus Andronicus*, and that he was well pleased with it. Had he attached my name to it? I hoped not, for I had considered taking my name from it entirely. Thomas Kyd seemed to have heard nothing about it.

Robin Greene's visit I liked least of all. Older than Marlowe, though not by near so many years as Watson, Greene came also to London by way of Cambridge. As one of the "university wits," he had also written (or collaborated upon) plays for the theater. Nevertheless, his natural mode was prose, and in the manner of that early day, he gained fame as a writer of "love pamphlets," so-called, and romances of greater length. He was far too haughty for one who had achieved little; and he was certainly no poet.

Not much was said when Greene came into the room I shared with Kit. He had not the grace to knock, for it was daytime, and I had known him to enter thus rudely before Kit had left. He caught me at the writing table with *Tamburlaine* at the left and *Henry* at the right, which was embarrassing. And thus caught out, I stupidly attempted to cover up what I was about; this had the effect of making him curious. He advanced that he might have a closer look,

"Where is he?" Greene demanded.

"You mean Kit, of course."

"Of course. And don't try 'gone to Canterbury' on me. That may have done with Kyd, but I know Kit well—well enough, in any case, to know that no matter what pressure was put upon him, he would not retreat to Canterbury to write. He hates the place, hates the people, hates it all."

By this time he was hulking over me, hands on hips, staring me down. He was a big man and something of a bully. I could do naught but hold tight to my chair and hope he would simply go away.

Then did he move suddenly and push me back so swift and hard that I nearly tipped over. He saw what I had attempted to hide.

"*Thief!*—You little thief. You steal words and phrases from him who gives you shelter. As soon as he is back, you will confess to him what you have been doing, for if you don't I'll tell him myself."

Having said that, he left, not even bothering to shut the door after him.

"Remember what I said!" he shouted from the stairs.

And I in return could think of but one response.

" 'Tis I who give *him* shelter!"

As for Thomas Watson, he came at night, as before, knocked thrice upon the door and identified himself. I threw it open and greeted him.

"Is he here?" he asked me.

"Why, no," said I. "Were you not with him?"

He ignored my query. "Well, if he an't here now, he will be soon."

XI

Is stealing words truly theft? I think not. Words, of themselves, have little value. What worth, as an instance, have "a," "an," or "the?" Or "he," "she," or "it?" They are so common, so indifferently employed, that they could almost be discounted altogether; and perhaps sometime in the future they may be. It is true, I grant, that nouns and verbs have greater weight, yet even they may be strung together in patterns of absolute nonsense in the manner of certain French poets. Thus it becomes plain that it is not the words themselves that have value, but rather the manner in which they are arranged. The number of words which I took from both parts of *Tamburlaine* would, no doubt, have numbered not much more than a hundred, and perhaps less. Think of it! A hundred out of thousands, or perhaps even a hundred thousand. (Marlowe was nothing if not verbose.) No, the words themselves had little value. It was their arrangement, his style, that I wished to duplicate. Often it was no more than the rearrangement of my own lines that was required, perhaps a stronger verb here or there, rarely an adjective (for I thought that in general he was too free with his adjectives); and does such judicious tampering with my own work constitute theft? I think not. And mark you well, I did not "steal" his manner of writing, for it was still his own long after I had adapted it to my own use. So go to, go to, Robert Greene! What would you know of such matters? You who have neither the style, nor the soul of a poet! If I do explain it all to Kit, then it will be in a manner that he, as a poet, will be sure to understand (or so I assured myself at the time).

Yet I never really found a proper opportunity to do so, for Marlowe arrived the day after Thomas Watson's brief visit. Thus given proper notice, I had tucked away the sewn copies of the two parts of *Tamburlaine;* they were now at their original depth in their original pile. I had before me only my own *Henry VI, Part Two* when I heard his familiar step upon the stair. I ran to the door and flung it open; and there did he stand, key in hand, aiming it where the lock might have been. He looked exhausted, fully spent, from the journey home—and who knows what ordeal may have preceded it.

"Ah, Will," said he, "I am so glad to see you!"

"And I you."

"To be home!"

"To have you back."

I fumbled at the travel bag upon his shoulder.

"Here," said I, "let me take this from you. And please—lean upon me, if you like."

He had no need for that, but gladly gave up his burden to me and tossed his outer garments to the floor as he made his way to the bed. Once there, he collapsed upon it and chuckled soft to himself.

"Ah, how good it feels to lie down in this old bed," said he. "Do you know? I walked all the way from Dover."

Though I had never walked to Dover, nor from it, that did not sound to me as might be a great distance. Kit was clearly not used to traveling by foot.

"Why did you not take the Dover coach?" I asked him. "You left here a wealthy man—or so it seemed to me."

"The money vanished, as money will. Those Dutchmen must have their drinks before getting on to business, and I must pay for them. And I found a little Fleming lad in Flushing who was quite irresistible. He worked me for a pound or more—ah, but he was worth it, I vow." Kit sighed. "Yet tell me, Will, have you still that hourglass you once showed me?"

"I have, right enough."

"Then get it down, will you? I must make my report to Walsingham by mid-day, and I'm in dire need of an hour's sleep. I'll tell you a few things about my journey this night, though I cannot tell you all."

I did as he bade me and fetched down the hourglass. He was asleep by the time I set it a-right upon the table.

Though he was gone most of the afternoon, when he returned, he was most forthcoming, though he did make me promise that I would repeat none of it as gossip to others. Certainly I promised—and came close to keeping it, as well.

After we had disported ourselves in celebration of his return, we lay together in bed and, having drunk little or naught, talked on a bit into the night of the threat of the Spanish. He predicted war.

"You talk of it as a certainty," said I to him, thus expressing my doubt.

"It is certainty. All that I learned and have passed on to the great spymaster"—Walsingham, of course—"says that the Spaniards will attempt an invasion by summer at the latest."

"But did not the raid on Cádiz—"

"Angered them more than it hurt them," said he, interrupting.

"Yet word came that their admiral—what was his name?"

"Santa Cruz," said Kit.

"Aye, that was it. That this Santa Cruz had died a month ago or more. People talked of it in the streets and in the taverns."

"Just so," said he. "And that was why I was sent."

Was this more of Kit's posturing? He did delight in presenting himself as more than he was. And I had even come to doubt the rumors I had heard that he had spied for Walsingham—doubted them, that is, until the visit paid us by Thomas Watson a month before. Yet there was that in me that doubted them still, and so I sought to test him.

"You say that was why you were sent," said I, "but why, truly, were you sent—that is to say, why you and not another?"

He then put on an expression I had come to know quite well. Some might call it a smile, yet to me it seemed nothing better than a supercilious smirk.

"Ah, Will, you question me, do you? You wish to examine my bone-fides?"

"Well, I . . ."

"Yet, why should you not? You ask why I was chosen to go and not another? Chiefly for two reasons, I suppose. The first is that I know Dutch better than any other in Walsingham's service." Then did he blurt out a sentence or two of gibberish of the ugliest sort which I took to be Dutch.

"How did you learn it?" I asked.

"That matters little," said he. "That I knew it and had a good understanding—certainly better than any Spaniard—that was what they wished of me. And the second reason why I was chosen—and of this I'm certain—is that I have worked successfully for them in the past."

"Who is 'them'?"

"Believe me, Will, you don't want to know—not names, not positions in the government. It's best not to know."

"So you say, but what does it mean to say you worked successfully in the past?"

He was silent for but a moment. Then, all in a rush, he threw at me four names: "Ralph Bickley, Thomas Pormount, Edward White, Richard Cotton," said he. "Do those men mean anything to you?"

I thought, groped, ransacked my memory, and then came up with something.

"One of them does, I believe—the last mentioned. Richard

Cotton was the brother of my schoolmaster in Stratford. He . . . well, he died."

"Died you say? Oh no, Will, that doesn't tell it—by no means does it. He was tortured, hanged, mutilated, eviscerated, and finally, decapitated, all in public view. In short, he was executed as a traitor. I ought to know, for I sent him to the scaffold, and I watched him—as you so delicately put it—die."

"He was a priest," said I, not much liking what I had heard but beginning now to understand.

"That he was," said Kit, "as were the rest of those I've named—Jesuits to the man. I betrayed them all, sent them to the executioner, and for each I was paid a bounty, a rather handsome sum."

"But that's monstrous!"

"Ah, you think so, do you? Perchance, dear Will, you have been hiding from me all these months that you, too, are a Papist. How say you to that?"

Would he betray me? Could he? I considered myself not so much a Catholic as one who had never properly declared—thus as neither Romish, nor Protestant. Could he put my head up there beside cousin Edward's on London Bridge? I did then, of a sudden, become aware that Kit was laughing at me. He quite took my breath away with his audacity—nay, not audacity merely, but cruelty. How could he laugh? Mayhap all that he had told of betrayals and the like was but a bad joke—though, alas, I suspected it were true enough.

He did at last calm himself sufficient to speak.

"Oh, Will, if you could but see your face—the terror, the fear, that is writ upon it! Calm yourself! You've naught to fear from me. I care not whether you be Catholic or Protestant or Musselman. It is all one to me. All are equally deluded. Forsooth, if I were to choose between them, I should probably choose to be Catholic. I like the ceremony so much better."

"You quite amaze me," said I, and it was true.

"Do I? I'm glad."

"Yet a monster, nonetheless." I paused, hesitating, wanting to know more, but not knowing quite what to ask. "How . . . how did you recognize these men as priests? They must have been in disguise as—"

"Clerks, common laborers, et cetera, yes they were. But I had known them well in France. I had prayed with them at the seminary in Rheims."

"*You* are a priest?"

"No, of course not. But for most of my years at Cambridge, I had pretended that it was my intention to become one. I made friends with the Catholics, dined with the Catholics, went with them to Rheims and pledged my future to them. While all the while I took money and instruction from the government that I might ensnare them when they returned to England."

"And you admit all this?"

"Of course I do. I believe that each of those men deserved his punishment."

"For propagating the faith as they believed in it?"

"No, for propagating a myth."

"I recall that you said sometime before that you do not believe in God," said I. "It seems now that you say that again, choosing different words."

He gave that a moment's thought, then with a nod of his head, "That would be correct. Yes, it would. Yet do not suppose that I give to the Protestant version any greater belief. They are, as I said but a moment ago, equally deluded."

Then neither of us spoke for a long moment, I fearing what he might say next, and he planning his next bit of mischief. And of a sudden, having decided, he threw a hand up and pointed a forefinger at me.

"Get dressed, Will, I must prove a point to you."

There was something in his manner, or perhaps his urgent tone, that prompted me to obey with neither argument nor question. I pulled on hose, thigh leggings, shirt, and doublet, as he did on the other side of the bed.

"Are you taking me far?" I asked, pulling on my boots. That was my only question.

"Farther than you've ever been, but no, not far—not as you mean it—yet—wear a coat. The nights are chill as ever they were when I left."

How odd, thought I. He speaks in riddles whenever the chance does present itself. Thus he adds to the general air of mystery about him, and this he seems so to love.

"So," said he, slipping on his hanger beneath his coat, "ready, are you? Then let us hence into the night. And lock the door after us, will you? It would not do to give entry to night sprites and demons."

(He was at just such times as these capable of exactly this sort of childish nonsense.)

In those years, Shoreditch had not near so many buildings upon it. There were farms, open fields, orchards, and the like, some of them quite close by Norton Folgate. He found a field to suit him and we struck off across it. He took us in the direction of a copse of trees, along what seemed to be a stream. The night was damp from rain that had fallen during the last two days; by the time we reached the trees, our boots were muddy. And yet the sky was clear and bright with stars and a perfect half-moon. I commented upon this to Kit. He made no reply. Glancing at him, I saw that he was preoccupied by some great matter, eyes ahead, lips moving soundlessly. What was it? Here he went before me and led the way through the trees, as if he followed a path. He knew the way. The stream was in sight when he brought us to a halt at a fallen tree in a narrow clearing.

"This is the best place," said he. "I've been here before."

"The best place for what?"

"The best place for doing what we are about to do. Kneel down here—knees upon this tree. It may still be wet, but it's clean—not muddy. You see?"

Reluctantly, I did as he said. The tree in question was an oak of middling size. Mayhap it had been struck by lightning but a year before, or had been felled by that great wind of last December. I'd no way of knowing. What mattered was that it had broken near-clean about a foot and a half above the ground, and the trunk was at a comfortable kneeling height, a *prie-dieu* found here in the woods (and that most fitting, as I would soon discover). It was, as Kit had promised, not muddy, though a bit wet.

"Now what is to be done?" I asked.

"You must pray," said he.

"Pray?"

"Yes, pray as you never have before to God for a sign, an appearance of some kind—a burning bush, a dove descending from the sky, some sign to show that He is there, that He listens, that He has granted you His attention. Or Christ, let Christ come down, or one of the saints, *any* one of the saints."

"But that would be presumptuous."

"Though not blasphemous."

"I . . . I . . . (hesitating thusly) I'm not sure. I would have to consult a theologian."

"I'm a theologian, or I might well be, for I know more of such matters than most of them, or all of them, for that matter. And I say 'tis not blasphemous to pray for a sign; for so prayed your Lord Jesus in the Garden of Gethsemane."

True enough, thought I, it was as he said, for I remembered that passage well—sweating blood, He did. And so I nodded, said nothing, but clasped my hands before me and prayed in the most humble and undemanding manner possible for just such a sign as might satisfy Kit Marlowe. For myself, I needed no such sign; that I attempted to make clear to the Most High. Yet since Marlowe was a doubter, it would convince him, as he seemed to require it. I repeated the prayer thus similarly, and then repeated it again, elaborating upon it in poetic fashion; "if, in Thy infinite wisdom," et cetera, et cetera. Then did

I pray it through a fourth time as the sweat stood out upon my brow. I had not felt so pious since my final lesson in the Catechism.

I was about to start through again when I felt a hand grip my shoulder, and I jumped near a foot off the fallen tree, fearing that I had just felt the touch of God. Then did I hear that familiar laugh and realized that it was Kit and no other.

"That should be quite enough, don't you think, Will?"

"Oh, well, all right, if you think so. They do say, however, that repeated entreaties are—"

"No," said he, interrupting, "your prayers were sincere and fervent. None, I think, could have bested them."

"But—"

"It was a nice touch, introducing me into them, asking that some sign be shown in order to convince me. And if, forsooth, the sign had been given, I would indeed have been convinced. You may be certain of it. But stand, Will, stand and look about you and tell me what you see—or better put, what you *don't* see. There is no burning bush, no dove flying about the trees, no Christ, no Blessed Virgin, no angel, no St. George—and, let us rejoice, no dragon. You see, Will? There is but the stream which flows in the same direction as before, the same trees, the same mud beneath our feet. Nothing is changed."

"But that proves nothing. Faith alone is—"

"Oh, it proves something. It proves that faith alone is plain foolish."

"We must argue that out," I declared right boldly, though I feared I would have been no match for him in any sort of debate.

"Later, perhaps," said he, "but first I have another exercise. In this one, you do not participate. You will observe. Come, stand close beside me here."

He had stepped back from me, and was now in the middle of the little clearing. I took a place next to him, as he had directed and saw him giving the ground around us careful study, as if making calculations. He then gave me a start by drawing his hanger from its scabbard. He made no threat toward me.

"Stay where you are," said he.

I did as he told me while he took three full steps to the outer edge of the clearing. Then did he walk round me, trailing his sword in the ground, so that when he had done, there was round me a roughly drawn circle. He stepped inside it and traced two symbols of a rather obscure sort into the dirt.

"If anything happens," said he then, "just stay close beside me, and you will be safe."

" 'Safe,' you say? What in God's name do you intend?"

"I intend to summon a devil."

"What say you? Not with me about! I am gone, sir!"

So saying, I stepped forth, to make a quick departure. Yet to no avail, for Kit grabbed me and held me where I stood and held me tight.

"Too late, I vow, Will. You must stay in the circle to remain safe from harm—or so it is said."

This left me in a turmoil. Two opposing fears fought within me, and the greater won out. I remained where I was—but a step away from Kit. He then pulled me roughly toward him, so that next I knew I was shoulder to shoulder with him.

"Now, stay where you are."

Then did he begin a kind of chant in an ancient tongue, thick and guttural, which I had never before heard. And as he chanted in rising and lowering tones, he touched first one of the odd symbols with his sword and then the other. That done, he began a slow and careful recitation in what seemed proper English yet one that made no sense at all. He was near done with it before at last I realized that he was reciting the Lord's Prayer back to front. And finally, having completed that blasphemous exercise, he called out in Latin for Satan to appear. He waited a few moments and repeated it. Never had I known such feelings of fear and awe as when I stood there with Christopher Marlowe awaiting the appearance of the Prince of

Darkness. Therefore, was I shocked when Kit thrust the point of his sword down into the dirt before him and shouted out his summons, this time in a loud and threatening manner.

"Veni, Satanus!"

It seemed unwise to be rude to the Devil. I held my breath, waiting, cowering, turning left and right to see, not daring to speak a word for fear that I might offend His Fearful Eminence. Marlowe, by contrast, seemed visibly to relax. He wiped the mud from the tip of his sword upon his boots, then sheathed it in his scabbard.

"There, you see?" said he to me.

"See? See what?" I whispered, looking round me. "Naught has changed. It is now exactly as it was before you drew the circle about us."

"That, Will, is exactly the point."

"I do not follow your devious logic."

"Nothing devious about it. Satan did not come, nor did he send one of his lesser devils, because he does not exist."

"If you thought that, why did you draw that circle? Why did you insist that I stay within it for my own safety?"

"Ah, well, I wanted you to be properly respectful of what I was about. But come, help me rub all this out. I would not have some peasant putting it about that someone was trying to raise the Devil on his master's property."

He did then walk to the perimeter he had drawn with his sword and began scuffing it out with his heel. I did the same at the rear of the circle, thinking ill of him as I went for all that he had put me through. I was still trying to understand his true purpose when he spoke up once again.

"Forsooth, Will, I must confess that I have always taken such precautions in the past. The circle seems merely prudent."

"'Always in the past' you say? How often have you performed this cursed ritual?"

"Oh, a number of times since I began *Faustus*. Quite naturally I wished to see if I could raise a devil myself."

"And did you succeed?"

"Of course I did not. Satan does not exist. There is no Devil. There is no hell."

"But still you draw the circle about you for your own protection."

"I have for some time found it easier to believe in the Devil than in God. But if there is no God—as *you* yourself demonstrated to me some moments ago—then there be no Devil, no Satan. There be no need for one without the other. Don't you see?"

"I see no such thing," I declared staunchly. "Have you not heard that Satan's cleverest guile is to teach us that he does not exist?"

"Ah, Will, I'm disappointed in you. Is that you or your catechist speaking? I urge you to think upon it. If there be no God, then there is no Devil. We are free to do what we will, for there is no sin. Think of all that gives us! If there be no sin, there is no hell, no punishment, no need for it."

"And," said I, concluding the conversation, "if there is no God, there is, alas, no hope for us at all."

Then did I turn and walk away, indifferent to Kit and his arguments. He would gladly depopulate heaven, throw out the saints and angels together with the Holy Trinity, if he might thus justify his sins and misdeeds. What he presented as philosophy was no more than an apologia for his own ill-spent life. And he did prove this by pursuing me, catching me up, and seeking to explain himself—in terms most metaphysical—with regard to the four priests he had betrayed and sent to the scaffold. That, to me, seemed beyond justification, yet this entire, grotesque play of prayer and occult ceremony, all of it, had been an attempt to do just that.

Yet I do remember reflecting, in a most humble way of course, how much more fortunate I was to have the simple faith that I had. I thanked God I was not the sort of hypocrite that Kit Marlowe was. Yet I said naught of this to him. Once he was at my side and babbling away in his fashion, I gave him a semblance of attention—enough, in any case, that he might be satisfied. In this way we returned down Shoreditch.

When we reached our place in Norton Folgate, the candle we had left burning upon the writing table was guttering out. Kit sought out another to replace it.

"Let it go," said I. "The evening has left me tired, and you, too, must be quite exhausted."

"As you say."

"Then let's to bed."

"I'm for it."

By the time the candle had flickered its last, we were under the blanket, warming the bed. Kit wished to have at me one more time, but I did put him off, telling him that I had not the strength for it.

Of what passed between us in the following months there is much to tell, though what there is has little place in a simple work of confession such as this. In a way it might be said that a sort of gap opened between us. We did not pleasure us near so often. Kit sought his corporeal delights elsewhere and had the decency not to bring his catamites back to our bed. For my part, I simply had not the lust for it. Yet oddly, as my desire for bodily pleasure seemed to wane, I seemed to take even greater interest in my work. I went at it not fitfully, waiting for inspiration, as I had been wont to do in the past, but regularly, as a matter of discipline. The lines seemed to flow from my pen upon demand. And when, as seldom happened, I found myself at an impasse, I had the courage and the good sense to consult Kit; we thus became colleagues, as we had not been before. I recall that once he read through an entire scene of mine and afterward commented that it was really quite good.

"It reads a bit like my own," said he. Did he know? Had Greene told him? Perhaps, yet by then I cared not.

Working so, I finished part two of *Henry VI* in a matter of weeks. Only then, as I read through what I had writ, did I realize that there was still more of the story to tell. And so, after consulting Holinshed, and without so much as asking Henslowe's permission or Kit's counsel, I began part three of *Henry VI*. It was completed by the beginning of May; Henslowe was delighted to have it and paid me well for the second and third parts; he did also accept my rewritten text of the first part, complete with emendations and a whole new scene (that in which La Pucelle is sent off to burn).

I learned my craft on *Henry*'s three parts, transformed myself into a true playmaker with it. I did feel my strength grow from day to day and act to act. I knew when I had done that I could write quite anything—comedy, history, or tragedy. When at last Henslowe brought the three plays to the boards at the Rose Theatre, they proved a great success. He was eager to get more from me, but he never did—no, and he came to resent it greatly. Years afterward, as I looked back upon this time in my life, it occurred to me that I had thrown myself thus into my work that I might put behind all that had befallen me there in that copse by the stream. As time passed that ordeal took on much greater importance.

Marlowe, too, worked as I had never before seen him. The reason, I suppose, was want of coin. He finished his *Doctor Faustus* with little difficulty and was paid no doubt double what I'd received for any one of mine. Yet he, who was always short of cash, was soon running low again, and his only recourse was to write more and write faster—and thus *The Jew of Malta*. I believe that it, unlike those which preceded it, suffered somewhat from its hasty composition—not, of course, that there are not good things in it; indeed there are, and I made good use of them in *The Merchant of Venice,* an altogether better play.

I do recall something that was said by him during one of his periodic cash crises. Again, it took on greater significance much later—though it seemed to be said casually enough when it was spoke.

He grabbed deep down into his purse and pulled out a coin of no great worth—perhaps a shilling or perhaps half a crown—examined it close and picked at it a moment or two with his thumbnail. Then did he hold it out for me to see.

"Look here, Will," said he. "This coin is of base metal. There is naught to prove its worth but what is stamped upon it. Am I not right?"

I took the coin and examined it. What the metal was, I could not say, but I was sure that it were not gold or silver. Then did I turn it over and see upon its other side the image of the Queen. I pointed this out to Kit.

" 'Tis this that gives it worth," said I. "She is our sovereign and therefore has the right to coin."

"Why should she have the right to coin and no other have it?" He posed it as a question of philosophy, a kind of puzzle.

Yet I, having no taste for such, simply shrugged and repeated my answer. "Because she is the sovereign, and the other is not."

"I've as much right to coin as she has." Wherewith, he laughed, took back the coin, and dropped it into his purse. Then did he offer a wink, as one might do when he had made a proper jest.

I had all but forgotten the matter when it came up again a few years later.

With the goodly sum paid me by Henslowe, I determined to set off for Stratford in the first week of May in that year of 1588. There were there many who had sneered and talked behind my back when I had set off for London. (Dick Whittington they had called me.) I wanted to still their flapping tongues. There were other reasons.

Because of the money I carried, I went armed and by post coach. I thought it worthwhile, as well, to let them know just how far I had come in half-a-year's time. And did they not goggle and stare when I stepped down from the coach in Stratford! At the inn, there were ever people about to meet the coach—those who expected letters and those who merely hoped. Among the latter there were familiar faces. I heard my name called out two or three times, and I waved back in answer, yet none were eager to approach me. Among the former was one who stood apart from the rest. I could not ignore him. He would not allow it. Coming to me direct, he held me where I stood waiting for my travel bag to be handed down. 'Twas his eyes kept me, for he gave me as cold a look as ever I had got. Only when he was upon me did I know him for who he was. Then did I feel an urge to run from him as one might from a distemper'd hound, for it was none but Arthur, Sir Thomas Lucy's man. Yet I conquered the urge and held my ground, and I managed, being an actor, to meet him with a smile upon my face.

"It's Will, an't it? Will Shakespeare?"

"Why, it is indeed," said I. He seemed civil enough in his greeting, which reassured me somewhat. "I cannot greet you by name, except to call you Arthur, for which familiarity I ask your pardon."

"Arthur will do." He looked me up and down. "Well, you've the appearance of a young gentleman, and you talk like one, too. I b'lieve Sir Thomas will be glad to see you."

"Do you mean Sir Thomas Lucy? He and I have no business together."

"Ah, you'd be surprised, you would. He's putting together a regiment of militia, and you're just the sort he'd want in the first rank when we go to meet the Spanish."

The prospect did not please me. Nevertheless, I attempted to treat it lightly.

"The Spanish? Here in Stratford? You must be joking, Arthur. Or is it Sir Thomas' jest? The Spanish will never come so far. They will be met and turned back at sea."

"Is that what they say in London?" I had angered him. His eyes flashed, but he held his tongue.

"Yes, that is what is said in London."

"Sir Thomas will be interested to hear that. Oh yes, he will indeed. Why not come round and tell him that yourself?"

At this point I realized that perhaps I'd gone a bit too far. I must use discretion in framing my response.

"Sir Thomas does not need me to counsel him in military matters," said I with a smile. "No doubt he is privy to matters of which I am ignorant. I only repeat what is said in London."

He did then smirk at me in a manner which seemed to say he believed that he had bested me. I saw no need to add to what had been said and desired only to be away. Then, as if the fates had granted my wish, the coachman called from above and reached my travel bag down to me. I took it and, eager to be away, began shuffling rearward.

"I shall pass on to him what you've told me," said Arthur. "My master is always eager to hear what is discussed in London. And let me repeat that he would be glad to hear it direct from you. He may even have a few things to tell you—and one or more questions to put."

I wondered not what they might be!

"Goodbye, Arthur."

"Goodbye, Will, I shall see you later, no doubt."

I waved, turned, and moved quickly away. Perhaps it was but my imagination, but I thought I heard him chuckle aloud as I left. Was his laugh one of anticipation?

As I walked down Henley Street, I mused upon that ill-starred meeting. It seemed that because of it I must again make my visit shorter than I had intended.

So Sir Thomas would think me just the sort to put in the first rank of his militia? How thoughtful of him. There I would make a fine target for a Spanish arrow or a pike. I had not come to Stratford to defend the Lucy holdings against foreign invasion. Forsooth, I had left London to escape all such danger of mortal combat, though Kit Marlowe had assured me that Drake and Hawkins and the Sea Dogs would stop the Spanish in the Channel. He had been the source of my information, and in the past he had always proved reliable on such great matters. Still, even the possibility of war discomfited me: I was not meant to be a soldier. (Nor do I now consider that a sin—a failing perhaps, but not a sin.)

It was the year of the Spanish Armada, after all. In London people in the streets talked of little else. It was brave talk, for the most part—"just let them try," et cetera—yet well I knew how swiftly their bold resolve would melt in the heat of battle. Thank God it never came to that. I leave to the chronicles and the historians the details of how the invading Spanish were driven back by our Navy and providentially swept away by a storm. It all happened as Kit had said it would—yet not even he could have predicted the many militias and private armies raised by the country aristos and the lesser nobility. Considering what had passed between us, I had no intention of putting myself under the command of Sir Thomas Lucy, and even less would I wish to be at the whim of his man, Arthur. No indeed, I saw it as my duty to myself to vacate Stratford as swiftly and inconspicuously as practically possible.

But first there were a few things to which I must attend. There were financial matters to be discussed with my father. After the first kisses and hugs, I heard the news of the family from my mother and from my father received a report on how his business went. That led to a confidential discussion of *our* business, for in the last couple of years he and I had begun an enterprise of our own, wherein I had contributed what pounds and pence I could raise from my own activities, and he loaned them out for me. The interest from these small loans he loaned out further, and so on. He had been engaged in a like enterprise since well before my birth; the original sum had come to him as a small inheritance left him by his uncle.

It was usury, right enough, and as such was it a crime in

most (perhaps all) of the Christian world by Papal edict. Yet I would not deem it so; even less would I call it sinful, as all the popes had done. Ever since our marrying King Henry altered things so profoundly, much of what the popes had called sinful has been judged quite acceptable, even desirable, as I feel certain this practice will be, too. How could usury be sinful? People often find themselves unexpectedly needful of money; it is, alas, part and parcel of the human condition. They will pay for the use of that money; the greater the need, the more they will pay. So, as it proved, this enterprise which my father managed, was most profitable to me. With the greater sum I had now brought him to lend out, it would certainly do even better.

We finished our discussions on these matters by dark. Then did I hie off to Anne and the children who awaited me in our little cottage next to the Hathaway house. I was expected. I had written of my coming some days before setting out upon my journey. Her father or one of her brothers had no doubt read the letter to her, for as I sighted the cottage, I spied her in the doorway. She did then run to meet me halfway up the path, with our children trailing along behind. It was thus quite a perfect homecoming, replete with hugging and kissing, laughter, and the cries of children. I found myself wishing that I had brought more than I had to this occasion—gifts for Anne and the children perhaps, yet also more in the way of warmth and tender feeling for them. They seemed genuinely glad to see me. Why could I not be equally and just as genuinely glad to see them? It was but another instance of a deficiency in myself of which I have been aware for quite some time. Only to John Cotton, who had been my schoolmaster, did I give myself completely and that when I was but a lad. Since that had gone ill for me, I had ever held back from others something within myself. My experiences with Kit Marlowe, while often strong, did tend to confirm this scheme of behavior. Anne, who is not an insensitive creature, seemed to detect something of this in my manner, though not to the depths which I have described.

"Will," said she to me, "is there anything wrong? Something you wish to tell me?"

Wherewith I gave her a description of my meeting with Sir Thomas Lucy's Arthur as the children ran on ahead to the cottage. I told her what he had said and laid particular emphasis upon the half-threat of the visit to me by Sir Thomas.

"Do you think he still holds against you the death of the doe?"

"I think he may, and if he do not, then Arthur does."

"Then you cannot stay long, I suppose."

"I suppose not."

We were by that time quite near the cottage. The girls, Susanna and Judith, had run on ahead. Hamnet, my son, toddled along beside me, holding tight to my hand. Anne brought us to a halt.

"You never do remain for more than a week," said she to me. "And seldom so long as that—or so it seems to me."

"That is unfortunate, I suppose, yet it is just so that many live their lives. What if I were a sea captain—or a soldier—away perhaps for years at a time."

"For all I know, that is what you are."

"Well, I assure you I am neither seaman nor—"

"The children hardly know you," she said, interrupting.

I glanced down at Hamnet. He returned my look, quite unintimidated. He seemed interested in what we were saying, though not distressed by it.

"He seems to know me well enough," said I in a reasonable and conciliatory manner. "Forsooth, Anne, what would you have of me? The sort of husband who mucks about in the dirt, tilling and digging, or a glovemaker, like my father?"

"What our fathers do is fair labor and ought not be held to ridicule."

"I do not ridicule," said I. "Still, I would know what you want of me. If I were here, I could not keep you and our children near so well. You know that as I do. And if I were here, eking out some sort of living for us all, I should find it very difficult indeed to avoid Sir Thomas. Can you not see that?"

"Indeed I see that, but—"

"Do you want for food or for clothing? Do the children?"

"No, but still—"

"Do you not understand that I must work in London to provide these?"

"I understand," she wailed most pitiably, "but what I do not understand is why we cannot go with you to London and live with you there."

And with that, Hamnet, who was but three, after all, and had held up well until then, began to weep most bitterly and inconsolably at seeing his mother thus upset.

There was always that bone of contention between Anne and me, and it has continued always to be so: she would go to London, and I would not have her there. In the next minute or two I must have given her ten good reasons why living in London was not a good idea; why it was impossible for me to consider it; why she, and most of all the children, would only be unhappy there. And through the dinner hour I must have given her twenty more. I spoke truly. I told not a single lie to strengthen the case against London; I had no need to do so, for I knew the city to be horribly expensive, morally corrupt, violent, dangerous, unhealthy, crowded, and altogether bad, bad, bad.

Susanna, the eldest of the children, listened during dinner with deep, serious eyes to my bill of particulars against the city, understanding most, though perhaps not quite all, of what I said. And when at last I had done, she directed at me a most searching stare and asked how, if it were indeed so bad, I could endure the pain of living there—or childish words to that effect.

"Yes," said Anne in agreement with her daughter, "I had wondered so myself."

Then did I patiently explain to Susanna that which I had already told her mother: that it was because of the work which I did.

"And what sort of work is that?" Susanna inquired.

"Writing plays and acting in them," I explained.

"What are plays? What is acting?" Et cetera. Once the curiosity of a child was brought to life, it was as a ravening beast which consumed all in sight or hearing; it certainly ate up the rest of our evening.

I fear that neither Anne nor I was sincere with regard to our reasons. Anne implied, if she did not actually state, that it was for myself alone as husband and father that I was missed by her and by the children; and that it was solely for this reason that she wished to join me in London with our children. Yet I had known for long that she nursed a desperate desire to leave Stratford-upon-Avon, to go to London, to see the great world. I do believe that if I had not married her, she would have gone off to the city on her own, and probably wound up as one of Henslowe's whores—or worse.

And just as Anne was not entirely frank with me, I was less than honest with her about my own reasons for wishing her to remain in Stratford. I enjoyed my separate life in London and wished to keep it secret from her. If Anne and the children were with me, I should have to do without my male companions, my evenings at the Duck and Drake, my nights at the World's End. I should have to give up Kit altogether. As I had no intention of doing without, then it was certain to me that Anne must stay in Stratford. I could not, at that moment, think of a single man of the London theater, who had with him a wife and child, though doubtless there are a few today.

Owing to this slightly deceitful discussion, I had not great hopes for the obligatory exercise of our conjugal rights—yet she gave me something of a surprise. As soon as the children were tucked away in their beds, prayers said (she was most punctillio in this), and the last cup of water brought to bedside,

Anne took me behind the curtain to our marriage bed and set about purposefully to strip herself naked.

When she stood before me as she was born, she gave me a queer, twisted smile and spake to me thus: "Will, I know not whether you keep mistress or whore with you there in London, but if you do, then I shall this night make you forget her. Just see if I don't."

And that indeed was what she did. She left me gasping for breath, tied in knots, drained of seed thrice over. Indeed, she played the more aggressive role, nor did that prick my pride in the least; *quite* the contrary. We played our games in bed so long and so agreeably well that it was near dawn when at last we fell together into a deep sleep, wrapped together, each in the arms of the other. My last glimpse before dropping off to sleep revealed her as that young woman who had first tempted me there along the garden path. Six years and three children had not aged her in the least.

I woke next morning to the smell of cooking and was given a fair feast before setting off for the inn, where the London coach would stop. Before leaving Anne and the children, I took her strongly in my arms, embraced and kissed her, and gave unto her my promise that next time I came, it would be for a proper visit—that is, one of some duration.

"How long will you stay?"

"That I cannot say exact. It will depend upon when I come."

"Then when will that be?"

"Anne, I cannot fix it so, but I promise I shall come as soon as ever is possible."

Thus satisfied, she lifted the children up to me, one by one, that they might receive and bestow parting kisses. Then did she grasp me in her arms and embrace me once again.

"Make it soon," she whispered in my ear.

With that, we parted. I shouldered my travel bag and, with a wave, set off down the path which led me eventually to Henley

Street, the inn, and the post coach to London. Though understandably wearied by our exertions of the night before, I was nevertheless filled with a great sense of well-being as I went my way. While I did not comprehend this fully, I had a sense of what became much clearer to me later on: that these visits to Stratford would become of more and more importance to me as the years went by.

All my efforts to avoid military service went for naught. I had not been back but a few weeks when Tom Watson, who had been given a captain's commission in some Earl's regiment of militia, came by to collect Kit for service, promising him a commission, as well. As I helped Kit gather up such articles of clothing and necessaries as he ought to take along with him, Watson looked me up and down and decided upon the moment that I might as well come along, too.

"Are you offering me a commission?" I asked him.

"Go to," said he. "What have you done to deserve one?"

Rather than parade my accomplishments before him (which, in any case, would not have impressed him greatly), I thought it best to decline his invitation.

"You misunderstand me," said Watson. "What I offered was no polite invitation, but rather an order. You have no choice in the matter. You may consider yourself pressed into service. And if you object too strenuously, young Will, then I shall have those two great oafs out on the porch truss you up and toss you into the cart below."

At that Kit Marlowe laughed with delight. He told me later that the wretched expression upon my face was what had then so greatly amused him.

Having no choice in the matter, I submitted with fair grace, gathered up my things and made ready to go. I took with me no other book but Holinshed. It was, I admit, Kit's copy, and I asked no permission of him to take the book, yet he would not need it whilst writing of that Levantine Jew—and besides, he did not see me slip it into my bag.

After moving us here and there up and down the Channel coast, a few hundred of us found ourselves under tents in a great field outside Tilbury town. Neither Marlowe nor Watson was with me there; I was in amongst the dregs of Southwark and London. The low quality of my companions did vex and distress me. If I were to die, I would that it were with my own kind. Yet there was no question of dying lest that be a death of dreary *ennui*. There was naught to do but run up and down the hillocks in formation and receive instruction in the handling of a pike. It was a dangerous enough weapon, true enough, yet would have been of little use against a line of Spanish harquebus. Thank God we were never put to the test. I believe I should have perished altogether had it not been for Holinshed in my pack.

The closest we came to combat was when, in early August, the Spanish Armada came up the coast with the Sea Dogs in pursuit. What we heard first was the sinister sound of thunder under a clear blue sky. We were puzzled as, through the day, the thunder grew louder and lasted into the night. At last word came down to us from the officers who were quartered in Tilbury that what we heard was the cannonade delivered by our ships against theirs. If the running battle continued at the same speed and intensity, they would be opposite us sometime during the next day, so we must be ready to move, should they try a landing.

When this was announced I fair pissed myself in fear. Yet during the night the sky in the east unexpectedly lit red, and we muttered amongst ourselves, trying to suppose just what it was should cause this strange state. We later heard that it was on that night that the fireships were launched from the shore and into the Armada, causing fire, confusion, and great panic among the Spanish. Then did they pass on beyond us and escape north into a great storm.

It was only then, long after the danger had passed, that a most peculiar sight appeared in our camp. A woman rode in, surrounded by an escort that numbered near a hundred (I spied Kit and Tom Watson among them). She was dressed in a manner most outlandish, wearing armor which was burnished so bright that it glistened and shone in the summer sun. She reined in and took her place atop the highest hillock in the field. There, well shielded by her bodyguard from the gathering crowd of militia men, she made a speech. I heard that it was meant to inspire us to do battle with the invaders. And no doubt it would have inspired some—those who were able to hear—yet most caught only a few words out of the many, and I, who stood in the farthest rank from the hillock, heard none at all.

Then, having shouted thus against the north wind, she waved her goodbye and trotted off on her steed to the cheers of all who had heard her—which was not a great number. Had they known that it was their Sovereign, Queen Elizabeth, who had just appeared before them, they would all have cheered quite lustily whether they had heard or no.

I never liked the woman, nor did I hold her in great respect. Even on those occasions which were to come when she would applaud works from my pen, I could not find it in me to be much more than polite in my expressions of gratitude. She was brutal to the Catholics, cold to Francis Drake, who had saved her island realm from the Spanish, and later on, a betrayer of Essex; she was altogether a dangerous woman to know.

After the great hurly-burly of the Armada was done, we were free to hand in our pikes and return to London. Kit was there in the room we shared, and had been for several days, when I at last entered after an absence of more than a month. We exchanged stories of our experiences in the militia, and it became evident that his were neither more exciting, nor more interesting than mine; all that could be said for them was that they were passed in greater comfort and better company.

It seemed to me that we adjusted to our former life together fairly well—except as lovers. Whatever pleasure we had given, one to the other, we now counted as gone. We neither argued, nor discussed it. We simply accepted, knowing that without it we would soon part company. I wondered which of us should leave—probably I, since the room was first his, and since it was that I had refused him thrice. For the nonce, however, we got on well, until some months on an event took place which long after did puzzle me near as much as, at the time, it had afrighted me.

As it happened, I had won a role in Kit's play of Barabas, the Jew. Rehearsals were to begin a day in the future. He and I walked together up Hog Lane in the direction of the Curtain theater. As I remember, he was relating to me his views on the part I was to play (Ferneze, governor of Malta, as I am now certain). I paid him the tribute of listening closely to what he said, for though, as an actor, I was inclined to feel that once the role had come into the player's hands, it belonged to him as truly as it did to the poet, I was also poet enough to believe that what was written by him would always be his own. To put it differently, I was of two minds on the matter: the player and the poet struggled within me. Thus I thought it best to hear Kit out, though I was also determined to form my own thoughts in the matter. After all, this was to be my first venture upon the London stage, and I wanted all to go right.

So intently did I concentrate upon what was said to me by him that I failed to notice the figure who stepped out before us from a space between two houses as if to confront us. Kit Marlowe certainly noticed, however. Though he did not draw his sword most immediate, his hand went to its hilt. He stopped about twelve feet from the figure who now blocked our way.

"So it is you," said Kit to him. "Will you let us pass?"

"Not without having a go at you," said the young man who, leaving no doubt as to his intentions, drew his sword with his right hand, and with his left pulled a dagger from his belt.

With a great flourish, Kit pulled his own sword from its scabbard. Then did the combatants fall to.

(I may as well say at this point that I had at that time no notion of who the young man was, nor of the nature of his quarrel with Kit. Though I discovered later that his name was William Bradley and his father owned an inn in High Holborn, I never learned why the two fought so bitterly.)

I had never before seen a duel of this sort. Immediately I fell back, lest I be sliced or skewered by some errant thrust. A group formed round them, most of them bolder than I, for they crowded in close and shouted encouragement and comments to first one and then the other. If I had never seen such a duel, I had certainly never seen Kit in such an action. Yet I had always assumed that he was most capable in his own defense. Still, the young man, Bradley, appeared to be more than a match for him. He was the younger, taller, and apparently the stronger of the two. He whirled about the narrow circle, thrusting with his sword, feinting with his dagger. It was all that Kit could do to parry his opponent's fast-moving blade. I feared for his life.

Then, pushing through the crowd, shoving me aside, came a familiar figure: it was indeed Tom Watson, he of the midnight visits, the captain of the militia, et cetera. He moved faster than I had ever seen him move previously, drawing his sword and slamming it down between them in a gesture apparently intended to end the hostilities. Nevertheless young Bradley would not be so easily deterred.

Looking at Watson, and evidently recognizing him, he called out, "Ah, now you've come. Then I will have a bout with you."

With a wild swing of his sword, Bradley drove Kit away, sending him stumbling back into the ditch which ran down one side of the lane. Immediately did he turn his attention to Watson, pressing him back so swiftly and aggressively that with little difficulty he inflicted a slight wound up on the right shoulder of the older man. The spectators would do naught to impede their sport. They cheered and bet upon the outcome.

Meanwhile, as Tom Watson labored to keep his opponent at a safe distance, Kit had managed to creep round to the rear of young Bradley. What was his intent? Surely not to stab him in the back.

No, not quite—yet his tactic proved nearly as effective. He came as near as he dared, a distance of about ten feet, and shouted a loud warning at Bradley's back.

"Look out!"

Then did Kit run rearward to an even safer distance. Bradley turned back to discover whence came the cry. Seeing only Kit behind him, he turned back to do further battle with Watson—too late. Watson, seeing his opportunity, advanced quickly upon Bradley—ran at him, he did—and buried his sword six inches into the latter's chest. Bradley fell dead then and there. In less than five minutes a constable was present and took the two survivors off to Newgate.

XII

She has been here—indeed here, *inside New Place. Of this I am quite certain. I returned home from my afternoon walk round the town and found the door open. (Well, not "open," quite, but unlocked, leaving the house accessible to any and all who might wish to come in for a visit.) If it were open to any and all, then why am I so certain that the invader was none but Goody Bromley? Why, because I had not laid eyes upon her at all during the day. It had become her habit to pursue me on my afternoon strolls, shouting things at me and about me for all of Stratford to hear. Yet except for that first occasion when I exchanged a few words with her, I have successfully managed to ignore her. The people of the town look upon me with rueful smiles of sympathy, and I pull the sort of long-suffering face that would have done justice to a saint. In this way, I created a store of good will for myself amongst the townsmen upon which I might wish to draw sometime in the future. Yet upon this day I received no such looks of sympathy, nor did I add to my store of good will, for Goody Bromley did not trail me, chanting my name, nor did she call after me her childish rhymes. She was nowhere about. I went without escort.*

But mark this well, Will: She could have been hiding in your copse, pushing aside the bush branches that she might spy to see when I would emerge. (It was Anne's practice to leave earlier in the day to assist one or the other of our daughters in their day's work.) Still, how would she, how could she, enter through a locked door? And then came the answer, clear and simple as could be: she was of Satan's party—in short, a witch. The notion had occurred to me before, yet I had pushed it from my mind, thinking it too far-fetched to be seriously considered. I, who had thought myself so much more clever and worldly-wise than these benighted indwellers of Warwickshire, had come round at last to their way of thinking, convinced at last that the pitiful creature who was thought to be a witch, was truly a witch. In a way, it seemed that her base state was perhaps the best possible disguise. If indeed she had wisdom and powers given her by the Great Fiend, then what better way to hide them than to go about as one bereft of human sense and dignity. Yet the powers are there to call upon whenever they are needed. Did not the Devil tempt Eve from paradise? Has he not brought wars, pestilence, and famine to the nations of the world from the beginning of time? And having done all that, could he not impart to one of his minions the proper spell for unlocking a locked door? Of course he could. Opening such a door would be no challenge at all to him, nor to one of his disciples.

Yet how, apart from her absence from her usual place behind me (no proper proof at all), can I be so certain that it was Goody Bromley who entered New Place and not a burglar with some special talent as a picklock?

There are two reasons for this, chiefly, and the first of them is this: she left her smell behind. At some earlier point in this writing (I believe it occurred in my account of her first pursuit of me through the streets of Stratford) I attempted to describe that smell which seemed to me then, as it does today, altogether unique—not foul, as I expected, but earthy. Yet that does it scant justice. Ah, now I remember that I also called it "eastern." That, I believe, is nearer to the mark, for I was reminded of something in my past when first I came close enough to sniff the smell of Goody Bromley—and that something, I later realized, was naught but Raffaela. She, born in

Venice, was ever familiar with the aromas of the East. There was one scent she favored above all others; I know not its name, though from India it came—or so said she—and so pungent was it that once smelled it would take residence in the nostrils for an entire day—or night. Yes, there was much of that in the air when I entered New Place late this afternoon. What was I to think but that Goody Bromley had thus paid me a visit?

My second reason for believing this so is not perhaps so firmly founded, yet it is nevertheless frightening in its implications. As I roamed through New Place, with that peculiar smell all about me, surveying our possessions to see what, if any, of our valuables had been taken. In the cupboard I counted our stock of silver plates and the eating pieces—knives, forks, et cetera—and found that nothing had been taken, or even moved. Upstairs I took the strong box from its hiding place and opened it, even reassured myself by counting all the coins therein and tallying their worth together; all was in order. And so on, through the house—until I came to the room wherein I now sit, writing in this manuscript, by now so much longer than any piece of work I had ever previously undertaken. It was out and open upon the desk. Had I left it so? Were the pages so disordered? And if this were not enough, I went up to the bedroom, looked within my closet and found that my spare codpiece was missing. That did, upon reflection, send through me a shiver of something quite like terror—as indeed it should have done.

Though what I have written so far should make it most plain that I count myself no expert in the black arts, I have learned enough through Marlowe and other sinister sources to know that all spells and such manner of enchantment directed toward a specific individual do require something belonging to that individual to be in the least effective. And I have heard it said that to be truly *efficacious, such an object or item should be worn or used next to the skin and should be of a personal nature. What then could be more personal to any man than his codpiece?*

At just about the time that I discovered that the codpiece was missing and had begun to reflect upon it, I heard a door at the other end of the house open and shut. Had Goody Bromley returned? I looked round me for a weapon of some sort—any sort! Not in the habit of arming myself in my own home, I knew not what I might use against an intruder. I had no dagger about, no sword nor club. Ah, but the fireplace yielded a poker. I grabbed it up, took a station just inside the doorway, and raised it above my head. Footsteps approached. My heart beat within me so loud that I wondered, could it be heard in the hall? Still I waited. I was just about to strike when she burst into song—and what is more, she knew to sing, Lillibulero," Anne's favorite tune—and sing it, what is more, in Anne's voice. What witch's trick was this? Just as I started the downward arc with the poker, a most troubling thought occurred: What if, indeed, it really was Anne who was about to enter the room? I did then manage to check my swing just as she came through the doorway.

"Will?" *she cried aloud, shrinking back in terror—or its counterfeit.*

"Anne?" Indeed the figure before me, crouching in fear, looked like her. She was dressed as Anne was when she had left that morning, and the voice was, as I said, like unto hers. "Is it truly you?"

"It is! Of course it is. Who had you thought me else?"

"The witch," said I.

"Witch? Who do you mean?"

"Why, Goodwife Bromley, of course. How many witches do we have in Stratford?"

"Not a single one, I would say. But why do you think that poor creature a witch? What has she done to you of harm?"

"She pursues me on my walks and shouts rudely at me."

"So I have heard, yet I have also heard that you take her

rudeness as the gentleman you are. I hear you praised and applauded for it. Why now do you think her an agent of evil? What did she to you?"

"She came into this house whilst we two were out of it. She is a burglar."

"You saw her?"

"Well . . ."—I hesitated—"no."

"Then how can you think that of her? She has no sense, Will. She's to be pitied."

"She has the sense that Satan gave her. She knew enough to cast a spell to open a locked door."

"You truly believe that, do you?" Anne looked at me in a manner I can best describe as dismayed. "Which door was it?"

"The front door, of course. I would call that the proper door by which the master of the house should enter and leave, would you not?"

"If that be so, I would say that the proper door for the mistress of the house to use entering and leaving would be the back door, that which leads up from the kitchen. It is that one I use and have always used. And I never lock it after me."

At that I was quite dumbstruck. I could scarce believe the words I had just heard from her mouth. At last, after struggling a bit, I managed to put together my thoughts, and then my words.

"And how long has this been your practice?" I asked her.

"I have ever done it so."

"How could you? How could you not lock the door after you? We have things of value here. I . . . well . . . perhaps you do not have a key? Has it been lost?"

"No, there is one somewhere about." She then looked narrowly upon me as if in suspicion. "Will, are you sure you locked the front door after you?"

"Of course I am. When I lock it, I put the key away in my purse, and you see?" I rummaged for a long, awkward moment *in my purse, yet could not find it for the life of me. "It doesn't seem to be here," I said at last, giving up the search.*

"No, and I'll tell you why," said Anne. "Just before I came up the stairs and you came so close to braining me with that poker, I happened to notice the key was stuck in the lock on the inside. Go down, and you can see for yourself." She waited, hands on hips—a challenging posture—for my response. It was some time coming.

"That proves nothing. There were other proofs that she was here."

"Oh? And what were they?'

"She left her smell all over the house. Just sniff the air. You'll find it quite heavy in this room."

She did as I charged her, walking about, turning her head first left and then right, working her nose like the very hound on a hunt.

"I smell nothing," she declared.

"But you must smell it."

"Nothing." *Said with a shrug.*

She could be quite the most infuriating woman in all of England. The odor was all about us at that very moment.

"Well," said I, "the smell is *here, whether you will or no. And it is here because she came into this room and stole my spare codpiece."*

"Your codpiece?" She laughed. "Why should she do that?"

"So that she might use it to cast a spell upon me."

"Perhaps I should have told you," said Anne, "but 'twas me took it. I threw the smelly thing out. I washed it over and over, and I couldn't get the smell of piss out of it, so out it went. I've been meaning to make a new one for you. I'll get to it this evening. I promise."

And so she will, of course, and I cannot say that she lied in these matters that we discussed, not in any way jot, or tittle. Anne would not lie, I'm sure. Nevertheless, I remain sure as can be that on this day Goody Bromley paid me a visit.

It is one thing to speak of a "smell" and quite another to attempt to recreate in words a "stink." As I return now to the body of this narrative, I realize that I must now accept that burden in describing Newgate Gaol. The stink of the place is what one remembers best, yet it is that which is most difficult to put into words. Still, I can do naught but try.

Newgate, it seems, is near as old as London itself. None I have asked could give me a satisfactory guess as to its age. Thus, for untold centuries its notorious stink has permeated the rocks and wood of the place so that when the wind blows south it can be smelled all the way to the Thames. To enter Newgate, as I did on the occasion I shall describe, is to experience far worse. The occasion to which I shall now call your attention was my single visit to Christopher Marlowe, him with whom I had shared room and life for over two years. Though I felt that my time with Kit was near ended, I knew I must see him after I had heard the results of the coroner's inquest. Witnesses testified that it was the young man, Bradley, who was the aggressor, and 'twas he who had been given ample opportunity to break off the fight. All of which was true, but naught was made of Kit's action to distract Bradley that he might prove an easier target for Tom Watson; I wondered at that. In any case, Watson was charged with homicide in self-defense and returned to Newgate to stand trial at a later date. Marlowe was charged with nothing at all but would remain in gaol until persons could be found who would post a bond guaranteeing that, if released, he would return to Watson's trial as a witness. I found one such, Richard Kitchin, a lawyer (also from Corpus Christi College, Cambridge) who agreed to look for another. This then was the situation when I made my first visit to Newgate: I had a report to make to him; I also had questions to ask.

Even before I entered the prison I discovered the principle upon which it operates. When admitted through its gates, I was stopped and asked whom I wished to visit. Since Kit was in no wise a special prisoner, he was kept in one of the common cells, the first to the right as one entered, as it happened.

"That'll cost you a shilling, it will," said the gatekeeper. "If your business with the prisoner takes longer than the quarter part of an hour, then you must pay more."

I assured him that a quarter of an hour was all that I should need as I pressed the shilling into his palm.

"Well and good," said he, "now listen close. Jack here will lead you to the cell and put the prisoner before you. He will then come collect you when your time is done. Tuppence is what's usual for him."

Jack presented himself, a pink-cheeked lad of seventeen or eighteen, a sort of apprentice to the gatekeeper. There was something of a resemblance between the two. It occurred to me that Jack might have been son or nephew. Whatever his relation, he wished to make a good impression upon me, for as we walked together to the entrance of the prison he kept up a steady stream of comment. Wasn't it a fine day? Did I believe that the wind from the west betokened rain? Et cetera.

Having thus ingratiated himself, he held me a moment at the entrance that he might deal with one of the harsh realities of life inside the walls of Newgate Gaol.

"Now, your man, Marlowe, he's a wondrous smart fellow, but he's in a bit of difficulty just at the moment."

"And what is that?" I asked, all innocent.

"It's this, you see: he spent all his coin getting free of his irons and fetters. Now he has naught with which to improve his diet."

"I take it the normal Newgate diet is insufficient?"

"It's not much good for nothin' but starvin'."

"Well, I should not want him to starve. What would it cost to supplement what he now receives?"

"Sup-plement? Is that like makin' it bigger?"

"Bigger *and* better."

"Ah, well, for a florin your man will get fat on all we serve him. For a shilling he'll keep his weight steady."

"Let's keep him as he is, shall we? I shall give him a shilling and he can pass it on to you himself."

"Well . . . that might work so." Yet he seemed dubious. "Best would be if you gave it straight to me. See, if they saw him getting money, they might not let him keep it. Fact is, they probably wouldn't."

"Oh? Who is this 'they' you speak of?"

"The other prisoners in that common cell—they're a vicious lot."

It seemed likely to me that that young Jack was simply trying to take me for all that he could. After all, I had no guaranty there would be any improvement in Kit's diet. It was, in fact, doubtful. "Nevertheless," said I, "you must allow me to do it as I see fit."

"Indeed, sir," said he with a polite little bow, "as you will."

His response surprised me. I expected to hear further arguments, blandishments, and inducements—yet they were not forthcoming. Instead:

"If you will then follow me, sir?"

And I obeyed, thinking myself prepared for what lay ahead. Had I not smelled the inside of the gaol through its very stones? Did the noise of the place not penetrate the very door which Jack now reached to open? Still, I was in no wise prepared for what lay behind that door.

The noise of the place—shouting, screaming, laughing, sobbing—hit me with a powerful force which was like unto some physical barrier, a wall perhaps. Yet there was no sense of walking *through* the wall, for there was no far side to be reached: simply more noise—louder, it seemed, with each step. It was truly what they mean who talk of a "bedlam." And I would know, for I have been within the walls of St. Mary's of Bethlehem; I have heard the mad, lunatic extremes of noise; I have witnessed the fantastical limits of mad behavior for which Bedlam is justly notorious. Yet I daresay that there in Newgate the supposedly sane had quite outdone those certificated as insane.

And now to the stink—and what a stink it was! It would be well to say that the place smelled of shit and piss (defecation and urination, if you prefer) and have done with it. Yet that does it no justice—not by half. It is age, I reiterate, which gives this foul odor its fundamental foulness. Were it simply old, the smell would have dissipated long ago. Yet each day of each year, perhaps each hour of each day, the supply of human filth was replenished. Why, when we stopped before the proper cell—dark and large as a cavern it was—I could see fresh turds upon the floor just the other side of the bars. I know not if this be worth noting, nor even if it be truly reasonable, but the great stink of the place in all its murky nastiness had something of the darkest sort of purple about it; it was as if the odor itself had tinted the entire scene. It was thus indescribable in ordinary terms. Leave it then that the stink stank.

There was such an ungodly hub-bub that I wondered how Jack, the young gaoler, would manage to call Kit out that he and I might talk together. Jack, however, had a surprise for me. He pulled from his pocket a whistle of no great size and let forth three great blasts upon it. Then was I quite amazed that the multitude behind the bars quietened down most immediate; there were whisperings and mutterings among them as they crowded forward curiously, yet now could young Jack be heard.

"Christopher Marlowe," he shouted out, "step up to the bars, for you have a visitor."

Then, from the farthest reaches of the great cell, there appeared to be a bit of movement. A figure came through the crowd which proved to be Kit. He looked frail and wasted already, or so it seemed to me, and he had been in Newgate but two days. Perhaps indeed it was the food had made him ill.

"Is this your man?" Jack asked me.

I nodded.

"Well and good then. I'll be back in the quarter part of an hour." And so saying, he turned and moved away right quickly.

Kit came forward to me. Most of those who had showed interest in the interruption returned to their former concerns, and soon it was that the former din of voices was nearly as before. Some few of the prisoners, however, stayed close and made to eavesdrop. What then did they expect to hear?

"You're looking well," said I to Kit, lying to him as one might to a sick friend.

"I doubt it," said he.

"I have good news for you."

"That would be welcome indeed."

I made my report to him. He attended closely, as did the three or four who had remained to listen. They made Kit ill at ease. He cast glances at them whilst I gave him the details of my efforts to raise bail for him—whom I had seen, what had been said, and which of them had actually agreed to help.

"Ah, good Richard," said Kit of his benefactor. "I teased him unmercifully regarding his poor Latin, yet he of all them proved willing."

"He said that he had another in mind who might indeed help but thought it best that he, rather than I, approach him."

"Did he mention his name to you?"

"Yes, as it happened, he did. It was Humphrey Rowland. He said you knew him, but not as well as he did."

Kit rubbed his chin in thought. "True," said he, "I do know him, yet I would not . . ." A gesture of dismissal, and then: "Ah well, what does it matter? If Richard can persuade him to come up with the other half of the bail, I would not mind if he were Satan himself."

"You forget," said I, "that you proved to me that no such exists."

"I believe you hold that against me still," said he with sudden anger. "That was scarcely more than a joke, Will."

"But *something* more than that, you admit," said I, matching him anger for anger.

"All I intended or hoped for was to free you of that burden of guilt which you carry about with you wheresomever you go. And if not free you, then to ease that burden somewhat."

"You chose a strange way to go about it—raising the devil!"

This had an immediate effect upon our listeners. They pushed forward, eager to hear more, to miss nothing, whilst at the same time Kit was signaling me that I was to drop the matter. Drop it I did. Then did we both fall silent, mayhap embarrassed at our brief loss of control. It was an awkward moment.

Kit eyed those who hovered so near, and then quite wisely he changed the subject. "How do the rehearsals go?"

"Wondrous well," said I, "though Alleyn grumbles that he must play so evil a character—and a Jew in the bargain."

"But 'tis by far the biggest role."

"So I have reminded him. That always serves to quieten him down."

And at that we did join in laughter, for the vanity of leading actors, no matter how able, is ever a matter of amusement to those who write the plays. Yet of a sudden Kit left off laughing and looked at me rather sharply.

"You said *you* reminded him?"

"Uh . . . yes," said I, looking ahead and liking not what I saw.

"By what authority? Who now supervises the rehearsals?"

"Well . . ."—I hesitated, betraying my unease—"I do."

"How did that come about?"

"How indeed! You are obviously in no position to supervise. The rehearsals must go forward. *The Jew of Malta* must open in two weeks' time. Someone had to take over in your stead. You understand that, don't you, Kit?"

"Who better than my bed-mate, eh? Why, I wager you told them that I let you know just how I wanted things done, didn't you, Will?"

"No!" I denied it most emphatically.

"But with hints and implications, a wink and a nudge, you managed to create just such an impression. After all, you, too, are a poet, Will, and have written plays. Who would know better?"

"Well," said I, a good deal less certainly, "they were free to infer what they liked." Forsooth, he had me to rights. He knew me far too well to suppose I would claim boldly to speak for him direct. Indeed no, that was not my manner, at all. For me, it was always a matter of presenting myself in the right light, inviting the invitation, and then modestly stepping forward to accept it.

"I should not have bothered to ask," said Kit. "It was all there in your face."

Was he trying to extract an apology from me? He'd get nothing of the kind, nothing at all. I noted that the eavesdroppers had drifted away, no doubt bored by theater talk of which they understood little or nothing. This, it seemed to me, was the proper moment to change the subject.

"Just in passing, Kit," said I in a neutral manner, "what was that fight in Hog Lane about? Did you even know that fellow Bradley? What had he against you and Watson?"

"Did someone tell you to ask me that?"

"No, certainly not," said I, speaking the truth. In the space of two days he had grown over-suspicious. Yet who would not there in Newgate?

He studied my face a moment, then did he say to me: "I fear I must disappoint you, Will. Yet you must believe me when I say that it is for your own good. There are truly some things it is best for you not to know."

"Hmmm," said I, pondering right judiciously, "my memory tells me that I have heard that from you before."

"And so you will again if you insist upon asking such questions."

He could, you see, be quite exasperating when he took unto

himself such airs. Seeing little chance for ordinary discourse with Kit in such a state, I found myself wishing that I might leave a little early. I began looking this way and that, wondering when Jack, the young guard, might come to show me out of this disgusting place. Then was I reminded of the matter he and I had discussed just outside the door. I turned back to Kit and found him looking off to his left in an abstract manner, as if he, too, wished our interview to be ended. Well, in a short time it would be.

"The guard who brought me along said the food here is such that one such as yourself might be in some danger of starving," said I with a smile to Kit, attempting to make a joke of it, "but that for a little money—"

At the mention of that single word, 'money,' those who had hung so close before rushed back again with more of their fellows, crowding Kit and hanging upon the bars, their hollow eyes alive with greed. They sensed that coins would be passed through the bars. I stood staring at them with my hand in my purse, amazed at such a display, afraid to draw out a single coin that it might be grabbed by one of the hands that reached through the bars. They called and whined at me for pence and food.

Kit, by this time, had retreated to the rear of the rabble. He caught my eye by waving briskly at me. Then, cupping his hands, he shouted over the pleas of the prisoners.

"Give it to the guard," cried he. "You can trust him."

I nodded my understanding and agreement.

Then did he wave once more and return to the murky dimness from which he had emerged. I then felt a tug at my sleeve and gave a start, yet when I saw that it was none but Jack, the guard, beckoning me away, I followed gladly. Nothing was said between us, however, until we emerged into the daylight and away from the stink.

"Well," said he to me, "did you have a good chat with your friend, Marlowe?"

"Quite good, thank you, and while I think of it, he advised me to pass on to you the florin as what it will cost to supplement his diet."

"Ah, the florin, is it? You've decided to fatten him up a bit."

"He looks a bit sickly, I fear."

"Well, a better diet will do him naught but good."

As we talked, I had been rummaging through my purse for a coin of the right denomination. Finding it, I offered it; and it was accepted with thanks.

"Your man, Marlowe, he's quite popular, an't he?"

"How do you mean that?" I asked.

"He's got two more at the gate waiting to see him. That's three in a day. More than most get in a year. Come along, and I'll show you. Maybe you knows them."

I followed along, thinking to see Richard Kitchin, who was standing surety for Kit, perhaps with Rowland; they may have come to report that the matter of bail was now settled and that Kit was free to go. Indeed I hoped that it was so.

Having thus supposed, imagine my disappointment in finding Robert Greene and Thomas Kyd there at the gate house. Though I had little against Kyd, I could not abide Greene's smirking air of superiority and the scorn he displayed so openly since he had discovered me pilfering from Kit's *Tamburlaine.* I counted every encounter with him a trial. There were few I should like less to meet.

"Ah," said he when he caught sight of me, "if it's not the crow."

"Crow?" I echoed him. "Why do you name me such?"

"Because the crow is a bird that steals from other birds and can learn to talk without ever knowing the sense of what he says."

At that Kyd chuckled and grinned like a schoolboy. I decided he was no better than Greene, and he proved that to me the moment he opened his mouth.

"You made a great, foul jumble of my *Titus*—or that is what

I have heard. I would not pay the penny it would have cost to see it."

"Your *Titus,* is it?" I laughed merrily as I was able, then sobered sudden to say: "Ah, but perhaps you have it right. In spite of all the work I gave to it, there was naught could be done to rescue it from its plot—and that, as we know, was yours—and Seneca's, too, of course. The groundlings liked it well enough, though."

My thrust seemed to wound him deep. I know not why, for it was no more than the truth.

"And as for you, Greene," I continued, "you are naught but a prose writer—and a writer of pamphlets, at that. A poet's work is beyond you and indeed always will be. You rail against me, calling me a crow, but you, knowing nothing of nature, have chosen the wrong bird. Say 'magpie,' rather, for I, as all poets, steal—each to build his own nest."

(As I write that from memory, I may have changed a word or two, but the substance is nevertheless what I have recorded here. It is fair proof that even though deprived by circumstance of a university education, I could have bested any of these "university wits," Marlowe included, in argument or choice of language. And I blush not to say it!)

Having effectively disarmed both with my own wit, I saw no need to remain and listen to them hiss and growl. Had we been permitted to carry weapons within the walls of the gaol, I should have by then been facing their drawn swords, no doubt.

Jack and the gatekeeper looked ill upon our quarrel, though they understood little of it, and took that moment to separate us. As the gatekeeper propelled me through the open gate, Jack took charge of the others, grasped each firmly by the arm, and swept them toward the gray walls and the high arching entranceway of the gaol.

Christopher Marlowe spent a total of thirteen days in Newgate. Bail was promised by the two I have named, but then one of them—Rowland, I believe—had difficulty getting together his half of the amount. Papers were to be signed, et cetera; there were the usual delays, and so it was near two weeks before Kit properly saw the sun.

(Thomas Watson fared even worse. He had to wait over three months before his case was heard. Then, even though the criminal court agreed with the self-defense verdict of the coroner, he had to wait another two months for a full pardon to be issued. Those five months in Newgate near broke his health, and he a reasonably young man of thirty-four.)

Because I had done what Kit had asked of me in locating those who stood bail for him, and since we two did not get on well at our single meeting there in Newgate, I decided there was no need for me to return. Let Greene and Kyd keep him company. With all this then I was in no wise surprised when upon the day of Kit's release, I received a visit fairly early in the morning. It all began with a loud knock upon the door. I, who was not at that moment fully dressed, ran to the door and asked to know who it was had knocked.

"Tom Kyd," came the strong response from beyond the door.

"Are you alone?"

"I am."

Accepting his word on that, I threw open the door and found him, as promised, alone on my doorstep; he held out to me a letter.

"What have you there?" I asked.

"It's from Kit," said he.

Without another word, I took the letter, broke the seal, read it where I stood.

> Will—[it began]
>
> Please oblige me by allowing Thomas Kyd to collect my books, papers, and clothes. All the rest you may keep, though in truth most of the furniture may belong to the landlord. I'm a bit vague on that.

This means, of course, that I shall not be returning to the room we have shared these many months. In fact, I am now ensconced with Kyd in his new place in Aylesbury Street. If any come looking for me, you may tell them that—but use discretion. Since you are the most discreet of mates, I shall trust you completely in this.

I should like to have stayed on with you, but in truth it became a bit dull. You work far too much, Will, more than I could and certainly more than I should want to do. I hear only good from the rehearsals of my "Jew" play, and so it seems that you filled in for me quite well. I shall be in the audience tomorrow night, and so you shall hear from me if I am displeased. I do not expect to be.

Yours,
Kit

P.S. Thank you for all the work on my behalf in putting together my bail,

P.P.S. You may keep my copy of Holinsheds' *Chronicles*. You get more use from it than I do.

There was silence then for a moment as I lowered the letter and looked steadily at Kyd. I set my face so as to betray no emotion.

"Surely," said I, "you do not propose to carry Kit's belongings by hand to Aylesbury Street?"

"I have a cart below."

"Then come in. I shall help you."

Stepping to the rear, I gestured him inside. He seemed taken aback by my cooperation. The expression upon his face as he stepped into the room was one of keen puzzlement. Yet I made no attempt to explain or justify my attitude.

"Let us start with the books," said I. "He has made a gift to me of the *Chronicles* of Holinshed. It is here in the letter if you wish to make sure."

I offered Kit's letter to him, but he waved it away.

"Oh no, no," said he, all eager to assure me. "Kit said you were to have something from his library."

"Then, after laying them aside, we shall begin with the top shelf and work our way down."

"Most practical."

The rest was all up and down work with no pleasure to it at all. I had done no real labor for years, and it was not long until I fell to huffing and puffing and wheezing like a baited bear in a pit. Kyd, no more accustomed to such efforts than I, was soon breathing in chorus with me. He did, however, have a bodily advantage over me. He could carry more books in his longer arms and felt called upon to prove it at each trip down the stairs. Yet in this way Kit's considerable library was disposed of in a short time.

Kyd had brought boxes in which to put the papers. Here I insisted upon going through them as he packed them away, lest my own be swept up with them. There were but two boxes filled when we finished and a single box of clothing, as well. These I let him take away and then hurried to finish dressing.

On this day the last rehearsal of Kit's play, *The Jew of Malta* took its place. It would not have been at all proper had I been late. 'Twas I, after all, who had presided at all previous rehearsals, taking Kit's place, to the satisfaction of all. My acting, in the role of Ferneze, governor of Malta, seemed to surprise all, most specially when I played the part in full makeup, adding twenty years at least to my true age. There be no need to dwell overmuch upon that last rehearsal. Leave it that all went well and that Mr. James Burbage, the master of the company, applauded our efforts just as I spoke the last lines of the play. Let me, rather, offer my recollections of the next day, upon which the play was first brought before the public. It proved to be a most significant event, for it was the last time that I was to see Christopher Marlowe for a considerable time, and the last time ever that I should see him under happy circumstances. It would only be fair to say that as Kit departs the drama as might be said, for an act or two, another enters to take his place, one who for a while filled a space in my life as large as Kit had done, and whose ultimate departure occasioned just as much pain. It does sometimes happen that the events of a single day can alter the course of a life. If I were to point to a single such day in my own, it would have been the one on which *The Jew of Malta* opened at The Theatre. It was not that so much happened on that day, but all that later did happen seemed to have found its beginning thereupon.

Edward Alleyn, who was called "Ned" by all who knew him, played three of Kit's heroes in turn—Tamburlaine, Faustus, and beginning on the night in question, *The Jew of Malta*. These were among many other parts he did play at The Theatre and the Curtain for the Burbage company of actors, yet it was agreed that these three were his finest roles. 'Twas on the strength of his performance in the last of these that he was invited by Henslowe to form a company of his own in Southwark to play at the Rose theater. I suppose that the point of all this history is that Ned Alleyn enjoyed a great triumph in the part of Barabas, and it led him on to greater successes still.

It should be understood, however, that his was not a triumph easily achieved. Because of the size of the role (Barabas is present in nearly every scene) and also because of its unsympathetic nature (Alleyn seemed to reject speeches and even lines which he felt would make people dislike him) he found it very difficult to master his lines. Yet I worked at him, as much as with him, and by the second week of rehearsal, he had at last begun to hold them in mind. He required prompting, and since I had a prominent part in the play I could not give it to him. For that first performance Kit Marlowe, only a day out of Newgate, was pressed into service. He prompted, just as he had done for *Tamburlaine* and *Doctor Faustus* before, and Alleyn paced about the stage, throwing his arms about, shaking his fist at fate as he waited for his next line. Thus it went through five acts. There were some awkward moments, but the audience seemed not to notice, so absorbed were they by Kit's dark poetry.

Thus it was that Kit saved the day twice o'er. Had he not prompted with the same skill he had in the first performances of *Tamburlaine* and *Faustus,* Alleyn would no doubt have been jeered off the stage. But best of all, he saved performance and production by writing a play so strong that it was proof against grievous lapses and short memories.

At play's end there was much applause and a bow to be taken. I pulled Kit out of the wings and fetched him to the front and center of the stage (which Ned Alleyn should have done), and I was pleased to hear the roar of the applause rise as he took his place; there were cheers, as well. At last the tumult stilled, then ceased altogether. I turned to Kit and took the first proper look at him I had had since the performance began, so busy was I running about, organizing the actors for the next scene, giving an eye and a touch to my makeup. Simply put, Kit looked bad—far worse than he had on the occasion of my single visit to Newgate; worse indeed than I had ever seen him. He looked so bad—thin, pale, and sick—that I did not even bother to tell him how well he looked.

"I'm glad to see you out of that hellish place," said I.

"No more than I am to *be* out of it."

"Your prompting was magnificent. I don't believe anyone in the audience even guessed at his troubles."

"Ah well," said Kit, "Ned and I are used to one another by now. I believe he finds the sound of my voice steadying. He'll be all right now. All he needs is to hear the applause and be reassured that people like him. And . . . well—" He hesitated but pressed on: "Ah, Will, I owe you much. You put together a good production in my stead. I doubt I could have done as well." He drew me close in a one-armed embrace. "Thank you." I could not but note that he still smelled foully of Newgate.

Then did he release me, and those who had been crowding round us pushed me aside to offer their congratulations to him. There were actors, and there were members of the audience, as well. Among the latter were gentlemen and ladies of quality—or perhaps better said, gentlemen of quality and their ladies.

But Kit Marlowe had not done. He had yet something to add, and he did call after me: "Will! Will!" Turning, I gave him my attention. "Your acting surprised me. You were really quite good."

Then was he lost in the swarm of well-wishers. One, however, held back. She was young, very well dressed and apparently quite pretty. My hesitation on the last point had to do with the mask which she held over her face; the entire upper half of her face was hid, so that only her eyes were visible through the holes cut in the mask. She had turned from her escort, who was dressed as a nobleman might be, and seemed to be staring at me. But I, thinking little of it and having no better place to go, proceeded backstage.

Kit's last remark, though he meant it in praise, did rankle somewhat. My acting surprised him, did it? I was really quite good, was I? I ought to be good, after all, for I'd been at it since I was sixteen. Ah, these Cambridge fellows, they do sit in judgment upon the rest of us, do they not? I should like to see Kit up there on the stage some day. He would trip over his own feet, wouldn't he? Mumble and stumble about like a Billingsgate porter, he would.

In just such a nasty mood did I arrive in the dressing room. There were but a few members of the cast inside who had preceded me there, and most of them were players of those small roles which may be parceled out two or three to an actor. They wished to be out of the theater and into the Duck and Drake as quickly as they were able—as did I. Without another thought I sat me down in front of the looking glass, lit a candle on either side of it and began the work of removing my makeup.

There came talk out in the hall of a noise and intensity so that I expected a great number to enter. Yet when they stepped inside, I saw there were no more than four—James Burbage, his son, Richard, he whom I had taken for a noble from the look of his fine apparel, and the woman in the mask who had stared at me.

Mr. Burbage led them straight to me and introduced Lord Hunsden "and his friend, Raffaela." I gave to each a deep bow in the French style and listened with a smile fixed upon my face as it was explained to the visitors that I had generously filled in for Christopher Marlowe when the poet was "indisposed," rehearsing the play and preparing the production.

"Well, you certainly did a fine job of it," said Lord Hunsden in a manner most pompous. He was old, sixty at least, and at such an advanced age it is difficult to say anything without sounding pompous.

"Meester Shake-a-speare, he is also a poet and write plays," said she to her lord and master. "Is this not so, Meester Shake-a-speare?"

"Why, yes it is," said I, brightening considerably.

"Raffaela is a great lover of the theater," said Hunsden proudly. "She sees every new play, absolutely every one." He smiled foolishly. It was obvious that the man doted upon her.

"That must keep you very busy," said I to her.

"I see one of yours. The name is *Titus Andronicus*. Very bloody." She tapped me on the shoulder with a paper which she carried rolled in her hand, as if she were dealing punishment to a naughty child.

"Too bloody?'

"No, is about Rome, and Rome was like that." She spoke in a jesting manner, as if there were some hidden meaning to it.

Then from out in the hall, I heard a great rumble and a roar. It came from none but Ned Alleyn, and the laughter that followed issued from his usual train of admirers. As he entered, boasting, Lord Hunsden and the Burbages, father and son, turned to meet him. Only Raffaela delayed.

"Perhaps we meet again, Mr. Shake-a-speare," said she with a rather mysterious smile. And once again she tapped me playfully on the shoulder. Yet this time the rolled paper, which I took to be a program, fell from her hand.

"You will take care of that for me, please?" She said it as she turned away.

"Of course I shall," said I, stooping to pick it up. Yet already she was gone.

XIII

It was an invitation to call upon her Monday morning of the coming week to discuss a matter of "mutual interest." An address in Little Gray's Inn Lane was given and a time suggested. It was unsigned, yet there was no doubt whence it had come, nor for whom it was intended.

I might have missed it entire, thinking it indeed no more than the program for that day's performance. Yet my vanity persuaded me to open it up and look once more at my name listed for the role of Ferneze, governor of Malta. As I unrolled it, I found within the program another, smaller scrap of paper whereon was written the invitation. She was still in the room as I made the discovery. I fought the desire to look in her direction and nod my assent to her proposal. It might well have been that I would look in her direction and find her protector looking in mine—and that would never do. So I wadded all together and tossed the ball in the waste bin before me, and then did I continue the task of removing my makeup.

I wondered a good deal about the note she had passed me. First of all, I asked myself who might have written it for her. Even if she were able to read, Italian was her language, was it not? That seemed odd. Who was she? Certainly not a whore off the streets; she was far too well-dressed, too sure of herself, for that. And what need would there have been for her then to wear a mask? No, she must be a courtesan, at the very least, and perhaps even the old man's mistress.

And for that matter, who was he? Lord Hunsden, of course.

Yet how important was he? Had he a position at court? I had only a vague notion of such matters of hierarchy and prestige. In the past, when I had such questions as these, Kit would answer them; none had such exact knowledge in these areas as he.

Later that evening, as I drank with the company at the Duck and Drake, I put the questions—those regarding Lord Hunsden—to Richard Burbage. He had praised me most lavishly for my role as Ferneze. Sitting next to me, he had lowered his voice a bit and muttered in my ear of how they needed me in the company.

"My father did comment most favorably upon your work," said he, "and particularly upon the way you filled in whilst Marlowe was in Newgate. Well, of course you heard what he said to those two in the dressing room. He was indeed most grateful."

"Yes, but what of those two—the old man and the girl?"

"Well, what about them?"

"Who are they? Oh, I understand he is Lord Hunsden, but has he some special eminence?"

"Certainly he has. He is Lord Chamberlain to the Queen herself. Do you know nothing of life at court?"

"Next to nothing, I fear."

"Well, you should learn, Will. All in London depend in some sense upon the Court—and we players more than most."

I did but nod, yet I realized as I did so that young Burbage had just stated one of those truths which could not be challenged. Yes, London was all-dependent upon the presence of the reigning monarch; she was the giver of boons, the bestower of favors, the granter of petitions. And yes, I should know more of life at Court—whose star was rising and whose was falling. But with Kit gone, as I believed, for good, who was there to teach me?

"And as for the woman, the girl, call her what you will," said Burbage, "well, she's no whore."

"I gleaned as much, certainly."

"She, too, is at Court in her own way—one of the Royal entertainers. A singer she is, and a player of the dulcimer. 'Tis said that the Queen herself sends for her to sing songs of consolation and ballads of love that she may be put in a proper mood. Then of course she must also entertain at all state dinners . . . the usual occasions."

"But," I offered, "she—this woman, Raffaela—she is Italian, is she not?"

"Oh, indeed—from Venice."

"Then she is Catholic," said I. "Would they allow a Catholic so near the Queen? Surely they see danger of assassination, or of spying, at least."

"Ah, that is where the Queen demonstrates to one and all just how clever she is."

"I don't quite understand."

"Don't you see? She is Italian, but she is no Catholic."

"No Catholic?" said I. "Nonsense! All Italians are Catholic."

"Not those Italians who are Jews."

He gazed at me in triumph, eyebrows raised and a silly smirk upon his face. He seemed to think that he had riddled me proper. Let him think whatever he liked; still, it seemed a most singular circumstance.

"Indeed? a Jew?" said I. "In truth, I had never met such."

"Well, forsooth, you have met one now."

"I did not know there were Jews in Italy. Are they in the Papal States? In Rome, where the Pope sits?"

"Possibly, probably." He shrugged. "Why not? I have heard, in any case, that there are many in Venice—moneylenders and the like."

"Ah yes, they escape the ban on usury, do they?"

"Since they are neither Catholic nor Protestant, nor even Christian, indeed they do."

"Interesting," said I. "Finally, to have met a Jew."

I had expected something more, something different. She was dark—darker than an Englishwoman. Not so dark as a

Moor, but no darker than I should have supposed any Italian to be—and evidently quite pretty, too. But should she not have had some distinguishing mark? Something like "Jew" emblazoned upon her forehead. No, of course not, nor would she have horns, as I had earlier heard was the rule with all her kind.

"Fascinating," said I to myself. Of a sudden did I then look forward to my meeting with her as I had not to any since my arrival in London.

"She's his mistress, you know." It was Burbage, interrupting my musing.

"What?" So abstracted was I that his intrusion had confused me somewhat. "Who is it you speak of?"

"Why, Raffaela, of course. Who did you suppose we were speaking of? She is the mistress of Lord Hunsden."

"Well, naturally," said I with a rather grand shrug. "I had not believed otherwise."

"Just so you keep it in mind," he cautioned. "You've far too excellent a future to lose it to your yard."

"Let me assure you, Richard, that I—"

He never received my lying assurances, for at that moment Christopher Marlowe did hove into view, predictably in company with Greene and Kyd. It struck me, as I viewed him approaching across the large room, how like that moment when I first met him here at the Duck and Drake was this one. He appeared in escort as I had seen him that first time following *Tamburlaine.* Yet this time he did not stop to visit our table and accept our congratulations. Without a look in our direction, the three of them walked past us toward their fellows at the farthest location, near the window.

Richard Burbage, who had risen to give Kit his congratulations was left standing and looking after the trio. It must have been embarrassing for him. That was not wise, neither for Kit, nor for Kyd, nor Greene.

Upon the Monday in question, I did not dawdle but rushed about starting early on to put a shine upon my face and a proper scrub to my body. Though I did forego a true bath, I applied water generously to my parts and used good lye soap wherever necessary. Once done, I applied sweet-smelling lotions to this place and that so by the time I had done, there was not a rude odor to be smelled anywhere on my person.

Ah, to be clean in such a way! It gave me a feeling of well-being. I took care with my clothes, rubbing and scraping them so that by the time I pulled them on, they were near as unsoiled as my body. As I walked the distance to Little Gray's Inn Lane, those I passed looked upon me in such a way as if I myself were courtier or noble; they stepped aside and sniffed me proper; the women smiled, and the men did frown.

Thus, as I walked, my feet bare touched the ground, so filled was I with anticipation. The image of her masked face played in my mind. The glimpse I had been offered of the deep cleft in her generous bosom seemed to appear before me with each step I took. And that voice of hers, so much lower than I had expected, was almost (dare I say it?) like unto that of an hermaphrodite; it played in my ears as I went, charging me with lust as I had not felt since last I lay with Anne in Stratford.

The house in Little Gray's Inn Lane may have been small, but it was, nevertheless, a house. She did not live, as I did, in a single room which was ill-lit by a single window and ill-served by tottering stairs. I later discovered what I should immediately have perceived: that the house was the property of Lord Hunsden and was hers only so long as she was his. Thus are artists (and she was that many times over) ever beholden to their patrons and women to their protectors.

Looking up and down the narrow lane, I saw that it was empty at that moment of idlers and passers-by, so I did walk swift to the door and knock loud upon it.

It was flung open in immediate response. An arm reached

out from inside and grasped one of my own. I was pulled with surprising strength into the house. For a mere fraction of a moment I feared that I had been trapped by Lord Hunsden or one of his lackeys, then I saw 'twas Raffaela herself had pulled me in. Still holding tight to my arm with one hand, she pushed the door shut with the other.

"We mus' hurry," said she.

"Hurry?" said I. "Why? Am I late?"

"No, no, you on time. But they come early for me today. I find out jus' yesterday and could not sent a note since I don' know where you live."

Then did she give me a most intense look, as if searching out the very secrets of my soul. She must have been satisfied by what she read, for she nodded in the way of one who has just come to a firm decision.

"Come. We go an' do it quick, eh?"

Then did she wink at me in the most friendly manner and pull me through the next door into the bedroom. There a large four-poster stood, taking up most of the space in the smallish room. She sat down upon it and began to unlace my codpiece with a well-practiced hand. At the decisive moment, my man, feeling himself free, leapt out at her. She recoiled slightly at his eagerness, then murmured a few words in appreciation and threw herself far back upon the bed. Pulling her skirt back and raising her knees, she exposed herself to me, hose, shift, bum roll, and all. Her "all," which was thus made available to me, was exceedingly handsome of its kind—generously proportioned, with a thick pelt of dark fur upon it—altogether pleasing.

"Come, come!" she urged. "What you wait for?" She propped herself up on her elbows and looked at me curiously. Then did she nod in sudden understanding. "Ah, I know!"

And so saying, she resorted to the device employed by countless hurried women before her. She spat two or three times into her hand and spread the spittle over her nether lips.

"There, should be all right now."

And it was. I entered her without too much difficulty, and, enjoying the snug sense of tightness within that narrow room, I began moving slowly up the hill to that distant peak. All-too slowly to suit my partner.

"Faster!" she whispered urgently in my ear. "We mus' hurry."

Just to make the point, she began bucking beneath me. Though I did wonder just then who was riding whom, I picked up her rhythm and posted swiftly up to a full gallop. But then, feeling a great outpouring imminent, I thought to do the considerate thing and withdraw—but she would have none of that.

"No!" she wailed, "in me—all of it."

Just to enforce her desire, she grasped me to her, a hand to each buttock, and held me tight in the saddle. 'Twas only a moment later that I quite exploded within her, groaning loudly in delight; she clamped a hand over my mouth to silence me. As I squeezed out the last of my seed, I began to kiss the hand over my mouth, each finger, the palm, all of it.

"Enough of that," said she, pushing me away, "*basta, basta.*"

"But I only wished to—"

"We do kissing and talking, all of that, next time, eh? Now you mus' go."

I felt vaguely offended by her dismissal of me. Was I some cow to be milked, then sent off to pasture? Nevertheless, I did as she told me, if reluctantly, and pulling free of her, I rolled off to one side.

"Out! Out you go."

"I need time to collect myself."

"Do that later."

"All right," said I, ever so reluctant.

As she blotted the precious fluid that none of it escape, I sent my man back into captivity and laced up the codpiece which had been so hastily torn asunder. I managed to finish just as she jumped from the bed, still holding the towel between her legs.

"Out, out, out," said she, "you come tomorrow, same time, and we don' need to hurry so. I love-a-you better then. You like to?"

The question was put to me most innocently. She looked wide-eyed and hopeful. No matter that I felt oddly used at that moment, I simply could not deny her.

"I shall come tomorrow," said I, "at the same time if you wish it so."

Satisfied, she pushed me toward the door to the street and gave me a buss upon the cheek. Then, throwing open the door, she urged me out and bade me goodbye in her own tongue—or one of them.

"Addio," said she. "Io ti amo." When you come *a domani* bring a play—one of you own, eh?"

A play? I nearly stumbled over my own feet at that. What had she in mind? Were we to read together? Would she have questions? What role was I to play in this, her tuition? When I turned round to put these questions to her, I found the door shut tight and the curtains closed.

I was halfway along Holbourn and on my way to see Henslowe across the river when a black coach, trimmed in gilt and drawn by four matching whites, did pass me by. Though I could not then be certain, I later confirmed that this was indeed Lord Hunsden's coach. I was only minutes away from the house in Little Gray's Inn Lane. I had proof then that Raffaela had fit our meeting dangerously close to Lord Hunsden's arrival. Or perhaps Lord Hunsden himself had not come for her. It may well have been that he had merely sent his coach for her. Even so, when it passed by, I thought it best to turn away and feign interest in a shop window, lest I be recognized by him from our brief meeting two days before—unlikely, of course, but minds do work in strange ways when by stress oppressed.

I remember that once the coach had gone by, I could not but laugh at myself, for it came to me that insofar as recognition was concerned, I could not even be certain that I would have recognized Raffaela if I were to pass her at that moment on Holbourn. She had answered the door when I had knocked at the appointed hour; there was no mask to cover her face, but the voice was the same, and the size and shape of her were right, so I assumed this was the woman I had come to see. As for what had come to pass after she pulled me inside, it was all as an indistinct blur upon paper. Indeed I had a better picture of her quim in my memory than I had of her face. Could she remember mine?

And so it had been a meeting between two strangers, almost as one might take a whore and have her up against a wall—almost was it so, yet not truly the same at all. For one thing, no money had changed hands, and for another, each knew something of the other that had aroused interest; we were not, in that sense, absolute strangers. But how strange it seemed to begin an *affaire de coeur* (again, the French have the right phrase) in such a way.

Yet how satisfying to begin where most affairs end! Thus to dispense with all the pretty lies, all the little hurts and deeply felt apologies, all the slavish efforts to please—in short, to be rid of all the falsity, flattery, and flummery that is the very essence of love as it has been given to us by the poets—this, say I, is a very great and noble gesture. I wondered at her surprising desire to collect all my seed and allow not even a drop to drip down her leg; yes, I wondered at it, though it did not bother me overmuch. It seemed likely that this had to do with practices common to the Hebrew confession. Perhaps, I thought, there were strict injunctions against wasting seed in their part of the Bible. I seemed to remember verses to that effect being quoted to us by the catechist and wondering what in God's name they could have meant.

Well, if it be a sin to "waste seed," then there be no sin in what we two did in that little house. We wasted naught. It's true, alas, that we were a bit rushed, yet I count that no blame upon her but rather on Lord Hunsden—or perhaps better to put the blame on mere circumstance.

What fine lust it was! It may be, after all, that the hurry helped us upon our way. Given the possibility that Lord Hunsden's coachman, or even the Lord Chamberlain himself, might come banging upon the door at the very moment I howled out so loud in delight, given *this* possibility, there may have been a particular illicit pleasure, a spice added to our enjoyment. The threat of discovery is ever a great spice to carnal pleasure.

Ah, but here we are again—"carnal pleasure." Is it a sin? Not in the marriage bed, so it is said. And I do readily admit that Anne gave me a great deal of pleasure (as well as a surprise) when last we copulated in Stratford town. But Raffaela gave me equal pleasure—and I hardly knew her. Was one sinful and not the other? That, I fear will not stand the test of reason, for if the good be truly good, it will be consistently so. And so, if carnal pleasure be good in the marriage bed, it must then also be good always and everywhere. What is equally good is then equally proper.

And from that time on, what did once give me carnal pleasure—playing wife to Kit Marlowe and whore to others too numerous to mention—no longer pleasured me in quite the same way. Why? I should be hard put to explain. Yet in such matters I thought it be best to follow the urgings of the flesh. Even today it does puzzle me, though.

Next day it was as Raffaela had promised. We took our pleasure, though at a far more leisurely pace. There was, she assured me, no need to hurry. And so we did dally, each preparing the other with kisses and loving caresses. (I vow she had the lightest touch of any man or woman that I had ever felt.) She taught me, too, that the tongue could be used for purposes quite other than speech. Ah, that day and during the many days that followed she taught me much and flattered me that I was an apt pupil. Yet all that preparation brought us at last to the pleasantest rut I had heretofore experienced. It was as different from our first as any could be—unhurried, imaginative, probing—until at last we found our rhythm, and she, it was, who sang forth first; moments later I joined in, and we did sing a proper duet. She was, nevertheless, just as frugal of my seed on this occasion as on the last. When at last I withdrew, she milked the last few drops from my man and with her fingers fed them to that open mouth below. Fascinated, I watched, half-expecting a tongue to flash forth and lick those hairy chaps. I did roll over then and lay down beside her. Nothing was said. The only sounds to be heard were the measured pulse of our breathing and the scrabbling and scratching of the rats in the thatched straw roof above us.

At last I asked how she could be so sure that on this day we might proceed with our pleasure without interruption. It was a question that troubled me no little.

"The Queen go to Bristol. She take the Court with her. Everybody go."

"But not the court musicians?"

"No, not the court musicians," said she, then did she give a sudden laugh. "You know about me, eh? How much you know? What you hear?"

In rough sum I told her what I had heard from Dick Burbage. She listened with care, giggled once or twice at my presentation, but grew most grave when I mentioned that I had heard she was Jew.

"Yes," said she, "that is my burden, my affliction. It is how I was born. That can't be changed."

"Would you change it if you could?"

"You mean *conversa?* Be a marrano?" She turned away, as if considering it for the first time. Then, having given it thought, she shook her head in the negative. "No, it doesn't interes' me."

"May I ask why not?"

"Is not hones'. You will find, Shake-a-speare, that I am very hones' person."

"And you will find that I am not."

At that she laughed a great full-throated laugh which caused her breasts to shake quite pleasingly.

"Is very hones' of you to say so," said she. "But I knew that."

Which caught me off guard and caused me to join in her laughter. My hand went to her belly which, too, had begun to shake. I glanced down upon it and noted the contrast in complexion—mine an ordinary English pink, and hers, not so much dark as sallow, but certainly of a Mediterranean hue.

"Oh?" said I, "and how did you know I was not honest?"

"Because you are a poet, and all poets lie. The most big liars of all are the poets who write plays."

"Why do you say that?"

"You write about kings and queens, but you don' know about them, so you lie. Why you don' write about men and woman like you and me, eh?"

"Because," said I, "those in the audience *want* stories of kings and queens—not about people like themselves. People like you and me are not interesting to them."

"Ha!" said she, "*I* am interesting to them. *I* am interesting even to the Queen. Her mouth hang open like so at some of the stories I tell her."

Raffaela thereupon demonstrated by letting her mouth gape open in a manner most comical.

Then did she continue: "The Queen, she say, 'Raffaela, tell me another story from you life.' She want to hear them all. I tell you my life, then you un'erstan'."

At which time she began a task of telling which extended o'er many days and later visits. There were indeed so many incidents and events, and some of them so strange, that I fear I came to doubt their truth, in spite of her claims of honesty. There were tales of narrow escapes from *banditti,* capture by pirates, imprisonment in a mussulman harem, travel through the air in the claws of a great bird, et cetera. I once discussed her account with one who had read a book I had not, a collection of stories supposedly told by one of a sultan's harem that she might keep him entertained and herself assured of his favor. The similarities were such that I am inclined now to believe that Raffaela did simply retell some of these stories as she remembered them and claim them as her own. But that is of no matter, for she kept me as well entertained as the sultan, and if it pleased her to think of these adventures as her own, there could be no reason to discourage her from it. I doubt that she ever told them to the Queen; to the Lord Chamberlain perhaps—but not to the Queen.

The only knowledge of her in which I put much faith can be put down in a comparative few lines.

Her full name was Raffaela Agostina di Abramo. She was born in 1567 in the ghetto of Venice, where had been collected all those of her kind, most of them Jews who had taken flight from Spain at the end of the previous century. Her father was a cantor—like unto a choirmaster—at a Jewish church, which she named in the Hebrew way as a "synagogue." From him she acquired her interest in music and her talent for it. He taught her to play the dulcimer, the guitarra and the virginal and to read music; she, as a young girl in that most romantic of Italian cities, had learned every *canzone,* air, ballad and madrigal sung thereabout. She, of a headstrong and willful nature even then, would in no wise accept the Jewish suitor chosen for her by her father. Embarrassed by her, her father sent her off to London on an English ship to the care of a cousin, a physician who happened to have close connections with the Court. It was once she had left Venice, according to her, that her great adventures began; or, to put it another way, it was once she had left Venice that her imagination took hold of the telling.

Ah well, the point is, eventually she arrived in London; the cousin used his connections well, and soon she was installed as one of the court musicians. The Queen, it seemed, was specially eager to have someone with whom she might speak Italian, for circumstances of state had made it difficult to maintain her command of the language, and she feared she was in danger of losing it altogether. It was not long before the Lord Chamberlain himself took an interest in her, and she had been installed in the small house in Little Gray's Inn Lane. There, theoretically, she was to be available to him whenever she was not with the Queen, or engaged in court entertainments in some way. In practice, however, he came by only two or three times a week.

"*Which* two or three times?" I asked her quite reasonably.

"What you mean?"

"Which days of the week? Monday, Tuesday, Saturday? Which?"

"Oh, can be sometimes one, sometimes another—different days."

"Well, I fear that won't do," said I. "Much as I enjoyed our first meeting—the thrill of it, the danger of discovery—I do not wish to risk it again. It was simply too close, far too near a thing."

"Why, what you think he do if he find us together?"

"First of all, and most important to me, he would kill me, or have me killed. Of that I'm quite certain."

"You think so?" She seemed genuinely surprised and distressed at the notion.

"Yes, certainly, indeed," said I redundantly, wishing to impress her with the seriousness of the situation. "And if he did not also kill you, he would throw you out into the street."

She gave serious consideration to this, sitting up in bed, her arms wrapped round her knees, her eyes drifting slowly back and forth across the room. At last, having given the matter a full measure of thought, she shook her head in the negative manner.

"No," said she with great certainty, "is not possible. Henry would not do that."

What did she mean by that? "Who is Henry?" I asked.

"Henry is . . . Henry—Lord Hunsden. Henry Carey is his true name. I call him that way."

"Ah," said I, "but I'll not argue the point with you. It remains that we must work out a way of signals which will tell me if he is here or if he is coming."

"You mean like ships make the signals with flags?"

"Exactly," said I.

What we devised had naught to do with flags but was nevertheless effective in a crude way. Like many of her sex, Raffaela was quite fond of flowers. There were pots of them placed in corners all round the house. And so it was agreed that on those occasions when I would be at risk to approach her door, she was to put a small pot of flowers in the window. When the Lord Chamberlain was present, his coach awaited him before the little thatch-roofed cottage; there was no need at such time even to look at the window.

All this was decided on the day before the Queen's return from Bristol and her tour of the West Country. We had better than two weeks together. There were days when she would play her dulcimer and sing to me, oft in Italian but occasionally in the language of her own people, a kind of Spanish dialect she called Ladino; these last were sung to the most mournful airs that e'er I heard. Yet for the most part we did make sport in bed. Glutted and sated were we with every sort of carnal act. We had tried tricks we had but heard of and erotic exercises of our own creation. I was certain as could be that I would be happy for a rest when the Lord Chamberlain returned in the royal party.

Yet 'twas not so. Quite understandably, he came back with a great hunger of his own to be satisfied. He may have been old—sixty-five by Raffaela's estimate—but with the proper stimulation he was still capable. And so, for more than a week that potted flower remained in the window, and the gilt-trimmed black coach stood at her door. Even the first day without her I felt the loss. On the second day I was quite beside myself with yearning. On the third day I dallied with myself in my own bed. On the fourth I was entertaining thoughts of a visit across the bridge to Henslowe's whorehouse next the Rose. But at that point I took charge of myself, sat down at my desk and began inditing a poem. A sonnet it was, nor had I written any such for years. It did not pour out of me as I hoped it might, yet I bled it forth, drop by drop, each line a victory over the turmoil within me. Still, I deem it no worse for the difficulty it caused me in composing. You may judge for yourself (whoever you be). I quote it here from memory:

> **How oft, when thou, my music, music play'st**
> **Upon that blessed wood whose motion sounds**
> **With thy sweet fingers, when thou gently sway'st**
> **The wiry concord that mine ear confounds,**
> **Do I envy those jacks that nimble leap**
> **To kiss the tender inward of thy hand**
> **Whilst my poor lips, which should that harvest reap,**
> **At the wood's boldness by thee blushing stand!**
> **To be so tickled, they would change their state**
> **And situation with those dancing chips**
> **O'er whom thy fingers walk with gentle gait**
> **Making dead wood more blest than living lips.**
> **Since saucy jacks so happy are in this,**
> **Give them thy fingers, me thy lips to kiss.**

My intention was to offer it to her when next we met, yet as that time came to seem ever more distant, I wished simply to knock upon her door, flower pot or no flower pot, and when she made open the door, to present it to her. Yet reason prevailed, as it does all too often with me, and so I did hold to my intuition. I set aside the sonnet and waited for my next opportunity.

This aspect of our relations—call it the poetic side—has not been touched upon at all, so eager was I to speak of the rest. But indeed such a side did exist. You will remember perhaps that she did call after me as I departed from our first tryst and ask that I bring along one of my plays when next I came to call. That I did. I brought with me *Titus Andronicus*. She read it that evening in my absence and asked me to bring another; then did I bring all three parts of *Henry VI*—and so on, until she had read all my works—even *Arden of Faversham*. Of them all, she liked best the Henry VI plays. And so, for that matter, did I.

"It was with them I taught myself to write," said I.

"Oh, you knew always to write," said she. "God give you that."

"Perhaps that is so, but I did not always know to write plays."

"You do that better than anyone," said she with a dismissive wave of her hand. "I know. I see all the plays here in London."

"You see them all? Yes, so I have heard. But could you perchance be more specific?"

"Pacific?"

"No, not the ocean. Could you be more particular? What do you think of my plays compared, say, to Christopher Marlowe's?"

"Who is he?"

"He wrote the play in which I had the role of the Governor of Malta. You remember? We met then."

"Yes, *o sì*. How could I forget, *mi amore?* Compare to *Enrico Sesto?* What you write is much better. You don' know that? You write much better than this man—how is he call? Marlowe?"

"Marlowe, yes."

"You know why you write better? You make a song with each line. I am a singer, a musician, so I know this. Here, I show you."

She grabbed the third part of *Henry VI* off the table near the bed, and at random chose a page near the end. Then did she sing out in deep full voice:

> **". . . To London, all in post; and, as I guess,**
> **To make a bloody supper in the Tower."**

It was a solemn song as it came forth from her, well-suited to the meaning of the lines, which she well understood.

"You sing them well," said I, "better than any actor could."

"The music is there for them to find. In that Jewish play, there is no music."

"*The Jew of Malta,* you mean?"

"If that is how it is called."

"Perhaps you do not like it because it is insulting to your people?"

"To the Jews? Worse things are said against them."

"Well, I know, but—"

Again she gave that dismissive wave of her hand, silencing me.

"You don' know who you arc, what you arc, eh? Shall I tell you?"

I said nothing and did naught but wait to hear what she would say. She, for her part, strained forward and peered into my eyes deep as any soothsayer or sibyl might.

"*Bene,* I tell you," she continued. "You a prodigy, a wonder, a poet with a talent so big you can do anything you want to do. I know that even when I see that Titus *qualunque cosa*. In many ways is a silly play, but it have the music in the lines, and if it have that, all the rest can be forgive."

I knew not what to say to that. Had I stood before her all the rest of the day, I would have known no better than I did at that empty-headed moment. My impulse was to laugh in embarrassment, yet she looked at me with such deep seriousness that I dared not do such a thing. There was yet another restraint which I felt, one that I would ever after carry with me, but one that was no more than a whisper in the ear just then.

And what was that whisper? What did it say? It said, "It is so. She hath said it right."

Only one other had spoken thus to me, and that was John Cotton. He it was who had inspired me as my schoolmaster, and then as my lover had sent me forth on my path in life. Now I hear similar words from Raffaela, an echo from years before. Though it was not immediate, a question would eventually form in my mind: Is this prodigious talent of mine only to be recognized by those who claim to love me? Which is to say, is it me or my talent they love? Yet that question, as I say, was to be put by me in the future, and much would have changed by then.

She had said to me all those memorable words as we sat, half dressed, upon the bed, speaking hopefully of our future. This was on the eve of Lord Hunsden's return. Would our flower pot signals buy us time enough to keep love at a boil? It was uncertain at best. I could but hope.

Bear in mind, if you will, that after we had disported ourselves each morn, I would hie myself off to The Theatre each afternoon and transform myself, by means of costume and makeup, into Ferneze, Governor of Malta. It was often a strain, for our exertions did sometimes leave me tired. Yet once I stepped upon the stage I never failed to rouse and rise to the occasion. By the end of the day, when the performance had done, I had little more strength than it took to accompany Dick Burbage, Alexander Cooke, and Will Kemp (Tarlton's replacement) to the Duck and Drake for a proper dinner. They were quite content to sit and drink the rest of the evening away. I, however, having quite exhausted myself, would soon after dinner make my excuses and drag me off to Norton Folgate and the bed I once shared with Kit Marlowe. In such a way did I acquire my reputation as a temperate individual who did practice moderation in all things.

Though I continued to attract praise and favorable comment

of every sort with my portrayal of Ferneze, I did in no wise wish to desert the writing of plays. Still, acting in such a production set me in good stead with the company. There was interest not only in my acting, but also in the plays I had written. James Burbage, father of Richard and Cuthbert and head of the acting company, asked to see a copy of my *Henry VI,* not knowing I had written it in three parts. Quite surprised was he when I delivered to him all three; and quite flattering was he after he had read them. Yet flattery was one thing and an earnest bid to produce them quite another. He begged off, declaring that a three-part play required too great a commitment than he could make at this time. (Alleyn soon produced it in its first part when he went into partnership with Henslowe.) When I mentioned to the elder Burbage that I had just begun work on another play, he was all eager to see it as soon as I had done with it, which I understood to mean, before I showed it to Henslowe. Again I was flattered.

Nevertheless, I kept in close communication with Henslowe, and it was from him that I received news of Christopher Marlowe from time to time. Kit had remained to prompt Alleyn only for two or three performances. By then the actor had the role by heart and had no need of him. Then was I surprised to learn that Kit had gone cross London Bridge and asked Henslowe for work of any sort that he might perform quickly. Coming out of Newgate, he was much in need of money. Henslowe took advantage of the offer and presented him with my *Arden of Faversham*; Kit was to rewrite it and give it a stronger ending. That was quickly done and, I readily admit, he did much to improve the play. True, I did ask to have my name taken from it, but I had long before lost interest in it and had no wish to work on it further myself. Yet Kit could not resist thumbing his nose at me in the rewriting of some of the lines. And in renaming the villainous murderers "Black Will" and "Shakebag," I hold that he went a bit too far. Before the next year was out, he would write two more plays, *Edward II* and *The Massacre at Paris*. Both were written following his ill-fated trip to Flushing. Both, in quality, were well below his best work.

Thus did we two, Christopher Marlowe and I, drift away, each from the other. Until early 1592, when he came back from Flushing, he lived with Thomas Kyd. Whether Kyd played whore to him, I cannot say; he did, in any case, loan him money and share food with him that he might not starve just as I had done. Kit was known to be one of Sir Walter Ralegh's circle. Ralegh and his friends met per occasion at his residence, and there (so it was said) discussed abstruse matters of the intellect as they smoked pipes of tobacco. Most of the talk during these meetings (again, so it was said) was of a blasphemous nature—blasphemy masquerading as wit. From one who had been present at one such gathering I heard Kit quoted verbatim: "All they that love not tobacco and boys are fools." I need not have heard that direct from Kit's lips to know that he said it. Having lived with him as long as I did, I knew well his style of speech, as well as his opinions.

At last came the day when there was neither coach at the door, nor flower pot in the window. I quite gaped as I went past the house the first time, hardly capable of grasping the meaning of their absence. Yet I circled round and came back again for another look, fearing that perhaps my eyes had misread when first I glimpsed the little cottage. I stopped opposite it and as casually as I was able, gave a thorough inspection to the place. No, there was most certainly no flower pot to be seen in the window or anywhere else. I looked up and down the lane, saw it to be empty, and ran for the door.

It opened before me—she had been waiting. Taking time only to kick the door shut, I threw my arms about her and felt her arms wind round my neck. She began attacking my face with kisses. I picked her up, threw her over my shoulder and staggered into the bedroom with this considerable burden, fearing every step of the way that I might collapse beneath her. Then did we fall onto the bed all in a tumble. Up came her skirt, out came my man, and we had consummated the act before there was so much as a word spoken between us. She did naught but giggle. I grunted and snorted like a bull in service. Noise we made aplenty, yet all of it inarticulate and unintelligible. When we did separate there was still no proper speech between us—only long minutes of panting and groaning.

"What?" said I at last, "have you no greeting for me? Will you not even say you are happy to see Will?"

"Ah, Shake-a-speare, I am *so* happy to see you that if I am more happy I mus' get a new bed."

"But if you do that, the Lord Chamberlain may become suspicious and wish to spend another week alone with you just to keep me away. And that would surely be more than I could bear."

"What happen to you then?"

"What would happen to me? Why, what happens to all sorrowing lovers? My heart would break in twain."

"In twain? I never hear this word before. What it means?"

"To break in two, to sunder."

"Ah," said she, "now I un'erstan'. An' you know? I have a song for that."

I laughed at her. "You have a song for everything." Forsooth, it did truly seem that she did.

"*Così?* You have words for everything. Why not I have a song, too—eh? You like to hear?"

And without waiting for an answer, she jumped out of bed and ran into the next room to fetch her dulcimer. Returning, she unwrapped it carefully from its soft leather covering, took a moment to test and tune it. Then, satisfied, she laid it aside and took a moment to describe to me the song that she would sing.

"Is a very sorrowful song," said she. "A young man, he sing

of his great sadness to be so far away from his true love. He say his heart is broken, and only she can put it back together."

As she sat up with the dulcimer in her lap and made ready to sing, I put to her a question:

"Is this a Ladino song?"

She nodded. "Jews are all over the world. They know well these feelings."

And having said that, she sang the song. She had described it in words so commonplace, so unexceptional, that I was quite amazed to hear it, for it seemed to go beyond sadness and take upon it an unexpected dignity. Rather than the song of a disappointed lover it became a mournful anthem of separation. Was it the song, or was it the singer? I wondered how it would sound if sung by another.

I did not applaud her, such a gesture of appreciation seems near silly when the audience numbers but one. Yet I believe that what I felt did show in my eyes. She looked deep into them and was in no wise disappointed by what she saw. And more, I reached into an inner pocket in my doublet and pulled from it the sonnet I had written for her and to her. I offered it to her.

"What have you?" she asked.

"'Tis a poem which I wrote you during our long divorce."

"Is it mine for true and forever?"

She took it and ran her eyes over it. Then did she hand it back to me. Was she refusing my gift? By no means would she do so. I saw then the tears in her eyes.

"You read it to me," said she.

I nodded, took it from her, and began. Though I be not greatly practiced at reading my own work aloud, I am actor enough to get sense and feeling from lines of any sort, and all the more from lines I had indited. I may have stumbled once or twice during the reading—though I think not—but it mattered little to her. When I had done, the tears coursed freely down her cheeks. She sniffled so deep and free that I could not withhold from her my linen kerchief; she took it, blew her nose and wiped her eyes, and returned it to me. Then did I give to her the paper from which I had just read. (Naturally, I had made a fair copy and left it in the drawer of my writing table.) Indeed she was quite overcome by my gift; I knew not quite why this should have been so. Her eyes roved o'er the paper in her hand. She studied it for a great long minute, and at last looked up and declared her love for me.

"Shake-a-speare, I like to show this to someone. He is very young, a nobleman and very rich. He could help you. You permit me to show him?"

XIV

His name was Henry Wriothesley, and he was the Third Earl of Southampton. Raffaela had told true: he was young (just nineteen) and also quite rich. With my permission, she had done as she asked and shown the sonnet to him. He, according to her, had danced for joy about the room upon reading it and cried aloud, "I *must* meet him!" (Meaning me, of course) I thought, when she told me, that she was exaggerating grotesquely in the Italian manner. But, forsooth, once I had met the boy, I had no difficulty believing hers to be a truthful account.

She had known him since he graduated from Cambridge at the age of sixteen and had come to London to take his place at court. They were friends. Still, there could be no possibility of Raffaela and I going together to meet him that she might introduce me to him direct. Yet after showing him the sonnet I had indited to her, she made an appointment for me alone, leaving the work of ingratiating myself to me.

Upon the designated morning, I made my preparations as careful and complete as I had on that first morning meeting with Raffaela. I came away from my room smelling like one who had just departed a French *parfumerie.* And I was truly as clean as I smelt. I had even bought a handsome new doublet for the occasion; it was not near as heavy as that which I usually wore—and a good thing, too, for the Inns of Court, which was my destination, was some distance beyond Norton Folgate. 'Twould take me the better part of an hour to walk there. If I were to arrive in a sweat from the journey, I would have undone the good impression I wished to make. The new doublet which I wore—brown with gold-colored thread worked into a pattern of posies—made it possible for me to arrive all fresh and dry.

I knocked upon the door with a degree of authority. After some delay, it was opened to me by a servant of a cold, suspicious mien. I gave him my name and added that I was expected. He looked upon me in a dubious manner but invited me in and led me down a hall to a room of considerable proportions wherein were hung all manner of pictures, most of them presenting stern-faced forbears of a sort who might have produced one like the servant who had brought me to this remarkable room. Would Lord Southampton be another such?

No, most emphatically, he was not. There was a prelude to his arrival—a flurry of footsteps upon a staircase which was hidden from my view—and then his appearance. He did pause in a most dramatic fashion at the room's entrance and threw a hand in the air in such a way as he might if shooing a fly away.

"Ah," said he, "the poet!"

At that I announced myself—"William Shakespeare at your service, m'Lord"—and bowed low in the French style.

He answered with a nod of his head, then ran—nay, pranced—across the room to me.

"I am *so* pleased to meet you," said he. "Dear Raffaela has told me *all* about you." (All about me? I did forsooth hope that were not true.) "She reminded me that I had seen a play of yours, *Titus Andronicus,* which I thought to be quite *marvelous* and at the same time terribly *frightening.* I do not believe I have *ever* seen such a bloody play—quite *dripping* with gore it was."

"And did you enjoy the play? Were you edified?" I hoped thereby to wring from him more direct and particular praise.

"Did I not say so?" He gave that a moment's reflection. "No, I suppose I did not, but to me, you see, what seems marvelous is always enjoyable, and to be made to feel fear is also to be edified."

"Then are you a true judge of art," said I, flattering him quite without shame, "for most who go to plays do so only to laugh. They count that play best which makes them laugh most—or so it does seem to a poor poet."

"Poor poet indeed," said he in a jesting manner. "You are *rich* in those gifts that only God can give. Your *talents* are your wealth. And note that I express myself in the plural, Shakespeare, for your talents are manifold and many. That I say with assurance, sir, for I have seen your work in the sonnet form, and I know you cannot be bested. Your poem to dear Raffaela was quite perfect of its kind. Have you written many sonnets?"

"Not many, no. Yet I trust you will keep in confidence that the poem was written to her. It could prove an embarrassment—and perhaps more than that."

"I understand completely," said he, "and I shall treat it as my deepest secret. There need be no worry on your part." Then did he remain silent for a spell. He took a step back and studied me. "And what else have you done?"

"Oh, other plays, and I have just begun a long poem recounting the love of Venus for Adonis."

"So you . . . keep busy, do you?"

"Oh, indeed I do," said I. "One must."

"True, all too true."

Then did he begin to talk on matters slightly different. What seemed odd and rather difficult for me was that as he talked, he began circling about me, so that I became near dizzy from turning and trying to follow him round the room.

He talked at length of the possibility of founding a circle of the sort that had formed round Sir Walter Ralegh. "What is it he calls them?"

"The School of Night," said I.

"Ah yes, so it is. Clever, don't you think, that he should call it so? It does suggest the darker side of things, don't you think, and lends a certain wickedness to the enterprise? Whilst in reality, all they do is sit about smoking that disgusting sotweed."

"I understood that there were philosophical discussions and debates," said I.

"Oh, so they claim, but I have heard otherwise."

"No doubt you have heard it a-right."

"But I should like to bring together a circle of my own for the discussion and debate of art and all related matters. It would bring together artists such as you and lovers of art like myself."

"Ah, now I begin to understand your purpose."

"And do you approve?"

"That I do, sincerely, and completely," said I, hand upon heart.

At last he ended his travels about the room. He clasped his hands together and rushed across the space which separated us.

"Ah, Shakespeare, how *wonderful!* May I then count upon you to . . . bring your friends, your colleagues?"

Friends? Colleagues? Could he mean that pack of drunken actors and poets who are each night at the Duck and Drake? If there be free wine and victuals to be had, there should be no difficulty persuading them to come. Keeping order amongst them would be another matter, however.

"I believe that with proper notice I can find a few," said I.

"Well and good," said he. "I shall then invite a few of *my* friends, but only those among them who are most sensitive, most attuned to the beauties of art, those such as Lord Hunsden and . . . oh . . . others whom you might not know—Sir Robert Cecil perhaps."

"Lord Hunsden, the Lord Chamberlain? With all due respect, my Lord, do you think it wise to invite him?"

He stared at me, blank-faced, for a moment—no more than that—and then, having grasped the sense of my demurrer, he brightened and sought eagerly to reassure me.

"I understand your objection," said he—"Raffaela, of

course—but, truly, you need have no fear. I am the very soul of prudence in all such matters."

I had no choice but to put my faith in him, though forsooth I liked it not. To him I bowed, yet not so deep as before.

"As you say, my Lord," said I.

"Perhaps in a week? Ask about, and I shall, as well. When I can give you an exact date, I shall send word by Raffaela. Will that suit you?"

"Oh . . . yes . . . certainly, I suppose."

"Then goodbye, dear poet. I shall look forward to our next meeting."

That said, he left me with a wave of his hand, covering the distance to the entrance in four or five bounding strides. He was out of sight but moments when the servant who had brought me thus far appeared in the doorway, and with a slight inclination of his head, he gestured into the hall, and I allowed myself to be led away.

I was, however, to be surprised, for he brought me not to the door by which I had entered, but to another halfway up the hall. He knocked upon it, and from within I heard a muffled invitation to enter. The door was opened by the servant, who then stepped aside and bowed me in. There a woman waited, seated in a chair. The gray in her hair and the lines in her face told me that she was near fifty, or better. Her queenly manner indicated that she was used to obedience from those round her; obedience, as it turned out, from all but one. I bowed low to her, and she inclined her head in my direction.

"You are Shakespeare, the poet?" There was the barest sense to it of a question. As it came from her, it seemed more in the nature of an accusation.

"Your humble servant," I replied.

"I am Henry's mother," said she.

"Lady Southampton," said I, with another bow.

"I am Henry's mother," she repeated. "And it is as such I now address you and appeal to you."

"You have but to ask and—"

"Oh, please, none of that courtly nonsense. I've something to discuss with you about my son. He is my only son, the last male in his line. If he does not marry and have a son, the line—and the title—will die with him." She paused at this point that she might emphasize what next she said: "I do not wish this to happen." Then did she come to a full halt, as if expecting some response from me.

"That would indeed be a pity," said I. "What stands in the way?"

"*He* stands in the way. He was promised to one, the daughter of Lord Burghley, yet he says now that he will not marry her. *Now* he says that he does not wish to marry *any* woman. He is very stubborn in this and will talk with me no more about it."

"And what do you wish me to do about it? Do you wish me to talk with him?"

"No, I wish you to write to him."

"Write? Write what?"

"Henry has a very high opinion of your work. He says that you are a true artist. He told me of that poem you wrote to the Jewess. While I do not encourage you in such . . . matters, I recognize that you have proven your talent with this poem and can write others as good. Would you say so?"

I pretended to give the matter fair consideration. "I would say so, yes."

"Well, then, I should like you to write a number of such poems to my son. He is sensitive to flattery and praise."

"What sort of poems had you in mind?" I asked.

"Why, good ones, of course. They should praise marriage and urge him toward it. Praise women to him. Speak enthusiastically of their good qualities." She then gave me a sharp look. "That should not be difficult for you, should it?"

Making a pretense of careful thought, I delayed my answer for some time, and then I said, "No, not difficult. I believe I can satisfy you—and your son, as well, of course."

"Well then, Mr. Shakespeare, we come round to the matter of payment. My son has no money of his own until he comes into his majority. He receives a generous allowance till then. But I have a few thousand of my own, *Deo gratias*."

My heart leapt at that. Would she offer me her entire fortune? Of course she would not, yet for a moment a brief shiver of avarice, almost amatory in nature, passed through me. I knew that she wished me to speak, to set a price for my services, yet somehow the thought of all that money had struck me dumb.

She prompted me: "What would you say, Mr. Shakespeare? You are a craftsman, and a craftsman deserves to be paid for his work. What value do you put upon your work?"

"Well, I . . . that is, what is it worth to you?"

"A great deal, if it sways him toward marriage, but let us say a pound per poem, and I would then place an order for fifteen at that price. Who knows? We may have need of more—but let us begin with that."

After a moment's hesitation, I agreed, while at the same time damning myself for failing to name an amount, a much higher amount than that which I had accepted from her. I promised myself that ever in the future I would come forth and not be shy in such matters—and by God, I never was again.

Even so, I might still have demanded more, for it developed that she required a sonnet a day from me. She proposed that she send a servant to me with the day's payment, and he would return with the day's poem for Lord Southampton.

"And I would continue it so for fifteen days?"

"Well, perhaps not—Sundays, after all. I would not have you violate the Sabbath on my account. So let us say fifteen poems in seventeen days. Does that not seem fair?"

"It might be a bit burdensome."

"Oh, come now, Mr. Shakespeare, how long was that poem you wrote to the little Jew?"

"Fourteen lines."

"Do you mean to tell me that you cannot write fourteen lines, given one whole day?"

"Well . . . there are times when inspiration flags."

"Let me hear none of that." She made a quick motion with her hand intended to send me from the room.

It seemed that I was indeed obliged to deliver at the rate she had demanded. Yet as I was bowing my way out of her presence, a thought occurred, one that I felt compelled to express.

"My Lady," said I, "you said that each day the servant will deliver the poem to your son. But will you not see it first? Do you not wish to read it before Lord Southampton?"

"Don't be silly, Shakespeare. I know nothing of poetry, nor do I wish to learn."

That much was evident, I told myself, as I made my way out the door and tramped cross the park to the street. The woman thought to buy poetry as a seamstress might purchase so many yards of silk to make a dress. Little did she know—or care—that poetry cannot be bought; it can only be borrowed. It belongs only to him who indites it.

Ah well, said I, offering consolation to myself, the bargain has been struck. If I can keep to her terms, I shall be fifteen pounds richer before the month is out. And that, it came to me at last, is a bit more than I might expect to receive from Henslowe for two plays at which I might labor two full months. Raffaela had told me that I could do anything I wished to do. Now was the time to prove it to myself.

The following are notes from the meeting I have just attended with Rev. Francis Stoner, vicar of Trinity Church, Stratford-upon-Avon in the shire of Warwick. It took place upon March 8, 1616. There were no others present. That is why I think it wise to commit my memory of it to paper before certain details pass from my mind.

I had made an appointment to speak with the vicar "on a certain matter" shortly after that day upon which Goody

Bromley intruded her foul presence into New Place. He received me in his place of office which had lately been added to the church. Rather proud of the place he did seem—perhaps excessively so—for he insisted on showing me much in which I had little interest, such as the repository for church records, a detailed plan of the town of Stratford, et cetera. I know not how long he would have held me there calling my attention to that and this, had I not rather abruptly brought him to the matter at hand.

Shakespeare:	*All very interesting, Vicar, but I have come to address a rather special matter.*
Vicar:	*Ah yes, so you said. And what might that matter be?*
Shakespeare:	*As you should know, I had chosen for myself a burial plot out in the churchyard.*
Vicar:	*Yes, I know it very well. It stands out beyond the south wall of the church, one of four together. Your mother and father are, I believe, buried there, and there are two more unused plots, one intended for you and another for your wife. It is, in that way, a family plot. Is there something you wish to change?*
Shakespeare:	*Indeed there is. I do not wish to be buried there.*
Vicar:	*I do not understand.*
Shakespeare:	*I wish to be buried in the church.*
Vicar:	*Well, that is certainly your right. You are, after all, a tithe-holder, and—*
Shakespeare:	*Exactly. It is my right.*
Vicar:	*What then do you wish us to do with the plot wherein you had previously intended to be lain?*
Shakespeare:	*Nothing. Keep it. My family will no doubt find a use for it after I am gone. The one intended for my wife is still intended for her.*

Vicar:	*I see. May I ask a rather personal question?*
Shakespeare:	*Indeed you may* ask.
Vicar:	*What is your health? Why do you wish to make this change?*
Shakespeare:	*Those are two quite separate questions. The first is truly none of your affair, and I shall not give it a proper answer.*
Vicar:	*Forgive me for asking. I meant no harm.*
Shakespeare:	*I know that, and you are certainly forgiven. I will go so far as to say that my health had nothing to do with this decision of mine. And that is all in the way of an answer that you will have from me. But as to the second question—* why *do I wish to make this change—I shall be happy to answer it. I was, forsooth, hoping that you would ask.*
Vicar:	*What then?*
Shakespeare:	*I fear that if my grave were outside and in the open, that it would soon be desecrated.*
Vicar:	*Truly so? Why should you suppose such a thing?*
Shakespeare:	*You have here within the parish a woman named Goodwife Bromley.*
Vicar:	*Yes, and an unfortunate creature she is.*
Shakespeare:	*Our views differ. You say she is unfortunate. I say she is evil. I believe her to be a witch.*
Vicar:	*Well, I am surprised.*
Shakespeare:	*I know not why you should be. There has been talk about her for years—or so I understand.*
Vicar:	*That's true, but in a town such as Stratford, there will always be talk of that sort among the ignorant and malicious about such persons as she. No, when I say that I am surprised, I mean that I am surprised at you.*
Shakespeare:	*Oh, really? And why do you say that?*

Vicar: *Because, sir, you have spent the better part of your life in London. You have lived and worked among the celebrated and worthy. How can one such as you voice the same suspicions which one hears from the unlearned?*

Shakespeare: *Would you put our late sovereign, our Queen, in that same class? She, it was, who put forward the present law against witches and witchcraft, and King James is its avid enforcer.*

Vicar: *I know, I know, but could they conceive of Goody Bromley as a witch? Surely not! Have you, sir, any proof against her? Is there evidence could be brought against her in any court, ecclesiastical or criminal? What have you against her?*

Shakespeare: *She follows me about continually. She knows things about me which, in the natural order of things, she should not.*

Vicar: *What things?*

Shakespeare: *That I . . . I would rather not say.*

Vicar: *If you are to witness against her, then you would have to say.*

Shakespeare: *She managed by spell or other occult means to enter my house through a locked door.*

Vicar: A locked *door? Are you sure? Did she leave something behind that you were able to identify as hers?*

Shakespeare: *Yes, her* odor.

Vicar: *(laughing) That, I'll grant, is all her own. Did anyone else smell it? Anyone besides you?*

Shakespeare: *No, my wife denied it was there, denied the door had been locked, denied Goody Bromley's visit altogether.*

Vicar: *Well then . . .*

Shakespeare: *Yet I am* certain *of it.*

Vicar:	*Let me do this, sir: let me speak to Goody Bromley on this matter. If she admits it or any part of it, I shall take the matter up with the Bishop.*
Shakespeare:	*What if* I *were to go to the Bishop?*
Vicar:	*Well, of course you're free to do that—a man of your position . . . But do let me advise you to prepare for him. I know from my own experience that he puts no great value upon suspicions. And so, sir, why not do as I suggest and let me talk with the woman first. Whatever she may be, she is one of God's creatures, and she is more likely to respond to a kind word than to a harsh one. So is it with us all. Even if she denies your complaints, such a talk may discourage her from continuing her ill-behavior. Let me then try.*
Shakespeare:	*I shall give the matter some consideration.*

Thus it was left unresolved. The Vicar is, I fear, rather a fool. I know not why I should have thought that it would serve some purpose to discuss these matters with him. He did give me a good bit of advice, however: I shall be better prepared and better organized when I go to visit the Bishop.

I dislike making such intrusions into my narrative as I have just made. Why then do I do it? I stare down at the question I have put to myself and find that I cannot readily answer it. Why indeed? I can only guess that at the back of my mind I find some parallel between this strange episode with Goody Bromley and some other in my past toward which I am blindly proceeding in this account. Or perhaps there is a pattern to my life, one into which the current intrusion fits neat and snug. I can only press on and see what, if anything, shall emerge.

———

At last I gave in to Richard Burbage and took a clown role, as he had been urging me to do ever since Dick Tarlton dropped dead in the Duck and Drake. He won me over by extending to me the opportunity to write my own lines. The play was, I believe, Michael Drayton's first (and he may since have disclaimed it). That Drayton was, as I, from Warwickshire led him to his subject—*The Tragical History of Guy, Earl of Warwick*. It also inclined him to be quite open in the matter of my contribution to his work; briefly put, he didn't care how much of it I wrote, so long as it made it to the stage. And so I made my clown a bumpkin and took him out of Stratford-upon-Avon. (I may have had dear Ned in mind—who is to say?) In any case, the play was cast, I had written my scenes, and we were about to begin rehearsals, when we received the first portent of things to come.

Three of us sat at table in the Duck and Drake, sipping ale and talking of the latest. There were Dick Burbage, his younger brother, Cuthbert, and I. Oh yes, Drayton was there, too—of course he was. Indeed, we began by talking the new play through before getting on to other matters. Richard B. was specially eager that all be right with the piece, for Ned Alleyn had just left the company to form his own, the Lord Admiral's Men; and young Burbage was taking his place and acting as Guy of Warwick, a role written for Alleyn. Yet having talked of little else but the play for near a week, there was little left to say. We sat silent for a moment as we awaited the next round of ale. I myself was in no wise ready to leave, having glimpsed a flower pot in Raffaela's window early that morn. 'Twas then that Cuthbert came forth with a report that interested us all.

"Hast heard the news of Marlowe?" he asked, lowering his voice to a whisper.

A chorus of urging ran round the table. We pushed our heads together that we might listen better.

"Well, you knew that he'd been sent back from Flushing in chains?"

Yes, all of us had heard that—except for Drayton, who was recently come to London. He wanted to know why. "What was the charge?"

"Coining," said Cuthbert.

"Making counterfeit shillings," said Dick Burbage, "Dutch and English."

"Though only the Dutch were circulated."

"But coining is come under the rubric of treason," said Drayton, "and is a hanging offense."

"He will not hang," said Cuthbert. "That is the news I bear."

"I should hope not," said Drayton. "He has a great talent."

"That may be," said Dick. "He is nevertheless a great pain in the arse. He cannot keep out of trouble long enough to write a new play."

"Will he be imprisoned?" I asked, at last breaking silence.

"Nay, not even that. Lord Burghley questioned him and then let him go. The fellow has more lives than a cat. Forsooth, he has more friends in government than the Queen herself."

"Indeed that may be," said his brother, "for as she grows older, she seems to have fewer."

"Well, I, for one, am right glad he will not be put a term in gaol," said Drayton. "And it gladdens me greater that he will not be hanged."

"Make no mistake, Michael," said Dick Burbage to him. "We rejoice with you that Kit Marlowe is now safe from the rope and from Newgate, as well. And we know better than you, perhaps, that he has a great talent. Still, he treats that talent with great scorn. He pisses it away. Mark my words: he will be in trouble again before summer is come."

(And he was! In the month of May Kit was cited for his part in a scuffle in Shoreditch.)

We nodded in glum agreement and not a snicker amongst us. Drayton, chastened, offered us no argument and no further response in the matter.

"Oh, and by the bye," offered Cuthbert, "what say you to this? I heard just yestereve that three cases of the plague have been reported in Southwark."

"In Southwark, is it?" said I. "Why, I would say that may prove to be rather awkward for our former colleague, now a competitor, Ned Alleyn."

"Oh, well it may!" said Dick with a ready smirk. "And it may prove the undoing of Philip Henslowe, as well. Henslowe's Rose has been contracted by their company, for the season, and it stands fair in the middle of Southwark. Alleyn may well regret leaving us—not that I should now want him back." Then did he add this question to his brother: "Were those plague cases fatal?"

"In faith, are they not always?"

"Nearly so," said I. "Word of them will be out before you know."

" 'Tis already. *I* heard, did I not?"

Quite suddenly Drayton pushed from the table and jumped to his feet, quite astonishing us all. He attracted much attention from those nearby.

"You three make a proper trio of vultures, so you do!" said he with a great show of offended virtue. "You see the plague as no more than your good fortune at Henslowe's bad luck? Do you believe that if there are cases on the south bank of the river, there will be none on the north?"

"Well . . . sometimes it is so," said Cuthbert.

"That's true. Why, I remember back in—when was it? '85, was it not?—it started in Southwark, spread to Bermondsey and every place on that side the Thames, and it never made it over here at all."

"There were a few cases, couple of hundred, no more."

"But that is not the usual—is it?" Drayton demanded, resuming his seat. "Christ, I'll never get *Guy* upon the stage!" He was quite fretful, and I was quick to note that the pious Drayton himself was not above looking to his own interest in the face of plagues, calamities, and other such acts of God. Naturally, however, I kept that observation to myself.

This reminder plunged the two brothers into a gloomy discussion of what might be done if the plague did spread quick across the river and into London. The Privy Council would then shut down *all* the theaters, sure, making no discrimination between those in the areas where the plague was rampant and those where it had not yet broken out; for it was widely supposed that in such crowds as theaters attracted the dread illness could move swiftly from one man to the next. If the Curtain and The Theatre were shut down, along with the rest, the company would have no choice but to go out on a summer tour of the provinces. Having lived that life for years in Lancashire, I had no wish to return to it—nor, for that matter, did the rest of them at the table wish to leave London. And so it did seem to me that there was, of a sudden, an excess of melancholy there. It suited my own mood not at all. I drained my tankard and took my leave of them—though not before I had invited all to Lord Southampton's residence upon the appointed evening. These, my fellows, would have to do as artists for the young earl's circle. They, for their part, were quite delighted by the prospect; I, for mine, wished that I might have done better.

On the evening in question we met outside the Drake and Duck and hied off together for the Inns of Court. Talk bubbled freely between them, as it usually did. They fair rubbed their hands in anticipation at the thought of mixing with the nobility. I, who had spent some time with Lord Southampton, was not near so glad at the thought of spending more. I wondered what, if anything, he would have to say about the sonnets I had been writing each night and sending off to him each morn. I only hoped that he kept his comments in confidence between us.

The chief difficulty in writing them had proved to be finding suitable material. So far I had found just one theme: that he was so beautiful and well beloved by so many that it was his bounden duty to marry and reproduce himself; the world needed more like him. I found, as I struggled, that the number of variations which could be played upon that theme was far from infinite. Up to that time I had done eleven. As we four took the long way to the Inns of Court, I found myself torturing out the lines and rhyme of the twelfth: ". . . the clock that tells the time"—oh, weak, obtuse! "When I behold the violet past prime"—near as bad, alas! Ah, what misery to try to write upon demand!

Upon our arrival we were ushered swiftly to the room wherein Lord Southampton and I had held our interview. I realized it was the same only after I had been inside it for some time. It was much altered from what it had been previous. Whereas before it had been bare of table and even chairs, it now offered seats scattered all about; one in particular, a kind of throne, dominated the rest, and in it sat none but our host, Mr. Henry Wriothesley, third Earl of Southampton and my prospective patron. Then did I note that there was an order to the arrangement of the chairs I had not at first noted: all were set in a half-circle facing the young nobleman. We four were shown to places at Southampton's left hand; those at his right were three—the first whom I did not recognize, except as one of about my own age who was handsome and quite richly dressed; the other two were known to me, and one of them quite well indeed. Lord Hunsden sat, arms folded before him, his head inclined toward the man unknown to me, with whom he conversed in deep, murmuring tones; beside him, bearing an expression that betrayed naught, sat my own dear Raffaela. She did not so much as look in my direction, and I returned her show of indifference. Thus none would ever guess our true feelings, one for the other.

A nudge at my elbow. "Hsst! Will!" came Dick Burbage's earnest whisper. "Dost know the who of that fellow sits farthest?"

I did not move my head left or right, nor did I shift my eyes.

"Lord Hunsden, is it not?" said I in a voice softer than soft.

"No, t'other one. 'Tis Lord Essex."

I moved my gaze to him. I had heard him talked of freely and often in tones of awe. He was quite the handsomest man in the room, a bit like Kit Marlowe in the face, though stronger-featured. Indeed he was handsome enough to turn the Queen's head—a dangerous game, that. He had, it was said, suffered for it.

Our nineteen-year-old host, nearly as handsome and clothed for the occasion in silk and linen, did rise and bow right and left to each separate group.

"Welcome," said he, "welcome. This will be a memorable night, I'm quite *certain* of it. That it has come about at all is worthy of remark, for in this room have been brought together two quite different parties who have something in common—and that something, dear friends, is art. Here, the artists"—he gestured toward us who sat at his left hand—"and here the art lovers." With a nod to his right. "Indeed, I count myself among the art lovers. I must, for I *know* that I am *certainly* not an *artist!*" At that he himself giggled, and the brothers Burbage joined in with a chorus of restrained cackling, merely (I'm sure) to offer sympathy to our host.

"It will be left to Mr. William Shakespeare to introduce each of the artists and explain something about each of them, be he poet or actor. The artist will make his presentation, and then the art lovers will have the opportunity to comment, to discuss the work, and perhaps to question the artist and—who knows?—make so bold as to suggest how a particular work of art might be improved. And so, without wasting words further, I turn the chair over to Mr. William Shakespeare." (Yet still he retained his throne, retiring to it as I rose to perform my duties.)

I introduced Michael Drayton to those on the far side of the room. Since I had not been put on notice that it would be my duty to present each of my company, I had not prepared and knew not quite what to say. Nevertheless, I managed, hailing him as "lately come to London and already recognized as one of our finest poets." And I did note that his new play, *The Tragical History of Guy, Earl of Warwick,* was in rehearsal and would be the next play presented at the Curtain theater. With that and no more, Drayton rose, came forward and read that tiresome sonnet of his, "Since There's No Help." I, at least, find it tiresome; it has become so to me through constant repetition. I have heard lines of it tossed about upon the street in London. I have heard that lovers know it by head and heart. None of my sonnets has achieved that sort of currency—and I can think of a dozen of mine superior to that one of his. But do take note: I do not claim that all of mine are superior to all of his, nor would I say that "Since There's No Help" is a piece without merit. Indeed, I liked it well enough when I first heard it on that evening. Yet was any work by any pen worth the praise heaped upon that little sonnet? And was Drayton himself worth the applause (the actual clapping of hands!) offered him there in Lord Southampton's residence. Most dismaying was it to see Raffaela applauding with the rest. Had she no sense of loyalty? Ah, women! How fickle their tastes! How changeable their desires! And when Dick and brother Cuthbert stood to applaud their colleague, I myself was forced to join in. And the comment afterward—dear God! It was naught but the most lavish praise; there was nothing of criticism or judgment to be heard in it.

Then did the brothers Burbage take their turn. In introducing them, I cited them as "talented sons of a great father, and gifted actors in their own right." That could only be said of Dick in truth; though Cuthbert appeared often upon the stage, his true talent was for commerce—the business of the theater. At my urging, they had chosen a short scene (the second in the Fourth Act) of my play, which had just then been produced at the Rose, *King Henry VI, Part I.* It takes place at the gates of the city of Bordeaux and is a dialogue twixt Talbot, the English commander, and the French general who commands the defending forces. It is of the right length for such informal presentation. Full it is with bluster and threat as the two throw challenges back and forth before the battle begins. I thought that it might have special appeal to Lord Southampton, for I had heard that he had military ambitions; I had no expectation then that Essex would be present and knew not that he had not only military ambitions, but military experience, as well.

Though we were applauded, all three—the brothers Burbage for their skill in dramatic performance and I as inditer of the lines which they had performed—the discussion which followed was not near so approving as what had followed Drayton's timid reading. 'Twas Essex led the attack.

"That was not how it is done," said he with casual authority, "and even less how it was done in those distant days."

"And how was it done?" asked Lord Southampton.

"With much less braggadocio and boasting. They followed some sort of code back then, a strict etiquette in the conduct of such meetings—still do, to some extent. 'Twould all be handled with much greater politesse, no matter was the outcome foreordained or not."

"That's all most interesting, your grace," said I, addressing him direct, "but it would not be possible upon the stage."

"And why is that, sir?"

"Forsooth, your grace, because the stage is not large enough, nor our time great enough, to portray the siege of Bordeaux. And so it is necessary for the poet to convey the violence of the battle with the violence of his language."

That seemed to satisfy Lord Essex, at least for the time being, and should, to my mind, have ended the entire matter there. Yet somehow, because of a question thrown out by Lord Hunsden, it opened the much larger question of the debt which the theater must pay to history, to fact, to reality. They chewed upon this for a quarter of an hour or more, it seemed.

I suggested that the need for verisimilitude varied from play to play and type to type. There was, I admitted, a great obligation to fact and reality in historical plays, and a similar debt in tragedies, but comedies had little to do with the world as it is, was or will be. "They may as well be set upon the moon," said I, "or upon the seacoast of Bohemia."

"But Bohemia has no seacoast," said Lord Southampton with a frown.

"Exactly," said I.

The comments offered to the brothers Burbage were all very favorable—this in spite of the inequality of their separate performances. Richard, as always, was both polished and powerful; Cuthbert had got all the words right, yet said them with little feeling.

I knew not then what the young earl might have in mind to conclude this first meeting of his "circle." It did, however, seem a bit early to offer refreshments. Thus was I somewhat taken aback when, rising, he called for me to stand, and then, approaching, made unto the small assembly a speech which caused me some embarrassment.

"Let me now approach Mr. Shakespeare and ask him to read something aloud," said he. "Though I now take him by surprise, he should have no difficulty with this text, for he is its author. Some days ago, after meeting him for the first time, I began to receive missives from him. They were quite short, each one fourteen lines long—a sonnet a day is what I have received from him. This may not seem much to some, but I'm sure that Mr. Drayton will agree that a sonnet a day would be a great task for any poet. Nevertheless, it is their quality which I most admire. Let me warn you that the matter of these poems is of a personal nature—personal, that is, to me. I suspect the poet has heard something of the tittle-tattle about me which buzzes round the court, yet I mind it not, for he has approached the matter whereof I speak with such delicacy and argued it in words and phrases of such beauty that I feel that I must share it with you all. Mr. William Shakespeare, will you read this sonnet to all here?"

He thrust the sheet of paper he had been waving about into my reluctant hand. And of course I had no choice but to read aloud what was writ thereon. As Lord Southampton returned to his throne, I glanced over the sheet and saw, with considerable relief that it was the first in this brief sequence of sonnets. At least in the beginning my inspiration was fresh; I was not straining to find new approaches to this most difficult subject. I cleared my throat and began to recite:

From fairest creatures we desire increase,
That thereby beauty's Rose might never die,
But as the riper should by time decease,
His tender heir might bear his memory:
But thou, contracted to thine own bright eyes,
Feed'st thy light's flame with self-substantial fuel,
Making a famine where abundance lies,
Thyself thy foe, to thy sweet self too cruel.
Thou art now the world's fresh ornament,
And only herald to the gaudy spring,
Within thine own bud buriest thy content,
And, tender churl, makest waste in niggarding,
Pity the world, or else this glutton be,
To eat the world's due, by the grave and thee.

(Let me make it clear that I do *not* consider this one of the dozen sonnets of mine which I hold superior to Drayton's best.)

At the last line, having read the whole of it aloud, I stood before them, my face burning in humiliation. My listeners did evidently share my embarrassment, for there was no response from them—absolutely none—they simply sat and stared at me.

Before I could seek sanctuary among my colleagues, the young earl had leapt from his chair and covered the space that separated us in three bounding leaps.

"No discussion," he piped forth. "I absolutely forbid it. The matter is *far* too personal. I shall only say thank you, thank you, thank you, dear Mr. Shakespeare—and relieve you of . . . this."

Having said that, he took from my hand the paper that had written upon it the sonnet. Then, surprising me and shocking some, he planted a buss upon my cheek. I then slank back to my chair and sought to nestle so deep within it that I might make myself invisible.

Yet Lord Southampton remained. He had not done, nor would he allow the evening to reach an early conclusion. There would be more entertainment.

"And now artists and art lovers, one and all," said he, "you will be entertained *royally*—truly royally, for Lord Hunsden has persuaded one of the most distinguished of the court musicians, Raffaela di Abramo, to come here tonight and sing for us a few songs, favorites, she tells me, of the Queen herself."

With that, he returned to his chair, and she sprang forward to the center of the room. A *guitarra latina,* which heretofore had been hidden from view, was now in her hand. She took but a moment to tune it, and as she attended to that she told her audience something of the songs that she would sing them. There was a bit of story to each, which I no longer remember. Yet in forgetting, I have retained the essential common thread upon which the three were strung: All were love songs.

And all three were sung in Italian. I know not how I was able to distinguish that language from the far less familiar Ladino; perhaps it was that the Italian was much more heavily accented, and in that sense more musical. Latin helped a bit, for I heard *"amore, amore, amore"* repeatedly and a few other predictable words and phrases of that sort. And naturally she sang the songs well—such was her work, was it not? Yet I gave less attention to the songs and her singing of them than I did to—how shall I call it?—the total performance.

It was disgusting, scandalous, a crime against propriety.

I have seen a whore dance naked upon a tabletop in a low brothel in Southwark, and that exhibition was in no wise more crudely appealing to man's baser instincts than what I saw that night in the Inns of Court.

How can I describe it? It must be understood, first of all, that she performed only for one. Was I that one? Of course not. Was it then her protector, Lord Hunsden, the Lord Chamberlain? No, it was not. Raffaela sang those three Venetian love songs, one flowing into the next, to our host, the boy-earl who, only moments before, had succeeded in abasing me before all present.

It was her device to circle the great throne-like chair in which he had seated himself, dancing about as she strummed upon her *guitarra latina* and sang to him—and only to him. Yet she sang to him in a manner that seemed quite indecent. She teased; she more than teased; she tempted. Having cast aside the gauze shield which discreetly covered the open bosom of her dress, she was left free to shake her breasts under his nose, right down to the very tips of her dugs. And this action she duplicated during the repeated chorus of the last of these airs. I burned with shame for her, yet she apparently felt none, for she laughed and carried on quite merrily as she bounced about and threw her hips this way and that in a manner most provocative.

And what was the affect of all this upon our young host? He was quite overwhelmed, as one might suppose. When she thrust a near naked bub at him, he winced and giggled; the brothers Burbage joined him in laughter—though I then had the feeling that they were laughing at Lord Southampton, rather than with him. She ended this coarse exhibition quite unpredictably by giving *him* a kiss upon the cheek. So overcome was he that he could do no more than signal to a servant who stood in the doorway behind us. That was all that was needed to bring in a wheeled table quite loaded with wine—good claret it was, of course—meats and dainties of all sorts. The brothers Burbage and Drayton made for it straightaway; for myself, after all I had seen and endured, I had little taste for food, though I felt I needed some several glasses of wine.

I would see that woman, and to her I would vent my feelings about that sorry spectacle I had witnessed. Waking early next morning, I found myself forming angry, hurtful phrases to be used as ammunition against her, who had been so dear to me but a day before. Yet first, there was the twelfth sonnet to be copied out and handed over to Southampton's servant in exchange for the usual payment; it was surely the weakest of the lot. I could only hope that I should not be called upon to read it aloud to any group as I was asked to read the first of them. The courier came punctually at nine, as he always managed to do. He counted out the coins to the exact amount and took away with him those fourteen lines, so painfully produced, so poorly argued. And yet there remained three more to be done. I had a passing thought simply to end it at twelve, to refuse to write more. I had done enough, had I not? Twelve pounds should be sufficient, should it not? Still, I had the distinct feeling that Lady Southampton would not allow it. What she could have done to counter my refusal, I cannot imagine. No doubt it was simple greed drove me on.

Where was I?

Ah yes, having sent off the twelfth sonnet to the Southampton residence, I set my course for the cottage in Little Gray's Inn Lane. 'Twas not a great distance, and the haste with which I walked the way there made it seem shorter still. All the while I went, my mind continued to boil forth the most cutting insults, so that I was in a fine fury by the time I turned down the lane. When I did, I saw neither a waiting coach, nor a flower pot in the window. This was most fortunate, for by the time of my arrival, I was in such a state that if there had been either, in spite of it all, I would have burst through the door and into the little house, demanding to have some explanation from both of them for her crude conduct of the night before. What would Raffaela then have said to that? What, for that matter, would Lord Hunsden have to say? Nay, it is a good thing that he was not present.

I, usually so discreet in my entry into her cot, gave no attention to who else or what might be in the street. I went boldly to her door and pounded upon it most insistently. When there was no immediate response, I grasped the latch and rattled the door as a constable might if in pursuit of a villain. So noisily impatient was I that I heard no sounds of stirring and no footfalls from beyond the door. Therefore was I surprised when, unnoticed by me, the key turned in the lock, and then the door came open a little. I spied a sleepy eye in the gap between door and doorjamb.

"Who is there?" came the voice, deep and thick as a man's. "Oh, is you, Shake-a-speare." A sigh—and then: "Come in."

The eye disappeared, and this time I did hear the steps which took her away. I pushed the door open, entered, and locked it behind me. As I did so, I glimpsed her, naked, disappearing into the bedroom. I followed and was rewarded with an inspiring view of her full figure horizontal upon the bed. She was already asleep, or pretended to be. I wanted to rouse her, to shout into her ear, yet of a sudden all those sharp, dreadful words and phrases which I had been thinking of had deserted me. What was it caused them to flee? 'Twas naught but the sight of her upon the bed. I threw off my cape and eased down beside her. Before I was quite aware of it, my man had begun to stiffen and grow. I had little choice but to unlace my codpiece that he might have some space. Sensing freedom, he leapt forth to full length. Then, surprising me somewhat, Raffaela put her hand out and, pretending careless innocence, groped her way to my loins. That was indeed all the encouragement I required. And she, it seemed, was always eager. In a few moments we were hugging and kissing as wildly as two possessed. How long we continued, I cannot say, for time has little meaning during such play, nor can I say how long we took to consummate the act. Not long, certainly—though it could hardly have been done in an instant, as it seemed.

She then quickly repeated the rite which was performed each time we made the beast with two backs: milking my man of the last of his seed, wiping legs and lips of any drops of the precious stuff that had strayed from their target. Lately this curious practice had made me wonder. Someday perhaps I would ask about it.

That done, she did lie down once again, still panting from our delightful exertions. She turned to me, her eyes no longer clouded with sleep, but bright and lively.

"Is good way to wake up, you know?" And so saying, she shut her eyes, thus threatening to return to sleep.

"Do not—oh, you must not sleep!"

"Oh? *E perchè?* You ready to try again so soon?"

"No, but you must listen to me. I have many insults for you. I have terrible things to say to you." This I said still lying beside her, resting most comfortably. I do not think that I inspired a great deal of fear in her.

"Uh," she grunted indifferently, "why? I gave you no pleasure a few minutes ago?"

"You gave me a great deal of pleasure."

"So? What is this about?"

"About your performance last evening."

"Oh, *that!*" She laughed. "That was nothing, *caro.*"

"To you, perhaps, but to me—why, it made me quite mad to see you display yourself in such a way as to make every man in that room lust after you."

"Not *every* man," said she. "The young Enrico, he was *very* unhappy."

"But *why* did you do it? It was such a whorish display, and it made him quite miserable. You said he was your friend. Why would you treat a friend so?"

At that a change came. She became testy, rising up on her

elbows, giving me an angry look. "He is still my frien'. He tell me so. But you, are you still my frien'?"

"Yes . . . well, yes, I am."

"But you not so sure, eh? You love me still?"

"Have I not said so?"

"Not so often anymore. Maybe you get tired of me, eh?"

There was silence between us for long moments—far too long—so that when at last she did speak again, her voice was cold and hard.

"You like to know why I dance aroun' when I sing those songs and show myself to 'enry? I do it for the same reason you do it."

"What do you mean? I did no such thing as you."

"No, what you do is worse—for you. That *sonetto* you wrote for him . . ."

"Yes, what about it?"

"Is no good. You know that. It has no music in it."

She dared to criticize my work? How could she? What did this ignorant singer of street songs know of poetry? Did she think that I wrote poems as so many ditties to be put to tunes?

Yet she persisted: "You write it for money, jus' like I sing and shake for money. I am tol' to tempt him, to excite him. The ol' lady pay you, didn' she?—jus' like she pay me."

"His mother, you mean?"

" 'Course she is who I mean. You don' have to say. I can see in your face you do it. I could see it in your face las' night."

Had it shown so clear? Was it so plain?

"And what did Lord Hunsden think of this? Did you ask him before you took her money?"

"Oh, yes. He think is funny. Is big joke to him."

Having spoken thus, she gave me such a look as had never before passed between us. It was a sad look, yet there was something of pity in it, too.

"Ah, Shake-a-speare, don' you know? Don' you un'erstan'? We do what they tell us to do." She shrugged.

"Not so! I write as I please!" said I in a fit of vainglory. "It's true I work for money—and only for money—yet I would rot, no matter what amount I might be offered, say what I do not believe, nor express what I do not feel."

"Ah then, I 'ave a rival—this 'tender churl,' eh?"

"What do you mean?"

"Maybe you 'ave to bugger 'enry before you get patronage. You think of that?"

I blushed in anger. I knew not what to say, for the thought she had just expressed had already occurred to me days before. And what at last I did say were words given me by the Devil, for they were meant only to wound. (Instead 'twas me they wounded.)

"And you," said I to her, "if you had been successful in tempting and exciting Lord Southampton, would you then have given yourself to him? Perhaps teach the poor girlish fellow how the trick was done?"

She looked at me square and then did declare: "If Lord Hunsden said to do that, then I would have to do it."

"Then you are naught but a whore—and he your pander."

"But he would not ask me."

"How can you be so certain of that?"

"Because he is honorable man."

"He has proven that to you?"

"*Sì*, he give me a promise that if he make me . . . how you say . . . *incinta?*"

I could not suppose what she meant. I could but shake my head and shrug.

"You know—when I have baby grow inside me."

"Pregnant," said I.

" 'At's it—preg-nant. If I become like so, then he will marry me to any man I want."

I allowed that to hang in the air between us perhaps a little too long. Then, fearfully, I formed the question. "And what man would you choose?"

"You joke, eh?"

"No," said I. "Who?"

"You, naturally—you, *stupido.* Why you think I want all you seed in me? Why you think I squeeze last drops from you and put all of it in me? I want to be preg-nant by you. I want to make a baby with you. I want to make a poet with you."

"And not with Lord Hunsden?"

"No, no, no, he can't make a baby."

"And why can he not?"

"Too old," said she.

"And you're determined to marry?"

"Is natural thing, eh? He see when my belly is big. I have a baby in me. He think he put it there, and he say to me, 'Raffaela, I make you preg-nant. You pick out a husban'.' And I pick you because I love you. All we need to do is make a baby. You see, Shake-a-speare?"

"That is your plan?"

"Is good plan, eh?"

"There is but one fault to it."

"Oh?" She peered at me most suspicious. "An' what is that, eh?"

"I am already married. I have been for some years. My wife is in Stratford."

"Why you never tell me?"

"I thought you knew, or would have reckoned it so."

For a great space of time she said naught. I watched her until her tears began. Only then did she avert her face.

"You go now, eh? Go please."

I did as she said.

XV

Now do I take pen in hand to record my impressions of my meeting with the Right Reverend Andrew Bliven, Bishop of Gloucester. I see no use in attempting, as I did with Vicar Stoner, to reproduce our interview verbatim. First of all, because Bishop Bliven is a much subtler man than the vicar; he can convey more with a change of expression or a wink of his eye than dear Reverend Stoner could communicate in an entire paragraph. Forsooth, a reason for my choice of style in recording the vicar's remarks was my wish to reveal him in all his foolish, pious timidity—he was truly, in my view, a pitiable creature. Since the bishop had little or nothing in common with him save for their mutual Godly interests, there was no need to treat him in the same manner.

He was, in a way that surprised me, quite a worldly man. He knew my name and even knew something of my work. Had he actually seen my plays? No, he said, but he had read a number of them in the Quarto editions. In this he spoke true, for he did not merely praise those he had read (though that he did in sumptuous phrases), he asked many intelligent questions which could have been put only by one who had actually read or seen them. And so I felt at ease with him most immediate.

Knowing nothing of ecclesiastical reputations (though I'm sure he has an impressive one), I could not pay back his generous words in kind; nevertheless, I succeeded in winning his favor by offering repeated thanks for his generosity in agreeing to see me. It also aided my cause immeasurably that I was so well prepared for the meeting. (Wishing to be fair, I must give Vicar Stoner some credit for that.) Short of writing out my speeches and rehearsing them, I had done all that one could do in preparing my case against that fearful woman. When I presented my case to the bishop, it came forth in the most fluent and logical manner. He heard me out most attentively, neither commenting nor asking questions. Only when I had done did he speak.

"The vicar said that he would speak to the woman on this matter?"

"Why, yes—yes, he did," said I.

He said naught in response to that, yet his entire face seemed to tighten in a manner almost imperceptible, and his eyes shifted away of a sudden as if considering a matter of some significance.

"What is it, your grace, if I may ask? You seem to have been taken by a thought."

"How very discerning of you," said he, "but then you are a poet, and poets see more and understand better than the rest of us."

"So they say."

"Indeed you are correct," said he. "I am troubled, merely that, by the vicar's intention to talk to this woman about the matters which concern you."

"Ah yes," said I, "that seemed to me not quite as it should be."

"If your worst fears are correct, then such talk would do no more than warn her that she was suspicioned. Then would she slow her diabolical activities—perhaps stop them altogether—for a time. No matter how hapless those such as your Goodwife Bromley may appear, they are often very sly. Do remember that they receive the advice of the very genius of evil. No, the best thing is simply to collect information on what harm she has done to date. Do you know if the vicar has had this talk with her yet?"

"I believe he has not, your grace. I should be happy to deliver to him your caution against proceeding."

He considered my offer for a moment. "I think not," said he to me. "I shall write him immediate and make plain to him my feelings on the matter."

"As you wish, naturally. I'm sure that a message direct from you would have much greater force."

"Yes . . . well, there is but one matter I wish to make certain of."

"Anything, your grace."

"What you have given me today, Mr. Shakespeare, is not intended by you as a formal accusation of witchcraft?"

"No, I cannot, in good conscience, make such an accusation. I told you of my wife's doubts—well, I take them seriously. I wish, in a way, I could be more certain, for the idea of troubling you over what may prove to be nothing at all—"

"On the contrary, sir, your hesitation to make a formal accusation gives substance to what you do say. I myself tend to be skeptical of those who are overly certain. And as for your fear that nothing will come of it, my own feeling is that something *will come of it—enough to convene an ecclesiastical court, enough to call a few witnesses. You'll be called, of course.*

"I had assumed so," said I modestly.

"Will we know by the end of the proceeding where Goody Bromley stands? Perhaps and perhaps not. If all else fails, though, there is always the trial by water."

I ransacked my brain, yet I came up with naught. "I don't believe that I am familiar with the term."

"It comes to my mind that the country folk hereabouts call it 'swimming a witch.'"

"Ah yes," said I, suppressing a smile. There were stories.

"Yet, however it may turn out," said Bishop Bliven, "our proceeding will serve to announce to Satan that he is not welcome in Warwickshire. That must be made plain to him."

To resume my tale:

Despite our earlier discussion at the Duck and Drake, we of the theater were much amazed at how swiftly the plague spread from the South Bank across the Thames and through London. There was naught could be done, it seemed. At first the numbers of those infected this side the river were not so great—twenty-five or thirty of a week. Yet they crept higher and continued to spread over a wider area of the city.

Michael Drayton's *Guy of Warwick* opened, nevertheless, upon its appointed date to a considerable audience. It played well, drawing great applause from the gallery as well as the groundlings. My many clown bits went over equally well, winning laughter from all. I was left with but a few opportunities to scan the audience, which I did, hoping to catch a glimpse of Raffaela; yet I saw no sign of her. I did spy Henry Wriothesley, the Lord Southampton, however. And a good thing it was, too, for I was thus prepared for him when he came backstage visiting after the play was done. I was taking off my makeup when he made his appearance in the company of a lad his age in a red velvet doublet; I was near certain I had seen his companion a time or two in the World's End. This was as it had been when Raffaela came first to see me, and I was, for just a moment, thrown back in time to that sweet occasion. Thus caught between present and past, I was unprepared to greet him properly. I flustered and stuttered, unable to make my tongue behave.

"My Lord, this is a happy surprise. What—what—what—"

"What did I think of the play?" Lord Southampton's companion giggled.

"Yes . . . yes."

"I thought well enough of it," said he. "It gave me an evening's entertainment. But you! To find you in such a clown role—that did surprise me. Was it not you who complained that most go to the theater only to laugh?"

He gave me a wry, somewhat suspicious look, as if he had caught me out—yet I had anticipated this challenge.

"Indeed I did complain. Yet a man must eat, be he poet or player, and so you see that I am reduced to acting the clown."

"Oh, well . . ." He seemed puzzled. "In truth, I had never considered that aspect of an artist's life. Do you find it . . . trying?"

"Often," said I with eyes downcast.

"Hmm. Perhaps, when I come into my majority, I shall be able to do something about that."

"My lord, you are altogether too kind."

Then did we make to part. I bowed to him; he nodded to me. Still, he had made no effort to introduce to me the lad in the red doublet. And still, he hesitated at the door.

"I miss your sonnets, sir," said he in a manner rather wistful.

"I have more to write," said I, "yet with rehearsals for this play and trying to write another . . ."

"Of course, I understand."

"Perhaps, now that we've opened at last, I shall have the chance to write more. Will there be soon another meeting of your circle? I might bring others and . . ." Yes, said I to myself, and have the chance to see Raffaela once again.

"No, not likely," said he, "for there is now much talk of moving the Queen and her court to the Greenwich castle—because of the plague, you know."

"Ah yes, the plague. Will all go with her to Greenwich?"

"Do you mean, the court musicians along with the rest?"

"Yes, that is, I suppose, what I mean."

"Well, Raffaela is sure to go. She is a favorite of the Queen."

"Yes . . . as indeed she must be," said I.

Then, having no more to say, one to the other, we bade our farewells. The lad in red velvet, who had stood silent all through our conversation, hung back a moment to give a wave and a wink. "Toodle-loodle," said he. Lord Southampton threw a harsh few words back at the fellow, who then obediently turned and jog-trotted after him.

'Twas from Michael Drayton, who was ever about the theater during the brief run of his play, that I heard further news of Christopher Marlowe. As I remember it, I had gone early to The Curtain that I might meet with James Burbage, father of Cuthbert and Richard, in the matter of a new history play at which I worked. Again he expressed interest therein, yet he had also a few doubts when he heard that the subject of the play was no less than Richard III ("the arch-villain of English history," the eldest Burbage called him). The interview was thus concluded in a short space of time. I was left free to wander about till the hour came to don my patched clown's attire and apply my makeup. It was in my wanderings that I encountered Drayton backstage.

He greeted me eagerly, asking when there might be another meeting of Lord Southampton's "circle." I disappointed him by saying there might not be one for quite some time. Ever since that memorable evening he had sought me out, believing that I must have great acquaintance among the grand and the great. Perhaps also he felt a certain kinship with me because of the bond to Warwickshire we shared. As was usual with us, he would talk—and I would pretend to listen. Yet a familiar name did penetrate my dissimulation. I held up my hand to halt Drayton, who had (and still has) a way of talking *at* a fellow, rather than with him. He caught my signal and stopped of a sudden, midway through a sentence.

"What was that you said about Marlowe?" I asked. "I fear my mind was wandering. So much to think about, trying to write two or three things at once, you understand."

"Oh, I do—completely. 'Tis thus also with me. I often find myself engaged in conversation whilst inditing a line or two in my head. I remember that just a day past I—"

"Drayton, please," said I, interrupting.

"What will you, Will?" He giggled at his pun. "Ah yes, Christopher Marlowe. What was it I said about him? Indeed I do recall. I mentioned him as one of those who had returned to print, fearing the closing of the theaters."

"What is he writing? Surely not one of those prose romances such as his friend Nashe spews forth?"

"Oh, by no means. He works upon a long narrative poem, *Hero and Leander*."

"Swimming the Hellespont and all of that nonsense?"

"Well, yes, but it's what he *makes* of it, naturally."

"Naturally."

"I understand he has already found a patron for that work, perhaps for all that he hath planned."

"Oh," said I, feigning indifference, "and who might that be?"

"Sir Thomas Walsingham, so I hear." Drayton rubbed his chin thoughtfully. "Would he be the son of the late, lamented Sir Francis Walsingham?"

"No, the nephew. But mark you, the late Sir Francis is *not* lamented by me. Nor will he ever be."

"I would not question you close on such matters as that, but there are a few things I would like to ask you about."

"You may ask as you please, and I shall answer as *I* please."

"Fair enough." He took a deep breath and then plunged ahead. "I have heard it rumored that you and Christopher Marlowe shared a roof for a time." There he paused, waiting—I assumed—for confirmation or denial.

"That is true," said I.

"If it be so, then he must have conveyed to you something of his devices for ensnaring a patron."

At that I laughed, quite unable to help myself. At last I calmed enough to ask: "Why do you think that?"

"Why, he must have some special skill at it, because I have heard that he is never without money and has ever been so. Or was he a gentleman born? He does conduct himself so."

"While all you say is true," said I, "it is also true that Marlowe often spent money he did not have. It is not so difficult once you have the knack. And he got the knack at university. Those he met at Cambridge and whose favor he curried there have since proved his chief benefactors."

"But you," said Drayton, "you seem also to have acquired the knack. Have you not a patron in Lord Southampton?"

"In truth, no, I have not."

"Yet that sonnet you read?"

"Nevertheless, no."

"Hmm, well, I know not how to put this." He did then shrug and give a great sigh. "I need a patron in quite the worst way. It is just that I know not how to beg. It is not that I am too proud to do it—I would if I could. Yet I know not how to go about it, which words to use, whom to ask, how much to ask for, what I should promise in return, et cetera."

"I know no more than you, I fear. But is your situation so desperate? You've made money from *Guy of Warwick,* and more will come your way."

"No, I think not," said he with a resigned shake of his head. "You've seen the audiences shrink in size. People are afraid to gather in number, afraid that he who stands beside will be infected by the plague and will, in turn, infect them. The situation is such that even if the Privy Council does not close down the theaters, they may as well, for the effect is the same."

"Can you not return to Warwickshire?"

"I have nowhere to go, none to welcome me. I am the last of my family and my former employer sent me packing, said I was taking liberties with his daughter."

"And were you?"

"Yes—and she with me."

'Twas no great jest, yet enough to set us both chuckling, so doleful had our conversation turned just then.

"I have but one more question to ask," said Drayton.

"Ask it then."

He hesitated, and I noted that of a sudden he did appear distinctly uncomfortable. "This also goes back to that time during which you shared space with Marlowe," said he. "It is said that then he was a spy in the employ of Sir Francis Walsingham. Is there also some truth in that?"

"I fear I must choose not to answer that. Nevertheless—"

"Yes, what would you?"

"Nevertheless, it does seem to me that you were asked to put that question to me. Who asked you to do it?"

"Lord Hunsden, the Lord Chamberlain."

His answer did shock and amaze me. I demanded from him a full accounting, and this is the story he told:

It seemed that a week or two previous he had been summoned by the Lord chamberlain. And though Drayton supposed that the invitation had come as a result of his attendance at that evening at Lord Southampton's residence and was consequently most optimistic, he also felt the sort of trepidation that anyone would in meeting the mighty. For all the reasons he had discussed with me, he had become uneasy about his future, and he hoped that the matter of patronage might come up. In a way it did, for Lord Hunsden hinted broadly that there were great rewards to be reaped by one as talented as Michael Drayton; he mentioned stipends, pensions, and appointments "of the less demanding sort," all of which might come to "one who cooperates." What the Lord Chamberlain meant by cooperation, it seemed, was the provision of information: that was all that he was after—"information that might prove useful." He was most interested in whatever might have been said or done by Sir Walter Ralegh or those round him, the so-called "School of night." When Drayton told him that he had no direct knowledge of that group, Lord Hunsden said that he knew that already. "Yet there is one with whom you are well-acquaint who has known one of them intimately," said the Lord Chamberlain. He meant me, of course. He instructed Drayton to ask the question and to plant the notion that he was quite interested in what I might have to tell him. Why, I wondered, had Lord Hunsden not summoned me and told me direct?

Three days after this conversation took place, the Privy Council shut down all the theaters around London, citing the danger to the health of the populace. The number of those infected, dying, and dead had soared most frighteningly. Not even wild rumor could keep up with reality. I heard it said that each day fifty died in London. When, on the same day, I went to visit an apothecary in Norton Folgate, he assured me that if Southwark, Bermondsey, et cetera, were included, the number would be much nearer to a hundred a day.

I had gone to the apothecary to inquire if there were some medicament that I might take as preventative against the plague. Yet he, an honest man, assured me that there was neither preventative nor cure. "Few recover," said he, "and it is not known why they do. 'Tis the will of God who is to live and who is to die, and there is naught that man can do to alter the plan of the Almighty." To hear that from an apothecary, usually among the most practical of men, was indeed sobering. It was near enough to send me into church to pray.

I took to wandering the streets of London alone. They became emptier with each day that passed. It was not that so many had died, but a great portion had left the city for places—any place—where the plague had not visited. There were tales told of those who had fled the great city only to find themselves barred from entering villages a hundred miles distant. Travelers were attacked upon the roads in an effort to turn them round and send them back to London. The plague had infected a goodly piece of southeastern England, but the fear of the plague was rampant all up and down the island.

Those who remained seldom ventured into the streets, so fearful were they of contact with their fellow man. They simply huddled in rooms, living upon what food could be pillaged from empty houses. Lacking hope of survival, they could do naught but suppose that they were powerless before the plague, and that it would be best, if die they must, to do so in familiar surroundings.

Finally, there were those who, from a sense of bravado or a contempt for all the rest, did choose to celebrate this macabre season by spending it in taverns and inns all round the city. They drank toasts to Death and the Devil in ale and wine, committed unspeakably foul acts in public and broke all the commandments given by God to Moses upon the mountain. And though they drank without limit, they never ran out of cash, for they filched it from the pockets of the bodies which had been tossed out into the streets.

I cannot forget the first such corpus which I came upon one dark morning in April. It would rain later that day, but at that moment there was naught but the threat of it in the sky—dark clouds moving west to east. When I first spied the body in that dim and changeable light, I thought it no more than a pile of old clothes tossed out into the street for the scavengers. But on closer inspection, I saw that there were arms and legs filling sleeves and hose, and a head popping out the collar of the doublet. It was the head caused me problems. All swollen and spotted with gray splotches the face was, and the neck a mass of pustules. I ventured not close for fear of inhaling the deadly vapors issuing from the corpus. Nevertheless, I came near enough to see all I wished to—and more—and immediately did I understand why the plague inspired such panic. 'Twas the look of it frighted all.

My walks through the empty city always took me past the house in Little Gray's Inn Lane. While Lord Hunsden's coach stood never again at Raffaela's door during that plague season, the flower pot remained ever in her window, warning me away. As I passed the place each day, I noted that the plant in the pot had begun to wilt, and its flowers start to droop. It had been neglected. I thought it unlikely that she had been inside the place for over a week. No doubt she had gone west with the rest of the court to the Queen's castle in Greenwich. Had not Lord Southampton said that she would? There was little hope of finding her inside, yet still I came to look, to remember, to yearn.

No, I had not forgotten her; I could not. The experience I had had of Raffaela was the deepest of its kind I had known—perhaps truly the only one of its kind. What did I miss most about her? Our talks? her voice? her laugh? our lusting? It was all of that and more. Her very presence did sum up and contain them all. And now that presence had been taken from me—and with it, all those remarkable qualities. What was I to do? I walked for days considering the answer to that, thinking hard upon it. Yet whenever I did, I came up hard against an indisputable fact: though I wanted Raffaela, I could never have her so long as my wife were alive. Well, Anne wouldn't always be alive, would she? After all, she was six years older than I. Even in the ordinary course of things she would die some years before me—yet that might be a long time into the future, and I might not be able to take advantage of the changed situation.

What then? an accidental death? Accidents are, by their very nature, chance occurrences. I could not *depend* upon her dying as a result of some sort—unless I were to have caused the accident. And in that case, would such a death not be considered—murder?

Not necessarily—for if we consider the lamentable death of Ffoke Gyllome, these many years past, I would be forced to admit that indeed I did cause the death, and yet it was truly accidental. I have no guilt in the matter—of that I am quite sure. Yet if the circumstances of that could be duplicated, then would not the death caused thereby also be accidental? (Even a *similar* set of circumstances might do.)

But wait! Was I perhaps overlooking what would be the most convenient and effective manner of death? Indeed, it would seem so, for was I not on every side surrounded by the most convincing evidence? Why had I not considered death by disease? How, with bodies piling up on every corner, could I have ignored such a possibility? It seemed to me that I might simply fill a phial with the vapors emanating from the corpus with the ugliest black spots and the greatest pustules, cork it tight, and take it so to Stratford, and there infect Anne. Yet could that be done without risk to me? Perhaps, but perhaps not. And even supposing that it could be done in such a way, could I depend upon the phial of invisible poison to do what was intended? The apothecary had declared that it was according to the will of God who would live and who would die. At the time I heard it from him, I must say I was convinced, for what better explanation for the survival of those who pushed their carts through the city and collected the dead for burial in mass graves? God willed them to live, for without them, there would be no way to see the dead into their proper resting place. And it might also be, though I was loath to admit it, that I would find that God wanted Anne to live, too.

Such were my thoughts as I wandered round the city. So troubled was I by my separation from Raffaela that I saw no harm in thinking them. My hunger for the mistress of my heart (for such she was) had grown so great that I was near ready to set off walking along the Thames for Greenwich castle. It was either that, or leave London for one more trip to Stratford-upon-Avon to see what might be done about Anne. I chose the latter course.

Indeed such a visit was past due. I had fifteen pounds from Lady Southampton which I must entrust to my father for purposes of usury. I knew, too, that the longer I delayed my journey, the greater the risk of becoming infected by the plague. Enough of this moping about Little Gray's Inn Lane! If I could not discover some practical solution to my problem with Anne there in Stratford, I might at least be able to work while there. God knows why, but I could do nothing of the kind in London.

And so, packing light, I set off after dark by foot, vowing that this would be the last time I should ever walk my way to Stratford. In this case, I was not merely being frugal: it was generally agreed that the tightly crowded conditions inside the post coach were unfortunately most favorable for the spreading of a dire contagion, such as the plague. While I wished to go to Stratford, I hoped to end the trip alive. Therefore I decided to tramp my way home and do so by night, so as to avoid the gangs which roved the roads and turned back travelers from London. For my protection, and for the protection of the cash I carried, I wore my poniard in my belt and my rapier in its sheath hanging from my belt. My travel bag, which contained naught but a few pieces of clothing, some papers, and a book or two, I had thrown over my shoulder.

I traveled northwest to Oxford, which I reached upon the third morning of my journey. There I allowed myself a day at an inn that I might recover some of the sleep lost along the way. There I had the first glimpse of myself in a looking glass for days and saw a full beard forming upon my jowls; I liked the look of it, did no more than trim it, and let the rest remain. I slept the day through, then did I take a walk through the town to view the colleges. (I have ever thought it a place where I belonged.) I left the inn and the town of Oxford at about the time that most of the sojourners were arriving. I continued in a northerly direction for Warwickshire. The piece from Oxford to Stratford is fair empty of villages and wayside inns and is thought by some to be somewhat perilous. And so it proved to me.

'Twas at the end of a long night of walking, my first beyond Oxford. Dawn had come, painting the sky a strange pink-gray. In truth, I had had enough of walking and was looking left and right along the way for a likely place for me to lay my head and wrap me in my cloak; I was perhaps not so observant as I should have been of the road just ahead. There was a bend, and just to the right of it, a copse of thick-grown bushes. Quite without announcement a figure leapt from behind the bushes and into my path. The fellow was clothed all in black and wore a cape and a broad-brimmed hat. He brandished a sword most threateningly, and I came to a quick halt.

"Stay, pilgrim, and show what th' hast in that travel bag." It was the voice of a youth and not that of a full-grown man.

I allowed the bag to slide from my shoulder and down to the ground. Just as I did so, the sun's rays broke over the horizon. The sudden light from the east illuminated his features, and I saw he was no more than a callow-faced lad. And most clear did I see the fright in his eyes. I took a step back from my bag there in the road, daring him to come forward. Then, with a long, deliberate motion, I drew my rapier from its scabbard, while all the while I fixed him with a fierce stare.

"There it is," said I in a strong, steely voice. "If you wish to see what is inside, you must fight me first."

I pointed down at the bag with the sword in my right hand as I drew my poniard with my left. I eased my position over to my left, so that the brightening rays of the sun hit his eyes direct. Now in a crouch with a weapon in each hand, I stood poised for a bare fraction of a moment. Then did I leap forward in a feint, causing the lad to jump back in a manner most awkward. Forsooth, he did near trip over his own feet. Yet I pursued him, causing him to jump back once again, this time no more gracefully than the last. A third feint, and I had final proof that I had read his eyes aright: the lad in black threw down his sword, turned round, and ran fast as he could up the road. I jeered not at him, nor did I hoot, whistle, or sneer. I would not have him vengeful, for I kept in mind that I must find a place to sleep along the way. If I had wounded his pride, that poor oaf of a plowboy might come back and slit my throat as I slept just to see what was inside my travel bag. He might try to do so, anyway, and so I hid his sword well in a neighboring field—indeed, I buried it, though not deep. Then did I walk on later into the morning than I would have liked, looking for a safe place to lay my head. As it came to pass, however, I came into a village of no more than a hundred souls, yet in it was an inn of some size, respectable and secure. I slept in comfort upon a bed, woke to find it dark and made ready to resume my march to Stratford.

Something about the story I have just recounted may strike you as strange, even false, or at the very least, not quite consistent with my nature. Had I become braver? Was I more heroic than that poor fellow in a field outside Tilbury who had shivered with fear when told to prepare for battle with the Spaniards? Was I no longer a coward?

Nay, have no doubt of it. I was then a coward and am now still. If cowardice were a sin I should be damned a hundred times o'er, and were it a virtue, my salvation would indeed be assured. Nevertheless, it is neither sin nor virtue.

Still, even I, a convinced coward, am aware of factors which may alter my position from time to time. First, when I set off upon this journey, I armed myself not just for my own protection but also for the protection of the cash in my travel bag. In my mind, the two are not greatly distant, one from the other, for without the necessities of life, which only cash can provide, life simply cannot be lived.

Then there is the matter of the opponent: he must be chosen with care. I have ever followed one rule in this regard, and that is this: only do combat with one who shows you greater fear than your own. In the matter that I have just recounted, I was certain that the plowboy was more frighted than I, and that gave me all I needed to act the role of one far more brave than I. 'Twas not my swordsmanship that sent him scurrying, but rather, my performance as one confident in his abilities as a swordsman. An actor is better prepared than most for life's surprises and sudden trials.

But enough of philosophy! Leave it that I completed my journey to Stratford-upon-Avon without further interference from brigands. Yet was my experience with that robber by the road unique? Far from it. There is not a single male of my acquaintance who has not been robbed by threat or stealth at least once. Let none suppose that there is any single mile of English road, in country or city, that can be called completely safe, nor perhaps is there ever likely to be. And so a man must defend himself and his property by whatever means he has.

My arrival in Stratford was quiet, as was indeed my entire visit there. Arriving near midnight, I walked through the town and saw no one, and forsooth none saw me. This I noted with interest, remembering why I had come, for after all, if a man might come and go thus undetected so late at night, there could be no end to what he might accomplish.

The door to our little cottage was not locked—I had not expected that it would be—and all slept inside. The children were nearest the door, and as I went past them on tip-toes, Hamnet stirred in agitation and cried out without coming completely awake. But Anne, who slept beyond the curtain, was sitting up in our bed when I appeared; his cry had roused her.

"Will," said she in a whisper, "is it you?"

"Naturally," said I, "were you expecting another?"

"Don't be foolish. Come." She patted the bed beside her. "Sit down, and tell me the news. What brings you here?"

I did as she bade me, and as I took my place, my hand did happen to brush the poniard, which was tucked into my belt on the left side. That reminded me of why I had come—well, one of the reasons I had come, anyway.

It occurred to me at that I might put my hand over her mouth and stab her in the windpipe, then take my belongings and disappear into the night. Who would then be the wiser?

Yet soon as the thought had come, it vanished. I was tired, altogether too tired from my long walk from London to undertake any action as potentially exhausting as wife-slaying. Besides, Anne was a big, strong woman—it would be in no wise easy to subdue her. Our struggle might indeed be heard by the children—Hamnet was already half-awake—and I should be loath to murder them all, least of all him. And so I let go the notion as soon as it had come.

"What brings me here?" said I, repeating. "Why, my wish to see you and my children, naturally. And, I must confess, a strong desire to escape London, which is at the moment ridden with plague."

"Ah," said she, still in a whisper, "I believe I did hear something of that. Yet London is so very far away that we here think of it as a different world entirely."

She was right. London was a different world. It was, in this town where I grew up, a mere rumor. It was in London that the Queen dwelt (with occasional sojourns in such places as Greenwich and Windsor). It was to London where our taxes went. It was to London where all high court matters were sent by the local magistrate. It was to London I had hoped to escape, and it was to London that I had.

As I attained something close to manhood here, it never came to me that Stratford had attractions of its own. They were, however, of the secret sort, not likely to be recognized by a lad such as I was at sixteen. There was the beauty of the country all about which I had bare noticed earlier; squalorous, crowded London had nothing of the kind. And there was Stratford's quiet, the sort of God-given absence of noise which only a poet can appreciate.

'Twas in Stratford I hoped to do some writing and had, accordingly, brought along some books to help me on my way—Ovid for my *Venus and Adonis* and Hall's *Union of the Families of Lancaster and York* for *Richard III*. I had nearly done with the former and had barely begun the latter. Still, I found that I could work on both, morning and afternoon, in that space provided for me in my parents' home. There seemed to be no question by them or by Anne but that I was entitled to time, space, and quiet to write. I had had success in London and had brought home money enough to prove it.

I found, too, that there was great pleasure to be had once again in writing sonnets. No longer was I put upon the demanding plan at which I was forced to work earlier. I was able to produce new sonnets according to a plan of my own devising and at my own rate. They were all the better for it. When I had a fair quantity of them, I sent them on to Lord Southampton that he might have a proper reminder of my deserving talents.

All in all, I did enjoy writing there in Stratford through that long plague season in a way that I had not in London. I liked the sameness of it: each day I would go off to sit down at the writing table at the same time. If I needed a change during the day, then I would put aside *Richard III* and work a bit at *Venus and Adonis*—or perhaps I would start off the day with a sonnet.

All of what I had done up to that time while in London and Lancashire had been prentice work—mere preparation for what I now accomplished with fair ease. What I was doing then and there in Stratford, particularly in the writing of *Richard III*, I did truly enjoy—and I enjoyed because I sensed the excellence of my work.

Was King Richard truly, as James Burbage had called him, "the arch-villain of English history?" I think not. Let him be thought of, rather, as the most powerful of England's kings, and let us hear no more about his sins. His power lay in his willingness to do what others refused even to consider, and 'twas his ambition drove him on. In an odd way, I came to admire the man for his decisiveness, his strength of purpose, his daring. These were qualities that I myself could emulate—and did.

Though it was that this meant much to me, it meant little to my parents and to Anne, and nothing at all to my children. I, as many fathers will, did wish my progeny to have some knowledge of my work so that they might take pride in it. Yet what understanding of the writing of plays could they have, they who had never seen a play? Yet well into August, whilst out upon my morning walk, I saw a notice tacked upon a tree, which would change all that. The notice ran so:

"Lord Strange's Men, players from London, will come one day only, August 9, to entertain you with a performance of the play, *'The Tragical History, Admirable Achievements and Various Events of Guy Earl of Warwick,'* as offered in London before titled noblemen and women."

I could scarce believe the print upon the notice, but forsooth, there it was. Lord Strange's Men, which meant that the brothers Burbage, Alexander Cooke, Will Oster, and all the rest, would be here in a few days to present the play in which I myself had played the clown's role. I should then have the opportunity to take the children to see a play that they might better understand what it was that I do—and why I do it.

I had them all prepared when the great day came, and as soon as ever I heard the fife and drums in the distance, I took Anne and the children that we might see the parade. Hamnet and Judith were then seven years of age, and Susanna was quite a mature girl of nine. I rushed them all to the side of the road, where most of the town had gathered. As the noise of the fife and the beat of the drums grew louder, the children grew more elated. Then at last the parade appeared, moving round a bend in the road, led by the three boys who played the parts of women in the play. They beat no drums, tootled no fifes, yet they set the crowd clapping as they cartwheeled down the street, danced in the Morris style, and turned a handspring now and again. They put on a fine show; the fifers played their tune recognizably well, and the drummers kept fair time. Hamnet, Judith, and Susanna were altogether bewitched by what they saw, and so, indeed, were all those who crowded in on both sides of the road. I had heard it said in town that it had been many years since strolling players had come this way—Thus the excitement that seemed to touch Stratford and the many here from outlying villages and farms. I knew most among the marchers, and in the beginning I waved to catch their attention. Yet I soon saw that all round me people were waving, calling out, and cheering, and that my greetings were lost among the many. Only when the wagon came by, bringing up the rear of the procession was my wave seen and acknowledged by one of the paraders. 'Twas none other than James Burbage driving the wagon and scanning the crowd.

Upon seeing me, his hand shot up in greeting, and he shouted out: "Will, Will, we hoped we might find you here. Come see us after the show!"

Ah yes, the show—I'd played it through ten performances to dwindling audiences, so that I knew it quite well. I could tell, for example, that *Guy of Warwick,* as performed by Lord Strange's Men here in the courtyard of the inn, was near half an hour shorter than it had been at The Curtain in Shoreditch. I knew, too, that the fellow they had got to play the clown role—my old part—was something of an amateur. I recognized him not at all—nor was that surprising, since his makeup was thick and quite preposterous (another sign of an amateur). He was not from London, surely; they must have picked him up along the way.

Ah, but what cared the Stratford crowd whether he be amateur or professional! This was theater, and more real to them than the life they knew. The children loved the play. Hamnet and Judith stood throughout, next to their gallery seats there above the courtyard, cheering at Guy's feats of combat, shrieking with laughter at the interruptions of the clown. (I do allow that the lines written by me for the clown, Sparrow, came off well in spite of the player's poor sense of timing; and I admit his Warwickshire accent was quite convincing.) Susanna, quite serious in her demeanor, remained seated throughout but concentrated mightily upon the action of the play; she, it was, who reminded me most of myself. As for Anne, her response was veiled, a bit mysterious, and far more difficult to read.

I recall that when the play was done and the applause had died, Anne turned to me and said, as one might to a child, "So this is how you've been spending your time all these years?"

"It is, right enough," said I. "Would you have wished it otherwise?"

She hesitated, as if giving the matter some thought. "No," said she at last, "we live as well as some and better than most."

To that I gave no response, simply stood and proceeded to herd the children from our gallery seats down to the place behind the temporary stage, which served as a dressing room. Let Anne come along as she liked, but I would bring the children, all three, backstage. Indeed, she came.

There was a proper reunion in the dressing room. I was there among my mates once again, embracing my colleagues. I had in no wise supposed how much I missed them all—nor indeed how much they missed me. I introduced Anne, Hamnet, Judith and Susanna so often that I became quite dizzy with it all and began confusing their names. The children took that rather badly, but for the most part they were happy to stand, stare, and listen.

Dick Burbage was most eloquent: "Ah, Will," said he, "now I can well understand why you chose not to go out on the road with us. What a fine family you have. To live in two places, as you do—that should indeed be every player's hope. How I envy you."

That last was said with a gesture toward Anne; she, unused to such playing-the-gallant round her, did blush with pleasure.

"Ah, but no, Dick," said I. "I'd no wish to go out on the road. I did seven summers as a traveling player. That was quite enough." Then, lowering my voice: "But who is that you have in my role? Did you pick him up in Southwark? I fear the fellow is rather bad."

"Didn't you recognize him?"

"Why, no. Should I have done?"

" 'Twas Michael Drayton—and no other."

I was struck quite dumb with surprise. Drayton was a fellow with whom I was well-acquainted. We had talked numberless times. Yet he hadn't for an instant revealed himself beneath his makeup.

"Perhaps he is a better actor than I supposed," said I. "I must greet him. Where is he?"

"Behind the blanket, changing. Go ahead, Will. I shall be happy to entertain your wife and young ones."

I thanked him a bit uncertainly. It occurred to me as I made my way to the blanketed space that Burbage had just given me another reason for keeping Anne in Stratford. She was, after all, a handsome woman, and I had no wish that she give me a set of horns. I might eventually murder her, but still, she was till then my wife—and that, by every court in the land, gave me prior claim.

Drayton and I did near bump heads as he exited the changing space.

"Will!"

"Michael!"

"I was hoping to see you," said he. "I remembered you were from Stratford, and I thought you might be in the audience." He sighed and gave me an expectant look. "What did you think of my performance?"

"Well, let me tell you, first of all, that you seemed to lose yourself completely in the role. I watched the entire show from beginning to end, and I never once recognized you beneath your makeup."

"When you speak of 'losing yourself,' you mean that in a good way, do you?"

"Oh, the very best."

"And you didn't mind the lines I changed?"

He had caught me out on that one. "Well, that is . . . I . . .

forsooth I did not notice them, so I couldn't have minded overmuch."

"True," said he, "true, but I own I rewrote near all the part. Dick Burbage said 'twas common for him who played the clown's role to do so and gave me his blessing."

"He did, did he?"

Burbage was becoming an annoyance to me. First he cuckolds me, and now I find he has given this beginner among playwriters, this not-yet-a-prentice, a free hand in rewriting lines which I did sweat and slave over. What justice in that? For a moment I was quite speechless. And Drayton, taking my silence for permission to exalt himself further, did begin again.

"I must say this chance to get out on the road with the troupe has been a great blessing to me. Well, in one sense that should be quite evident. If James Burbage had not invited me to come along, I should probably have starved to death, had the plague not taken me. Yet it has also done my understanding of dramatic writing a great lot of good. I do believe that when we get back to London I shall pursue acting as a sort of second career. What do you think of that, Will?"

As I had listened to him prattle on, I offered him only an indulgent smile. What could I say now, in response to all that I had just heard?"

"What do I think, Michael?" I gave him a pat upon the shoulder. "I think you had best work on your timing."

Then, having let him off most generously, I deserted him where he stood and made my way back to Anne and the children.

"Well," said I to Anne, "I see that your gallant has fled."

"He will be back," she replied with a flash of defiance in her eye. "He went to fetch his father, who would have a word with you."

I turned to the children and sought the proper questions to ask them. How had they enjoyed the play? Which was their favorite part? Et cetera. There must be something beyond the obvious. Then, from outside, came Burbage, father and son, and saved me from such tediousness.

"Ah, Will," said Burbage senior, "there was something I wished to say before we must away."

"And what was that?"

I noticed Dick Burbage settling into conversation with Anne. I made an effort to listen in to what they were saying, but with his father talking into my other ear, that proved quite impossible. What was it he was saying?

". . . that play."

"Which one?"

"The one you said you were working on—the one about Richard Crookback."

"Indeed? What about it?"

"Have you finished it?"

"Nearly."

"Been working on it here, have you? Good place for a poet to write, I can tell. Yes, well, I'd like to see it when you're done."

That took me somewhat by surprise. "You do? But you said—"

"I know what I said," he interrupted. "Just let us have a look at it before you sell it off for cash to Henslowe. Dick and I've been talking on it, how it ends the War of the Roses story, and so on, and Dick says I'm a fool to let it go without a look. An't it so, Dick?"

"I implied it, but didn't say it," said the son.

"Listen to him. He should've been a lawyer," said he with a shake of his good, gray head. "But I'll tell you what I'll do, Will. I'll pay a pound to you right this moment if you promise to let me have first look. What say you to that?"

"I say done!" Why not? God knows I had no special affection for Henslowe.

With that, James Burbage dipped into his purse and put into my hand a mark and the rest of the amount in shillings.

"Done and done. Now, I have your promise that we shall see it first?"

"You have it," said I.

"Good. When will you be back in London?"

"Why, when the plague has gone, I suppose."

"Well, if you mean gone complete, then you may have a long wait. But it'll slow down considerable after the first frost. That's when we're heading back. Should be safe enough. Shall we see you then?"

"With the play under my arm," said I.

Then did he bellow out a summons to his players. "Let's away! Must make Warwick by nightfall." And he did walk out the door with Dick close behind.

XVI

Four months later, I walked out of James Burbage's office in the Curtain theater with my future assured. The senior Burbage, head of the company, had read *Richard III,* pronounced it my masterpiece, and offered me seven pounds for it. We haggled, and I raised him to eight (which excluded the pound I'd received for allowing him to see it first).

But best of all was what he had to tell me of their plans for a new company. Lord Strange was fast falling out of favor with the Queen and with the Privy Council, and a new patron would have to be found when they reformed after the plague had spent itself. Nevertheless, when they did reorganize, it would be as a "stock company" in which all shared equally in the profits. Burbage told me that I would be wanted by them as an actor, but even more as a poet of the drama. As he put it to me: "What every theater needs is good plays—and they're what's hardest to get. Henslowe makes us pay dear for them. But if you can come up with two or three a year as good as this one about old Crookback, then there'll not be another company in London town can match us."

Forsooth, who would not feel elevated by such a discussion, such an offer! I walked aimlessly through the streets buoyed by my fantasies of wealth and fame. In a milder form, such had been my condition since my earlier encounter with Burbage in Stratford. I was so excited to be given cash merely to be assured first look at a work I had not yet quite finished—such implied a degree of enthusiasm for my work and confidence in me which was truly surprising. Had Dick Burbage tipped his father in my direction, as they claimed? If so, I owed him much. Dear old Dick, ever my friend, always my greatest supporter, I had long before forgiven him for attempting to seduce my wife.

So lifted was I by that meeting in Stratford that I went to work with even greater fervor than before. In a day or two, hardly more, I had finished the last scenes of the drama, those scenes which are set upon the battlefield. King Richard had repeated his mournful offer to trade his kingdom for a horse. He is slain by Richmond, who then calls for an end to all divisive civil strife:

> **Now civil wounds are stopt, peace lives agen:**
> **That she may long live here, God say Amen!**

Ah, it *is* good, isn't it?

Yet I immediately commenced the writing of another play. *Two Gentlemen of Verona* it was, and a comedy it is. The reason for that, naturally, was that to write it, I needed neither historical fact, nor biographical inspiration, which could only have been obtained from books unobtainable in Stratford. I chose the Italian setting as a bow to Raffaela.

Ah yes, Raffaela. During my time in Stratford, I thought of her often—though each day perhaps a little less. I had not given up the plan that had brought me down there, yet somehow the longer I remained the less likely it seemed that I should ever see it brought to fruition. Well I remember the last occasion upon which I gave serious thought and effort to its execution.

Anne had suggested that we take the children on an excursion to the riverside where we should celebrate the completion of *King Richard III*. She must have understood from me—and all that she heard said between the eldest Burbage and me—that this did represent a considerable achievement on my part, one from which much was expected. As so many of the illiterate west-country folk, she had a tendency to dismiss the importance of reading and of all that is in books; she questions its utility and value in everyday matters. And to her, that a man of obvious worth such as Burbage should pay a pound just for the privilege of being the first reader of the play was indeed impressive. Therefore, though she could not herself read the play, she was eager to celebrate it—an odd situation, that. Thus she gives me many occasions at which to wonder at her. Nevertheless, I assented, not least because I, too, felt it an occasion for celebration, yet also because I thought it might prove an opportunity to see if the circumstances of Ffoke Gyllome's death might be duplicated.

'Twas following the repast of dainties and wine (cider for the children) that the event in question took place. The children slept in the shade beneath a tree. And whilst Anne gathered up the leavings of our little meal, I declared that I would have a closer look at the River Avon. In response, she gave me a shrug, as if in dismissal, and I went off to a point on bankside just out of sight of the children. Looking round me, I saw that there was no one else about, which was as it should be. Then did I look down at the river. Well, thought I, 'twas hardly the River Mersey in flood—the Avon was a gentler river at this time of year—still, it might do. There had been hard rains earlier, and it had risen a good bit. The current, if not terribly swift, was at least strong enough to be seen. Indeed, this river and this place might do. I called out quietly to Anne.

By and by she came. Taking her own sweet time, she was. I wished her to hurry. Could she be mindful of my intentions? Witnesses to the intended deed might appear at any moment.

Ah, but wait. What excuse might I offer to bring her close to the riverbank? I leaned over and found a bit of moss and a flower growing out of it. I was continually asking her the name of this plant or that, and so to ask her again about this one would seem quite reasonable.

"Yes, Will? What is it?"

"Come over here, will you?"

She came willingly enough, curious at my request. She stood by me, looking down where I pointed.

"That flower growing out of the moss there," said I. "What is that?"

"Where? Let me see."

She edged closer to me, so that her body was actually touching mine. Then did she bend down for a closer look.

"Can't you see it? It's just over the edge there."

Bending forward, she was so nearly off-balance that she put a hand upon the ground to steady herself. It seemed to me that if I could just persuade her to lean forward a bit more, it might not even be necessary to give her a shove. But quite unexpectedly, I felt the earth of the riverbank shift beneath my feet. I pushed back, scrambling for firm footing—and then of a sudden I found myself plunging down in a shower of dirt into the cold and wet of the river.

"Will!" Anne shrieked from somewhere above.

Then was I swept along by the current, flopping and floundering against it as I tried to keep my head above water so that I might breathe, yet at the same time fighting against the current that I might reach the nearest bank. Had I thought the current seemed weak? I could do naught but flail my arms against it. I had once known how to swim. Why could I now make no progress at all?

I know not how long I struggled thus, though it seemed quite an eternity. Indeed, I was weakening when a strong arm was thrown round my shoulders, and I felt myself tugged in a new direction. All I could do to help was kick my legs as

I was pulled along. Working together in this way, we reached the farther bank, which was not so steep as that which had collapsed beneath me. 'Twas only then, as we scrambled up the bank together, that I saw that my savior was my wife.

She had shed her gown and, dressed only in her shift, made quite a figure as she threw herself down upon the grass beside me. We could do no more than pant together for a considerable length of time. At last I managed to prop myself up on my elbows so that I might speak.

"Thank you." I managed to bring it forth between gasps.

"What? You thought I would let you drown?" She was not near as spent as I.

"No." Thus much I managed, but then did I lay my head once again upon her that I might breathe deeper and recover myself. But one question more had I to ask, and so I struggled up again onto my elbows.

"I . . . didn't know you . . . could swim . . . When did . . . you learn?"

"When I was a girl," said she, lifting herself to a sitting posture then taking a deep breath. "All those brothers of mine. But I thought *you* could swim."

"So did I . . . But it's years . . . since I tried."

"And where did you learn?"

"In the big pond south of town."

"Pond swimming an't the same as river swimming."

We left it at that. Ever afterward had I contending feelings over this incident. On the one hand I felt thwarted in my efforts to bring about Anne's death by "arranging" an accident, so to speak. Yet on the other hand, I felt properly chastised by Providence that I should come so near to drowning in the manner I had intended for Anne. Most of all, however, I felt gratitude to her, my intended victim, for saving me.

How could I not? The power of love was such that any sin might be forgiven if committed in its name—or so was it according to the tradition passed on to us from courtly times. Nevertheless, when one has been given such a lesson as I was there in the River Avon, it would be hard not to reconsider plans, even perhaps rearrange attitudes altogether.

What was it that Dick Burbage had said? That to dwell in two places as I do should be the hope of every player. Dick was no fool. There was a bit of wisdom in that. Had I not found Stratford a good place to work in this last visit? Indeed I had! Two plays written *and* a long poem, which would make a short book, as well as any number of sonnets (forsooth, I had lost count)—all done in half a year. I was ne'er so productive in London!

And what then had I got Anne out the way and then found that Raffaela could not or would not have me? Would I then be condemned to life as a lonely solitaire?

And what about my children—dear Hamnet and Judith, and stout Susanna? Who would then be mother to them? Oft-times the satisfaction of lust asked too high a price of a man.

Yet here was I, wandering the streets of London with such thoughts in my head—and on this day of all days! Why? Why could I not simply rejoice at my good fortune? I must open my heart to the well-wishes of James Burbage, his congratulations, his talk of my "masterpiece." This be all a man should need. I determined not to allow myself to be weighed down by considerations of the darker sort. Yet it occurred to me how much richer this occasion might be had I someone with whom I might share it.

Then did I note with some surprise—yes, truly, surprise—how near I had come in my aimless stroll to Raffaela's little thatch-roofed cottage in Little Gray's Inn Lane. Indeed, from the corner just ahead I should be able to spy it. What luck if Raffaela should be there at this very moment! We could meet as friends, and I would tell her of this sudden change in my situation, and all about *King Richard III*, which had brought it all about. She would wish to see it, naturally, so I would make a copy for her—and we would talk and things would be, for a while, as they had been.

I hurried to the next corner, whence I could see well enough to tell—yes, the space before her house was vacant of coach and horses, *Deo gratia*. As near as I could tell, the window was empty, as well. I approached carefully, making every effort to appear as a casual passer-by, thus confirmed that there was no flower pot placed in the window, and that the little street of like houses was quite empty. Only then did I walk most eagerly to the door; I was about to knock upon it when I saw that it was ajar. I listened, heard nothing, and gave it a careful push. It did not squeak when it opened, as it usually did. Still waiting, still listening, I remained for a moment at the doorstep; hearing nothing but a slow, light slapping sound, I stepped inside.

Though I was near certain that there was someone there, I did not wish to venture too far from the door, in case a hasty exit was necessary. And so I did call out most quietly, "Raffaela? Raffaela, are you there?"

In response, a face appeared in the doorway which led into her bedroom. It was a very familiar face—that of Henry Carey, the first Lord Hunsden. I had got myself into a predicament, so it did seem.

He frowned. "What will you—" Then did his face relax in recognition. "Oh, I know you. Sit down. I want to talk to you."

The face in the doorway disappeared as I looked about for a place to put my backside. Only then did I notice that the room had been emptied of furniture almost completely. There were but two plain chairs on either side of the fireplace; reluctantly, I took one of them. One does not disobey a direct order from the Lord Chamberlain.

Talk continued—or perhaps I should say resumed—in the next room. By what was said, it was evident that a good deal of discussion had gone on before my arrival. It simply happened that I had blundered in during a pause in their conversation. Now I had no choice but to wait, not knowing what I was waiting for and fearing the worst.

I heard Lord Hunsden dismiss him with whom he had talked with an expression of assent. "That will do it," said he to his invisible partner. "Yes, that will do quite nicely. Get as much of that as it will take to do the interior of the house and start tomorrow."

Then out came a painter—not a picture painter, but a wall painter, rather—with his painter's brush in hand. Uncertain as to who I was or what my station might be, he doffed his hat to me and gave a little bow, and then did he scamper out the door to the street.

Lord Hunsden popped his head out again. "Come in here. I wish to show you something, Mr. . . . uh . . . what is your name again?"

"Shakespeare, my Lord."

"Ah yes, very well, come in here."

Again, I did as he commanded and entered that room I remembered best. It was, however, much changed since last I had seen it. It was quite empty of furniture now, even the big old bed had been taken elsewhere. There was a great canvas cloth thrown over the floor. A middling-large section of the wall had been painted a light blue—a very light blue.

"How do you like that?" Lord Hunsden asked, pointing to the painted section. "What do you think of that color?"

I could tell by his manner that he was not baiting me. He did truly want my opinion, and so I gave it some consideration. "I like it," said I. "It's very . . . oh . . . restful."

"Yes, I like that—restful. You'd have the right word, naturally." He pointed a finger at the floor. "Be careful where you step. There's a bucket full of the stuff down there by your foot."

I looked down where he had indicated and put some distance between me and the bucket in question.

"In any case," he resumed, "it will cover all the walls in the next room, too. Do you think that's too much of a good thing?"

Again, I gave the matter proper consideration. "No, such a restful color should cover a multitude—"

"Of sins?" he put in, interrupting.

"No, well, I was going to say, a multitude of walls."

He laughed, as I did, too.

"May I suggest," said he, "that we go into the next room and sit down in those two chairs? With one thing or another, I've been on my feet for the last three hours. That's quite a test for legs as old as mine."

And naturally we did as he suggested. He stretched out and shifted this way and that in his chair in a bootless effort to achieve comfort. At last he settled down sufficient to talk.

"I'm getting this place cleaned up."

"I can see that. It should please Raffaela greatly," said I. Then, thinking it necessary to offer some excuse for my presence, I added: "I am lately returned from Warwickshire and had news for her of my work. She . . . she has taken a great interest in my work."

"Yes, I know that she did."

"That's why I came by, you see—just to tell her. I found the door open slightly, and so I stepped inside. I know I shouldn't have done but . . . but . . ."

"Let us be honest, sir, one with the other. You did not come here thinking to tell Raffaela of your work. Or let us say, you did not come here *only* for that purpose."

I opened my mouth to protest, but Lord Hunsden closed it with an impatient wave of his hand.

"No sir, nor was she *only* interested in your work. You two carried on a *liaison,* as the French have it, for many months—whenever I did not require her, nor her duties as court musician take her attention. That left her with a good deal of time, and she chose to spend it with you."

He said it without rancor, so that I was moved to dispense with the usual denial.

"How do you know this to be true?" I asked.

"You do not think, do you, that I would put something so valuable out where the world could have at it without posting a guard?"

"Well, I—"

"Indeed, no! Though I admit that the guard I provided would have frightened none away, at least I was kept informed. It was the old woman across the lane. She was always at her window, and she did faithfully report what she saw. Between the two of us we managed to break your flower pot code and kept count of your visits."

"Then why did you allow me to continue?"

"Ah, well, I've only a few good years left in me, and I wanted to provide for her. That's why I made that promise to her—if and when she were to become pregnant, I would see her married to a man of her choosing. She must have told you about that?"

"She did, yes."

"And so she chose you—a bit impulsively, I fear, but that was ever her way. She had a passion for the theater, and you caught her attention—an actor who wrote, a writer who acted. In her eyes, you would have been the perfect choice. In my eyes, well, that remained to be proved, and I was dubious. But at first, the news was good. I found that at least you were no whoremonger. That reassured me somewhat, for I wanted no pox nor clap from you. But it was a bit more difficult to get more detailed information about you because of your Warwickshire origin. But eventually I got my report, and I must say it did not please me."

I hung my head contritely. There was little could be said in my defense. And for his part, Lord Hunsden had no wish to hear that little.

"A wife and three children? Really, sir, how could you have kept that from her?"

"I . . . I wanted things to continue," said I most flustered. "Indeed, I never lied to her. I thought she would have assumed that I—"

There he cut me off: "Assumed, is it? What was she to assume? That she could trust you? What had you in mind? To practice bigamy as the mussulmen do? Or had you thought to keep her as a mistress once I was out of the way?"

"Nothing of the kind, my Lord."

"Or worse still, were you to solve the problem by murdering your wife and children?"

Inwardly I shuddered at that. He had no idea how close he had come; at least I hoped that he had none. An emphatic denial was called for.

"Let me assure you that such a thought had never and could never occur to me."

(All right, that was a lie—and therefore a sin, I suppose. I admit it so. Yet none but a fool would have owned to the accusation. And after all, 'twas only a thought, or some several thoughts, and not acted upon—successfully.)

He, who had been increasingly aggressive, did at last slump back in his chair, as if for a moment drained of all strength and purpose. His face seemed to pale for a few moments. Then, having recovered his color and presumably his strength, he began again in a quieter, more moderate style.

"Let me admit," said he, "that I was not without blame in this myself."

Please, please, I thought, share the blame, help me shoulder the burden.

"It is in this," he continued, "that the guilt be partly mine. I knew of your situation—your wife and children in Warwickshire—and told her nothing of it. It seemed to me that if I were to tell Raffaela of your situation, I should be, in part, blamed for your situation myself. This is a most common response. I have oft seen it so with the Queen herself. When she is brought news which she does not wish to hear, then he who has brought it is made to suffer. It has happened so again and again. She punishes by the uses of silence, or by actual expulsion from her sight. Ah, she can be cruel, have no doubt of it."

"If it's the Queen you mean," said I, "then I have none at all."

My response brought a sharp look from him. It was, I fear, a bit too bold under the circumstances. I resolved to watch my tongue.

"In any case," said he, "I neglected to tell Raffaela—though that is perhaps the wrong word. Let us say, I withheld the information, reasoning that she would find out for herself soon enough—and of course she did. I estimate that was just after that rather awful evening that we spent at Southampton's. You remember it, of course. The only thing that made it in the least tolerable was Raffaela teasing that young capon with those dirty songs. She was such fun."

"The *only* thing, you say?" Then was it my turn to offer him the gimlet eye.

"Oh well, there were your things, naturally—quite good, I suppose. And I did indeed like that short poem that the other fellow read. But all that talk—so tedious. Yet it must have been about that time, was it not, that she discovered your little secret?"

I sighed. "Yes, you have it exact. 'Twas the very next day."

"And how was it she found you out?"

"I told her. She talked of marriage, and I was forced to explain that it would not be possible—and why."

Of a sudden, a look of concern appeared upon his deep-lined face, a look that seemed to suit it well.

"Was she pregnant?"

"Not to my knowledge," said I, "though I think not."

He was much relieved. "Thank God," said he. "That would have been more than either of us could bear."

I struggled to suppose what he could mean by that. This was all too mysterious. What purpose had he to scold me, to put me through all of this? No matter who he was, nor how close to the Queen, I deserved to know.

"I don't understand," said I, raising my voice to something short of a shout. "I don't understand any of this. Why would it have been more than we could bear?"

"Don't you know? Haven't you guessed? Raffaela is dead."

I looked about me at this familiar room made unfamiliar by the absence of furniture whilst I attempted to accommodate this fact which had just been put before me. I found it most difficult to do so. In some manner it must be accepted: I realized that. Yet somehow the idea that there was no more Raffaela resisted my understanding.

"The plague took her less than two weeks after you saw her last," said Lord Hunsden.

The plague? My mind went immediately to that first plague victim I had viewed on the street corner last spring, the one whom I had first mistaken for a loose bundle of old clothes. I remembered the pustules on the neck of the corpus, the dark gray splotches upon the face. Then, without willing it so, the two pictures merged. I saw her in death—pustules, splotches, her open mouth pulled back over clenched teeth in a hideous grin. Then did the picture blur, the livid colors smear, and I found myself weeping quite uncontrollably.

"Here now," said Lord Hunsden. "Let's have none of that. We've a few matters to settle between us first. After that, you may blubber all you like. Here."

So saying, he produced a most beautiful silk kerchief from his doublet that I might wipe my tears and blow my nose. I put it to good use, and in a short time I was prepared for whatever he might have to say—though in truth I wished to be alone with my sorrow as quickly as might be possible.

"What then, my Lord?" said I to him, signaling my readiness to talk.

"Well enough? I see you are. Very well then, I should tell you that in my researches into your personal history, I found that you lived for a time—over a year it was—with a colorful individual named Christopher Marlowe. I should like to talk to you about him."

"I've little to tell," said I. "Michael Drayton, to whom you talked, told me you were interested in Marlowe, but only insofar as he had to do with Sir Walter Ralegh. And that, as I told Drayton, came after he had moved from the room we shared."

"Ah, but I think you can be of more help than you realize. First of all, the Ralegh proviso no longer applies. We are interested in Marlowe for himself alone. You probably know a good deal about him. You may know, for instance, where and with whom he lived when he left your company. Would you mind telling me that?"

"I suppose not. I'm unsure of the where—someplace in Aylesbury Street, I believe—but it was with Thomas Kyd, another writer of plays."

"Ah well, you see? You've already been of some help. I'm sure you can be of more in the near future. May I suggest we get together again, let us say in three days—at ten in the morning right here. That will give you time to collect your thoughts on Marlowe that you may tell me all you know, or may have heard about him."

"Have I any choice in this matter?" I asked after a moment's hesitation.

"I would say that you, as the son of recusant Catholic parents and the nephew of one whose head adorns London Bridge, have very little latitude in the matter. I'm sure that you wish no harm to befall your kin in Warwickshire."

"Of course I don't," said I.

"Then do as I say, and none will. I do have one additional request, however. You no doubt received an invitation from Lord Southampton for another evening at his residence?"

"Yes, I did, for tomorrow night."

"I know not what your plans are, but my request is that you

honor the invitation and attend. I shall not be there, but I believe you will find much to interest you if you go. It will not be a wasted evening. You have my word on that."

During that space of time which elapsed before my attendance at Lord Southampton's evening, I did little but roam restlessly through the streets, thinking upon the passing of Raffaela and of what might lay ahead in my interrogation by Lord Hunsden.

What was it he had said? That she had died less than two weeks after I had last seen her. That could only mean that whilst I paced past her cottage, wishing to be with her, she was inside sinking nearer and nearer to death. Why, I must have continued my watch at her door for many days past her death. The flower pot in her window had meant nothing: had I entered, she would have welcomed me. She must have ached to see me, as I to see her.

Yet what if I had gone boldly inside and seen her upon her death bed? In the final stages of the disease she would have worn the same ugly mask as all plague victims, and she would not have wished me to see her so. Or supposing that in the course of things our last meeting had been put off a week, no more. Then our last embrace would have been truly our last, for she would doubtless have infected me, as well. Did I love Raffaela? Yes, indeed I did. Yet did I wish to join her in death? No, in all truth, I did not. The fact was that I lived, and she did not. How fortunate for me then that my half-hearted attempt at drowning Anne had gone so dreadfully awry. Thus was my life twice saved—once by Anne and once by circumstance. Indeed it was clear that it be God's will that I live. It was plain that He had great plans for me.

Of my coming appointment with Lord Hunsden I thought not quite so much, nor to such a happy conclusion. The truth was that I knew not what to expect, and I dislike finding myself in situations which threaten to surprise me in unpleasant ways. Not that Lord Hunsden was himself the sort who would wish to create fear in one whom he intended to question. That was not his way. He approached me as a sort of stern but loving father. He felt that I had wronged Raffaela, as indeed I had, and he scolded me for it in fatherly fashion. Yet he was sympathetic, within limits, to my response to what he told me of her death. I suspicioned that all this had been thought out beforehand in order to persuade me to be pliant with regard to Marlowe. Yet why should I not be helpful? Kit Marlowe was no friend to me, nor was he more than a friend. Still, I made up my mind that I would tell Lord Hunsden only that which I knew to be true—no rumors, no hearsay (though he seemed eager to hear them) and no unsupported opinion.

Thus do I summarize the thoughts of a day's brooding in a few paragraphs. I was unable to work, knew not what better to do with myself, and in such a mood, wished only to pass the hours separating me from the meeting of what Southampton called his "circle."

What was perhaps most curious about the long conversation I had had in that thatch-roofed cottage the day before was Hunsden's concluding insistence that I attend the little party given by the young earl, and his promise that I would not find it a "wasted evening." Forsooth, I might have avoided that occasion altogether, yet not because I feared the time would be wasted; nay, what I feared were the memories of Raffaela at the last such meeting I had attended—not the proudest of occasions. It seemed possible that they might quite overwhelm me and send me sniveling from the gathering.

Of a sudden did it strike me that those of my friends and colleagues whom I had gathered up and taken with me that night months ago might also have been invited to this festal evening. I would seek them out and discover what I might then expect from it. And so, wrapping my cloak tighter round me, for it was a cold day in early winter, I set my path for the Curtain theater where I might likely find them.

And find them I did. Quite a number of players were about, for the troupe, just returned from the road, had set aside this day for the storage of costumes and props. The place was a hurly-burly of activity.

"Don't tell me you came to lend us your hands!" roared Dick Burbage. " 'Tis a thankless job, Will. You'd be best off at home, writing us another masterpiece."

"Well, that's a proper greeting, I must say. *Another* masterpiece?"

"What I quote to you is my father's opinion, for I've not yet had the pleasure of reading your Crookback play. But the old man's talked of nothing since finishing it and has already promised that I shall play the king."

"Not a bad choice." Actually, quite a good one.

"Look, I've been practicing his walk."

Whereupon, Burbage began scuttling across the stage, crouching sidewise, like a crab. Work ceased. Immediately did he acquire an audience, most of whom had no idea what he was about—and not knowing, they giggled and snickered and made other rude sounds of amusement.

"Good," said I, "but perhaps not quite so exaggerated."

"I'll work on it a bit more."

He jumped down from the stage and walked over to me.

"What news have you?" I asked him.

"Of the theaters being reopened? The rumor is that if the number of dead and dying continues to decline, they'll open them for the Christmas season. The number of new cases is just about nil."

"Then we should know in a week or two?"

"A week or two," he agreed. "Though how long they'll stay open is an open question."

"I came by to ask you if you received an invitation to Southampton's this evening. I assumed that you would."

"Yes, I'll be going, as will Drayton. Cuthbert received one, as well, but my father will be going in his stead."

"Really? Why should he interest himself in such amusements?"

"He's courting patronage. He said he'd told you of the company we'll be putting together and had invited you to join. That's going to require quite a lot—a lot of effort, a lot of patronage, a goodly lot of money."

I nodded my understanding. "What say you, Dick? Shall we make our journey cross London together?"

"As you wish," said he. "Let us collect at the Drake and Duck, say, at seven?"

I waved a farewell. "At seven then."

I turned to go and had even proceeded a few steps toward the exit when he called me back. He came close and beckoned me even closer.

"Something I heard just this morning I feel I ought to tell you," said he in a tone just above a whisper. "Tom Kyd was taken away for questioning."

"By constables? Was he formally arrested?"

"No, 'twas said that it was just to answer questions, but they were Sir Robert Cecil's men who came for him."

"The new spymaster."

"Aye."

"Will Kyd be tortured?"

"I don't know," said Burbage. "I don't want to know."

"When did this happen?"

"This morning, quite early—a knock upon the door at dawn. The usual thing."

"And how did you hear about it?"

"From Drayton. He's shared quarters with him since we came back from the road." Burbage gave me a most piercing look. "What's got you, Will? You look pale."

"Oh, nothing, Dick. It's just that, well, the news is shocking, quite shocking."

Again I must interrupt this narrative to post the latest of Goody Bromley. The Bishop of Gloucester, has convened an ecclesiastical court, and she, the prisoner, has been detained in a cell in the local gaol. The magistrate's men complained of her filth and odd smell and would like to have her out of the gaol as quickly as might be possible. She will be examined by the bishop and other members of the court, and depending upon their findings, will be put on trial. It seemed a certainty, to me at least, that she will be brought before the court in a full proceeding.

In the meantime, I have devised a few lines which are not so much an epitaph as an inscription for my tomb—and a warning. Here it is, such as it is:

Good friend for Jesus sake forbear,
To dig the dust enclosed here:
Blessed be the man that spares these stones,
And cursed be he that moves my bones.

It seems to me that what it lacks in poetry and art, it supplies in strength. I think it should frighten away Goody Bromley and her kind.

Certainly I did find the news of Kyd's arrest (for that, forsooth was what it seemed to me) quite shocking. And doubtless I turned pale at the news. Still, I did no more than tell Lord Hunsden the truth as to Marlowe moving in with him—and what sin, what wrong, in that? Thus did I reason with myself in preparation for my departure to the residence of Lord Southampton. I wore my best, smelled my best, and took trouble to trim the moustache and beard I had let grow longer whilst in Stratford.

Meeting the others outside the Duck and Drake, I set off with them, Drayton by my side. Though I often found him tedious, he was now the best source of information on Kyd. Indeed, the fellow talked of nothing else most of the way to our destination. Little new came out of it all, however. The only thing which seemed truly remarkable was that, by Drayton's account, the arrest was carried out with some degree of consideration. True enough, they waited without complaint as he dressed himself and gathered a few things to take along with him. He was not put in chains, and when he asked why he was to be spared that indignity, they told him they had been told simply to fetch him that he might answer questions. There was no reason for them to believe he might flee. Did he intend to do so? He assured them he did not, and that seemed to satisfy them. The three left quietly together.

I had but one question for Drayton: "How did they react to your presence in the room?"

"They gave no attention to me whatever," said he. "They were interested only in Thomas Kyd."

After he had gone over this two or three times, yet in much greater detail than I have given here, he asked me what I thought he should do. To that I had no easy answer to give.

"It might be best to seek a room elsewhere," said I, "if you feel it necessary to be abundantly cautious."

"Indeed I'd like to, yet I cannot," said he. "I paid Kyd well into next year. I cannot afford to pay another the same amount."

"Well, perhaps you'll not have to. From what you say, they've not detained him for serious matters. They were not interested in you—did they even ask your name?"

"No."

"Well, there, you see? It is most likely that you have no need to move away."

He thought upon that for a good long spell. "I suppose you may be right," said he most uncertainly.

From behind us, I heard chuckling from the Burbages, father

and son. I said nothing of it to Drayton, nor did he to me. In any case, he then let the matter drop and began talking of his latest project.

When we reached Lord Southampton's residence, we were swiftly ushered in to the same room as before. Again, we seemed to be the last to arrive: there were but four empty chairs, and they were set against the wall beside two which were filled. As I took the chair farthest from them, I leaned forth to find which two had preceded us. The first I recognized tentatively as George Chapman, a poet of no great skill and one of that group known as the "university wits"; he, it was said, had given Ralegh's circle its enigmatic name. The fellow next him, he who sat farthest from me, I could not recognize for the moment, for his face was turned from me. Yet even the back of his head was familiar. He seemed to be communicating in some silent way with our host, Henry Wriothesley, the Earl of Southampton, for the two stared, one at the other, as if they together were the only occupants of the room.

Then at last did Southampton manage, with what seemed a great physical effort, to tug his eyes away; he glanced round the room and rose from that grand chair which itself seemed like unto a throne. That fellow farthest from me did then show me his profile. And so was I quite amazed to discover that he was none but Christopher Marlowe. No wonder I felt that I should know him, even by the hair upon the back of his head!

This then was a strange assembly of men, for Chapman and Marlowe were clearly there as representatives of Ralegh. And just look who sat opposite them: 'Twas the great enemy of Ralegh—Lord Essex. He sat with three of his fellows, none of whom I could name. Were these two poets then emissaries of peace, or would we see blood spilled upon this grand Turkish carpet on this night? (Naturally, I exaggerate.) Perhaps Lord Southampton knew, or perhaps he was indifferent to the possible result. I caught the eye of Dick Burbage: he seemed slightly apprehensive.

Up to the end, however, all was conducted in gentlemanly fashion. Lord Southampton took firm charge of the proceedings, introducing each poet and player, leaving nothing to chance—nor to me. George Chapman read from the translation of Homer which he had just undertaken. He received favorable comment from all but Essex, who wished it known that he had a bit of Greek. Lord Southampton, who probably had none at all, defended Chapman and the poet's right to translate freely. The Burbages did two speeches from *Guy of Warwick*: the son offered Guy as a young man; James Burbage gave us Guy as an old man, a hermit looking upon the prospect of his death. And soon. I've no memory of what Drayton read, perhaps another sonnet. In any case, discussion of all these afterward was brief, off the mark, and without real purpose.

It fell to Marlowe and me to conclude the evening, and I immediately understood that we had been put into competition. All through the readings, he and Southampton had been carrying on what might be called a play at love—long looks, quick smiles, gestures of notice. It was all done so openly that I was embarrassed for both of them—in particular for the young earl, for he was the more open in his attentions. Now that it had come my turn to read, I knew not if my choice of material were the best. I would certainly not have read aloud any of those sonnets I had been dashing off in Stratford. No, what I had chosen was right enough, for *Venus and Adonis* was the finest work of its kind I had done. I was proud of it, yet this was surely not the best occasion at which to present it. After witnessing such loveplay as I have described, the audience might be further embarrassed by the poem. Nevertheless, I had naught else from which to read, and so I gave them the first dozen or so stanzas. What I had drawn from Ovid by way of inspiration and story charmed and entertained my listeners, and the language fair-enthralled them (as my language always seems to do). When I halted, Essex and his party called for more—and so more I gave them. After a few encore stanzas I retired and Marlowe stepped forward.

Unabashed he may have been in reading the lines of *Hero and Leander,* yet he was not skilled. Christopher Marlowe had not the voice for reading poetry aloud, nor had he learned the actor's art of giving unto spoken verse the style and rhythm of everyday speech. Alas, he allowed himself to bounce along from iambus to iambus like a tall man on a pony. Even Michael Drayton read his verses better.

Lord Southampton was the only one present who seemed to give the poet his full attention, and he, it seemed, could scarce take his eyes from him. The reason for this was surely that the lines read by Marlowe seemed written and spoken direct to the young nobleman. Merely as an instance, and not the only example to be found among the lines he gave forth that evening, were those which described Hero and "his dangling tresses that were never shorn." One had only to look beyond Marlowe to our host to find the inspiration for these words. (And just so there be no doubt of it, Southampton chose that moment to shake his long tresses that they might settle down upon his chest.) When Marlowe had read as far as he intended (and a good deal further than I would have liked), he was applauded by Southampton, who called for more. Yet more came only with difficulty, for as Marlowe explained, after reading only a few additional lines, the poem was incomplete and would take a month or more to finish. Quite undiscouraged, the young nobleman rose from his chair and approached the poet with something leafy in his hand.

Waving it about, he announced in a voice both loud and shrill, that this was the laurel wreath and from this time forward it would be awarded at every such meeting for the poet most deserving.

"And there can be no doubt," said he, "who is most deserving on this fine evening!"

So saying, he placed the laurel wreath upon the brow of Christopher Marlowe, who thus appeared rather foolish, as if he had been given a spinach to wear. He, who had been so honored, looked left and right, as if he would quite like to find a rubbish bin in which he might deposit it. He must have found none, for he was forced to wear the silly thing for the rest of the evening.

"Refreshments for all," cried Lord Southampton. "Wine! meats! sweetmeats! dainties!"

And those of us who had survived the long march from Shoreditch did flock to the table laden with plates of foodstuffs and bottles of wine.

I had a half-eaten sausage in one hand and a glass of claret in the other when Marlowe approached me. I raised my glass to him in mock salute.

"All hail the winner of the laurel crown," said I.

"You may have it for a farthing," said he to me.

"I would not wear it for a pound."

"Yet I must wear it for naught."

" 'Naught' say you? I thought your poem rather good, what there was of it. I'd heard you'd worked on it the better part of a year."

"You're too kind, Will," said he with a smirk of a smile. "But no, not near so long. It was begun at about the start of the plague season, as I assume yours was also."

"About that time, yes."

"When theaters close, poets must write for print."

"Aye, indeed, just as Chapman translates Homer and Drayton contemplates the writing of a sort of poetic geography of England."

"Better than writing sonnets." Then did he act out a fit of embarrassment. "Ah, but as I recall, that is a form at which you have tried your hand. Henry showed me some of those you showed him."

"Henry?" For some reason I had got it in mind that he meant Henry Carey, Lord Hunsden. But no.

"Henry Wriothesley—Southampton, our host."

"He showed you my sonnets?"

"Well, he gave me quite a handful, and I read a few of them. One can't read too many sonnets at a time. It's a bit like eating too much sweet apple tart." He smiled winningly. "Oh, but your sonnets were quite good, quite good indeed. You show a real talent for the form—a regular Samuel Daniel is what you are."

(It must be said at this point, as a reminder, that Samuel Daniel was a poet, a sonneteer, and a writer of plays of no real talent. Though he still lives, I speak of him here in the past tense, for he is largely forgotten and has, as I have heard, ceased writing and retired to a farm in Wiltshire.)

I put it to him squarely: "Is that flattery or an insult?"

"Take it as you will. For my part, I've never been attracted to the writing of sonnets. Much too restrictive."

"I rather liked writing them," said I in a manner most urbane. "The first fifteen were written on a commission. Those which follow are better; they were written during the plague season. I wrote a good deal during that spell."

"Oh? Where did you spend it? Surely not in London. I stayed long enough to know what it was like here then."

"A graveyard," said I. "No, certainly not London. I returned to Warwickshire, to my home in Stratford. I found it a good place to work."

"So you said."

"Two plays," I declared. "An history and a comedy, unquestionably my best to date."

"Then you are determined to prove Greene wrong, are you?"

"Greene wrong? Robert Greene? I do not follow."

"He died, you know, just this year."

"So I heard," said I. "The pox took him, as I was told."

"Yes, well, whatever. The point is, Will, that before he died he wrote one last pamphlet. It bore a title typical of him—*A Groatsworth of Wit, Bought with a Million of Repentance*. It is in the form of a cautionary letter to all of us."

"Us? To you and me?"

"No, not quite. To the university men who live by their pens."

"The university wits."

He shrugged grandly. "As you will. But he does have something to say about you."

"About me? Truly so?" I hoped I did not sound to him as eager as I felt.

"As it happens," said Marlowe, drawing from his doublet a worn and dog-eared pamphlet of the usual hand-size, "I have here a copy of said *Groatsworth of Wit*. It was rumored that you were out of town during the plague season, as indeed you were, and so you did not have the opportunity to see what had been written about you—well, more or less about you."

"I do not understand."

"You will. May I read to you what Greene wrote?"

I looked round me and saw that the lads from Shoreditch had gathered in a bit closer that they might also hear.

"By all means," said I, trusting creature that I then was.

Near as soon as he had begun, I wished I had forbade him, for he bellowed forth so the whole room might hear.

" 'There is an upstart crow—' "

(That was Greene! I remembered he had called me "crow" outside Newgate Jail.)

" '—beautified with our feathers, that with his Tiger's heart wrapt in a player's hide—' "

(There he parodies a figure of mine from the third part of *Henry VI*.)

" '—supposes he is well able to bombast out a blank verse as the best of you; and being an absolute *Johannes factotum*—' "

(Latin, naturally, for jack-of-all-trades. How Greene did love to parade his Latin!)

" '—is in his own conceit the only Shake-scene in a country.' "

As Marlowe finished, he had the whole room laughing along with him. Great gales of it circled round me, threatening to unbalance me altogether. I looked round me with eyes half-blinded with tears of chagrin and saw that even Shoreditch group had betrayed by making merry at my expense. I felt myself pummeled, slapped upon my back, mocked with that name Shake-scene. That, finally, was too much for me.

I ran from the room, ran from the house with their laughter still loud in my ears and the jeering voices which called after me, "Shake-scene! Shake-scene! Shake-scene!"

XVII

I slept little that night, and that little only by resort to the bottle of brandy I kept about for such occasions. As a result, when I woke the following morning I felt foul and sickly indeed. Still within my mind I heard the jeering cries of "Shake-scene," so that my head ached and my hands shook with the sense of humiliation that I carried with me from the evening before. Yet I controlled myself. I had an appointment that very morning that I would be loath to miss. I prepared for it as I might have for an appointment at court; for after all, an appointment with the Lord Chamberlain was quite near to one with the Queen herself, was it not?

He must have known that something had been planned for me the night before. Did he know what? If so, I asked myself, why had he not warned me? Why had he insisted I attend Southampton's evening? Unless . . . unless he wished to remind me with whom I was dealing. He knew that Marlowe was my enemy and wanted me to know it, too. Forsooth, possessing such knowledge, he had been more generous than I had realized in staying away. His generosity would be repaid.

Setting off to meet Lord Hunsden at the appointed hour, I considered the uncertain ordeal that lay ahead and realized for the first time that there were questions that I wished to ask *him*. I could but wonder if I would be given opportunity to ask them—or would there be naught for me but questions, questions, questions? I freely admitted to myself that I was fearful of what lay ahead, but as it loomed closer, I realized that I was more curious than fearful. There was a possibility of danger for me, should I misspeak or be caught in a lie. Nevertheless, I welcomed what lay ahead as a chance to speak my mind about Marlowe.

Upon my arrival, I saw immediately that my interrogator had preceded me, for there at the door waited the coach-and-four, whose presence in the past had always sent me scurrying away. This time, however, I walked boldly past coach and coachmen and knocked stoutly upon the door of the cottage. Hunsden himself answered the knock and, seeing that it was me, threw open the door and welcomed me inside.

Entering, my eyes swept round the room, and I saw first that all but the floor had been painted that same very light blue I had been shown in the course of my last visit. There was a smell of fresh paint in the air, yet I found it not so heavy that it was difficult to sit through the next two or three hours there with the Lord Chamberlain. We were not alone; as I looked round the room, my glance fell quite unexpectedly upon a young man who was at a writing table, newly added to a corner at the far side of the fireplace. He gave me an indifferent look and set about arranging his writing materials on the table top before him.

Making no effort to introduce him, Lord Hunsden informed me that the young man was here simply to act as scribe, taking down our conversation—and yes, the word used to describe what would follow was "conversation."

He sat me down in the chair opposite him, which put my back to his scribe. Then did he take the remaining chair, which gave him a view of the young man. He made a signal of some sort to him and began, not with a question, but rather with an explanation.

"You were doubtless surprised to hear that Thomas Kyd was brought in for interrogation," said he. "Let me assure you that he was not mistreated in any way. He was, as a matter of fact, discharged this morning after spending a night in a cell at the

Tower. That can't have been pleasant but certainly did him no harm."

At that point he stopped, offering space to me to ask a question. I asked it.

"What was the point, then, in bringing him in?"

"There were three points actually. First, it was our intention to inform him, as we have you, of our interest in Christopher Marlowe and tell him to gather his thoughts on that period when he and Marlowe were familiar and be ready to tell all that he remembers at some future date. Secondly, just to impress upon him that we were quite serious, I asked Richard Topcliffe, who administers questioning under duress, to show Mr. Kyd the instruments of torture and explain to him their uses. Thirdly, we wished to get Mr. Kyd out of the way, and Drayton, too, so that we might search their room."

"How did you know that Drayton shared the room with him? Those who came for Kyd did not even ask the name of his fellow lodger. I happen to know that as fact."

"Ah, you do, do you?" said he in a good-natured teasing tone. "Well, that information was supplied by Kyd himself. We did not ask him many questions, but that was one of them, and he did not hesitate to answer. It seems that our friend, Michael Drayton, had just joined him there. Kyd said that he had come in from a theatrical tour of the shires and counties."

"So I also had heard," said I. "In their tour—it lasted the length of the plague season—they appeared one day in Stratford. I saw them perform there."

"I've no reason to doubt Kyd or Drayton on that," said Lord Hunsden. "Besides, we've no interest at all in Drayton."

"Good," said I. "But perhaps you could tell me, my Lord, why I was not singled out for a lecture upon the uses of the instruments of torture, as Kyd was? And you have never specifically threatened me. Why is that, if I may ask?"

"Why, because we have every reason to believe that you will

be forthcoming in your answers. You do intend to be, don't you?"

"Yes I do, most truly."

"I should suppose so, after what you were put through yestereve."

"You've heard about that, have you? Did you know in advance?"

"Yes, I've had a report on it already. I stayed away because I knew those two were planning something for you—much whispering in corners. Your name was mentioned."

"Lord Southampton and Marlowe?"

"Naturally. Who but they?"

"I was humiliated."

"Of course you were. And in a rage, too, I've no doubt." Lord Hunsden leaned back in his chair and studied me in a manner most sympathetic. There was something quite warm about the man, almost priestly. "You must have been astonished to find Marlowe there at all," said he.

"Oh, I was—altogether amazed."

"He is soliciting Southampton's patronage."

I was, as one might say, shocked at the news, though not surprised. Looked at coldly, there was but one circumstance could persuade one so haughty and cold as Marlowe to debase himself before another so foolish as the young earl, and that be the expectation of monetary reward. But had I not heard that he had pledged himself to another?

"But," said I, "is it not known that Thomas Walsingham is his patron?"

"Perhaps Marlowe feels he is entitled to more than one," Lord Hunsden suggested. "Or, more likely, he sought Southampton out because Southampton has the deeper pocket—or will have when he reaches his majority next year. In any case, the young earl is flattered beyond measure at Marlowe's attentions. I do believe that the fellow thinks he is in love."

This news fair destroyed me. Though not completely dependent upon such alms as Lord Southampton might toss in my direction, I had counted on *something* from him when he came into his fortune. Indeed I had been prepared to dedicate *Venus and Adonis* to him if that were what it took. And if the theaters remained closed, I should then have to write another long poem in hopes of receiving a further donation. Yet now, with Marlowe to reckon with, could I count on *any* such largesse from the noble? It seemed to me that there was more than simple greed driving him on. What had Marlowe against me? Was it envy? Did he fear that my talent was greater than his (as it undoubtedly was)?

"Have you any idea what sort of villain you are dealing with?" said Lord Hunsden, interrupting my desperate ruminations.

"Why, I know not quite what you mean."

"Do you know what he is capable of?" He leaned forward and lowered his voice. "No doubt he asked what you had done to evade the plague? Where you had gone?"

"Yes, and I told him that I had returned to Stratford, my home, in Warwickshire."

"But he said nothing about where he had gone, what he had done?"

I thought back over what had passed between us before he had pulled that copy of *A Groatsworth of Wit* out of his doublet. No, as so often with Marlowe, he asked questions and demanded answers while offering nothing of his own in exchange.

"No," said I, "he told me nothing to do with himself."

"Well, he, too, went to his home which, as you may well know, is Canterbury. There, in August or September—I am unsure of the when of it—he killed a man."

"He did? Who?"

"That, too, I know not," said Lord Hunsden. "So much of Marlowe's past and present is shrouded in secret—and is kept secret even from me. He had the protection of Sir Francis Walsingham—uncle to his supposed patron—and it seemed for years that Marlowe acted as a law unto himself. As a result, we must now talk to people such as you and this man, Kyd, in order to reconstruct his past. He has no protector now. Sir Robert Cecil, who assumed control at the death of Walsingham, has grown tired of rescuing him from jails, and persuading magistrates to overlook criminal offenses for which many another would be hanged. Now," he continued, "unless you have further questions to ask . . ."

I had none. I shook my head in the negative.

"Good," said he. "I shall ask certain questions, for there are certain specific bits of information that I would have from you. Nevertheless, I don't wish you to feel restricted by my questions. If, for instance, in answering one of them, you are reminded of another bit of information which you think may be pertinent—then, out with it, by all means. I would say, too, that this is not a court of law. You may guess, conjecture, infer, so long as anything of that sort is labeled as such. But please tell no outright lies. We are preparing a bill of particulars against this rogue, and though Cecil has washed his hands of him, Marlowe does have a few defenders at court. If we present falsehoods along with truths, and the falsehoods be proven so, then the truths will be assumed false." He offered an encouraging smile. "Is all of that clear?"

"Quite clear," said I.

"Then," said Lord Hunsden, with a new signal to the scribe, "let us begin."

He did not ask how it came about that Christopher Marlowe and I shared the same roof, nor if we shared a bed, as well. He did not, in fact, ask anything of a personal nature, though he may have inferred much of the sort from a few of my more careless answers. And if I was careless, it was because I felt comfortable in Lord Hunsden's presence.

No, without further preamble and without reference to me,

he went direct to Marlowe. Rather than ask *if* Marlowe were in Walsingham's employ during the time we shared a room, as he had through Drayton some months before, Hunsden asked what I knew of Kit's activities for the Secretary of State at that time. I then told him of Marlowe's journey to Holland in 1588—of how Thomas Watson came bearing the commission and rode with him as far as Dover.

"Watson? He also has become an embarrassment," said he to me. "But how long was Marlowe gone on this trip to Holland?"

"More than a month but less than two."

"And when was that? Before or after the great battle with the Spanish?"

"It was in spring—early April when he returned. I'm certain of that. The fields were newly plowed and muddy when he took me out to summon Satan."

Hunsden's mouth flew open in amaze. He blinked in astonishment. "Marlowe did what?"

"Without success, let me assure you."

Then was I required to tell how Kit had sought to prove to me that there was neither God nor Satan by praying to both. I was to pray to God for a sign, and I did pray mightily, for I would have some appearance or wonder that would convince even a doubter such as Marlowe. But God in his infinite wisdom had given none, no doubt holding it to be a presumption. That, I explained, was when he drew a circle and began an incantation of the sort meant to summon Satan or some lesser demon. Then, when asked by Lord Hunsden to describe what was said, I told him that it involved the recital of the Lord's Prayer, back to front. When Satan did not appear, nor any other devil, Marlowe said that proved that just as there was no God, there was no Satan, no heaven and no hell.

"Oh, dear God!" said Hunsden. Then did he take a full minute to regain his composure. Then, when at last he felt ready: "You described Christopher Marlowe as a 'doubter.' Would you say that was an *accurate* characterization?"

I believed I knew the word he wished to hear. "Perhaps," said I, " 'atheist' would be more accurate, though one hesitates to use an epithet so hateful, so—"

"Yes, yes, naturally one does, but if the word fits—"

"Use it, of course."

"Indeed," said he, "but would you now object to telling that story once again?"

"The whole of it?"

"Oh, certainly, and don't scant the details. I would have them all."

And so I did as he asked. As for the details, far from sparing any, I added a few of my own invention. This was done simply to make plain my resistance to Marlowe's methods and to distance myself from his conclusions. No harm done.

When at last I was allowed to move on, I told Lord Hunsden of Marlowe's curious remark (made specially weighty later on by his involvement in a plot to forge and pass Dutch and English coins) regarding who had, and who had not, the right to coin. I could tell that my interrogator was greatly taken by the tale by his response when I came to the end of it.

"He said *what?* Repeat it," said he. "Tell all of it again—and give me more details."

And repeat it I did, putting my declaration perhaps a bit more forcefully than I did in the original circumstance: "He showed to me the coin in his hand, an English coin, of course, then asked what it was made the coin worth its face value. I said to Marlowe 'twas the image of our Queen made it worth what was claimed. 'She is our sovereign and therefore has the right to coin.' Then Marlowe asked, 'Why she and no other?' And he declared, 'I have as much right to coin as she has.' "

As I finished, Lord Hunsden addressed his scribe for the first time. "Did you get all of that? Shall I ask him to tell it again?"

"No, I have it all," said the young man.

"But my Lord," said I to Hunsden, "in fairness I must say

that Marlowe offered it as a philosophical question, a puzzle."

"That is conjecture on your part," said he rather coldly.

"Well yes, I suppose it is."

"All right, it can go in," said he, "so long as it is labeled as such." Then to the scribe: "Make a note of that, will you?"

And so it was that we came to the final tale I had to tell. I knew well that there would be room for it. Yet I did bide my time until I might present the story in response to a question by my interrogator. At last it came.

"What do you know of this matter for which Marlowe was held in Newgate for a matter of months? Have you anything to say about that?"

"I know a great deal about it, for I was witness to the entire affair and visited Kit Marlowe whilst he was in jail."

Whereupon I launched into the tale I had been saving, thinking it to be the most damning of all. Yet I was not long into the telling of it when I noted that my listener seemed to be growing impatient. I had reached that point in my description of the duel when Marlowe, near overwhelmed by young Bradley's attack, was rescued by Thomas Watson. Hunsden grunted in disapproval.

"Uh, Watson again," said he. "Keeps turning up, doesn't he?"

"Well yes, but then—"

"All of this is in the public record, you know. I've read through it myself two or three times. I know what happens."

"Still, what I saw was never made public, never even hinted at during the coroner's inquest, not mentioned before the magistrate, nor was it before the Judges of the Assize."

He sighed. "Indeed? Well, all right then, tell the story, but be quick about it. I must soon be off."

And so, I did rush through to the end, telling in a few short sentences, how, at the height of the duel between Watson and Bradley, Marlowe had rushed up to Bradley from the rear and shouted his false warning, thus distracting him sufficiently for Watson to strike him a mortal blow into his heart.

"That was all then?" asked Hunsden, obviously unimpressed.

"Well, it was indeed not fair of Kit Marlowe to distract the young fellow as he did."

"The worst one can say of him is that he acted in an ungentlemanly fashion."

"But surely Watson was wrong in taking advantage of the distraction to run Bradley through?"

"Wrong? The only wrong in such a street fight is to come out at the losing end. Have you ever faced a man from the wrong end of a sword? No, I thought not. Well, in truth I had hoped you might be able to give me some idea what the fight was all about. Can you do that? Do you know?"

"No," said I, feeling quite foolish.

"Ah well," said he, "I've no complaints. You've given me enough, more than enough, to work with. Believe me, sir, this has been a morning well spent." He rose from his chair. "But now, I fear, I must be returning to my routine duties."

Reluctantly, I also rose, oddly unwilling to end this interview. "How may I contact you?" I asked.

"Why would you wish to do that?"

"Perhaps I shall think of something to add to what I've told you."

"Perhaps you will, but as I said, you've given me a great deal to work with for the time being. If necessary, I'll contact you. You've been most forthcoming. I'm quite pleased."

"Thank you. I'm . . . I'm pleased to have been of some service to you."

I looked round the room, vaguely fearful that I might be leaving something behind.

"If things go as they usually do," said Hunsden, "it will take some time to get things under way—not until after Twelfth Night at the very earliest, and more likely sometime in spring. You may be required to testify when the proceeding begins. I hope you have no objection to that."

"No, none."

"Very well then. I have just one more matter before I send you on your way—a bit of advice to give to you."

"And what might that be, my Lord?"

"Tell no one of our meeting this morning—neither that you met with me, nor what we talked upon. All that you have said thus far about Christopher Marlowe should be kept secret because, as you know, he is a very dangerous man. He would not hesitate to silence you. Avoid contact with him. I would, if I were you, forgo any further visits to Lord Southampton." With that said, he nodded, indicating that our meeting was ended.

I bowed and departed.

While at my arrival my intention had been simply to slip past the coachmen and through the door, when I left I looked each in the eye, one after the other, returning stare for stare. I had naught to be ashamed of—indeed quite the contrary. With each bold step I felt more elevated and more prideful than with the last.

Thus did this sensation come upon me as something new, yet at the same time there was a way in which it was not an altogether new feeling. It was as if I could remember something quite like it—perhaps the same sense exactly—from my childhood. What was it?

I had walked many streets up and down on the way back to my room in Bishopsgate before it came to me just what it was that seemed so familiar. And that came not by rumination nor through a diligent search of my memory, but rather by a happy accident of association. I remembered how, toward the beginning of that taxing interview, I had reflected that Lord Hunsden's manner seemed almost priestly, and further, dressed in his dark robes of office, he did look the part. As I thought upon him in this role, it came to me that he was like unto a father confessor, and we two in that bare room together as if in a confessional. Oddly, I had been granted the right and duty to confess not my own sins, for I had none worth mentioning, but those of Kit Marlowe.

Little wonder that I felt so elated, so much at peace with myself. I had had the experience of confession without the burden of penance. And with it that post-confessional sense of having donned raiment of shining white. I had not known this since I was a child. How strange that confessing the sins of another should affect me so.

Remarkably enough, that heady feeling remained with me for weeks afterward. It seemed there was naught could bring me down, not even the evidence of death in the streets. For yes, though the numbers of the dead had continued to lower, the plague was with us still, and the evidence was there to be seen throughout the city in every precinct and parish (though nearest the river things were worst). The dead were brought out and left to be collected for burial or for burning. Some, I was sure, had simply fallen and died where they dropped, their grinning faces mocking us, the living.

Because I disliked viewing such scenes as I here describe, and disliked even more the smell of death which seemed then to hang over London like a fog, I determined to return to Stratford for Christmas. It was evident that the Privy Council deemed it too great a risk to open the theaters, if only for the holiday season. There seemed no reason for me to stay. And so, after notifying the Burbages of my intentions, filling a new portmanteau with gifts for all, and buying a new white linen kerchief for the trip, I took the post coach to Warwickshire—and home.

(That "white linen kerchief" may need a word of explanation. Those who journeyed by coach during the plague season would do so only with a kerchief over the lower half of their face. Breathing through the white linen was said to be the only sure way to avoid breathing the infectious vapors of the plague when in a crowded coach. And though I made use of the kerchief in just such a way, I am in no wise sure that it works in such an efficacious manner. According to what I later heard, many did breathe their last through white linen.)

I had written ahead to my mother and father that I would be coming and asked them to inform Anne. Nevertheless, I was surprised when I found the whole family, including the children, there at the inn to greet my arrival.

The occasion, it seemed, was the presentation of a balance sheet that father had prepared for me to prove his exemplary management of our usury enterprise. My money had been handled separately from his own, though with the same care. He had listed all who had borrowed money, how much they had borrowed, and at what rate of interest, et cetera. He tallied all the necessary figures over the seven years in which I had been contributing money for him to handle.

Needless to say, all of this was discussed in the privacy of my parents' parlor, since this enterprise of ours was illegal still. Anne had sent the children out to play and now sat beside me, as my father held forth pompously praising his own "good business sense," and so on. I nodded in sage agreement. My mother, who sat across from me, was clearly impatient for him to end so that she might get on with truly important matters—such as dinner, and so on. Anne simply looked puzzled.

"Now, all this I carried in my head," said my father. I must have exclaimed in disbelief, for I remember he assured me that what he had said was so.

"Aye, Will, 'tis true! For years I carried your accounts and mine right up here." So saying, he tapped his brow with his finger. "And it worked pretty well. But it occurred to me a month or two back that I wouldn't be here forever, and if I died sudden, all this would die with me. Since then I've been giving a little time each week to writing it all out, all that was in my head. I've finished, so I give it to you now, Will, the record of my handling of your money. I think you'll agree that I've done pretty well by you."

He handed to me a sheaf of papers which was quite impressive in size. As I thumbed through it I noted that each sheet was well-covered with names, comments, and numbers.

"By God and all the saints," said I, "it looks as if the whole town has borrowed money from me at one time or another."

"Not quite," said he. "The big borrowers—those who wanted more than you could lend—I took care of myself. But if you look at the tally number on the last sheet, you'll see that you've got a profit figure up to date of near fifty pounds."

"Oh dear," said Anne in a tone of dismay.

"Could it be so much?" I asked. "That's more than even I had expected."

"I'm sure of the amount. I used your money for smaller loans and put the interest I collected back into your lending pool, so that your money was working all the time. You understand?"

"Yes, I understand quite well, but I'm quite overwhelmed. I know not what to say."

"You may start with 'thank you,'" said he with a wink, "and get flowery after that. You're the poet. You'll think of something."

"Well, indeed you have my thanks most profound, Father."

"I've made a copy of my own so that I can add to it if you wish me to continue as I've been doing, putting profits in the lending pool, and so on. Yet I thought you'd be glad to see just where you stand right now. If you want it all right now, you may have it."

I needed but a moment to reflect. "No. Keep it working, by all means. Perhaps in a few years I shall want it, or some of it. Until then, could you give me reports—oh, say, once a year?"

"That I can do, certainly."

"Good, then it be settled!" shouted my mother, leaping from her chair. "Come along, Anne. Let's to the kitchen before our dinner is burned beyond eating."

It was not burned. It was, in fact, as good a piece of beef as

I had ever eaten. The children were so unused to the look of the slices of beef each had on his plate that they asked, almost in chorus, just what sort of meat this was which had been put before them. I resolved to increase Anne's housekeeping allowance so that she and the children might have meat more often and beef on special occasions.

Christmas proceeded through its rounds of gift-giving and eating as Christmas always will. All seemed well-pleased by the gifts I had brought to them from London—dolls, balls, and the like for the children; and for Anne gew-gaws of one sort or another, a ring which she wears to this day, and a good, warm cape which became her well. As for the eating, it continued from one house to the next. 'Twas as if it were all one great meal, and each separate meal in each separate house but a single course in this great orgy of eating. I quite enjoyed all this visiting about, for in each house I was welcomed and celebrated as if I might be a grand personage from some distant land. And in a sense, that is just what I was, for to come to Stratford from London was like arriving from another country entirely. It seemed that all we had in common was our language, and upon occasion I came to question even that. Still, they seemed to understand me well enough and never ceased to ask me questions about the great city and listened entranced as I spun my answers into tales. These were, for the most part, friends of Anne and members of her family—simple Shottery folk who liked nothing better than to hear of the grand and the famous; I simply gave them what they wanted.

Anne and I took to walking all round the town, talking of one thing and another, greeting acquaintances and strangers alike. Stratford was growing, and so also was Shottery. I had seen a number of new faces during my long stay earlier that year, and now I noted more. How, I wondered, did they earn their keep? Anne said that some worked at the new mill on the Avon and others for Sir Thomas Lucy, who had so expanded his holdings that many more were needed to work them.

"Is he so rich?" I asked. "I shall be so someday myself."

"If we are to believe your father," said Anne, "then we are rich already."

"Do you disbelieve him?"

"No."

We walked on in silence for a bit. By chance, we happened to be approaching New Place—the better to make my point.

"No, wife, when I say rich, I don't mean a mere fifty pounds-rich, I mean truly so—rich enough to buy New Place just ahead."

"Will, you joke, surely. New Place is much the biggest house in town. 'Tis owned by Mr. Underhill who would never sell it."

'Tis true that it was a bit huge, perhaps even over-large with its five peaked gables, its ten rooms, gardens, and outbuildings. Nevertheless, I wanted it and would have it for what it meant. New Place was to be a goal, a target at which to aim.

"I shall make more money in London than any," I declared. "And father will make of it more money still."

"There are those who say that your father's manner of making money is wrong."

"Because it is usury? The laws will change soon enough."

"No, I know naught of usury. They say he employs a porter at the inn to knock the heads of those who are late to pay."

"Well . . . they should not be late. Besides, he treated your father fairly enough, did he not?"

"Yes, but they say he has changed, that he cares more for making money than for making gloves."

"What if he does? And who is this 'they' you quote?"

"No one—just people."

We had come to New Place. I brought us to a halt there at the gate and gestured to it in an ornate manner, as one might upon the stage.

"There, see? Would you not like to call that your home?"

"I would rather have a smaller house in London."

"So you say, but if you knew how you would live there—"

"If it is never to be London—and I suspect it never will be—then come more often and stay longer when you do. Why must you leave just past Twelfth Night?"

"I have my reasons," said I, raising my voice to her, "and important reasons they are."

"The plague is there still. I have heard. They still die. The theaters are still closed, are they not?"

She simply could not be stopped, could she?

"Woman, why must you vex me so?"

Innumerable men have asked that of their wives, and none probably has received a satisfactory answer. As for myself, I believe that wives vex their husbands because it is their nature to do so. Or perhaps better put, it is in the nature of marriage that the two partners are set in conflict. The female partner, severely limited in the weapons she has at her command, must do with what she has near at hand. And what is closest at hand for every woman is the inborn ability to mock, irritate, anger, and annoy—in short, to vex. Therefore women refuse to argue sensibly with their husbands: they vex. It was always so, and it probably always would be.

As you might suppose, I did leave Stratford just past Twelfth Night, as I had intended. Though Anne fought me to the end, she walked with me to the inn and saw me off on the post coach to London. Out came my white linen kerchief, and through it I breathed during the next three days running.

Upon my arrival, I hurried to Norton Folgate and sought any sign of communication from Lord Hunsden. There was none—no note slipped between the door and the doorjamb, no letter under the door, nothing. Then did I go to the family on the floor beneath mine and inquire if anyone had come since I had been gone, searching for me. I was informed by the mistress of the house that there had been none such. When she asked me then where I had been, I told her that I had traveled home to Warwickshire for Christmas, she looked at me as if I were mad.

"Why ever did you come back here with the plague still upon us?"

I could give her no proper answer to that.

No doubt it was foolish to return to this disease-ridden city on the chance that what Lord Hunsden had called the "proceeding" against Marlowe would have begun. He had said indeed that it might well be that nothing would be done until spring.

Until spring? Dear God, could I wait so long? With all of the traveling and the visiting back and forth through the Christmas season, I had somehow lost the fine edge of the fury I felt toward Marlowe, yet now that I was returned, I sensed it come back strong as ever.

I knew that I must find work, for only work would divert and sustain me through the wait that lay ahead. Burbage had bought *Richard*; he also had in hand the comedy of the *Two Gentlemen*. With the theaters still closed, he would not, could not, accept more, and so I must undertake another long poem. As none other than Kit Marlowe himself had observed, "When theaters close, poets must write for print." And so having little choice and less inspiration, I took it upon myself to begin *Lucrece,* that tale of rape in ancient Rome. I fear that the poem suffers for it. Only by fits and starts did I myself become interested in the piece as I wrote it. Though afterward I did continue to write sonnets, more or less to amuse myself, I convinced myself in writing *Lucrece* that I was meant to write for the stage and only for the stage.

Still, it passed the time—and how else was one to do that? By reading? I returned to my studies of Holinshed for further histories, made notes, and looked indifferently at the first book I had bought in an age, *The Faerie Queene,* by Mr. Cotton's old favorite, Edmund Spenser. (Forsooth, I confess I have never taken much pleasure in reading the work of others.)

Thus I had little to do but work upon a poem for which I felt little sympathy, take walks out into the country to buy provisions that I might not starve, and brood upon my desire to have revenge upon Marlowe. Months passed so. Eating little, I fattened from inactivity.

Then one day it came upon me that I needed news of him. Like a hunter tracking his quarry, I wished to know Marlowe's movements. Was he still in London? What if he had gone off to some distant location to escape the plague? To Holland or France? If he were not present here in London, they could not begin the "proceeding," against him—could they? I felt a sudden urgency to know what it was had happened to this darling of the nobility. Where to find out? Though it could well be that the surest place to go for such information as I desired was the World's End. Yet therein lay difficulties: Marlowe himself might be there, and if not he then another, a lackey who would report to him that one of my description was about asking questions about him. He would guess soon enough the identity of the questioner. No, not the World's End. Lord Hunsden had advised me to avoid Marlowe at all costs, and I meant to take his advice.

That left the Burbage clan, who could and would be found somewhere in the vicinity of the Curtain. Though they would be a little less likely to provide information of the sort I wished, they kept up with gossip of all in their circle and might well know Marlowe's whereabouts. Here the difficulties were of a personal nature, for I remembered well that on that evening at Lord Southampton's, Burbage, father and son, as well as Michael Drayton, did laugh at me along with the rest. But of course I should have to achieve a reconciliation sooner or later, for I intended to be one of their company, that I might write for them and act. Thus was it better to see them sooner, rather than later, and allow them to make amends.

I was most generous. I swore to them I had not noticed that they, too, had laughed merrily at my discomfiture (though I was certain they had). In any case, they apologized and sympathized profoundly and declared that if Drayton were here he would join them in chorus. Though I assured them that there were no apologies necessary, I accepted theirs since they insisted—oh, and they did insist! They wriggled a bit, and I must admit that I enjoyed it. But then was I caught off-guard.

"When did you return from Stratford?" That from James Burbage.

"Just a few days ago," said I, lying of course. That much I had thought out beforehand. "But where did you hear I had gone there?"

"You may not credit this, but I heard it from no less than Lord Hunsden, the Lord Chamberlain himself."

"You don't mean it?" said I. "How could he have known?"

"No idea. To tell you the truth, I was too busy talking business with him to ask him. Besides, it's not the sort of question you put to the Lord Chamberlain."

"I suppose not. But business? What sort of business?"

"Ah well, that's the big news, an't it, Dick?"

His son nodded an emphatic agreement but left the telling to his father.

"You remember, Will, I wanted along on that visit to Southampton's place to court patronage. Lord Strange has fallen so far out of favor, he can do us no good at all anymore. We needed a new patron, and we needed one soon. It looks like the Privy Council won't be opening the theaters any time in the near future. But the rent is coming due on the Curtain here and on the other one, too, and as things were, we just couldn't come up with it."

"What about your summer tour? Surely you made enough in the provinces to tide you over?"

"No, you never make much more than your expenses out on the road. Country folk are too poor. Anyway, that's why I came along that evening when you was treated so poorly. But I had no luck with the illustrious lords and gentlemen that night nor the one that followed. I was about ready to give up altogether, except I went one more time to Southampton's—and that was when I broached the matter to Lord Hunsden, and . . . and . . ."

James Burbage was, of a sudden, too excited to tell his good news. He gasped and held one hand to his heart. So it fell to Dick Burbage to reveal all.

"And it seems sure now that the new company," said Dick, "the one you'll be in with us, Will, is going to be known as the Lord Chamberlain's Men."

"Oh, I like the sound of that," said I.

"We all do! You couldn't ask for a patron more highly placed."

"Indeed not," said father Burbage, who had at last recovered his voice, "nor more generous. He has already promised to cover the rent and asked us to prepare a list of what we'll need and what it will cost. Cuthbert's working on that."

"He should be done in a day or so if you'd like to look at it," said Dick. "He's putting together a whole plan, covering it all. I think you'd find it interesting."

"No doubt I would," said I.

"Oh, and Will," said James Burbage, "I believe it would only be fair to let you know that you played a part in all this."

"I did? What part?" (Forsooth, I could not guess.)

"When I got Lord Hunsden aside there at Southampton's and started telling him our plans were for sharing equal, for the number of theaters we'd operate, and the like, you know what he asks—first thing?"

"I've absolutely no idea."

"His first question—and he didn't ask too many more—was this: 'Will Mr. Shakespeare be a part of your company?' And wasn't I happy to be able to say that you were? I told him we'd proposed, and you'd accepted. That seemed to satisfy him. He looked like he might not have let me go on if you hadn't been in our plans."

"You haven't changed your mind about that, have you, Will?" Dick asked cautiously.

"Certainly not," said I, right ready. But then, seeing my opportunity, I smiled most ingratiatingly and proceeded in a new direction. "But tell me, was I in your plans from the first? Or did I perhaps take the place of another, say, one such as Kit Marlowe?"

The two exchanged looks.

"Marlowe was discussed," said Dick. "He's a great favorite with audiences, but he's difficult and undependable and has no sense of loyalty—as you yourself may have noted."

"Yes . . . well . . ."

"We didn't really settle on you, Will, till you showed us your Richard Crookback play," said James Burbage. "That's a remarkable piece of work, a bit in the Marlowe style—making a hero of a villain—but you do him at least one better in each scene. I called it your masterpiece, but you'll do better work. I know you will. Whereas, I have the feeling that Marlowe's best is behind him."

"Besides," said Dick, "you're a good actor, a fine actor, and Kit can scarce read his own verse aloud. It's painful to hear him try."

At that I was forced to laugh, remembering Marlowe's past attempts.

"There," he pressed his case, "you see? You're a man of business enough to see what a bargain you are—poet *and* actor. An't that so, Pa?"

His father gave a wise nod. "In all truth, Will, Christopher Marlowe never wrote anything so fine as Richard Crookback, and we know you'll write better. The thing is, he knows that, too, and that's what was at the bottom of that bit of nastiness a few months past."

My vanity surfeited, I allowed myself to smile in gratitude at each. "I know not what to say," said I. "You are both so generous in your praise. Surely, I am blessed to have such colleagues as you two. But tell me, what do you hear of Kit? Was he at all these evenings of Southampton's? Has he collected more laurel wreaths?"

"They do appear foolish, do they not? But no, he was not at the last," said father Burbage, "the one at which I had such a fortunate meeting with Lord Hunsden. I fear he has gotten himself into trouble."

"Ha!" said I, "when was he not in trouble?"

"Indeed," said Dick, "but this time it seems quite serious."

"More serious than murder?"

"In a way, for he seems this time to have offended the wrong people."

"What sort?"

"Well, according to Drayton, they've moved him to someplace in Deptford where he must stay whilst he journeys each day to the Queen's Palace in Greenwich. This is not of his own choosing. He must attend a trial of some sort—his own."

"How comes Drayton to know all this?"

"I know not. Perhaps from Kyd before he was taken away."

"He was taken away *again?*"

"Aye, and this time they did not keep him a single night, but many nights. He has not been heard from for near a week."

"And Marlowe?"

"For somewhat longer."

Well, said I to myself, whatever else is proven by all this, it does make one thing very clear indeed: the proceeding has begun.

They came for me at noon, near a week later, just at the end of the month of May. There were two, perhaps the same two who had collected Kyd. They said little but took the trouble to show me a document in which I was named and which bore the signature of Henry Carey, Lord Hunsden, Lord Chamberlain to

Her Majesty. They also allowed me time to dress properly, and one of them went so far as to offer advice.

"If I may suggest, sir, this would be an occasion to wear your best."

I took his words to heart and sought out my new linen shirt (a gift from Anne at Christmas) and my embroidered doublet. I dabbed rose-water upon my beard and through my hair, and at last presented myself as ready.

"Excellent, sir. You'll shine brighter than all but the Queen Herself."

I locked the door behind me, pocketed the key, and descended the stairs in step with my escort. We were but a short time under way when the second of the two, he who had not thus far spoken a word to me or to his companion, did turn to me with a question that struck me as odd.

"Do you live there all by yourself, sir?"

I answered him a cheerful yes but wondered at his powers of perception. There was no trace, no hint, of another in my little roost there above the world. Indeed there would hardly have been room for another. I had sworn after Kit moved out that I would never again share space with another.

"It's right snug and pleasant," said my questioner, "but do you not grow lonely all alone there?"

"No," said I, "I need the quiet for my work."

"And what sort of work is that, sir?"

"Writing. I am a poet. I write plays."

"Is that so, sir? Plays? Like them at the Rose and the Curtain? Till not so long ago I'd supposed those up on the stage made up their own words. So you write them, and they say them, eh? Just imagine."

He quieted down after that. We walked at a good pace through the empty streets of the city. Ordinarily they would have been crowded at this hour, and it would have meant a slower passage. Yet the plague had so emptied London that there was naught between us and our destination to hinder our progress. I don't believe I saw more than two or three wagons all the way to Little Gray's Inn Lane.

Oh yes indeed, I had calculated from the route we took that our journey would take us to that familiar two-room cottage. Still, I had asked nothing, made no inquiries whatever; that, I thought, would be the proper manner of displaying a confidence which, forsooth, I did not feel. Lord Hunsden's coach-and-four sat outside the door. The driver and the coachman gave nods of recognition as I was led up to the door. He who was nearest thumped loudly upon it. From inside, after a moment had passed, came the invitation to enter.

Lord Hunsden sat before the hearth where a small fire burned—all that was left of a much larger one. With him sat another man, younger but sharp-featured and possessed of the coldest eyes that e'er I saw on any man. (I later discovered he was Sir Robert Cecil.) Lord Hunsden made no introductions. He simply pointed to a chair between the two of them.

"Sit down, Shakespeare. I want you to repeat to us that story which you told me—that remarkable story, if I may say so—of the occasion upon which Mr. Christopher Marlowe attempted to raise Satan or one of his lesser demons."

"That was not truly his purpose," said I. "He simply used that as a method to—"

"I know all that," said Lord Hunsden. "Just tell the story as you told it to me."

"Yes, m'Lord."

Whereupon I launched into the tale as I had recounted it earlier. I had given thought to it and did add a bit, though naught which was untruthful, nor what would reflect badly upon me. And I believe I quoted him accurately when I put these words in his mouth: "If there be no God, as has been proven, then there be no Satan, no heaven and no hell. There be no need for one without the other."

The younger man looked at me sharply and waited to be certain that I was done.

"Did he describe these heretical beliefs to you as 'atheism'?"

His voice matched his appearance perfectly: harsh was it with a tone of complaint.

How was I to address this man whose name I had not been given? Better to aim above the mark, rather than below. "No, my Lord, I—"

He waved a hand at me, cutting me off. "You may address me as 'sir.' "

"I understand," said I. "No sir, Marlowe did not make use of the term, atheism, to describe his beliefs. 'Twas I who used that hateful word to describe his beliefs to Lord Hunsden."

"What about Sir Walter Ralegh? Did he, in any way, attribute them to him?"

"To Sir Walter Ralegh?"

"Yes."

"No," said I, "I cannot recall him mentioning Sir Walter Ralegh, except perhaps in passing, all the time we shared a room. So far as I know he had no personal acquaintance with him until afterward."

"Afterward? After what?"

"After he had been released from Newgate Gaol and moved in with Thomas Kyd."

"And when was that?"

"In October of 1589, sir."

At that he sighed and threw himself back in his chair most fretfully. There he sat and considered—considered what, I was not sure until at last he spoke up.

"All right then, here," said he. "This is what you must say when you appear before the panel. Tell the story exactly as you told it to me just now—you tell it very well, by the bye. And as you end it, as you say—how was it? 'As there is no God there is no Satan, no heaven and no hell. There be no need for one without the other.' Is that it approximately?"

"Quite close," said I.

"All right, after you have said all that, I want you to add, still quoting Marlowe, mind you 'And this I have learned from my teacher, Sir Walter Ralegh.' Is that clear? Do you have that?"

I did not immediately assent, but rather turned to Lord Hunsden for guidance. He nodded.

"Yes," said I. "I have it."

I had been told to sit upon the bench outside the meeting room. There I took my place, and there I waited through hours of that day, knowing little of what went on the other side of the thick wall which separated me from Hunsden, Cecil, and the rest.

What I have thus far described—the meeting room and the passage outside it wherein I waited—was all that I had seen and all that I would ever see of the Queen's Palace in Greenwich. It was not near so impressive as I had expected. I had seen country residences of the nobility on my tramps through the north country and the west which were far more impressive. The Greenwich Palace, however, had a considerable advantage, and that was its location. It was just near enough that the Queen and her counselors might dash into London should some urgent situation require them; and it was just far enough that it was supposed, and fervently hoped, that the plague could not reach her there.

We—Lord Hunsden, Sir Robert Cecil, and I—had entered through a rear door and had actually descended a few steps and then a few more as we moved down into the very depths of the building. I knew that the room in which the proceeding was conducted had been chosen, not for comfort, but rather for secrecy. It was also an advantage that participants and witnesses might be brought in without attracting attention.

So there I sat, waiting. And though waiting may seem no proper activity in and of itself, there were happenings whilst I sat there on the bench that proved near as important as any connected with these events.

The first of them came early. A party of men, four of them, came down the passage, talking softly amongst themselves. He who led the way was armed and watchful. Well he might have been, for behind him was Kit Marlowe who, though unarmed, was equally watchful. When he spied me, he showed surprise—nay, more than surprise. His eyes widened, and he came to a sudden halt, so sudden that he caught the two who marched behind him off guard, and they collided with him. I looked him in the eye from where I sat, expecting him to speak, but he had naught to say. The group reorganized themselves, and in a moment, they were under way again. The two who brought up the rear scowled at me as they passed. Then did all four disappear through the door which led into the meeting room.

Later came Thomas Kyd. I barely recognized the man, so twisted with pain was his face. He made the walk down the passage with the support of two men, the same two who had wakened me that very morning and accompanied me to the little cottage in Little Gray's Inn Lane. They murmured encouragement to him as he moved along quite gingerly, almost on tip-toe, unwilling or unable to put much weight on either of his two feet. Unlike Kit before him, he paid me little attention; perhaps indeed he did not even see me, so intent was he upon taking his next step. I wanted to help in some way, and so I jumped up from my place on the bench and hurried ahead to throw open the door to the meeting room. Then did I have my first glimpse inside. The place was dark and windowless, which should in no wise have surprised me since we were there below the level of the ground. There were, however, candles stuck in holders all round the room and in a candelabrum set upon the long table in the middle of the room. Though I spied Lord Hunsden, I saw no sign of Marlowe. Once Kyd and his two helpers had passed inside, I closed the door behind them.

I had barely enough time to sit down again and begin to reflect upon the poor fellow's state when the door came open again. The process was repeated in reverse. Yet this time Kyd was in such a weakened state that his two-man escort all but carried him back down the passage. Seeing him thus made it clear that this time Topcliffe, the royal torturer, had not only told him of the instruments of torture, but also demonstrated their uses. How long, I asked myself, would it take him to recover from such lessons? (He died but a year later.)

Then came the longest, the most unendurable period of waiting. I must have kept my place near two hours, leaving the bench only to stretch and walk about for brief periods. Even though the walls were thick I could hear sounds within the room behind me—sounds of talking, occasional shouting, though never the words, the sense of what was said.

Without notice, the door opened and a familiar face appeared. It took me a moment to realize that it was one of Kit's protectors, or jailers, or whatever.

"You, hi, they want you inside now, so they do."

"They want me now?"

(I don't know why I asked that. Perhaps because I'd been made to sit and wait so long that I could barely believe my term on the bench was ended at last.)

"'Course, *now,* didn't I just say so?"

I rose and scrambled for the door. Stepping inside, I found it a bit darker than at my earlier glimpse. Candles had flickered out and had not yet been replaced. I stood, looking left and right, trying to acquaint myself with the room.

"Over there, to your left," came the voice of Lord Hunsden. "You stand there and face us."

I did as he had ordered me to do and, as my eyes accustomed to the dim light, I made him out. He was, as always, an imposing figure, though it was evident from his peevish tone that he was grown weary with his role in this proceeding. On either side of him were three or four others, all of whom seemed to be wearing robes of some sort; farthest from him on his right sat Cecil. Then, a surprise, for next to Cecil, I saw Lord

Southampton. Could he, I wondered, take part in such a proceeding when he had not reached his majority—and then it struck me immediate that he probably had done so. This was the year that he was to turn twenty-one, and I knew not the month or day of it.

I still had not found Marlowe. But then almost as a response to that, my realization, I heard a cough and the shuffling of feet behind me and to my right. I looked and found him seated before his standing escort. This time he managed a smile, one perhaps better described as an ironic leer.

"State your name, please." 'Twas Lord Hunsden calling me to the matter at hand.

"William Shakespeare," said I, speaking calmly.

"And what is your relationship to Mr. Christopher Marlowe?"

"Formerly, he and I shared a room together."

"And when was this?"

"From 1587 to 1589."

"Roughly two years then, give or take a few months?"

"That would be right."

"You say that you shared space, but how would you describe your relation to him? Were you friends?"

"No doubt up to a point we were, but I would say it would have been more accurate to call us colleagues."

At this point came the sound of raucous, forced laughter from Kit's corner.

"I advise you, Mr. Marlowe," said Lord Hunsden, "to keep a respectful silence. You are here on sufferance to defend your name. We have granted you that opportunity. We have not granted you the right to cause a disturbance."

"Yes, my Lord, forgive me, please. It will not happen again."

"See that it does not," said Lord Hunsden. And then said he to me: "Mr. Shakespeare, I would put it to you so: you were colleagues in what sense?"

"In that we were both poets who wrote for the theater."

"You both wrote plays?"

"Yes."

"But it would not be accurate to call you friends?"

"No, not after a certain incident had taken place."

"And what was that incident? Will you describe it, please?"

"Certainly," said I, then did I tell the tale as I had told it twice earlier to Lord Hunsden and once to Sir Robert Cecil, and I concluded as I had been instructed.

" 'If there be no God, as has been proven, then there be no Satan, no heaven and no hell. There be no need for one without the other. And this have I learned from my teacher, Sir Walter Ralegh.' "

With that, the room quite exploded into a chaos of shouting. It seemed that every man in the room was upon his feet yelling at me or at each other. Lord Hunsden was crying loudest of all for the rest to be silent. Marlowe was shaking his finger in my direction and shouting, "Liar! liar!" at the top of his tenor. Yet Hunsden's commanding bass prevailed. He thundered for silence long and loud, accompanying his calls with his fist beating down upon the table. Thus did all eventually submit to his demand for order. Last to seat himself, however, was Marlowe, and he took his place only reluctantly, still asking to speak. But when all was once again quiet, it was me he addressed and no other.

"Mr. Shakespeare, as you see, you have caused a great commotion. Do you stand behind your testimony?"

I nodded and was about to assure him that I did when Marlowe piped forth: "Let him take an oath."

The cry for an oath was taken up round the room by two or three—but by no means by all.

"Would you agree to take an oath, sir?" Lord Hunsden asked me.

"I would."

"Step forward please."

I did as he directed. A Bible was produced and offered me. I placed my right hand upon it and swore by all that was holy that what I had said was exact and true as I remembered it.

"I am satisfied," said he, "as indeed you must all be." He nodded gravely. "Now, Mr. Marlowe, you may speak."

Kit rose and paced about for a moment or two before speaking up.

"It is all lies," said he loudly, throwing open his arms, addressing all in the room. "Him who was mentioned last in the perjured testimony you have just heard could not have been named by me as my teacher, could not have provided such arguments because we were not then so much as acquainted. I have submitted to you, my Lord, and all the rest of you have had the opportunity to examine, a sworn statement from no less than Sir Walter Ralegh himself to the effect that he and I first did meet in the year 1590. Since Mr. Shakespeare here says that the events he described took place in 1588, Sir Walter could have played no part in them." Kit then folded his arms and nodded victoriously, as if the matter were settled. "*Quod erat demonstrandum,*" he declared.

"Just a moment, Mr. Marlowe," said Lord Hunsden. "You began just now by saying that it—presumably Mr. Shakespeare's testimony—was 'all lies.' Then do you base the whole of your defense upon a single sentence there at the end. What about all the rest which led up to it? Do you accept it? Do you deny it? With or without reference to Sir Walter Ralegh, it seems to me that you had made what was intended as a strong argument for atheism. Did you intend it so?"

"As an argument, which is to say, as an intellectual exercise, I may have intended it so. Yet Mr. Shakespeare has neither the wit nor the education to recognize an intellectual argument, much less to take part in one."

"Then you do not hold with any of that which he attributes to you, except as an argument, an exercise?"

"Why," said Marlowe, "I don't know."

"What do you mean, you do not know? Either you do, or you do not."

"With some of it I do, or so it seems to me at the moment, and with some of it, perhaps most of it, I do not."

"How are we then to tell with which you do, and with which you do not?"

"I should think the only way, the only fair way, would be to have Mr. Shakespeare repeat his testimony from the beginning and allow me to interpret it, sentence by sentence, perhaps word by word."

A great groan arose from those assembled as if in a single voice. I may even have contributed my own to the many.

"There," said Lord Hunsden, "you hear the reaction to your suggestion. Though I do not dismiss it out of hand, Mr. Marlowe, it will be necessary, I think, to consider the proposal you've made through the evening. The decision will not be mine alone. I shall seek the counsel of others in this group and attempt to come up with the right judgment. It may not please all, but I hope that it does, at least, satisfy all. You will report here tomorrow, Mr. Marlowe, at the same time. Whether you must return, Mr. Shakespeare, will depend upon our conclusion. Until tomorrow then."

I had hoped that all might be done in a single day. The thought of spending tomorrow as I spent that day—or worse—seemed altogether more than I could bear. Nevertheless, I had no choice in the matter. I would do what they required.

Then did Lord Hunsden catch my eye and beckon me to him.

"Yes, my Lord?"

"You did excellently well. Have no doubt of it. Would you now wait for me, outside in the passage?"

I agreed and turned to go. And turning, I saw first Sir Robert Cecil in earnest conversation with the members of Marlowe's escort. Then did I spy Kit himself standing off to one side, staring at me. I frowned at him, signaling that I knew not what he wished to communicate. At last, after returning his searching gaze for longer than it warranted, I shook my head and turned away, then headed for the door.

I took my place upon the bench and resigned myself to another long wait. Yet it was not near so long as before.

First out the door was Marlowe and his three constant companions. I gave him no more notice than I had earlier. I simply waited until he would be gone. Yet when he was near he signaled to his escort that he would stop. They allowed him his wish, and he bent down; and I half rose to meet him, curious what he might have to say. When he was but a foot away, he spat in my face.

"Judas!" said he.

Then, snickering, his captors pulled him away and set off with him again down the passage. It was odd, but I knew not quite how to react. Ought I to jump up, shake my fist at him, and curse him? Or . . . what? The truth was, no such thing had ever happened to me before. Nor should it have, for of all signs of anger, disgust, and hatred, this one seemed the least English, did it not? I took that same linen kerchief I had breathed through to Stratford and back and carefully wiped my cheek dry with it. Something perhaps he had learned in France.

Judas? Judas, was it? Kit Marlowe named me such? He, who had boasted of the priests he had betrayed and joked of their sufferings on the scaffold? There was your Judas. Marlowe had made an art of betrayal. He was a professional Judas.

How fitting that he should be made to fall in the same way that he had trapped others in the past. Surely, thought I, this is a case of the divine interceding in human affairs. Did I feel upon me a burden of guilt? Not an intolerable one, certainly. But for that final sentence, authored by Sir Robert and contested so bitterly by Kit, my testimony contained naught but the truth. Let him reflect upon that. Nay, I was proud to have been chosen as God's scourge against Christopher Marlowe.

"Come along now. We've no time to sit about. There are important matters to be dealt with before the evening is done."

'Twas Lord Hunsden before me, in the company of Sir Robert. They must have been the last to leave the meeting room. Many had passed me by since Marlowe had insulted me and occasioned my musing. So deeply had I mused upon the matter that I fear I was not near as watchful as I should have been. I was caught completely by surprise by Lord Hunsden.

"Come along now," he repeated.

The two started down the passage. I jumped to my feet and hastened to catch them up. I trailed behind all the way to the rearyard of the palace, where Lord Hunsden's coach awaited. The footman scrambled to open the coach door. The two men had not spoken a word one to the other during our journey through the passages beneath the palace. Nevertheless, they did not hesitate to hop into the coach; they seemed to be acting according to a plan. I could but wonder if I were part of it—and to that I had my answer soon enough.

"Well, what are you waiting for?"—the voice of Lord Hunsden from the interior of the coach. "Get inside, Shakespeare."

Though the two had been silent earlier, they talked openly and without ceasing once the coach-and-four was moving.

"What did you tell them?" asked Hunsden.

"I told them to get him ready. That is, I told the one Essex appointed and my man, Frizer. The third one, Ralegh's man, Poley, I simply warned to keep out of the way."

"What's to prevent him from running off to tell Ralegh?"

"He won't," said Cecil with great finality. "Or if he does, Ralegh will do nothing."

"How can you be so sure?"

"Can you suppose that in his situation he would move against the Secretary of State and the Lord Chamberlain?"

"I see what you mean," said Hunsden. "And would he move to save one as troublesome as Marlowe? No, indeed I see what you mean, and I concede the point to you. But what about members of the committee? This was supposed to have been put to a vote."

"Who would complain? Southampton? Who would listen to that silly boy? As for the rest, we'll give them a story."

"What sort of story?"

"Oh, I don't know. We'll think of something. Say, for instance, that all four of them were drinking at a tavern, and there was a quarrel over the reckoning. They fell to fighting, and in the fray, Marlowe was killed. Frizer has already agreed to take blame, so long as the charge is self-defense, and he is given the Queen's pardon."

"Do you think that those on the committee will believe that?"

"No," said Cecil, "but I think they will accept it."

Lord Hunsden said nothing whatever for a short period. He simply sat, staring out the window at the dusk, considering the matter at hand.

"Perhaps it would be best if we put it off a day. We could spend tomorrow preparing the committee."

"What? Do you mean another day of listening to that popinjay play games with words and their meanings? What has he promised us for tomorrow? He will parse and interpret each sentence, each word if need be, of our friend Shakespeare's testimony, so that we may know what he did and didn't mean when he sought to raise Satan."

"Well, I can't say that I look forward to it myself. But perhaps I can attack that sworn statement he's so proud of. I might suggest that a man may learn from another without actually knowing him. He might read his work or hear his talk discussed."

"Really, Lord Hunsden, how long do you think you could keep that going?"

A pause, a sigh, then: "Not very long, I suppose."

The coach, which had slowed, came to a full halt. The two men exchanged looks. Hunsden, who sat nearest the window, looked out at the house where we had stopped. There were lights inside, though not so many.

The footman threw open the door.

"This is the place, my Lord," said he.

"We'll wait out here a bit," said Hunsden.

"As you wish, my Lord." After closing the door, he withdrew. Hunsden and Cecil lapsed into silence. Faint sounds of talking could be heard from the house. Though I listened intently, I could make out none of what was said. We were waiting, though for what we were waiting for, I was uncertain. Of a sudden and without explanation, Lord Hunsden began searching the pockets of his robes quite hurriedly, as if for something feared lost.

"Ah," said he, "here it is."

And so saying, he produced the object of his search—a small, narrow parcel wrapped in chamois leather. It was no more than ten inches long and not much more than an inch or two across. He offered it to me.

"Here, Shakespeare, I fear I nearly forgot."

I could tell what was inside from the hard shape of it. I unwrapped the parcel quite carefully and found, as I had expected, a knife. It was a poniard of a sort that Kit Marlowe had owned. In fact, judging from the chip in the shell handle just above the pommel, it was the poniard that Kit himself had owned.

"It's Marlowe's," said I.

"Well done," said Lord Hunsden. "You did know him well, didn't you?"

"Why are you giving it to me?"

"Why? Because the fellow must die. You must kill him."

"But . . . but . . . why me?"

At that Sir Robert Cecil laughed abruptly and rather cruelly. "You don't expect one of us to do it, do you?"

"My dear sir," said Lord Hunsden to me, "he has given you ample reason. He has insulted you, humiliated you. I thought you would welcome the opportunity. I assumed that from the start."

"Well," said Sir Robert to me, "whether you welcome the opportunity or not, Marlowe must die, and you must do the deed."

"But what about your fellow—what's his name? Frizer?—you said he was taking the blame, why not—"

"Because *he has declined*. He has that right. You have not. It must be done, and *you* must do it. Is that clear?"

As it happened, I never answered that question, rhetorical though it be, for just then the door of the house opened and a figure appeared, holding a lantern high. One after the other, three men marched out, and the figure we had first seen reappeared in the doorway and waved the lantern thrice.

"I believe that was a woman," said Lord Hunsden, "the one with the lantern."

"Oh yes, it was," said Sir Robert. "That would be the widow Bull. She has court connections, a cousin is one of the ladies in waiting, something of the sort. She has a big house and allows us to make use of it from time to time. For a price."

The three men who had filed out had now disappeared. Hunsden looked from Cecil to me, then rapped upon the door for the footman.

"I suppose we had better get on with it," said he.

"I'm for it," said Sir Robert.

I said nothing but held tight to the poniard, which was now wrapped in the chamois once again. The door to the coach came open and we descended to the road, then walked up the path to the house, I last of all.

"Where have they put him?" Cecil asked the woman with the lamp.

"In back," said she, "where it can best be washed down. I know what must be done, and I accept that, but do try not to foul things too badly. You understand, surely?" That last was spoken to me. She had picked me easily as the designated executioner.

Leading the way, she brought us to the rear room she had mentioned. The door was closed. There she left us, saying, "I shall be in front, should I be needed. Should I not, I ask only that you let me know when you are done."

Lord Hunsden waited till she had gone, then did he open the door and bring us in. The room was well-lit by candles which burned on each wall. Looking down, I saw that the floor was wide-planked with rough timbers which could easily be rubbed down with soap and brush. It occurred to me then that she must be expecting a proper bloodbath.

The room had been emptied of furniture, but for a single chair in the middle of it; and upon that chair sat a figure I took to be Christopher Marlowe. It was difficult to tell in any exact way, for he was bound to the chair, gagged, and blindfolded, so that there was little of his face to be seen. Yet the clothes worn by him in the chair were those in which I had last seen him. I thought that it was he, but could I kill him, not having truly seen his face and thus being certain beyond doubt? Could I kill him at all under that circumstance?

Hunsden fumbled inside his robes and brought out a scroll of no great size, unrolled it and began to read aloud. It was Marlowe's death warrant, no doubt written days before. I heard little of it, for I was too deep in my thoughts to give attention to it. Those thoughts were of Marlowe and of the past we shared. I thought of his arrogance, of the many occasions he had embarrassed me and worse, of his vanity and his self-conceit. How could I ever have lived with such a man, much less fancied myself in love with him? And most specifically did I think of that evening at Southampton's—of how he had led the crowd in jeering laughter at me and my work. "Upstart crow," indeed! "Judas," indeed! Even before Lord Hunsden had finished his reading of the death warrant, I was ready to execute it at his instruction.

Still, he droned on: ". . . and for teaching that most odious and unholy crime, that most accursed and despicable of all heresies, atheism, the punishment is death." He looked up from the scroll and over in my direction. "The sentence is to be carried out immediately."

Could Marlowe actually have heard the Lord Chamberlain's reading of the document? Not very well, I fear, for the rolled cloth which served to blindfold him did also fit over across his ears. Nevertheless, the moment Hunsden's voice ceased, Marlowe's voice began. It was not a voice that spoke words or sentences, for he had been gagged so thoroughly that I doubt he could move tongue or lips. What came from him came from far deeper down. Howls, they were—from his throat, or deeper still, his chest—sounds of the sort that might come from a wounded animal.

Yet I was not to be put off. I stepped forward and tore at the blindfold that covered his eyes. Did I then wish to make certain that it was truly Marlowe bound and trussed up in that chair? Perhaps. Yet more certain was it that I wanted him to see me.

Only one eye came uncovered. I hoped, even expected, to see fear in it. Yet what I saw was what I had seen when he spat in my face—arrogance, distaste, hatred. I liked not what I saw in that eye, and so I plunged the poniard into it.

Then what a howl came from him! It fair rattled the windows. And as I pushed the blade deeper into his brain, his body went rigid for a long, long moment until it relaxed in a slump of death.

The poniard was stuck in up to the pommel. Blood and the liquid of the eye trickled round the blade and down his cheek. There was a bit of brain matter there, as well.

"Well done, Shakespeare," said Sir Robert, "oh, very well done indeed."

And as we were leaving, Lord Hunsden turned back and called me aside. "You may not fully realize it, but you've done me—and your Queen—a great service," he said quietly. I said nothing, just nodded and tried to look both sad and worthy. "I think you'll soon find that you did yourself one as well," he added. Knowing what plans he had already made with the Burbages for his new theatrical company, I could not help but agree. But again I said nothing, and we all left that death house in silence.

I regret the killing of Kit, truly I do. Yet I regret it in a manner most particular. 'Twas not the act of killing which preys upon my soul, for I had been brought there for that purpose and was given no choice in the matter. Yet I confess that I took a certain pleasure in it, and one should never take pleasure in ending the life of another.

I learned from a remark by Lord Hunsden later on that in the week in which this took place, two thousand died of the plague in England. (By that time all the channel ports had been infected.) Was Kit better than any of these? Did he deserve death less? Nay, I say he was more deserving of the end he came to than any of them. He had killed more by his own hand and by means of betrayal than any soldier might kill in a great battle. And how many souls had he led astray and thus sent to eternal damnation through his specious arguments and pernicious preaching? Looked at in this way, I was no less God's instrument than Sir Robert Cecil's. And further, he died a more merciful death by my hand than ever he would have upon the scaffold.

Ah, but to take pleasure as I did in ending Kit's life, that were as sinful as killing an animal for naught but pleasure (and that, in a sense, is just what I did). I was guilty of such as a boy, as I made clear at the beginning, and I was guilty of it in killing the cunning, soul-less Marlowe. These sins I confess and for them I ask God's forgiveness.

In some unanticipated ways I gained from his death. I had the benefit of Lord Hunsden's counsel and friendship through the rest of his life, just as the Lord Chamberlain's Men had the benefit of his monetary support ever after. For sentimental reasons known to both of us, he made me a gift of the small house in Little Gray's Inn Lane. I thought that most generous of him, but there was never any hint, neither before nor after that night in May, that such would be my reward.

In fine, there may be little more to say here in this, my confession. I can in no wise claim that my life ever after has been without sin, but these later sins were not in kind or degree different from those I have already described—except, of course, for homicide. I killed none but Christopher Marlowe. And for that and other sins both mentioned and unmentioned I have assigned myself as a penance to attend church each Sabbath for the rest of my days. Some might consider that no penance at all, since it is required of us as a simple demonstration of faith, yet they would have no notion of what a trial it is for me to listen to the simple-minded nonsense spouted by Vicar Stoner from the pulpit. For me, though not perhaps for the rest of Holy Trinity's congregation, that was a cruel penance indeed.

To speak of Holy Trinity, as I have done, is to be reminded that it was in the churchyard there that all this began with Goody Bromley. Since, along the way, I have included bits and pieces of her story, I think it only right to tell how it all ended. As I recall, I left it that the Right Reverend Andrew Bliven, Bishop of Worcester, had convened an ecclesiastical court, and Goodwife Bromley had been brought there and detained in the Worcester gaol to await an examination by the bishop and his court for the capital crime of witchcraft.

Goody Bromley neither passed nor failed that examination. I was asked to testify before the ecclesiastical court in the course of this hearing. I did so readily but in the same conservative manner I had used to inform Bishop Bliven. That is to say, I did not exaggerate her powers nor her questionable deeds, and I made certain that wife Anne's objections to my conclusions were known and understood. I might not have been near so careful had I known that Vicar Stoner would follow me before the court to plead for her as "naught but a poor, unfortunate woman." As for Goody Bromley, she herself could not speak in her own behalf—or would not—for she was determined to present herself in the pathetic role that Vicar Stoner had created for her. And so the results of the hearing were declared "inconclusive." Bishop Bliven suggested that in such cases as this, it was sometimes helpful to employ the "trial by water." Objections were raised but voted down, and it was decided to hold the test next day but one. The intervening day was taken up by arguments over whether such an event would best be held in a pond or the river. There were objections to both, yet in the end, supporters of the river won out.

It was, as the bishop reminded me, often called in our part of the country, "swimming a witch," and that should do as well as any for a description of the exercise. I had never seen it done, and so I made it a point to attend, as did many from Stratford.

What happened is easily told. Goody Bromley was brought forth in a white shift, specially provided for the occasion. She was frightened, for she evidently had no real understanding of what was to happen. In short, she was to be thrown into the river; if she floated, it would be known that she was a witch; if, however, she sank, it was clear that she was innocent of all commerce with Satan.

The closer she came to the river the louder her objections became. Finally, the two constables who pulled her along had simply to drag her forward, for she refused utterly to go forward. This, naturally, counted against her, for it was assumed that what she feared was not so much the river as it was the discovery of witchcraft. They wrestled and tugged and brought her to the edge. She screamed loudly, chanting some indecipherable something in a language all her own (or per-

haps hers and the devil's). Then, with a great effort, these two large, strong men managed only on a third attempt to throw her off the riverbank and into the water.

This spot had been chosen with care, for there the river waters were almost still and clear. It was a calm pool near a bend in the river. It would not do to have her swept away by the current. She must be seen by all who came to witness this unusual event. I had chosen my spot well, for I had an excellent perspective upon the action.

She made a great splash, for she was no small woman. After going down, she then came up, flailing wildly with her arms, screaming in panic. This did her no good, of course, and down she went again. The expectation of the crowd was that she would reappear, but she did not. They waited one minute, two, perhaps three—and only then did the bishop signal to the constables that they were to pull her out. The two dove in unwillingly and together searched the river bottom. It was not near so deep as one might have supposed, but the near stagnant waters of the pool were murky, and there was further difficulty in finding her. In the end, she was under water for too long to be revived, though to their credit, the constables made every effort to bring her back to life. I understand that far more often than not such trials by water end in just such a way.

Frankly, I was surprised and disappointed by the outcome. So sure was I that she had made a pact with Satan that I had quietly made a wager with one of the Arden cousins. I was made a pound poorer by her drowning. Yet certainly I was pleased that Satan had made no inroads into our part of the country—or apparently he had not. The bishop and I have not discussed the matter since the event. I am sure that we will.

Rest easy, whatever lawyers, family members, scholars or the merely curious have read thus far: My confessions have almost ended, and I at least intend to round them off with a sound sleep.

Just one more scene remains to be described—the true start of whatever fame has attached itself to my name and work.

In 1594, as the plague receded and London life took on at least some of its old flavors and colors, the theaters reopened and the acting companies went to work again.

I suppose you could have called me a working playwright and actor at that point: I was able to earn enough from my chosen careers to survive, and to send money home to my family. But I was hardly anyone's first choice for future riches or honor. All that was about to change, however, in a most dramatic way—thanks to a hunchbacked villain and of course to my newly-won friend and conspirator, Lord Hunsden.

Under his patronage, plans for a new playhouse, to be called The Globe, were drawn up. It would take some years to finish, and the Burbages decided to use that shabby old barn called The Theatre until their new home could be built.

The Burbages also decided to launch their career as The Lord Chamberlain's Men with my *King Richard III,* which I had been smoothing and polishing at the same time as I wrote my poems for print and money.

During rehearsals, it was exciting to watch as Richard Burbage fell into the role of Crookback with so much devotion that he virtually became the character, onstage as well as off. (Doubtless you have heard the rather good—but I'm afraid also virtually fictional—story about the married woman so smitten with him in this role that she bade him come to her bedchamber and announce that Richard III was at the door. That part indeed might have had a tinge of truth to it, but the sting in the tale's tail—that I, hearing of this, arrived moments before and sent forth word that "William the Conqueror came before Richard III"—is cut from whole cloth. I swear it.)

At last came the opening night—which certainly promised to be a grand affair. Lord Hunsden and his circle were to be there, of course, and it had been broadly hinted that he was bringing along a particularly glittering party of guests. Some even whispered that the Queen herself would make a surprise appearance—even though it was her usual custom to have plays and players brought to her, and not travel through the rough streets in search of entertainment.

I confess to being somewhat nervous about the play's reception. I knew in my heart as well as in my head that this was my best play—much more shapely and interesting and modern than the three parts of *Henry VI,* for example. But would the world notice?

And would anyone remark on what to me at least became more and more obvious every day—that without Kit Marlowe, and especially his *Doctor Faustus,* there probably would have been no *Richard III*?

It certainly wasn't conscious on my part, but that magpie which lives in my brain could hardly ignore the dark energy of Kit's soul which poured out of his daringly alone and aloof main character—a man with an essential evil so strong that he pulsed with life and carried the play along with him.

Did I in fact set out to copy Kit? As I say, I really don't think so. I knew from the start that my own powers of poetic invention were superior to his, and that whatever stagecraft I still had to learn was mere mechanics. And my choice of character was perfect: Richard III's actions seemed, and still seem, to cry out for this kind of dramatic treatment, even granting the physical exaggerations I added to his body.

But there is also no denying the fact that audiences since then have loved him more than any other character I ever created—with the exception of that other great sinner, Sir John Falstaff. And if there was one thing Kit Marlowe knew well, it was how to catch an audience's attention.

Opening night of *Richard III* was a triumph—as the world knows full well by now. At the theater itself, the audience (after the usual stirring and shouting during the battle scenes) sat silent for a moment after Richard III's death. Then came a roar of approval such as I had never before heard—and not often since. We players looked at one another and knew we had struck some vein of dramatic gold which would change our lives.

The party afterward at a local tavern taken over for the occasion was even more of a triumph. Lord Hunsden's finest chefs and caterers provided a wealth of food and drink—meat pies filled with pork, beef, raisins and dates, topped with whole chicken pieces; soups flavored with wine and thickened with almonds; vegetables and fruit marinated in wine, honey, and herbs and savory sauces and stews of all varieties—followed by sweet pastries fried in oil, fruit confections, and sculptures made of sugar. But by that time I was blissfully awash in the flood of wines and ales of all sorts which were consumed during the entire meal.

That night opened up for me a wealth of possibilities from which I still profit and indeed revel in. For whatever part you played in that triumph, I thank you, Kit. I'm almost certain that I remembered to drink a silent toast to your memory.

Now, why not let the very last words in this odd document be Crookback's—from that very same play which flowered after Marlowe's death.

"Conscience is but a word that cowards use," Richard III says at Bosworth just before he dies, "devised at first to keep the strong in awe . . ."

The rest is—or soon will be—silence. I feel it coming. I'm about to be fifty-two. It is time to join my ghosts.